MAGGIE BLACK CASE FILES BOOKS 1-3

Vendetta - The Witness - The Defector

JACK MCSPORRAN

D1412280

inked entertainment

Series Guide

The main Maggie Black Series consists of full-length novels featuring secret agent Maggie Black.

The Maggie Black Case Files is a prequel series of self-contained missions which Maggie completed prior to the events of the main Maggie Black Series.

Both series can be read before, after, or in conjunction with the other.

Maggie Black Case Files

Book 1: Vendetta
Book 2: The Witness
Book 3: The Defector

Maggie Black Series

Book 1: Kill Order
Book 2: Hit List (Coming Spring 2018)

VENDETTA

MAGGIE BLACK CASE FILES BOOK 1

Chapter 1

Maggie Black watched her target from across the street.

She sat by Sigismund's Column while Jason Stroud enjoyed an alfresco dinner in Castle Square. Two men with ties to his shady dealings joined him, laughing and joking with each other before they got around to talking business.

Jason wouldn't be laughing for long.

Maggie had been tailing Stroud for three days now, and the man had yet to notice her. It was easy to spy on over-confident men who thought they were too smart to be found out. Jason carried on with his life while she followed him, ignorant to the fact that his days were numbered.

Night approached Old Town as the summer sun began its descent. Lights blinked on around the square, illuminating the historic castle from the ground up and giving the quaint area a warm glow.

The Krolewski Restaurant and Pub, situated across from the castle, was Jason's favorite spot; he'd dined there every night on Maggie's watch. A man like him should know better. Being predictable could get you killed.

The square around them was crowded. Tourists milled through, taking photos of the brightly colored buildings and gawking at the difference between Old Town and the modern metropolis they stepped in from. Locals weaved between the tourists as they headed home for the evening, while lovers linked arms and strolled off towards the Vistula river.

A horse-drawn carriage passed Maggie, clip-clopping over the cobbled roads.

Maggie's phone vibrated an hour and a half into her watch. She dug it out of her pocket and checked the screen. Bishop wouldn't call while she was out on assignment unless something was wrong. She had to take it.

"Bishop?"

"I need you to come in," said her boss.

Maggie got up from her bench by the monument and moved away from prying ears. "When?"

"Tonight."

"I'm not done here." She checked over her shoulder and found Jason settling his bill.

"Then wrap things up. It's urgent."

"What's wrong?"

"I'll explain when you get here."

Maggie sighed. "I'll be there soon."

As she hung up, a car approached and pulled up outside the restaurant. Jason bid his dinner guests farewell and got into the back of the sleek Lexus. Maggie glanced around, hand reaching to her back where she concealed her gun. It was too crowded. Too many witnesses.

With Jason inside, the black car took off and headed down the street, leaving Maggie and Old Town behind.

Shit.

Maggie raced around the corner to where she'd parked her rental. She hopped onto the motorbike and secured her helmet to conceal her identity. Rush jobs could lead to mistakes, and she wasn't taking any chances. Making sure her long blond hair was hidden, she flicked the kickstand away and put the key into ignition.

The engine of the Suzuki GSX-R1000R roared to life. Pulling back the throttle, Maggie planted a foot on the ground and spun the bike in the right direction before taking off.

Jason was out of sight by the time she returned to the main square, but it didn't matter. He was a man of habit. He'd return to his apartment and remain there for at least an hour before heading out for a night on the town.

Thanks to the layout of the city's roads, this would force his driver to circle back, going down Miodowa and eventually rounding into Aleja Solidarności, one of the main roads that veined through the city.

The road to Castle Square acted as an overpass to Aleja Solidarności, and Maggie crossed the street, peering over the edge of the bridge and down to the two-way traffic below. It was the perfect place.

Maggie swung right and took a short cut, bumping her way down the adjoining staircase to the road below. Pedestrians yelped and dodged out of the way as she careened down the steps, standing up from the bike's seat to avoid her teeth rattling with the impact.

At the bottom, Maggie waited at the mouth of the underpass for the right moment. The timing needed to be perfect.

Minutes passed like hours, and doubt crept into Maggie's brain. Perhaps Stroud decided to switch up his usual schedule. He'd just met with two of his business partners, after all. Something could have changed his plans.

His next shipment of unsuspecting workers could be ready. Jason frequently smuggled Polish citizens into the UK, all under the false pretense of promised employment. Instead, he'd use them for slave labor when they arrived.

The authorities had discovered Stroud's not-so-little operation in the West Midlands a couple of weeks ago and planned a raid for the following night. They couldn't allow his 'business venture' to continue. Three bodies had already been found, poor workers deemed useless after falling ill, thanks to malnutrition and the horrendous conditions in Stroud's factories. Each received a bullet to the head as payment for their services.

Maggie's employer had sent her to return the favor.

She narrowed her eyes to get a better look down the tunnel. A black car entered from the opposite end and headed her way.

Revving the engine, she held off for the right moment. *Three. Two.*

Maggie shot off like a bullet, the metallic blue bike whizzing through the busy traffic as she entered the tunnel.

Steering with one hand, Maggie reached behind for her Glock 19. She weaved into the next lane of the two-way traffic, narrowing the gap between her and the Lexus.

Cars filled the four lanes. Maggie swooped between them, running up the edge of her lane as the black Lexus approached.

Time seemed to slow as she drove towards them. Jason was sitting in the back, talking into his phone with no idea of what was about to happen.

Maggie raised her gun and aimed as she continued forward. Taking a deep breath, she held it and lined the shot.

She pulled the trigger and watched as the bullet reached its final resting place, buried deep into Jason

Stroud's temple. Blood spattered over the cracked window, and Maggie sped on forward.

The booming from the shot reverberated through the hollow tunnel.

Brakes screeched as drivers reacted to the noise and ran into the cars in front of them. But Maggie didn't stop.

She had a plane to catch.

Chapter 2

LONDON, GREAT BRITAIN

It was almost midnight by the time Maggie reached King Street. The two-and-a-half-hour flight from Warsaw went by without issue, Stansted Airport busy as always.

She swiped her pass at the door and entered the five-story office building. To the outside world, Inked International was a global stationery supplier. To those in the know, it was the headquarters to a covert intelligence agency simply known as the Unit.

Strictly speaking, the Unit didn't exist. Unlike the Secret Intelligence Service at Vauxhall Cross or MI5, everything about the Unit was underground. Only those with the highest clearance were privy to their inner workings.

Unlike their public counterparts, the Unit's activities weren't strictly legal. When the need arose to step outside the law for the greater good, Maggie and her colleagues shouldered the burden and did what others could not.

Jason Stroud wasn't the first person Maggie had killed, and he wouldn't be the last.

Maggie went inside the elevator and pushed the button for the top floor. Whatever prompted Bishop to call her in had to be time sensitive.

The cart stopped on her level and pinged, opening out onto a floor of offices. Bishop's door was open, and he stood in the doorway waiting for her.

"Thanks for coming, Maggie."

"Of course."

"Tea?" he asked, closing the door behind her as she shrugged out her jacket.

Maggie took a seat at the conference table. A projector screened the contents of Bishop's laptop onto the far wall. "I'm okay, thanks."

Bishop sat across from her and took a sip of his fresh brew. He wore his usual uniform: an expensive yet subdued suit with a silk tie over a clean white shirt. An army man through and through, he kept his brown hair cropped at the sides despite leaving the military years ago. He became an agent long before Maggie's birth, yet she bet the fifty-eight-year-old could still kick her twenty-seven-year-old arse. Bishop was one of the best, and he'd been her mentor ever since she was a teenager.

"Sorry about the short notice," he said, pulling her from her thoughts. "I trust there were no problems wrapping things up in Warsaw?"

"It was a clean hit," she assured him.

"Good, because something's come up, and I need you on it."

"What is it?"

Bishop tapped at his laptop and brought up an image on the projector. A man stared back at them with sharp eyes, his bronzed skin carved with age.

"This is Carlo Rossi. His family is one of two warring factions in the Italian region of Veneto."

"The mafia?" Maggie suppressed the urge to talk like Don Corleone.

"Of a sort, yes. Carlo is the Rossi's leader, and we've received intel from the Italian government that he's currently in negotiations with one of the UK's largest importers."

"Drugs?" Maggie guessed. While people like Jason Stroud trafficked people, the mob were prolific in shifting narcotics.

Bishop nodded. "The Rossis are looking for international distribution for their cocaine and heroin. Things are bad enough here without their product reaching our shores."

"Who's the importer?"

"Peter West." Bishop switched Carlo's photo out for another. "We've been after him for some time now, but the bastard's eluded us until now."

Peter West was a dapper, though not handsome, man. He looked as if he'd rushed into middle age and forgot to bring his hair along with him; his bulbous nose and chiseled jaw competed for the starring role on his face.

"Where do I come in?" Maggie asked, committing both men to memory.

"The Italians have someone on the inside, an agent named Isabella Valentin. For the last six years, she's worked her way up the organization and now serves as Carlo's trusted personal assistant."

"She must be good." Organizations like the mafia weren't trusting to outsiders. They liked to stick with their own and keep business in the family.

"One of their best, from what I'm told. She's managed to secure you a meeting with Carlo, under the guise of Peter's competition."

"You mean Rebecca Sterling." It had been a while since Maggie used Rebecca. Maggie now understood why Bishop called her in. The American drug lord was the ideal woman for the job.

"The Director has made it clear: under no circumstance is the deal allowed to go through. You have clearance to do whatever's necessary to stop it." Bishop slid a manila folder across the table. "Everything else you need to know is in here."

"When's the meeting?"

"Tomorrow afternoon. You leave for Venice in the morning."

Maggie got up from her chair. She had prep to do before her travels, and Rebecca needed to be ready before leaving the country. "Anything else?"

"Yes. You won't be going alone."

Maggie straightened. "There's no need. I can do it myself."

Relying on others could ruin a mission, or worse, and she wasn't about to die thanks to someone else's screw up. She'd proven herself more than capable over the years, and Bishop knew she did her best work alone.

"Nonsense," Bishop said, dashing her hopes. "There's no way someone like Rebecca would travel to Venice without a bodyguard by her side. Leon will join you."

Leon Frost.

Maggie cleared her throat and wracked her brain for a good enough reason to object.

Bishop gave her a look. "I thought you'd be glad."

"Things are..." Maggie searched for the right word. "Complicated."

Complicated was an understatement.

"I've warned you before about allowing your personal life to interrupt your work."

"It won't," she promised.

"Then it's settled." Bishop opened his door for her. "Go home and get some rest. You're going to need it."

Chapter 3

24 JULY

M aggie gave up on sleep and got up with a couple of hours to spare before she needed to head to the airport.

She padded through her riverside apartment and prepared a much-needed coffee. The rejuvenating liquid dripped through the filter, and Maggie stretched her stiff muscles while she waited, yawning her head off.

Sleep always eluded her the night before a new mission. The mixture of anticipation and dread was an uncomfortable combination, like wearing a ball gown to a shoot-out. Something Maggie knew a thing or two about.

A meow slipped in through the window in her living

room, left open to contend with the humid heat that clung to the early morning air. The sun was making a guest appearance, stretching toward its perch high above the city. Summer was never a guarantee, the British seasons often quite happy to skip it altogether.

Maggie crossed the open floorplan and shimmied open the balcony. The murky waves of the River Thames below created a soothing song with its constant hum.

The impatient cat slinked in and weaved between her legs.

Scooping up Willow, Maggie headed back to the kitchen.

"You're hungry, I presume?" she asked the stray, who purred at the attention and raised her head to allow Maggie to scratch under her jaw.

Willow jumped from her arms onto the counter and plopped under the cupboard where Maggie kept tins of tuna for her feline visitor. She opened one onto a little plate, filled a bowl with water, and left Willow to scarf it down.

Maggie slurped her black coffee and raided the fridge in search of her own breakfast. She sighed. All it contained was some expired milk and a pot of jam. She'd get something at the airport.

A suitcase sat by the front door, filled with clothes she wouldn't choose to wear herself, the name on the tag not her own. Getting weapons through security wasn't a worry. According to the file Bishop handed her, the Italian government would supply everything they needed when she arrived.

When *they* arrived.

Leon was out on a job when she'd left for Poland. For the last few months, they passed like ships in the night, one leaving as the other returned home. It was the nature of their work, and one of the many things that caused problems in their on-again-off-again relationship.

They were most definitely in one of their off-again phases. Had been for a while. No matter how many times they tried, something got in the way. Maggie concluded a few months back that they just weren't meant to be.

That didn't stop her from missing him though. Lazy Sundays in bed watching films. His infectious smile. How he made her feel safe and secure in his arms, one of the only things that fought off her nightmares. Yet another hazard of her job.

The things she'd seen and done...

Maggie shook the thoughts away and returned to her bedroom. She sat at her dressing table to get ready. Her luggage from Warsaw remained unpacked by the bed, but like most things in her life, it would have to wait.

Each agent at the Unit had a wide range of skills, everything they needed to protect and serve Queen and country. Back in training, Maggie learned everything from languages and foreign etiquette, to mixed martial arts and weapons skills. Most students displayed an affinity for a particular field. For some it was tactics, for others logistics.

For Maggie, it was undercover work. Namely, adapting herself into someone else.

"Hey, I'm Rebecca," she said, staring at herself in the mirror. The fake tan she'd applied the night before gave her pale skin the sun-kissed glow of someone who lived by the beach. The blond hair framing her vulpine features had to go.

Rebecca Sterling was one of many aliases Maggie had adopted during her time as an agent. For six years, she'd hopped from one country to the next, molding into different personas to infiltrate the criminal underworld and eliminate those within it.

It was like method acting, except she wouldn't get a bad review from a local theatre critic if she had a bad night. She'd lose her life.

Changing her appearance was the easy part. The real skill involved, the thing that separated Maggie from her less adept colleagues, was the internal change.

"Let's get to business, shall we?" Maggie paid close attention to her inflection. It had been some time since she last used her American alias.

Rebecca Sterling was born and raised in Miami, Florida to a small-time drug dealer father, and a mother who spent most of her time sampling his product. After her mother died of an overdose when she was eight-years-old, Rebecca was put to work in the family business. At first, she counted the money her dad brought home, piling it in little stacks and watching it grow. As time went by, she graduated to cutting the drugs and weighing them out into single bags ready to sell.

"I mixed powdered caffeine pills into the blow. No one noticed the difference, and it gives us twenty percent more product to sell."

Maggie pulled her hair back and placed a cap over it, ensuring no errant strands escaped. She only used the most premium wigs made from real human hair. It was vital not to stand out for the wrong reasons. Placing the hair over her own, she secured it in place with pins and brushed her fingers through the lush brown waves.

"Does it bother you that I'm a woman?" Maggie cocked her head to the side. Rebecca liked to cut through the bullshit and get to the heart of the matter, especially if it made her opponents uncomfortable.

By the time Rebecca was nineteen, the business had grown from the kitchen table in their run-down apartment to a lucrative, full-blown enterprise. Rising to the top wasn't plain sailing, however, and the father-daughter duo earned themselves enemies in the form of rival dealers. Like a lot of men, those rivals underestimated Rebecca.

When a Mexican cartel arranged the assassination of her father, Rebecca fought back with everything she had. Where they had brawn and greater man power, Rebecca had brains and a ruthless thirst for revenge.

Maggie smirked. "In my experience, money solves all problems."

Heading to the source, Rebecca met with the Colombian drug baron in charge of distributing the city's supply and secured a deal. As payment for agreeing to take over the Mexicans' contract for a substantially higher price, the baron would burn her rivals to the ground.

And that's exactly what happened.

Now, uncontested and with close ties to the Colombians, Rebecca reigns supreme and with an iron fist. Or so the story goes.

In actual fact, the Colombians decided to cut out the middle man and run the streets of Miami for themselves. Having no further need for the Mexican cartel, they simply got rid of them.

With no one willing to incriminate themselves and admit to wiping out the Mexicans, the persona of Rebecca did, creating an almost urban legend of an elusive young woman who didn't suffer fools lightly and liked to remain in the shadows.

From what Bishop told her, Rebecca was wanted for questioning by Miami state police and the Drug Enforcement Administration. That alone helped reinforce the rumors spread by agents in the field, and word of mouth did most of the work from there.

Maggie dug through the dresser drawer for a set of light brown contacts and slid them over her ice blue eyes, blinking them into place.

The Unit would never risk using Rebecca on her home turf. There were too many opportunities for things to go wrong. Too many things that could catch her out.

Elsewhere was another thing entirely. It always amazed Maggie how most criminals never paid much attention to the dealings of their peers overseas, unless they were directly involved.

Carlo and the Rossi family might be able to learn a bit about Rebecca through their contacts, but they wouldn't get much. Besides, people like Carlo were far more invested in their own domestic interests, and Rebecca would bank that if the money was right, they wouldn't care who they sold to.

Satisfied with her transformation, Maggie changed clothes. Willow was gone when she returned, and she closed up her barely lived in apartment and caught a taxi to Heathrow.

By the time she entered the airport and approached the check in desk, Maggie *was* Rebecca.

"Where are you headed?" asked the man behind the desk.

Maggie handed over her ticket along with Rebecca's US passport.

"Venice."

Chapter 4

Maggie touched down in Venice Marco Polo Airport a little after ten o'clock.

Leon waited for her by arrivals.

"Take these," she said in place of a greeting and passed him the luggage. She wasn't Maggie meeting a colleague; she was Rebecca ordering about her personal bodyguard.

The Rossi family could have people awaiting her arrival with orders to report back. Even if they didn't, it wasn't wise to break character in such a public space. There was no telling who was watching, and concealing her true identity was a major priority for Maggie.

The success of the mission depended on it.

As far as she knew, she'd successfully kept her identity a secret. Anyone who met the real Maggie never lived long enough to spread the word.

There was a first time for everything, but she wasn't about to slip up now.

"Nice to see you, Ms. Sterling," Leon said as he grabbed her bags and led them outside.

The port was a five-minute walk from the airport's main building. Passengers marched in an eager line of rolling suitcases that rumbled over the hot tarmac.

With a two-way stream of tourists using the same narrow walkway, the line was forced into single file. Leon took the lead, and Maggie appreciated the view from behind her dark-framed sunglasses. The white fitted t-shirt contrasted nicely against his black skin and hugged his defined torso, the fabric straining around prominent biceps.

"How was your flight?" he asked, peering over his shoulder. Like his hair, Leon kept his beard trimmed short, his full lips and deep brown eyes as alluring as ever.

"Not as bad as the long-haul from Miami to London." Maggie wished no one was around so they could have a real conversation. "You European's have it good. A little two-hour flight and you're in a new country."

"Our friend is meeting us at the dock." Leon's graveled voice rumbled deep in his chest.

"Good," Maggie said. "She can get us up to speed for the meeting."

They walked onto the dock where a line of water buses and taxis bobbed in the waves, waiting to ferry the new arrivals across the lagoon to the main city and surrounding islands.

Maggie spotted their ride beyond the string of public transport and private hires. A sleek speedboat was parked at the end of the dock, the polished mahogany topside shining under the intense sun.

A woman waited onboard, speaking to the driver as Maggie and Leon approached. Maggie recognized Isabella Valentin from the photo supplied in the mission files.

"Benvignùo," she said in her native tongue. "Welcome. You must be Rebecca."

Leon passed the bags to the driver who secured them up front while Maggie stepped down to board the boat.

"And you must be Isabella." Maggie greeted the woman with a kiss on each cheek.

In her forties, Isabella wore her long dark hair tied back smartly from her face, the beginnings of crow's feet appearing at the corners of her warm eyes as she welcomed them. She was impeccably dressed in a high-end fashion Maggie had grown to expect of Venetians, her designer blouse and skirt hugging every curve. Style was just as much a part of Italy's history as art and architecture.

Leon hopped onboard and the driver pulled out and headed off.

When they were a safe distance from the shore,

Isabella smiled wide at them both. "Maggie, Leon, it is nice to finally meet you."

Leon eyed the driver.

"He's one of ours," assured Isabella, leading them to sit inside the cabin as the waves picked up and sprayed the sides of the boat. The seats were upholstered in fine cream leather, and Leon had to lean his large frame back to stop his head from touching the roof.

Outside, they whizzed across the lagoon, staying between large wooden posts buried deep into the marshy depths below which sprouted out the water to guide the traffic. Salt clung to the air from the sea water and mixed with Isabella's strong floral perfume, the aroma inescapable in the close confines of the cabin.

"Carlo asked me to take you to your hotel," Isabella said, getting down to business.

"How's he feeling about the meeting?" In the cramped quarters, Maggie's shoulders brushed Leon's arm and she inched away. They couldn't afford any distractions.

Isabella considered the question for a moment before answering. "He is very set in his ways. Peter West has met with him several times now. I fear Carlo likes him. It will not be easy to sway him from a deal with Peter if he has already made up his mind."

"Then why agree to the meeting in the first place?" Leon asked.

"I advised him to do it." Isabella crossed her legs as

they picked up speed. The boat jumped over the waves, the outline of the historic city coming into view.

"He must respect your opinion," Maggie said. Carlo wouldn't listen to just anyone when it came to his business.

Isabella nodded, seeming pleased. "I've worked by his side for years, slowly gaining his trust. I've proven myself in his eyes. I do not make a habit of getting involved in his decisions, so when I speak, he listens."

"Tell me about him and his family." The more Maggie knew, the more ammunition she had in her artillery. Men of Carlo's age and position abided by a code of respect, and it would be a sign of bad taste to go against Peter West at such a late stage in negotiations. Maggie would need to make the man an offer he couldn't refuse.

"In the early seventies, my government exiled key members of the Sicilian Mafia to the north in an attempt to isolate and weaken their infrastructure and power."

"I'm guessing it backfired?" Maggie asked.

"Terribly," Isabella agreed. "Carlo was among those sent to solitary confinement in a provincial town in Veneto. Instead of settling down, Carlo sought out the local gangs and bandits and brought them all together under his leadership. What was once a scattered mix of criminals, became a group of mobsters, eventually growing to the widespread syndicate it is today with Carlo still at the helm."

The file Bishop supplied indicated Carlo had been

running the region of Veneto from his home in Venice for decades now, and the family showed no signs of slowing down. Despite attempts by the government and other opposing syndicates, the Rossi family still ruled supreme over the lagoon, their influence felt throughout the city.

"Carlo's old," Maggie noted. "Who's going to take his place?"

Isabella sighed. "It's generally acknowledged that Carlo's son, Stefano, will take over when the time is right."

Maggie took note of their ally's distaste. It was clear Isabella did not like Stefano. Maggie stored the information with everything else she learned, keeping it all in a mental file she could access when needed.

"How much influence does Stefano have on his old man?" Leon asked.

"Not much," replied Isabella. "They see things very differently. Carlo is traditional, but Stefano wants to bring the family into the twenty-first century. It's one of the main reasons Carlo is so determined not to hand over the reins."

No luck there then. Though there could be ways to use the contention between father and son to her advantage, if she played it right.

"What about rival factions? I read they were a potential threat to Carlo's rule." The more Maggie understood the pressures facing Carlo, the better she could exploit them.

"Carlo doesn't seem to think so," said Isabella. "The

Marinos are a younger set up than the Rossis. Less organized."

"Have there been any attempts to take over?"

Isabella shrugged. "There's been a few run ins, but nothing substantial. The Marinos are more of a nuisance than anything else."

Maggie nodded along, but she wasn't as quick to write off the rival family. They may not have the same level of influence and power as Carlo's gang, but being the underdog brought a level of bold eagerness and hunger.

If they had nothing to lose, they had everything to gain.

The boat jolted the trio forward as the driver slowed down. He bashed the horn and yelled at another boat which overtook them, waving his arms. Maggie gripped the edge of her seat. Driving in Italy was just as fraught in the water as it was on the roads.

"Bishop told me you'd have supplies for us," Maggie said as they drew closer to their destination.

"Of course." Isabelle collected the briefcase sitting next to her and opened it for them. Two Beretta 8000's, more commonly known as Cougars, winked up from the case. While not compact, it was a better alternative to the larger Beretta 92. The 9mm semi-automatic was similar to Maggie's Glock and would allow her to conceal the weapon without too much trouble.

Maggie nodded. "These will work."

Isabella and the Italian government kindly supplied

them with extra magazines and rounds, as well as a set of knives, just in case. Hopefully the weapons would remain unused and she and Leon could return them good as new.

Maggie passed one of the guns to Leon and tucked the other into the waistband at the small of her back. Being unarmed left her uneasy, and the presence of the weapon settled her nerves like a security blanket.

Outside, the outskirts of the city unfolded before them. Maggie ducked out to the back of the boat. Leaning on the roof to keep her steady, she drank in the view.

It wasn't Maggie's first time in the sinking city, but each visit felt just as magical.

Water sloshed up against the sides of buildings on either side of the canal as they slowed to a steadier pace. Layers of slime and algae showed how far the water rose during high tide. The walls were painted in vibrant shades of yellows and oranges with cracks spread across them like fractured glass. Holes dotted over the facades where the brick, fragile with age, had crumbled off into rubble.

Opaque water rippled at their presence and hid what lay below as they ventured deeper into the city. Leon came out of the cabin and joined her.

"It doesn't look real," he said after a while.

He was right. By all accounts, the city shouldn't exist.

Built by peasants on nothing but marshland, Venice was held up by wooden stilts. Somehow, it had persisted over the centuries. From the initial shabby little homes to the sublime city it became, Venice had endured the impossible and thrived under the unique conditions of living in a floating city.

"Is this your first time in Venice?" Maggie asked, a little shocked.

"Yes," said Leon, taking it all in.

They exited through the capillaries of connecting canals and found themselves in the main artery. The Grand Canal was a hub of activity as waterbuses, gondolas, kayaks, and taxis swam past each other, the chaotic traffic forming semi-organized patterns through the water.

The arched dome of the Salute Cathedral filled the horizon, a vital part to the city's skyline that had been painted by some of the best artists in the world.

Maggie and Leon watched as they passed the heart of the city. The Doge's Palace dominated the right-hand side of St Mark's Square, its arched architecture like something from a fairytale. The basilica lay at the far back, adding more domes to the landscape, while the cathedral tower loomed high above them all and offered the perfect spot to take in the wonders of Venice.

The city had many incarnations over the years, from being the center of maritime trade, to one of the world's major financial hubs. These days, most of its money came from tourism, and from the number of people clogging the square, it was rolling in Euros.

The boat jerked again to allow room for a passing gondola, and Maggie stumbled. She fell back and braced for a fall that never came.

"Steady," Leon said as he caught her in his strong arms.

Maggie placed a hand on his chest; his heart beat steady against her palm. She met his eyes and a flutter danced in her stomach.

Isabella called from inside as she made to join them. Maggie cleared her throat and let Leon go. "Thanks."

"Your hotel is right there." Isabella pointed to a lavish building on their right, situated beside the opening of the Grand Canal. A terrace jutted out to create an outdoor dining area with idyllic views across the water, the surface shimmering under the warm rays of the sun. Guests sat outside eating breakfast and drinking espresso from little cups, while a group of tourists sipped on prosecco despite the early hour and toasted to the trip of their dreams.

It was a remarkable location, and everything about it exuded luxury and decadence. Maggie grinned. It was the perfect place for someone like Rebecca Sterling to stay while on business.

"I will see you both at the meeting this afternoon." Isabella took Maggie's hand and gave it a squeeze. "Good luck."

There was a tremor in her touch, but the Venetian hid it well, showing none of her fear on her beautiful face.

"Look after yourself." Maggie knew what Isabella risked with the upcoming meeting. If her cover broke, there would be no getting out. People like Carlo were unforgiving, and if Isabella did return home, it would only be to send a message. One that required no words, only the delivery of her body in severed parts.

The boat pulled up to the private dock, and they were greeted by an elderly gentleman in an impeccable suit and two young porters who took their bags from the driver.

"Hello," he said. "Welcome to the Gritti Palace. My name is Guido. So nice to see you, Ms. Sterling."

"Hey, Guido." Maggie fell back into character with a flawless American accent. "Can you give me a hand?"

"Of course." The old man leaned over and helped her off the boat.

Maggie turned and waved off Isabella and the driver, but only for a moment. Rebecca wouldn't waste time saying goodbye to those providing her transport from the airport.

"We have the Pisani Suite reserved just for you. Very nice." Guido led Maggie and Leon through a lavish foyer with pristine marble floors, plush sofas in royal reds, and large mirrors and paintings hanging on the walls in gilded frames.

The elevators pinged open and they stepped inside. "At almost seven thousand Euro a night, I sure hope so," said Maggie. Rebecca may be rich—and she certainly enjoyed that wealth—but she never forgot where she came from, or what it took to get to where she was today.

As they stepped from the elevator and entered the suite nestled in the corner of the building, Maggie whistled. "This is a far cry from Miami, I'll say that much."

The suite screamed indulgence across every inch of the lounge area, bedroom, and even the bathroom. Floor-to-ceiling French doors opened out from the lounge to two balconies that offered stunning views of the Grand Canal and the adjacent canal that ran along the side of the building and led deeper into San Marco.

Majestic chandeliers twinkled in the breeze, created by the famed glassblowers of the neighboring island Murano. Venetians wouldn't hang anything else, viewing all others glasswork as cheap imitation.

Guido and the porters carried the luggage into the bedroom and offered to unpack their things into the ample storage provided.

"No, I'll do it myself," called Maggie from the lounge. The last thing she needed was for one of them to open the suitcase with the knives and ammunition. She shooed the men off, and finally relaxed now that she and Leon were alone.

Her calm didn't last long.

"Oh," she said when she entered the bedroom and spotted the problem making Leon's forehead crease.

There was only one bed.

A nice king-sized bed, perfect for a weekend getaway in one of the most romantic cities in the world.

Leon ran a hand over the back of his neck. "I can sleep on the couch."

"You can take the bed," offered Maggie, heat rushing to her cheeks. "I'm shorter."

"No, it's okay." Leon removed his bag off the bed. "I've slept in worse places."

"We can figure it out later." Sleeping arrangements were the least of their worries. In less than three hours, they would come face to face with one of the most notorious Mafiosos in Italy, and Maggie had to be ready. "I'm going to change."

Rebecca had a meeting to attend.

Chapter 5

The meeting was scheduled for one o'clock at the Palazzina Grassi hotel, which was named after the seventeenth century palace it sat beside. No stranger to the presence of celebrities and foreign dignitaries, the hotel was famed for catering to high-end clients, and it seemed Carlo Rossi was no exception.

The hotel housed the Krug Lounge, an exclusive place for the social elite to drink and dine among their peers. The lounge extended onto a roof terrace, tucked discreetly away from the busy streets and canals to create a hidden oasis.

Maggie had checked online before leaving for the meeting to get an idea of the location. She would have preferred to scope out the area personally, but given the time restraints and the fact Rebecca's presence could raise questions she didn't want to answer, she settled for digital.

32

The entrance was right on the Grand Canal, about halfway between her suite at the Gritti and the Rialto Bridge. Guido had arranged for transport, courtesy of the hotel of course. Maggie and Leon stepped out from the boat into the hotel's arched waterfront entrance and were each greeted with a bubbling glass of champagne.

Maggie tugged at Rebecca's fitted white suit, feeling confined in the expensive fabric. She was more of a t-shirt and jeans kind of girl and enjoyed lounging around her apartment in her pajamas on days off. At least she didn't have to wear a dress or force her feet into a pair of heels. Rebecca preferred flats, having learned early on that dressing with a masculine edge made men take her more seriously.

A waitress led them upstairs to the restaurant on the roof's terrace. Wrought iron chairs were tucked under round tables, surrounded by large pots with twisted trees canopying over them to create an intimate environment for guests. Beyond, the terrace looked out to the tops of surrounding buildings, a mass of close knit roofs crowned with terracotta tiles.

"You ready?" asked Leon by her side, decked out in a sleek navy suit that, if possible, made him even more handsome than usual.

"As I'll ever be," Maggie replied, taking a deep breath.

She straightened her back and put on her best Rebecca smile, a knowing grin that hinted danger. Rebecca was many things, but boring wasn't one of them. She exuded a charismatic confidence in everything she did. There was no doubt in Rebecca's mind that the meeting with the crime boss would go her way.

The waitress led them to the corner of the terrace where four people sat waiting on their arrival. They weren't alone, of course. Maggie clocked the armed guards dotted around the rooftop, none of them trying very hard to be inconspicuous. Carlo wouldn't go anywhere in public without a detail given who he was and the nature of his business.

Isabella stood from her chair. "Ms. Sterling, so nice to see you again. Please, take a seat."

Maggie complied and sat at one of the two chairs left out for her and Leon, directly across from the Mafioso.

Antipasto lay out across the table in a delectable spread of bruschetta, cured meats, soft cheeses, and ripe olives. In a normal setting, Maggie would have delved in and enjoyed the local delicacies, washing them down with the sweet champagne in her glass.

Only, it wasn't a normal setting.

"Ms. Sterling," said Isabella, playing her own role for the meeting, "it is my pleasure to introduce you to Carlo Rossi."

Maggie held out an expectant hand to Carlo. A rumble of unease rippled through the table, and she spotted one of the guards reaching inside their jacket. Touching, it seemed, was not allowed.

Nevertheless, Maggie waited until Carlo took her

offered hand and shook it. His grip was firm and confident. Maggie matched him and squeezed his weathered hand, earning her a surprised raise of his white bushy eyebrows.

Rebecca was used to men like him. Where most grew intimidated under the stare of men in power, Rebecca reveled in it and saw an equal. Someone worth doing business with. An opponent with whom to barter favorable terms.

"Pleasure to meet you, Carlo," said Maggie, holding his gaze. She doubted anyone there called the man by his first name.

Carlo looked well for a man in his twilight years. He had managed to cling on to his hair, a thick mop of white which was combed back with product and matched the bristled moustache above his thin lips. A portly stomach bunched up against the edge of the table from decades of over-indulgence, yet he didn't seem unfit or fragile with age. There was still fight left in the old Sicilian, and his dark eyes were sharp as he considered her.

"Likewise," replied Carlo in accented English.

It was far better than her Venetian or Italian. Maggie was fluent in several languages, including French and Russian, but her knowledge of Carlo's home tongue was limited to simple pleasantries.

Isabella motioned to the man at her boss's left and the young woman who sat at the bottom of the table. "This is Stefano, Carlo's son, and Angela, Carlo's granddaughter."

"Bondi," said Maggie, greeting them with a good afternoon and deliberately botching the Venetian. Europeans expected as much from Americans.

Maggie didn't introduce Leon. Like the armed detail surrounding the little terrace, Rebecca's bodyguard was to be seen, not heard.

Stefano nodded yet remained silent, regarding Maggie with open interest. He was much like his father, only a couple of decades younger, with a stalky build and dark hair. They both shared a prominent Roman nose which took center stage on their faces.

"How are you finding Venice?" asked Stefano's daughter, Angela. Her English was perfect.

"Beautiful, as always," Maggie replied, sending a subtle wink to Angela over the rim of her glass as she took a sip. Rebecca liked women, especially those like Carlo's granddaughter.

Angela was a vision. In her early twenties, she was a mixture of sharp cheekbones and small, rounded features, framed by thick, black curls that fell past her shoulders. Maggie looked between the woman and her father and concluded Stefano's wife must be a model.

"Would you like to order something from the menu?" Isabella asked, her usual brisk and efficient nature altered to one more subdued and subservient in her role as Carlo's assistant.

"No, thanks. Let's get to business, shall we?" Maggie replied, speaking to Carlo.

The old man shrugged and chewed on an olive before

taking a deep drink from his champagne. "I wasn't aware we had any business."

"And yet you still agreed to a meeting." Maggie shot him a smile, Rebecca unbothered by his slight. It was a play for power, and she was well versed in the art.

Carlo's hands made a steeple. "Only because I was advised to by someone I respect."

Stefano's face fell at his father's words and his eyes narrowed on Isabella. There was no love lost there, then.

"You were advised well." Maggie took note of Stefano's reaction in case she could use it. "I hear you're in discussions with Peter West."

"And how did you come to learn that piece of information?"

"It's my job to know these things."

"I wonder," mused Carlo, swirling his champagne. "Have you been sent by my rivals to disrupt my current negotiations?"

Maggie sat back in her chair and relaxed, like they were simply meeting for lunch. "I don't work for the Marino family. I have my own agenda."

If the man was shocked at her knowledge, he didn't show it. "Which is?"

"A counter offer." She took one of Carlo's olives and popped it in her mouth.

"I'm afraid you're too late," said Angela. "The deal has been agreed upon. Besides, we hardly know you."

"Quiet girl," Carlo spat, cutlery clinking as he

slammed a meaty fist on the table. "You speak when you're spoken to."

Angela's cheeks flushed, glaring at her grandfather as her eyes grew glossy. "Excuse me," she said, raising her chin in a gallant attempt to save face. "I need to use the restroom."

Without another word, she collected her purse and marched off.

Carlo shook his head as she left. "Bold youth."

"Not always a bad thing," said Maggie. Angela was right to be suspicious.

Stefano lit a cigar and blew a puff of smoke into the air, seeming unbothered by the transgression. Maggie balled a fist under the table and bit back a request for him to stop staring at her like she was a piece of meat. He blew a mouthful of smoke towards her, and Maggie considered how it would impact negotiations if she stabbed him with her fork.

Leon's body was tense beside her, and he stared at Stefano with open distain. Maggie placed a hand on his leg, a reminder of where they were and why.

"Angela is right, though," continued Carlo. "The deal is set."

Maggie focused her attention back to the boss. "Not from what I hear."

"We're simply ironing out the details."

"I think we should at least hear what this fine lady has to say," commented Stefano, speaking for the first time.

Carlo spun on his son. "And I think you should shut your mouth."

The air grew thick with tension. Was Stefano testing his father? Were he not family, the repercussions of speaking out of turn could have been severe. Did Stefano think it was time for his father to retire and give up his throne? It seemed Maggie wasn't the only one in a power play with Carlo.

Maggie cleared her throat. "If you're both quite finished, I'd like to propose my offer." Rebecca nor Maggie may speak Venetian, but they spoke the only language that mattered. Money.

Father and son broke their contentious gaze and listened.

"I will offer you double what Peter West is offering for the distribution deal."

Carlo narrowed his eyes. "Why would you do that?"

"It's simple. You have an overabundance of quality product, and I have a market that's always hungry for more."

"You're from Miami, no?" Carlo held his plate out to Isabella, who piled on the antipasto. "Why not have the Colombians supply you?"

Carlo was no fool, but neither was Maggie.

"They do," she replied, "but I need a more stable supplier. My government's cracking down hard on imports, and I've lost too many shipments to their raids."

Over the years, the US had waged a hard war against

drug trafficking, especially from south of their border. While the drugs still managed to find their way through, it was becoming increasingly difficult to ensure the safe passage of Colombian narcotics. Dealers in places like Miami had to adapt and be more inventive when it came to slipping their supply past the authorities.

"What makes you think a shipment from us would fare any better?" asked Carlo, tucking into a slice of bruschetta.

"I have a contact in immigration who can ensure safe passage of stock brought in from Europe. Border control isn't as stringent with European cargo. I plan to have it land in Virginia and transported the rest of the way by road."

"Why not direct?"

"There are too many random checks and security measures in place for my state. The authorities have gotten too good at weeding out deliveries coming into the ports at Miami and Orlando. It's a risk I'd rather avoid."

Maggie couldn't gauge if she was winning Carlo over. Back in training, the Unit taught her to read body language, yet the man before her was an enigma. He had years of practice at these kind of sit downs, more decades than she'd been alive.

"And the Mexicans?" he asked between chews. "Surely they can help you?"

Maggie frowned and lowered her voice to a growl. "I don't deal with those fuckers."

Isabella whispered into Carlo's ear. He put down his

fork and knife and met Maggie's eyes. "My condolences about your father."

"Thank you," she replied, making a show of recovering from the mention of the people who murdered Rebecca's dad.

Carlo wiped his lips with his napkin and tossed it over his empty plate. "That said, I'm afraid I cannot take you up on your offer. A deal is a deal, and I am a man of my word."

Shit. She was losing him.

Stefano leaned close to his father and muttered, loud enough so everyone at the table could hear him. "She's offering twice as much as Peter."

"And I can order more than him, too," she added, grasping for anything to seal the deal. "The US is a much larger market than little old Britain. I have a lot more customers to satisfy."

It wasn't like she needed to follow through on any of it. All she had to do was ensure the deal with Peter West fell through. It would sour things between Peter and the Rossi family, enough that no further agreements would arise between them.

Carlo sat in silence for a while, brows burrowed. Maggie's heartbeat quickened, and a trickle of sweat ran down her back. She fought the urge to bite her lip.

"You make an enticing offer, Ms. Sterling, but my answer is no. It is too late to–"

Carlo never got to finish his last words.

A bullet to his neck saw to that.

Chapter 6

Blood spurted from the bullet hole in Carlo's neck and sprayed over Maggie's white suit.

Isabella shot up from her seat and shoved the table away to reach Carlo, who sat wide eyed and gurgling. Carlo cupped his neck, but the blood flowed through his fingers in a scarlet fountain that wouldn't stop until it ran dry.

It was too late.

Someone had fired a kill shot.

A waitress screamed and dropped a tray of drinks, the glass shattering across the floor as the guests dining on the terrace scraped their seats back and ran for cover.

Carlo's detail sprang into action. Two grabbed Stefano by the arms and dragged him away from his dying father. Isabella went without a fuss, her face pale and splattered red. The rest of the men picked up a squirming Carlo and carried him inside the building to the covered safety of the restaurant. A guard stood at either end with their gun raised and eyes on the lookout for the culprit.

They weren't the only ones.

Maggie and Leon ducked behind one of the large potted plants for cover in case the shooter wasn't finished.

She scanned beyond the terrace, searching to the west based on the location of the entry wound in Carlo's neck. Her heart drummed in her ears, and Leon held a protective arm over her as she narrowed in on the gunman.

"There," she said, spotting a man on the roof a few buildings away. Maggie looked around. The terrace was abandoned, empty in a matter of seconds. "I'm going after him."

Leon was by her side seconds later, his long legs catching up to her. "Not without me."

The streets were so narrow in the San Marco area, that there wasn't a huge gap between the terrace to the nearest rooftop, but it was still a deadly fall should they slip. Maggie climbed the railing surrounding the terrace and jumped.

Reaching out, Maggie caught the edge of the roof and hoisted herself up. Leon landed on his feet beside her and held out a hand to help.

The shooter saw them coming and took off at a run.

They followed, charging over the tiled roof. The shooter reached the edge of his building and hurdled across to the next one, taking off again as soon as he landed. Maggie caught sight of his face, but she didn't know it.

Italian. Five foot ten. Dark hair. Fast.

A spurt of ruble burst from the tiles near Maggie's feet as the gunshot echoed through the air. The killer aimed another shot at them, and they dived out of the way as he turned and hurtled through the rooftops.

"Bastard," spat Maggie. Killing Carlo was one thing, but trying to end them too was a big mistake.

She and Leon raced forward and came to the end of their building. They looked at each other in silent agreement and leaped. For a moment, all that lay under Maggie's feet was air and the hard, unforgiving ground four stories down.

The roof was a few feet lower than the one they had jumped from, and Maggie landed in a roll to break the fall, scuffing Rebecca's ruined suit. She reached inside her jacket and brought out her Beretta.

Aiming as she gave chase, the shooter ran past a chimney and blocked her shot.

They continued, narrowing the gap and springing over to the next roof. An old woman was hanging her washing out on a line from a window below and yelled at them with a wave of her fist.

A flock of fat, tourist-fed pigeons burst from a coop as they rounded the corner their target took. The birds flapped at them with coos of surprise, flocking around them with frantic wings. Maggie charged through them, Leon swearing at them to piss off.

"We're going to lose him," said Leon, as the bridge between them and the killer lengthened.

Maggie studied his trajectory and took in the layout of rooftops around them. "No, we're not. Take the left. I'll go this way." She pointed to the right. "We'll round in on him."

Leon nodded and dove across to the next set of buildings, zeroing in on the shooter. Maggie ran further down until she reached her opening and sprung off the edge.

A shooting pain shot up her leg as she landed down on the conjoined building, the impact making her muscles yell in pain. Maggie gritted her teeth and surged on.

Across the way, Leon kept pace and narrowed in on the killer from the sidelines. Maggie pushed herself, ignoring her complaining muscles and the heat from under her brown wig.

Focusing on the shooter, she counted two more jumps before she was on him. The killer risked a look over his shoulder and spotted them coming in from either end.

Maggie quickened her pace.

The first gap was nothing, and she was over to the other side with little effort, her chest heaving as sweat beaded across her forehead. The second jump approached, and her heart plummeted.

The gap was wide. Too wide.

Her feet sped forward, propelled with momentum and

getting closer and closer to the end of the building with each step. If she tried to slow down now, she would topple over the edge. She would never make it.

With no other option, Maggie leaped forward and soared into the air.

She flew, inching closer towards safe ground like she was moving in slow motion.

But it wasn't enough. Her feet wouldn't clear the gap.

Below, people walked through the narrow street, smiling for photos and browsing the line of little shops selling trinkets and cheap souvenirs.

Maggie reached out as the rooftops fell from her line of sight.

Her fingers gripped the drainpipe running along the roof, and she clung on tight. She cried out as her fingers took on the burden of her weight.

The metal dug into her fingers, but she fought through the pain. Her mind raced as panic threatened to take over. She squirmed in the air, her feet scraping over the wall of the building to find purchase.

Her foot snagged on something, and Maggie tested it, her fingers slipping from the drainpipe. It was a loose brick, the hole just wide enough to fit her shoe in.

Maggie shifted her weight to her foot and allowed her fingers a slight reprieve, but she couldn't just stay there. If she lost her grip, she would fall back and plummet to the street below.

With one final push, Maggie tightened her grip on the

drainpipe and pulled herself up with everything she had. Her arms shook, and fatigue settled in her muscles. She managed to swing her right arm up over the edge and elbow her way high enough to release her foot from the brick wall and kick it up over the roof. She rolled to safety, panting and struggling for air.

With no time to lose, she stumbled to her feet and hurried along the rooftop.

Leon was almost at the shooter now, who had come to an abrupt stop. The killer had run out of roof. The next set of buildings were far across the way, separated by the murky turquoise water of the canal below.

Leon ran up by her side as she aimed her gun at the shooter.

"There's nowhere left to run," she said. "Put your hands on your head and don't move."

The shooter clung to his weapon, even though it was two against one. He stepped back until his heels hovered over the edge and peered over his shoulder. His chest heaved, and he looked as exhausted as Maggie felt.

She and Leon stepped towards him, guns at the ready. "Don't do it," she warned.

Before she even finished her sentence, the shooter stepped back into open air.

Maggie and Leon ran to the edge as he landed in the canal with a splash.

Two people on a boat below helped the shooter out the water. At first, Maggie assumed they were passersby, but one of them reached for their waist and sent three rounds their way.

They dropped for cover and lay flat on the tiles as an engine roared to life. Maggie crawled to the edge and peered beyond as the boat sped off down the canal with the shooter on board.

Chapter 7

Maggie walked out from her second shower since the disastrous meeting. There was something about being covered in someone else's blood that made her feel especially unclean.

Unlike the blood, she couldn't simply wash away the memories. There was no doubt Carlo was dead. Even if Maggie never saw the body, there was no coming back from a shot like that.

The Rossis were short of a leader. For now.

Maggie wrapped herself in a silk robe and padded out into the lounge. Her mouth watered at the aroma filling the room.

"I ordered room service," said Leon, sitting at the dining table. "I figured you'd want to stay in."

"Thank you." Going out for something to eat meant having to be Rebecca. After the day they'd had, being shot at and running across the rooftops of Venice after a killer, they deserved to kick back and relax for the evening.

"Prosecco?" Leon pulled a chair out for her.

Maggie held out her glass. "Please."

Leon filled her up then sat down across from her and raised his own flute. "Cheers."

"Cheers." Bubbles danced over her tongue, and she drained half the glass. "Though I don't think we're out of hot water yet."

They hadn't heard from Isabella since the meeting turned deadly. No messages were waiting for them when they returned to the hotel after stopping to change into new clothes on the way back. Arriving at a place like the Gritti Palace covered in blood and dirt was bound to raise some eyebrows.

"You think the deal will still go ahead?" Leon asked, topping off both their glasses.

"Carlo may be dead, but business won't stop because of it." If syndicates stopped their dealings every time they lost a don, there wouldn't be any left. A new leader would rise.

"Nothing will be done tonight. Hopefully, we'll hear from Isabella tomorrow and we can take action from there."

"You're right." Maggie leaned back in her chair and rolled her shoulders, muscles aching from the chase. She had garnered more than a few bruises from it, too. "There's nothing we can do for now."

"We can eat," said Leon. "I don't know about you, but I'm starving."

Six different dishes sat between them, concealed beneath silver cloches. Maggie's stomach growled. "What did you order?"

"A bit of everything," he replied, taking the covers off.

Steam rose from the dishes, and Maggie's mouth watered. Leon had ordered a selection of local specialties from squid ink risotto, thick bigoli pasta with mussels in a garlic and butter sauce, and carpaccio sliced paper thin and garnished with parmesan cheese.

"Oh, you got prawns." Maggie filled her plate. The hotel would have bought them fresh from the Rialto Market that very morning. "I thought you didn't like them?"

"I don't, but I know you do." Leon skipped the shell-fish, filling his plate with gnocchi.

They ate in quiet for a while, falling into the comfortable silence gained from having known each other for years. No matter how long they were apart, things with Leon always started back like they had never ended. It felt normal. Right.

"How did things go in Warsaw?" he asked after a while, a drop of sauce stuck to his beard.

Maggie smiled and reached over the table to wipe it off with a thumb. "I wasn't there long. I had to wrap things up a little sooner than expected, thanks to this. What about your job in Dubai?"

"It got a little hairy, but it worked out in the end."

Knowing Leon, 'a little hairy' meant he almost died at least twice.

"How have you been?" she asked, focusing on her food. "You know, aside from work?"

What Maggie really wanted to ask was if Leon was seeing anyone, but she wasn't sure she'd like the answer. They never agreed to be exclusive. It wasn't fair on either of them to expect it of the other. Not when their lives were so up in the air, spending most of their time apart in separate countries. Not when they had tried and failed so many times to make it work. With no promises came no expectations, and it stopped them from getting hurt in the long run.

Maggie knew it was better that way, but it didn't make it any easier to accept when Leon sat across from her, their legs touching underneath the table.

"Good," said Leon, after a while. He stopped eating and met her eyes. "I've missed you."

"I've missed you, too." She hadn't realized how much until the moment he picked her up at the airport. It was vital to push her feelings aside while out on a mission. She could hide her emotions beneath the tough exterior of her aliases and forget about her own troubles.

It was another thing entirely now she was face to face with them.

"How are your parents?" she asked, changing the subject before the feelings of loss could take hold. They'd done well so far keeping things professional. Maggie got up and piled the empty dishes on the service cart, returning with dessert.

"They're doing well." Leon tipped what was left of the bottle of prosecco into their glasses. "Mum always asks about you."

"I'll need to pop round for a cuppa," she said and meant it.

Maggie liked Leon's parents. Having never known her father, and losing her mother when she was a child, it was always nice to be around a real family. She'd spent many Sunday afternoons at the Frost's house for dinner and enjoyed watching Leon's parents fuss over their only son. They still believed Leon worked as a manager at the stationary supplier the Unit used for their cover, and they couldn't be prouder.

Leon took a bite of his tiramisu and moaned. He scooped another spoonful and held it to Maggie's lips. "Taste this."

Maggie opened her mouth and allowed Leon to feed her the dessert. Her taste buds sparked to life with the perfect mixture of strong coffee, light sponge, and fresh whipped cream dusted with coco powder. "That's delicious."

She returned the favor and fed Leon some of her panna cotta.

Leon nodded in approval, licking lips that had kissed

every inch of her. "Much better than that dodgy stew in Lebanon."

Maggie laughed, recollecting the mission from a few years back. "Yeah, I never want to know what was in that."

"You should have seen the stuff they called food back in the army." Leon crinkled his nose.

"I will see your army slop, and raise you expired cans of cold soup."

Leon conceded and raised his glass to her. "Touché."

While Leon had spent two years in the army before being recruited into Bishop's covert program, Maggie had spent her time homeless on the streets of London, fighting her own kind of war. Without Bishop, the mistakes she made trying to survive would have sent her to prison for a very long time.

"Speaking of bets," said Leon, polishing off the rest of his tiramisu, "this stuff might beat the food at the Venetian on our Vegas mission."

"The view here gives it a one up, that's for sure." Maggie got up and took Leon's hand, leading him to the balcony.

"Wow," he said, looking out over the horizon.

It was nearing ten o'clock, and the summer sun had just set, leaving the sky a deep blue. Traffic had slowed to almost nothing along the canal, and across the way, a few straggling tourists sat on the stone steps on the Salute Cathedral. The street lamps ignited in a rose-tinted gleam that twinkled across the water like stars.

Below, a gondola floated by with two lovers kissing as a baritone gondolier, dressed in the traditional striped t-shirt and straw boater hat, serenaded them with a timeless song.

"See," said Maggie. "Gondolas on a real canal. The Venetian in Vegas doesn't have that."

"But they do have poker and blackjack tables," countered Leon, no stranger to a bet or two.

"There's a casino up the canal in Cannaregio," Maggie countered. "The Lido across the lagoon has one, too."

Leon smiled and wrapped an arm over her shoulders. "Well you've got me there. You win."

"I always win," she teased, nudging him.

Maggie leaned her head on his chest and watched the night go by. "Do you ever wish we could sit back and enjoy all the places we go?" she asked, almost somber. Maggie had travelled across the world, yet never got to be tourist.

"I'm enjoying myself right now." Leon peered down at her. "A beautiful view with my favorite person. What's not to like?"

He tipped her chin up and leaned down with parted lips. Maggie didn't bridge the gap, but before she knew it, they were kissing like lovers on vacation.

Leon cupped her face with one hand, the other placed on the small of her back and roaming further down. Maggie reached up and ran her hand through the bristles of his cropped hair, pulling him towards her as their passion intensified.

Maggie bit Leon's lip, and he moaned from deep in his

chest, brushing his tongue against hers. His hands travelled over her curves and slipped inside her robe to explore within. The tension built between them until it was only a matter of moments before they would reach the point of no return, neither of them willing to tear themselves away from the other.

But they had to.

Maggie stepped away, her lips plump and tingling from the taste of him. "Leon," she whispered, catching her breath.

His shoulders slumped. "I know, I'm sorry."

"I'm sorry, too. We agreed."

"You're right," he said, rubbing the back of his neck. "I shouldn't have started anything."

Maggie tightened her robe. "I didn't exactly push you away, either." Heat rushed to her cheeks.

Leon reached out, and she laced her fingers in his. "I better go to bed," she said, kissing him once on the cheek. "Goodnight."

He let their fingers untangle and watched her go. "Night, Maggie."

Chapter 8

Maggie woke to a text message from Isabella, asking to meet her and Leon by the Rialto Bridge at noon.

They sat outside a restaurant by the bridge, a canopy covering them from the blazing sun. Maggie fanned herself, playing the role of Rebecca in shorts, a white blazer, and blacked out sunglasses that allowed her to scope out the surroundings. Being a Miami native, Rebecca may be used to the weather, but Maggie struggled against the hot, humid day. The heat hung heavy in the air and intensified the scent of salt water from the Grand Canal.

Leon turned his neck to the side and winced in his seat across from her.

"You okay?" asked Maggie in Rebecca's accent.

"Yeah, my neck hurts, that's all."

Maggie lowered her voice. "I told you, you could've had the bed." The street was thick with tourists wandering by, the other diners loud and too interested in ordering to care about two strangers sitting in the corner. Nevertheless, it was prudent to be cautious.

"Don't be silly," said Leon, shrugging her off. "It's probably from all the running around we did yesterday."

Maggie sipped her iced coffee, in need of a cool down and a perk up. She slept uneasy knowing Leon was outside her bedroom, feeling bad about leaving him to sleep on the small couch. The temptation to invite him in was enticing, but she didn't trust herself with him. She couldn't share a bed with the man without wanting more. It would have been a bad move.

Leon stared at his hands. "Listen, about last night."

"I'm sorry," Maggie said, fighting the urge to touch him.

"Me, too." He sighed. "I know we talked about not falling into old habits. It was a moment of weakness."

Silence hung over them, each lost in their thoughts. They knew better than most that old habits die hard. Ever since their days in training, their connection was undeniable. Leon saw through the walls she'd built, a fortress constructed high to protect herself. To stop people from seeing the lost girl inside.

Even as a young child, Maggie could be in a room full of people and still feel desperately alone. She'd had no one after her mother died. No family to run to. No one to make her feel safe or loved.

Maggie went through countless foster families growing up. Uprooted and moved from place to place, house to house. Nowhere ever felt like home. She didn't belong with them. She didn't belong anywhere.

All of that changed when Bishop recruited her to the Unit and she met Leon.

He was open, and honest, and listened to her when she spoke. He had a genuine interest in her thoughts and opinions. Asked about her hopes and dreams; two things she never dared think about until then. Hopes and dreams weren't for people like Maggie.

After training, the world was open to them. They travelled all over on missions, and snuck away between jobs on secret trysts, high off young love. Making plans for a future that could never be. For a normal life that wasn't possible given what they did.

It didn't take long for reality to set in. For the high to fall, and for them to realize just how hard it was to make things work. Weeks would pass without seeing each other, sometimes months. Deep cover missions didn't allow for any contact with loved ones, semi-regular check-ins with the Unit the only thing letting them know the other was still alive.

Death was a real threat in their line of work, and there was no telling if the next mission would be their last.

Romantic dealings were frowned upon between agents, but when Bishop found out about them, he never reported it to the Director. Maggie suspected he saw things coming to an end before they did.

Eventually the pressures grew too much and they went their separate ways. They didn't talk for a while, but that didn't last long. Somewhere over their time together, their young, carefree love had developed into something much deeper. Stronger.

They always found their way back to each other. And when they did, it was like they had never parted. When Maggie was in Leon's arms, he made her feel like she was home. With him, home wasn't a place. It was a feeling, and she longed to return there.

Maggie stared at him behind her glasses and her chest grew tight. Leon was always honest with her about how he felt, and she braced herself to do the same.

"Look," she said, "I know we agreed that we're better off as friends, but–"

"Ms. Sterling," called an approaching voice. Isabella sat down next to Leon, her cheeks flustered and strands of hair jutting free from her ponytail. She wore no makeup, and bags hung under her sad eyes.

Maggie placed her hand on Leon's knee under the

table. Her confession would have to wait. Molding back into Rebecca, Maggie gave her full attention to their inside contact. "Isabella, how are you?"

"I'm fine," she said, fooling no one.

Maggie couldn't tell if Isabella was acting, or if she really was upset over Carlo Rossi's death. Her show was very convincing, even by Maggie's standards. "Carlo's dead, I presume?"

Isabella nodded and bit her lip, like she didn't trust herself to speak.

Leon eyed Maggie and she returned a slight nod. "Did you come by the boat you picked me up on yesterday?" she asked. They couldn't talk freely sitting there, and Maggie had questions.

"I walked," said Isabella. "Things are understandably up in the air, and I've only now been able to slip out. I can't stay long."

"Then what have you come to tell us?" Maggie used Rebecca to be short with the woman. There was something about Isabella that led her to suspect her grief was real. Maggie raised her guard and scrutinized the woman as she spoke.

"Stefano requests a meeting with you," said Isabella.

"Stefano?" asked Leon.

Isabella gave a weary nod. "He's taken his father's place."

"That was quick." Maggie wondered if the son had grieved his father at all.

"He needs to establish himself as the new don before anyone thinks to usurp him." Isabella fumbled with her fingers. "It's his birthright, after all."

Maggie leaned forward. "When and where does Stefano want to meet?"

"The Antico Martini restaurant at Campo Teatro Fenice after the orchestra. The theater is dedicating tonight's performance to Carlo's memory. The whole family is attending." Isabella's eyes glistened at the mention of the man she'd spied on for six years. "He loved attending and donated a lot of money to them over the years."

"Stefano doesn't suspect my involvement in his father's assassination?" Maggie asked. After all, he was shot at their first meeting. The idea must have crossed Stefano's mind that Rebecca may have had something to do with it.

Isabella shook her head. "We suspect it was the Marino family."

Maggie narrowed her eyes. "We?"

"Stefano does," corrected Isabella. "They made threats about their plans to take over Venice. It appears they carried through with them."

Maggie leaned back in her chair and tapped the table. "What about Peter West? Could he have arranged it? Carlo was meeting me about a counter offer. Perhaps he felt Carlo betrayed him."

"Carlo never told anyone about the meeting," said Isabella. "Peter didn't know."

"He must know now, given how the meeting ended." Maggie studied Isabella as the woman winced at the mention of her subject's death. Her unease grew.

It was possible Isabella was simply worried about her safety now that Carlo was dead. He respected her, but his son didn't seem to view her in the same light. Either way, Isabella needed out. Her handler should have done it the second they learned Carlo was dead. Bishop would have gotten Maggie out if she found herself in the same situation.

"Stefano has already spoken with Peter on the phone," said Isabella. "He plans to meet him, too."

"He means to start a bidding war?" Maggie guessed.

"Yes."

It seemed Stefano didn't hold the same values as his old man when it came to loyalty. It was a good business move to lock two interested parties in a bidding war. But Stefano dealt within the criminal underworld, and sometimes a good business move could also get you killed. Especially if one of the parties felt disrespected.

"And what about you?" Maggie asked Isabella. "I got the impression there was no love lost between you and Stefano."

Isabella cleared her throat. "He's asked me to remain his assistant for the time being. At least until all of Carlo's affairs are in order."

Whether it was an act or not, Maggie couldn't stand to sit there and watch Isabella mourn the death of a crime boss any longer. Men like him infected beautiful places like Venice, spreading pain wherever they went. They didn't care who got hurt from their shady dealings, or the lives that would be ruined from their supply of cocaine and heroin. Syndicates like the Rossi family were a living, breathing plague.

"Anything else?" Maggie asked.

Isabella made to say something but stopped. "No."

Maggie dug in Rebecca's Louis Vuitton bag and dropped some Euro's on the table to cover the bill. "We'll see you tonight."

Getting up, Maggie left Isabella at the table and walked down the street without another word.

"Where are we going?" Leon asked when he caught up to her.

"To get you a tux."

"Why?"

Stefano was attending a show in his father's honor, and some of the city's heavy hitters would be there to pay their respects. Maggie couldn't put her finger on exactly what, but *something* wasn't sitting right. There was more to it, and she intended to find out what.

"We're going to the orchestra."

Chapter 9

Getting last minute tickets to the orchestra hadn't been an issue. The Gritti Hotel owned a private box for their high-end guests, and Guido was more than happy to arrange their attendance.

Maggie checked herself over and ensured the knife hidden above her ankle was stored tight. Ready to go, she stepped out the bathroom and went to the lounge where Leon waited for her.

She wore a red jumpsuit in line with Rebecca's taste and styled it with a gold belt and matching clutch bag which contained her Beretta. The jumpsuit allowed the kind of movement a dress wouldn't. A deliberate choice, given how things went yesterday.

Leon stood by the windows, taking in the spectacular view. He turned around when he heard her and his eyes widened. "You're breathtaking."

Maggie couldn't help the smile that tugged at her lips. "You scrub up well yourself." The black tux was cut just right for Leon's large frame, the formal wear mixing well with his rugged features. "That bow tie could use some help though."

Leon undid the tie and started another attempt, but she stopped him and took over.

"I'm used to clip-ons," he admitted.

Wearing a full tie was usually a bad idea for an agent. You never knew when you'd find yourself in a fight, and a long tie was the perfect leverage for an opponent to choke you. Bow ties weren't as dangerous, and Maggie stepped close to him to fix it around his neck.

Their bodies touched, and Maggie peered into his deep brown eyes as she worked.

There was so much she wanted to say to him, and while she may not hesitate to jump rooftops or dodge bullets, her courage crumbled when it came to talking about how she felt.

When it came to him.

They couldn't be together; they both knew that. She'd almost fallen into their usual trap earlier, ready to bare all to him and ask for another chance to make things work. It hurt every time things failed, cutting deeper than any wound she'd taken from an enemy's blade. Yet it hurt more to be apart. To deny her feelings and try to move on.

Maggie pursed her lips. Some things were better left unsaid. "There you go."

"Thanks." Leon tucked a strand of her hair behind her ear, his fingers brushing along her jaw. He caught himself and pulled back, straightening his jacket. "Ready?"

Maggie nodded and they left the suite, the tension between them thicker than the humid nighttime air that teased at another hot day to come.

The Teatro la Fenice was only a short walk from the hotel. Maggie and Leon strolled along the path with the mass of tourists, walking through the streets and over the bridges connecting the fragments of the sinking city together.

The world-renowned theater sat landlocked within San Marco, surrounded by art galleries, the San Fantin church, and numerous restaurants. Including the one where they were to meet Stefano after the orchestra.

People stood outside the front entrance, dressed to the nines and awaiting the call to be seated. There were more locals than what Maggie suspected was usual, most of them there to pay their respects to the dead Mafioso.

Leon offered his arm. "Shall we?"

Maggie complied. It would help them blend in with the other attendees. Or at least, that's what she told herself. They walked up the stone steps and entered the foyer.

Most attendees waited inside, the hum of chatter bouncing off the rose marbled walls and high ceilings. Royal red carpet led upstairs to the theatre, and extravagant crystal chandeliers twinkled above the guests, casting glittering light over the room.

Somber faces mixed with the excited ones of the tourists, the latter unaware they were mingling with some of the city's unsavory elite.

Heels clicked behind Maggie, and she and Leon turned to see Isabella. She was dressed in a mournful black dress, the fabric covering her figure from neck to wrist. "Hello, Ms. Sterling," she said, her smile forced. "I didn't expect to see you here."

"I wanted to pay my respects," said Maggie.

"I appreciate it," came Stefano's voice. He stepped from behind them, dressed in a black suit with Angela on his arm. She, too, wore black, her dress covered in sequins that glittered under the chandeliers. Sadness etched over her beautiful features, striking even in her sorrow.

"I'm sorry for your loss," Maggie said to the pair.

"Thank you." Stefano nodded, but he didn't look half as mournful as Isabella. Someone called him from across the room. "Please, excuse us."

"I'll see you after the show." Maggie watched Stefano and his daughter greet a group of attendees who'd just arrived. She turned her attention back to Isabella. "Stefano looks real cut up over his father's death."

Isabella led them away from the crowd, hiding behind a marble pillar, and lowered her voice. "Stefano can't show any signs of weakness." Isabella nodded across the room to a group of stern-faced men huddled in the corner. "Those men over there are the Marinos. The one in the middle is their leader, Enzo. The two beside him are his brothers, Franco and Jovanni."

Maggie ducked her head around the pillar to get a better look. The three brothers were far younger than Carlo, but Enzo, the oldest Marino, looked about Stefano's age. The siblings were flanked by five other men: large, brutish figures with dark eyes and faces that promised even darker intentions.

Maggie studied their features. Was one of them the shooter?

"Why are they here?" Leon asked.

"To show off and gloat over what they've done," said Isabella. "They know Stefano won't do anything in front of so many people. Coming here tonight is an open display of defiance, and Stefano won't have any other option than to retaliate."

"They're starting a war," Maggie said, taking note of the room. Enzo and his brothers' presence wasn't going unnoticed. Attendees spoke in whispers and stole glances over their shoulders at the men, looking between them and Stefano.

"Yes, I'm afraid so," said Isabella. "I only hope it doesn't spill onto the streets."

"Sounds like Carlo won't be the only dead member of the mob soon."

Isabella flinched, and Maggie clenched her hands

around her clutch, keeping her face neutral in case they were being watched.

"You know," she said, pulling Isabella in for a hug and whispering in her ear, "for someone working against the Rossis, you sure seem to be taking Carlo's death hard."

Isabella pulled away. "I won't deny that part of me grew to care for the man during my six years undercover. Outside of his business, Carlo could be kind and fair, and he treated me well. But that doesn't mean I've forgotten exactly who and what he was or why I'm risking my life to take down his family. Instead of worrying about my allegiances, perhaps you should focus on your job and secure the deal before the night is through."

Isabella shot them both a glare, gritting her teeth. She spun on her heels and stormed off to return to Stefano's side.

"We need to watch that one," Maggie said as a gong rang through the foyer to call for the attendees to take their seats.

She and Leon joined the crowd, and a member of the staff led them upstairs to their seats. The private box sat four people, but Rebecca requested for her and her guest to be the only patrons for the evening. They took the two seats at the front and waited for the show to begin.

Maggie had already checked the layout of the theater before coming, just in case. The trouble spies must have gone through to obtain such information before the internet didn't bear thinking about. Now, a quick search online gave Maggie access to the theater's blueprints. She'd made a mental note of all exit routes and counted them off in her head.

"It's like we've stepped into the past," Leon leaned on the booth's bannister to get a good look at the intricate facade.

"It was all done this side of the century. The theater burned down in the nineties, for the third time, and everything had to be restored." According to the theater's website, at least.

The reconstruction succeeded in creating the ambiance of the old theatre, designed to resemble the nineteenth century incarnation which was built after the first fire. The name of the theater was no coincidence, *la fenice* meaning 'the phoenix.'

The ceiling was painted in a cornflower blue and framed by a gilded filigree design, like golden Burano lace. The lacework travelled down and encompassed the stage, running along the boxes and the gallery above. Below them, the rows of crimson seats filled up on the ground level, anticipation dancing through the room.

The crowd clapped as the lights dimmed, and the ninety-eight members of the orchestra walked out onto the stage.

Maggie was much more interested in the audience than she was the musicians. They were one row up and four booths to the left from the royal box. The seats of honor offered the best view in the house and looked

72

directly at the stage from above the main entrance to the theatre.

Blood red curtains draped on either side of the seats where Stefano sat with Angela by his side. Neither of them clapped when the conductor entered, Stefano too busy staring across the theater to his right.

Maggie followed his gaze to a box halfway down the row where the Marinos sat. Enzo shot a brazen smile Stefano's way.

"Peter West is here." Leon nodded to the row of boxes below them and over to the left.

Maggie brought the brass binoculars provided by the theater to her eyes and narrowed in on the man. He looked just like the picture in his file: well-built, bulbous nose, bald head. Two people sat behind him, but darkness cloaked their faces as the conductor led his orchestra into the first number.

The song opened with the melancholy cry of cellos, the minor keys resounding through the entire room thanks to the amazing acoustics. The tiny hairs on Maggie's arms stood on end as the violins joined the procession.

She turned her attention back to the Marinos, getting a closer look with her binoculars. The brothers were deep in conversation, none of them paying any attention to the delicate music enveloping around them.

The conductor picked up the tempo as the woodwinds and brass joined the fray, offering a balance of rich and bright tones to compliment the lush strings.

Maggie crossed her binoculars to the royal box; Stefano stood by the door, stabbing his finger into the shoulder of one of the men standing guard, his lips moving in rapid succession. The men nodded and left. Stefano slammed the door shut behind them and returned to his seat.

The percussion section entered in a crescendo, the timpani rolling like thunder, the marimba skipping like rain. The conductor swooped his arms high then flourished them downwards as symbols crashed as the storm reached its peak.

Moving to Peter West, Maggie spotted him watching Stefano with narrowed eyes.

The music was wild now, erratic and thrashing out in bursts of anger and panic that coursed through the room.

"Something's wrong." Maggie could taste it in the air. Feel it in her bones.

Leon straightened in his chair. "What?"

Maggie shook her head. "I'm not sure."

Leon took the binoculars and zoomed in on their people of interest. "Stefano isn't happy."

"Neither is Peter West."

Maggie checked on the Marino brothers, who watched the angry Stefano with stone faces.

"You think one of them is going to make a move?" asked Leon.

"I wouldn't rule it out." She reclaimed the binoculars and checked each of the men again. Stefano glared over at the Marinos, Enzo's expression cool and calm. Neither of them paid any attention to the British man watching them from across the theater as the music built up to a ferocious crescendo.

Peter West slipped his hand into his suit jacket, and Maggie caught a glint of metal.

"Peter," she said, dropping the binoculars and getting up. She swung open the door to their box and took off at a run with Leon by her side. "He's got a gun."

They sprinted down the corridor and reached the stairs, taking two at a time to the floor below. A member of the staff yelled after them, but they didn't stop. Maggie pricked her ears for a gunshot.

Two men stood outside the door to Peter's box, both as wide as the frame. They blocked the door when they spotted Maggie and Leon charging towards them.

Neither of them stopped. Maggie lunged for the man to her left as Leon took out the other, smashing his fist across the guard's cheek.

Maggie needed to end things quickly, before Peter West got off a shot. She ducked under a hook from her opponent and feigned a punch to his face. The guard raised his arms to block the blow, and Maggie used the distraction to slam her shin hard against his crotch.

The guard fell to his knees, red faced, the vein on his wide neck bulging.

Maggie left Leon with the other guard and ripped

open the door, barging in to stop Peter from taking the shot.

But the guards behind the door must have heard the commotion. They pounced the second she stepped inside. The men grabbed her, one on each arm, and she struggled against them, clipping one in the face with her fist before the other caught her with the back of his hand. The blow made her vision spin and her mouth filled with the metallic tang of blood.

Peter West turned in his seat and looked at her, lowering his own set of brass binoculars from his eyes.

Maggie's heart sank as she realized her mistake.

It wasn't a gun.

An earth-shattering scream pierced above the music. The orchestra faltered and fell silent. The musicians on stage looked out into the audience. The conductor's eyes widened as the screaming continued and the rest of the audience turned to the sound.

Angela Rossi stood inside the royal box with a haunted face. Behind her, Stefano's security men charged inside, Angela's heart-wrenching cries calling them back from wherever their boss had sent them.

In the center of the box, Stefano swayed on his feet. Blood slipped free from his mouth and ran down his chin. He reached for his daughter, and Maggie spotted the knife buried deep in his back.

The newly appointed Mafioso stumbled and lost his

balance. Angela tried to catch him, but she was too far away.

Stefano toppled over the bannister and plummeted to the hard floor below, landing with a sickening thud.

Silence settled over the theatre. One beat. Then a second.

Then chaos erupted.

Fresh screams joined together in perfect unison. A symphony of blind panic. People sprang from their chairs and raced for the exits, pushing and shoving each other out the way. The lights turned on and the musicians clutched their instruments to their chests, cradling strings and wood and metal like children as they raced backstage.

Maggie struggled in the guard's grasp and caught sight of the Marino's box across the theater. It lay vacant.

Maggie closed her eyes. She'd been right about an attack. She just picked the wrong culprit.

Leon's muffled struggles carried in from the hallway and she tried to fight her way free to no avail.

Peter West stood in front of her, blocking her view, unafraid of her while detained by his personal guard. "You must be Rebecca." Peter raised his fist and caught Maggie square in the jaw. Her head whipped back, and she tried—but failed—to fight the darkness that approached.

Her body went limp and someone dragged her away, her legs trailing behind her.

Then everything went black.

Chapter 10

A wave of nausea crashed through Maggie as she came to.

An engine hummed beneath her, the floor vibrating from its purr. A dull pain throbbed over her face and drops of water sprayed over her skin, stale and salty as she licked her dry lips.

Maggie blinked her eyes open and came face to face with Leon.

His eyes were closed, one of them swollen and growing purple. His chest rose, and though he appeared to be asleep, his breathing was controlled. Maggie tried to reach for him, but her hands were bound behind her back. She shimmied her arms and rope scratched into her wrists, rough and damp like it had been pulled from the lagoon— perhaps taken from the very boat they were on.

Risking a look, Maggie tilted her neck back while

feigning unconsciousness. Through slit eyes she could make out the shape of the vessel. It was some kind of speedboat, similar to the ones used for water taxis. The night sky loomed overhead, the stars blotted out by a mass of clouds. Mist lay thick over the lagoon, hanging over the surface of the water and cloaking the surroundings in a hazy shroud.

Rows of derelict houses lined the canal, a far cry from the preened residences around the tourist hub. An eerie silence lingered, only the engine and the sloshing of water filled the night. Two pairs of legs stood at the front of the boat, but the inside cabin blocked her view of anything else.

She dug her nails into her palms and bit back a frustrated groan. She'd messed up.

Pushing herself forward, Maggie nudged Leon with her knee. "Leon," she whispered.

He pried open one eye at his name. "Maggie."

Maggie inched closer to him on the floor at the back of the boat, the engine low and indiscreet as they slowly sailed through the canal. "Where are they taking us?"

"I don't know. I just came around a couple of minutes ago. Are you okay?"

"Fine," she said, though she was far from it. "You?"

Leon gave her a little smile. "I've had better nights out."

The boat slowed further and turned right into a narrower canal. A fetid stench of stale water and dead fish assaulted Maggie's senses. "I'm going to get us out of this," she promised.

A rusted screech echoed off the crumbling walls on either side of them, and the boat ducked out of the canal and through an iron gateway, pulling into a shabby building that may have looked nice a hundred years ago.

Maggie waited until her eyes adjusted to the darkness and struggled to a seated position. There was no point pretending to be asleep. The engine turned off, their captors arriving wherever the hell it was they were taking them.

Brick walls surrounded them, damp and slime the predominant décor of the place. The boat had stopped by a docking station that ended by a set of stairs. Like a lot of properties in Venice, the ground floor acted as an aquatic parking garage, the rest of the living space needing to be above sea level to avoid flooding when the tide rose.

Maggie doubted anyone had lived upstairs in a long time.

A figure hopped off the boat and tied a rope around a rotted wooden post to keep the craft steady. Someone called orders, and a few moments later, two burly men came to the back of the boat and hoisted Maggie and Leon to their feet.

Neither of them fought. They knew when to pick their battles, and this wasn't one they could win. They needed an opening. A distraction to give them enough time to get away to safety.

Maggie winced as she stepped off the boat and onto the dock, a sharp pain stabbing at her ribs. The fuckers must have continued to beat her after their boss knocked her out. She made a mental note for later. No one touched her like that and got away with it.

The men lined her and Leon up by the wall, and Peter West disembarked his boat. The craft's headlights flicked on and lit up the room, coating Peter's smug face with an eerie shine.

Rats squeaked at the shock of light and scampered off into the shadows.

"Rebecca Sterling," Peter said, walking up to her.

Maggie kept her mouth shut, calculating the best way to play the situation. Peter still thought she was his opposition. Perhaps she could use that.

Peter grabbed her jaw with his meaty hand and forced her to stare at him. "You fucked up my deal with the Rossis."

"You did a pretty good job of that yourself by shooting Carlo," she replied in an American accent. Revealing her true identity would only make things worse. If Peter knew she was a British agent, he'd kill her right there and then. At least with Rebecca, Maggie had a chance of whittling her way out of it. Rebecca spoke Peter's language, and she was no stranger to negotiating terms, even if it was to save her life.

Peter frowned at her accusation. "I didn't shoot Carlo."

"You arranged it though." Maggie kept up the act.

She'd chosen the wrong advisory at the orchestra, but Rebecca would still be suspicious.

Peter let go of her and paced the dock with his hands behind his back. His stride was confident and relaxed, knowing full well he had all the power. Maggie sensed a part of him enjoyed it, saw the thrill in his eyes.

"Let's stop the charades before they start," he said. "You had Carlo shot."

"And why would I do that? I was about to secure a deal with him," countered Maggie, Leon remaining silent beside her. Rebecca would do all the talking in a situation like this. If her hired muscle started getting chatty, it would ruin the illusion and tip off Peter as to who they really were.

"Not likely. The old man would never agree to your offer after already meeting with me," said Peter. "That wasn't his way."

"And you think Stefano would have been any different?"

"He set up meetings with both of us tonight. He clearly planned to pit us against each other, which is a step further than Carlo was willing to go with you." Peter shook his head. "Stefano wasn't half the man Carlo was. Useless. Dumb as a box of rocks."

Maggie counted Peter's guards. Two holding her and Leon, a woman with a gun ready to shoot them if they so much as shuffled their feet, and the man driving the boat. Five against two. Those were decent odds for people like her and Leon, but not when they were tied up.

None of his crew were the shooter from the roof, further confirming what she already believed. Peter didn't kill either of the Rossi men. She had jumped the gun back at the theater, and now it could cost her and Leon their lives.

"If you think I killed Carlo, then how do you explain Stefano?" Maggie asked.

Peter mused over it for a moment. "You could have hired the same person to kill him as you did his father. With you otherwise accounted for on both occasions, you could ensure alibis to keep you in the clear."

Maggie raised an eyebrow. "That's a bit of a stretch. Besides, I needed Stefano to secure my deal. Now we've both lost out."

Peter laughed, his deep voice booming inside the cavernous room. "You have, but I haven't."

"How so?" Maggie's stomach tightened.

"With Carlo and Stefano gone, the Marinos are free to take over the city. I'm sure they'll be more than willing to set up a deal with me." Peter checked his watch, like he had somewhere to be.

"Maybe that was their plan all along." Maggie was running out of time. Peter hadn't brought them there for a sit down. "To eliminate their competition so they could take over the narcotics and export them to you."

Peter shrugged. "Could be."

"Which means I didn't kill the Rossis. They did. If they hadn't killed Carlo, then your deal would have gone through after he rejected my counteroffer."

Peter stepped towards her again and lowered his lips to her ear. "Perhaps," he whispered, "but that doesn't change things between us. You ruined a perfectly good deal. No one crosses me like that and gets away with it. Not even someone as pretty as you."

Maggie sneered. "Hurry up and shoot us then. I'm sick of your self-important yammering."

"Oh, that would be too quick." Peter scoffed. "You royally messed up my business deal, and for that, I'm afraid you'll have to suffer."

Peter moved back and clicked his fingers. The men holding them yanked Maggie and Leon by their bound hands and led them to the edge of the dock.

Maggie dug her heels, but they pushed her forward until she was inches away from the water. Her heart drummed in her ears with rising panic.

She pivoted in the man's hold and stamped her foot down on his with every bit of energy she had left. The man cried in pain and she spun on him, ignoring her aching body, and prepared to attack.

The woman with the gun was waiting on her, though, and she shoved the weapon in Maggie's face. She tutted at Maggie with a smile and waited on her boss to give the order.

Maggie raised her chin in defiance and stared death

right in the eyes. She refused to show them fear, to give them the satisfaction.

"Now be a good girl, and do as you're told," said Peter. "Get in the water."

Maggie considered her options. A bullet to the brain would seal the deal right there and then. Complying with Peter's orders gave her time to come to an agreement.

Clenching her jaw, Maggie turned and allowed the woman to shove her down a set of stone steps leading to the water. The water was ice cold and thick with sludge.

Leon followed close behind, and they continued deeper into the water with the woman's gun trained on them. The water rose to Maggie's shoulders. Leon's height gave him an advantage, the water only reaching his chest.

From the boat, the driver leaned over the edge and pointed to a wooden post at the other side of the vessel. Maggie and Leon sloshed to the post and stood with their backs to it as the driver wrapped more rope around them, tying their torsos to the wood in a tight sailor's knot.

Maggie spotted the seaweed and barnacles stuck to the walls, noting how they grew way beyond the surface level of the water as it sat now.

Her heart sank as she realized what that meant.

A rising tide may float all ships, but it would also fill up the room and rise above Maggie and Leon's heads.

"You don't have to do this." Maggie's leg brushed Leon's under the surface, his back turned to her from his end of the post.

Peter stepped onto his boat and leaned over the edge to smirk at them. "You're right. I don't have to." His face spread out in a wide, sinister grin. "But I want to."

"We can come to a deal." Maggie called after him, her voice rising in pitch. "I can purchase the Rossi stock from you, just name the price."

Peter leaned his elbows on the side of the boat and looked down at them. "I already have buyers at home."

"Something else then," said Maggie, desperate now. "Surely you can put aside our differences for the sake of business. We can make a lot of money together."

Peter shook his head, and dusted the shoulders of his formal suit from non-existent dust. "Sorry, Love, but that's not going to happen. As your American mobsters say, you and your bodyguard are going to swim with the fishes."

"Bastard," cried Maggie, fighting against the bounds. The rough rope cut into her skin, her fingers growing numb from the cut off circulation and the cold seeping through her sodden clothes.

The boat's engine roared to life and reversed out of the building. Peter waved a bon voyage to them, laughing with his guards. "Ciao."

"Wait," Maggie yelled after him, but it was too late.

Peter West sailed out of the building, closed the iron gates, and left Maggie and Leon to drown.

Chapter 11

Darkness enveloped the room.

Maggie waited for her eyes to adjust, but it never happened. Without the light from Peter's boat, it was pitch black and impossible to see anything around them. Maggie and Leon were cut off from the outside world.

There was no use calling for help. No one would hear them. Peter made sure of that.

The water around Maggie sloshed as Leon wriggled behind her. "The knots are too tight," he said.

Maggie tested her own binds and discovered the same thing. The driver certainly knew what he was doing with the rope. With their hands locked together behind their backs, they couldn't even try the knots that secured them to the post.

Leon thrashed behind her, sending splashes of water

over them both as he forced all his weight against the ropes, pulling away from the post.

Nothing happened.

The wooden post may be rotting, but it was still solid enough to withstand Leon's strength. He tried again and swore in frustration.

Maggie struggled, but that only made the ropes hold tighter. If Leon's strength couldn't do anything, then hers was useless. Where he had power and brute force, Maggie had speed, but that wouldn't help them now.

Time passed, somewhere between an hour and an eternity. The tide rose quickly now, the surface of the water now past Maggie's shoulders. She bowed her head. "I'm so sorry, Leon. This is all my fault."

"Peter left us here, not you."

"But I moved too fast." Guilt stabbed into Maggie's conscience. "I should've waited until I saw the gun."

"If you had, and Peter really was about to shoot Stefano, then you would've been too late to save him."

It was too late for Stefano, either way. Peter may not have killed him, but the man was still dead.

"But he didn't," Maggie's teeth chattered as the water froze her to the bone. "I messed up. It's my fault we're here."

"You were right about something happening," Leon said. "We just chose the wrong player."

Maggie leaned her head back against the wooden post and closed her eyes.

"Do you believe what you said to Peter about the Marinos being the ones to take out Stefano?"

"I don't know." She couldn't concentrate on any of that. The water level crept up and up their bodies with each passing minute. Taking deep, deliberate breaths, Maggie tried to slow her racing heartbeat, to squash the rising panic before it reached the surface, moving faster than the approaching water.

It didn't work.

"Leon, I–" Maggie stopped, her voice breaking.

"I know," he said, brushing his leg against hers under the water.

She cleared her throat and tried again. There were so many things she'd left unsaid over the years, keeping her feelings to herself to avoid facing the truth. Their lives would never allow them to be together. Not in the way they wanted or needed, anyway. It was easier to hide all the messy parts of her life beneath her many aliases.

But she didn't care about that now. Not when this might be her last chance to tell him how she truly felt.

"Do you remember when we first met?" She grounded herself in the memory, an anchor amid the oncoming waves.

Leon laughed, perhaps a little forced as they tried to ignore the life and death situation they found themselves in. "How could I forget?"

Maggie was sixteen when Bishop rescued her from a police station. She was facing a murder charge for killing the abusive monster who masqueraded as foster-father, and Maggie was sure her life was over.

"I was so scared then." It was easier to open up to Leon in the darkness, where she couldn't see his face and read into his expressions.

She wasn't the religious type, but Bishop was her guardian angel that day, turning up with an ultimatum that changed everything: risk a life sentence in prison or join the Unit and start a new life. One where she could make a difference.

It was the easiest decision she ever made.

Maggie shook her head. "We were so young back then. We thought we knew everything."

"You certainly did," Leon teased.

"It was all a front," she admitted, sobering at the thought. In truth, she felt way out of her depth. Training to become a member of the Unit was tough. The rigorous regime had pushed her body and mind to the absolute limit, breaking her and the other recruits before building them back up again, molding them into weapons.

"I know," said Leon, quieter now.

"You were so nice to me when I arrived." Maggie arrived at the Unit late. Leon and the other recruits had already gone through several months of training. "At first, I assumed you wanted something from me, playing games like a lot of boys do at that age, willing to say anything to get what you really wanted."

A lump formed in her throat, and Maggie forced it

back. The water passed above her shoulders and showed no signs of stopping.

"But you weren't like that. You listened to me. Worked to get to know me, even after I embarrassed you and pushed you away. I wasn't used to that kind of attention. I didn't know how to react. You never gave up on me though, like so many had done before."

Eventually Leon wore her down, slowly breaking down the walls she built to protect herself, brick by brick. They became friends, their relationship soon developing into something more.

She remembered their first time, how scary and new it all was, yet how right it felt. How their young love developed over time and grew to something she never even knew she was capable of feeling. Something she never felt she deserved.

"My life has never felt stable. Even now. Yet you're the one constant that remains, the person I know I can always rely on. Who will be there for me no matter what happens, no matter how messy our lives get, how full of death and the evil of others. When I'm with you, all that goes away. You make me feel like I finally belong somewhere, and I love you for that. I love you for a hundred other things. I love you so much that it scares me."

Tears ran down her cheeks and dropped into the water, which crawled up her neck like a silent assassin.

"I love you, Leon," she said again. "I don't tell you that enough."

Maggie sniffed, not caring if he heard her cry. She hated showing emotion. It always felt like a sign of weakness, but not with Leon. She never had to hide anything from him.

"I love you, too, Maggie." Leon's deep voice was thick with emotion. "I'll always love you, no matter what happens. Nothing will ever change that."

Maggie smiled as the tears continued to fall. "Even after this mess?"

"Always."

Leon struggled against the rope and inched ever so slightly to her left. His fingers brushed her own, and they linked them together.

"Now let's think," he said. "We need to get out of this, because I refuse to die down here."

Maggie shook her head, her hair floating around her like snarling seaweed. "I don't know."

"We better think fast. This water isn't going to wait for us."

The tide was at Maggie's chin now. She would go first, and soon. Struggling against the ropes as she slowly drowned, lungs on fire. Every nerve in her body screaming for help.

A shudder ran through her. Drowning would be a horrible way to die. Leon would witness her death before he met his own, a pain that would kill Maggie before any water reached her lungs if their roles were reversed.

Maggie had brushed against death before. It was part

of the job, and she was under no illusion about her expected lifespan. Agents in the Unit weren't exactly known for growing old and dying in their sleep. They lived fast and died young.

She made peace with that fact a long time ago. Maggie couldn't do her job otherwise. Yet being down there in that stinking cesspit with Leon caught her by surprise. She could accept an early death for herself, but she couldn't accept the same for Leon.

He deserved to be the exception. The anomaly. One of the few Unit agents to live a long and happy life. She wanted him far away from the risk of being murdered. Wanted a life for him where he wouldn't go out on a mission and never return. He deserved a full life, packed with love and free from the worries of their profession. Maggie could never offer him such a life, not while she worked as an agent. While they both remained fighters to the cause. Soldiers on the front line protecting the British public who would never know what they sacrificed to keep them safe.

Leon squeezed her fingers. "Don't give up on me now."

Maggie's rushing thoughts ground to halt. Leon never gave up on her, never stopped believing she could accomplish the impossible. He never gave up on her, and she couldn't allow herself to give up either. Not on Leon. Not on herself.

His words evaporated her panic and dried her tears.

Their story wouldn't end this way. She wouldn't let Peter West destroy everything she'd built for herself. And she sure as shit wouldn't let him kill the man she loved.

Not tonight.

"My knife," she said, her mind clearing now. "I have a knife."

"Where?"

"Strapped to my ankle." Maggie stretched her arm down, bringing her leg up to bridge the gap, but the rope pinning her to the post stopped her from leaning down with her upper half. "I can't reach it."

"Maybe I can." Leon strained against the ropes. "Kick your leg up behind you and hold it still."

His longer arms reached down her leg, the rope tugging tight across Maggie's chest as Leon pushed down with everything he had.

Leon swore through gritted teeth as he tried—and failed—to reach her ankle.

"Try again," said Maggie, bringing her leg back up behind her.

The water was near her lips, and she had to lean her head back to keep it from filling her mouth as she spoke.

"Almost got it," Leon said, his fingertips on her shoe.

Their movements caused the water splash around them, and a wave of it washed over Maggie's face. She tasted salt and choked as the water invaded her mouth, coughing it up as she struggled to keep her head above the surface.

"There," said Leon in triumph.

Maggie reached out and Leon passed her the knife as the water rose past her mouth. She stilled as best she could, breathing through her nose while she struggled with the knife, her fingers numb and ice cold.

Maggie hissed as the edge of the blade brushed past her hand, the wound stinging as salt from the water bore into it. The knife slipped in her fingers, and she was forced to submerge herself to catch it before all was lost. She gripped tight to the handle and ran the sharp edge along the ropes around her wrists.

It was slow work, Maggie unable to saw the rope thanks to her trapped hands.

The water continued to rise, and when she leaned back for air, she found there was none. The water had risen above her nose now, leaving her with nothing but the air already in her lungs.

Maggie guided the knife up and down her confines, frantic now as her lungs struggled to cope and her chest tightened.

The fibers finally splintered enough for her to snap the rest free, and she moved to the ropes that bound her and Leon to the post.

With her hands free, she cut faster, sawing the coils of rope wrapped around them.

Her mind grew foggy as she worked, the lack of oxygen stealing her clarity, her focus. Nevertheless, she persisted, and finally the ropes loosened around her.

Maggie passed the knife to Leon, allowing it to slip through her fingers as her lungs begged for air she couldn't reach. She sank deeper into the water now that the ropes no longer held her up, her body too tired to fight for air.

Strong hands wrapped around her waist and pulled her up. Her head broke through the surface as Leon hoisted her in his arms, and she sucked in the fetid air of the abandoned building.

"You did it," said Leon, brushing the hair off her face.

Maggie had him set her down when they reached the dock, and she swayed on her feet, straightening her back.

"I'm done playing games," she said, her throat hoarse. She took Leon's hand, and they trudged up the stairs of the old house and slipped out into the fresh night air. "Rebecca can go back to Miami as far as I'm concerned. It's time Peter West, and whoever else is messing with us, met Maggie."

Chapter 12

It was well past midnight when Maggie and Leon finally reached their hotel.

Peter West had taken them to a secluded spot in Cannaregio, the northernmost district of Venice, and it took them almost an hour to traipse back to the Gritti Palace on foot. Their sodden clothes dried in on the way, the dirty salt water making the fabric coarse and deeply uncomfortable.

Maggie itched to rip them off; the smell was bad enough, never mind how they rubbed against and irritated her skin.

The Gritti Palace was quiet when they entered, only the night manager manning the front desk and a few guests still out by the terraced bar. Maggie and Leon slipped past without any trouble and made it to their suite.

Maggie closed the door behind her and leaned against it, her muscles aching and tight. "I feel filthy."

Leon shrugged off his tux jacket and dumped it straight in the bin by the door. "Take a shower. You'll feel better."

"No, you go first." It was the least she could do, since it was her fault they almost died.

"You sure?" he asked.

"Of course, go on."

Leon nodded and headed through the bedroom and straight for the bathroom, yanking off his tie and unbuttoning his shirt at the neck on the way. If he felt half as grimy as Maggie did, she understood. Everything chaffed, even her underwear, and the temptation to take off her clothes and burn them was strong.

Maggie crossed the room and poured a double measure of whiskey from a decanter into a crystal glass, her hands tremoring from the residual shock of almost drowning.

Tossing back the drink, Maggie closed her eyes and focused on the burn of the amber liquid washing down her throat and warming her insides. She helped herself to another and sipped at the drink, walking out to the balcony and opening the French doors.

A light breeze swept past, rustling the curtains and dancing through her hair. Her fake hair. Maggie fumbled with the pins keeping her wig in place and yanked it off, throwing it on the floor. She had no need for Rebecca now.

Peter West had made things personal, and he was about to learn who he was really dealing with.

No one tried to kill her, or Leon, and got away. Ever.

Maggie brushed her fingers through her blond locks, ratty despite being covered by the wig, and peered over her shoulder to the bedroom door.

Leon.

They had come so close to dying, slipping free mere seconds before death clutched them in its eternal grasp.

A future together may not be set in stone, but they were still alive. Still able to wake up and fight another day. Their past may be troubled, and their future unclear, but they still had today. Maggie didn't know what lay in store for either of them, but she knew one thing: the man she loved was two rooms away. And that was two too far.

Maggie gulped down the rest of her drink and abandoned the glass. She peeled off her jumpsuit, the fabric sticking to her skin, and dropped it on the floor. Then went her bra, adding to the pile of ruined clothes. She stepped out of her lace panties and tiptoed through the lounge to the bedroom.

The shower hissed through the cracked doorway, tendrils of steam slipping through into the bedroom. Before she could change her mind, Maggie eased open the bathroom door and slipped inside. Anticipation tingled in her stomach, mixed with the dread of possible rejection.

Leon hadn't noticed her come in, too busy washing off the dirt and grime from his toned body. Soap bubbles coated his muscled arms as he scrubbed at them, his black skin glistening where the light hit the water as it caressed over each and every part of him.

A warmth flooded Maggie that had nothing to do with the whiskey, and the feeling made its way south. She bit her bottom lip and reached for the shower door.

Leon spun as she entered, his body tense with surprise, and she closed the door behind her to show she had no intension of leaving any time soon.

His eyes travelled over her naked flesh, filled with hunger as he took in the curves of her body. Maggie stepped closer, her breasts rubbing against his torso, close enough that she could feel him breathing in and out, faster than normal as his excitement grew.

Steam circle round them, tickling Maggie's skin. "Is this okay?" she asked, starring up into his dark eyes and trailing a finger down his chest.

Leon cupped her face. "I've wanted this since the moment you stepped off that plane."

Maggie couldn't take it any longer. She pulled him towards her and kissed his full lips, the bristles from his cropped beard brushing over her face as she tasted him. The fear of death and the thrill of escaping its clutches added a desperation to her lust. A need that wouldn't be denied.

Leon wrapped his arms around her, holding her close while he explored every inch of her skin with his calloused hands, his erection hard against her leg. He tightened his grip as his own need grew, brushing his tongue along hers. Maggie nibbled at his bottom lip, and the groan that resulted sent a titillating shiver down her spine.

Leon broke away from her lips and kissed along her jaw, travelling down her neck. Maggie's eyes fluttered shut as he reached the spot just under her ear.

Reaching for the soap, Maggie ran the bar over Leon's back, feeling the bumps of his raised scars, battle wounds from years of missions that matched her own. They washed each other clean before they got dirty, fingers lingering in all the right places, replaced with lips once the soap was washed clean.

Leon lowered to his knees and pressed her against the wall, the green marble cool against Maggie's back as she arched in response to his touch. Her breathing hitched in her throat as Leon drew a moan all the way up from her belly.

Maggie waited as long as she could, letting him take the lead until she couldn't bear to wait any longer. She pulled Leon to his feet and begged him to take her, leading him inside and wrapping her legs around his firm waist.

They remained in the shower until their fingers pruned, then fell into the king size, gripping the sheets as they lost themselves in each other. Reacquainting themselves with their bodies, neither of them willing to stop.

Chapter 13

Maggie woke to weight shifting on the king-sized mattress as Leon returned to bed.

"Are you watching me sleep?" she asked, eyes still closed.

"Maybe."

She laughed and reached out for him. Leon brought her into his arms and kissed her forehead. She opened her eyes and smiled, leaning into him and appreciating the view of his bare chest.

It wasn't the first time they'd woken up in the same bed, and Maggie hoped it wouldn't be their last.

Leon laced his fingers in hers. "I ordered breakfast."

"You're the best." Maggie's ravenous stomach rumbled in complaint.

The morning after was never like a one night stand with Leon. She never felt the need to scramble over the floor to collect her discarded clothes, shove them on, and escape as fast as possible. There was no awkwardness. No regrets. He was Leon, and no matter how much Maggie tried to move on, it felt right. *They* felt right.

A knock on the door came soon after.

"I'll get it." Maggie hopped out of bed and shrugged on her housecoat, wrapping a headscarf over her blond hair. Rebecca's wig may be a filthy, tangled mess, but it was still prudent to keep up appearances to the hotel staff.

"Hello, Guido." Maggie held the door for him.

Guido wore his same crisp uniform as always, not a hair out of place. "Good morning, Ms. Sterling. I have your breakfast."

Maggie stepped to the side and widened the door for him. "Come on in."

Guido wheeled in the trolley, the scent of strong coffee and bacon wafting past. He placed everything out just so on the table, leaving the cloches on to conceal the heat.

"Is there anything else I can do for you?" he asked.

"That will be all," Maggie said, offering him a pleasant smile. That smile dropped when she spotted something on the man she hadn't noticed before. She frowned and narrowed in on his name tag.

Guido Marino.

Maggie grabbed Guido by the collar of his jacket and pulled him back inside the suite, slamming the door closed. She dragged him into the lounge and threw him down on one of the chairs.

Guido tried to get up and run for the door, but Maggie shoved him back down on the seat with her foot, pressing it over his throat.

"Your name is Marino," she said, abandoning her fake accent.

"Yes," Guido stuttered, holding his hands up.

"As in the Marino family? The syndicate?"

The old man's eyes bulged. "They are my nephews," he said, the words toppling out as he rushed to explain himself, "but I don't have anything to do with their business. I am an honest man trying to make an honest living."

Maggie pressed her foot against his neck, making it clear he wasn't leaving until she got what she wanted. The commotion had alerted Leon, and he walked out of the bedroom in his boxer shorts like a Calvin Klein model ready to fight.

His shoulders relaxed when he took in the room and saw that Maggie was in control. She gave him a little nod, and he ventured to the table and helped himself to a coffee while she continued her interrogation.

"What do you know about Carlo and Stefano Rossi?" she asked Guido.

Sweat beaded over the man's forehead. "I know they're dead."

"Did Enzo Marino and his brothers have them killed?"

Guido shook his head emphatically. "No, the boys wanted to do business with Carlo, to become partners. They would never have killed Carlo, or his son. Carlo was a self-made man. They looked up to him and his family."

"Carlo didn't see them that way," said Maggie, keeping her tone sharp. "He said they were his rivals."

Guido squirmed in his seat, gripping on to the armrests. "Anyone doing illegal business in Carlo's territory was a threat to his leadership. In his eyes, I mean. The man was suspicious, and rightfully so given what happened to him."

"How do you know all of this if, as you said, you don't involve yourself in your nephews' business?"

"They are my brother's sons. He tells me all about them and what they are up to.' Guido sighed, appearing troubled. "He's proud of them."

"And you're not?"

Guido shot her an offended look before he remembered himself. "I am a man of God," he said, like that should be explanation enough.

Maggie believed him, but he wouldn't be the first person to call themselves religious while living a life of crime and 'sin.' Some people hid behind their beliefs like a shield, using it to justify their actions, despite said actions conflicting with what their religion taught them.

"If Enzo and his gang didn't kill the Rossi men, then who did?" asked Maggie. "What do they know?"

"I don't know. I called my brother this morning after hearing what happened at la Fenice, and he said the boys were trying to find the culprit. Enzo seemed to believe Stefano would be more willing to work together than his father."

Maggie nodded. She'd had the same impression of Stefano when it came to Rebecca's offer. Carlo may have been old school, but Stefano came across as more progressive. Not to mention greedy. Peter West had even called him an idiot.

"Stefano wasn't happy to see Enzo at the theater last night," Maggie said, remembering the way Stefano glared over at Enzo from the royal box.

Isabella had said the presence of Enzo and his brothers was a sign of disrespect, insinuating that the two families would end up at war. Could it be the very opposite? Had Enzo turned up at the theater as a show of respect for Carlo? As a way of showing Stefano that he wasn't their rival, that they wanted to be allies?

Had the gesture been taken the way it was intended, it would have been a good approach to initiate a business relationship with the new leader of the Rossi family. But it seemed Enzo's olive branch didn't come across the way he had hoped. Not from Stefano's end, at least.

"Enzo and Stefano have a history," Guido said.

"Go on."

"Back when they were both young, Stefano next in line to his father's business and Enzo wanting nothing more than to make something of himself, they both fell in love with the same girl. Carmella."

Guido settled down a bit, the shake in his voice subsiding.

"Carmella was very beautiful, and the boys ended up in a fist fight over her, trying to prove their love. In the end, she chose Stefano, breaking Enzo's heart in the process."

"Then why would Enzo want to do business with Stefano?"

If there was bad blood between them, it didn't make sense for the men to become partners. At least, not to Maggie. Then again, when it came to holding a grudge, Maggie held it for life.

"That was years ago," said Guido. "They were only boys back then. Carmella has since died, and Stefano's daughter, Angela, is a woman herself now. Enzo has his own wife, and two lovely children. The men may not like each other, but in this city, enemies make deals all the time. It's just business."

Now that, Maggie could accept. All was fair in love and war in the criminal underworld, and she had witnessed mortal enemies coming together as one, even if only temporarily. Assuming, of course, each party stood to make money—and lots of it—from the arrangement.

Confident she'd squeezed all she needed from the butler, Maggie released Guido from her hold. Enzo and his brothers wouldn't be too pleased to hear their old uncle spilled their business, but the old man was harmless. The nephews may have held their tongue under Maggie's questioning, but Guido wasn't a part of their world.

She leaned down until her face was level with his. "This conversation never happened. Do I make myself clear?"

Guido gulped, and tugged at his buttoned shirt collar. "Yes."

Maggie stepped back, holding his gaze until he cowered away from her. "You can go."

Guido didn't need to be told twice. He got up on shaking legs and scampered for the door.

"And thank you for bringing breakfast, Guido," she said as he left, a niggle of guilt coming over her. "I appreciate it." She'd need to leave him a sizable tip as an apology.

"That changes things," said Leon from the table. He waved her over, dishing out breakfast for them both and pouring Maggie out a black coffee, just the way she liked it.

Maggie plopped on the seat across from him, the happy glow from their lustful night together zapped as she went over everything Guido said.

"I believe him," she said, taking a sip from her cup. The coffee was a dark roast, and strong, the caffeine just the thing to give her a boost after a long night of being knocked out, almost dying, and glorious sex.

"The man had no reason to lie," Leon said as he tucked

in to his breakfast. "Not to mention you had him scared shitless."

Maggie leaned back in her chair and tapped a finger on the table. "But if the Marino brothers didn't kill Carlo and Stefano, then who did?"

Leon put his fork down and buttered some toast. "Peter thought it was Rebecca, so that rules him out. He had no reason to lie about it, considering we were supposed to die down there. If he'd had them killed, he would have said so."

Maggie agreed. "The pompous prick would have boasted about it."

She hadn't forgotten about Peter West in all the drama. While he may not have killed the Rossis, he had tried to kill her and Leon. Maggie wouldn't leave Venice until he'd paid for that particular crime.

Maggie stabbed her fork into her scrambled eggs. "If neither of them did it, then who?"

Leon crunched his toast and considered her question. "The best thing to do when lost, is to go back to the beginning."

"You think we've missed something?"

"Something's amiss. I just can't put my finger on what."

Maggie massaged her temples, going over everything that had happened since she arrived in Venice. Going back to the beginning, like Leon said. Eliminating Peter West and the Marinos from the equation didn't leave many people with the means to kill Carlo or Stefano. The motive behind it was another thing entirely.

Then it came to her. Something they'd missed amid all the blood, and conflict, and mess. Something that was right in front of them the whole time.

Maggie grabbed her phone and texted Isabella to arrange a meeting.

It was time they had a serious talk.

Chapter 14

Isabella asked them to meet her at the Isola di San Michele. Maggie couldn't deny the idea of meeting her in Venice's cemetery island felt a little foreboding, but they agreed to go.

It was time to end things once and for all.

Leon talked Guido into letting them use the Gritti Palace's boat—Maggie figured it best she avoid the man after their little Q&A session earlier that morning—and they crossed the lagoon, entering near the front gates of the island and maneuvering into a docking station.

A shiver ran through Maggie as she tied the boat to the wooden posts. The memories from the previous night would take a lifetime to erase.

Isabella said to meet her in one of the subdivisions of gravesites at the back of the island. It was secluded, which suited Maggie just fine. The tourists would be well out of their way, confined to the gravesites surrounding the San Michele church, searching around for the final resting places of famous historical figures.

Like most of Venice, the cemetery was well tended, the grass kept short and walkways free from weeds or litter, yet it still maintained an air of decay which carried on throughout the city, even in the hot spots and central hubs. It provided the city with a sense of charm, but there in the cemetery, all it emitted was the eerie presence of death.

Back home in Britain, Maggie was used to ancient cemeteries with lichen covered stones that crumbled with age. The headstones on the island, however, remained intact and free from wear and tear. Real estate was in high demand all over Venice, and the cemetery was no exception. Most Venetians were only guaranteed a short ten years to rest in peace on the island. With so little space, and so many dead, bodies were regularly exhumed and stored in ossuaries.

A pit of dread weighed heavy in her stomach as Maggie and Leon crossed the island. Thanks to Peter West, they were both without their Berettas. He'd disarmed them before leaving them to drown under the rising tide.

Maggie tied her blond hair in a tight ponytail away from her face, the wind skirting across the waves of the lagoon and sweeping through the little macabre island, whispering in her ear like ghosts. There was no need to keep up her alias of Rebecca. Not when she knew the truth.

Crossing into the next subdivision of graves, it appeared the class system that lived and breathed throughout the city lingered even in death. Freestanding chapels and family mausoleums were scattered all around, surrounded by contemporary monuments and sculptures that made the area look like a modern art museum.

Glassed-in photographs of the dead watched them as they reached their meeting place, another tradition that seemed so foreign to Maggie. She averted her gaze from the still faces and waited on Isabella.

Neither she nor Leon spoke, the location instilling a mourning silence.

A few minutes later, the crunch of boots on gravel grew louder and headed towards them. At first, Maggie thought that it was a group of tourists, coming to unknowingly interrupt their clandestine meeting.

But it was something much worse.

Armed men and women stormed in from all angles and circled them like a pack of predatory wolves.

Maggie suppressed the instinct to fight. There were too many guns pointing at them, but no one made to shoot. Yet.

She counted six in total, three women and three men,

before another set of footsteps approached. Maggie stiff-ened as a familiar face rounded the corner.

"Isabella," said Maggie through gritted teeth. "How could you?"

Isabella shook her head and stared over her shoulder as another woman entered.

Angela Rossi.

Carlo's granddaughter followed behind Isabella and held a gun to her back, shoving her into the man-made circle with Maggie and Leon.

"It was you?" Maggie gaped at the woman. "You had your own family killed?"

"I did." Angela nodded to the man standing to her left with his gun trained on Maggie. "Ricardo helped with Carlo, but I stuck the knife in Stefano's back myself."

Maggie recognized the man as the shooter from the roof. He sniggered at her behind the safety of his weapon, and Maggie's fingers itched to punch the expression off his face.

It wasn't lost on Maggie how Angela referred to the men in her family by their first names. She could almost taste the venom that laced her words. Her beauty took on a vicious edge in the light of day, now that the truth was out.

"Why?" Leon asked. "Why would you kill your own family?"

Angela narrowed her eyes. "They're not my family. My mother was the only family I needed."

"Carmella?" Maggie asked.

"They killed her." Angela's gun wavered in her hand. "Covered it up to make it seem like some tragic accident, but I knew better. Mother always told me that if anything happened to her, to look no further than them."

"What happened?" Maggie didn't particularly care, but she needed to keep the woman talking long enough to figure out how to keep her and Leon, and even Isabella, alive.

Thankfully, Angela was in a talkative mood, finally able to admit to what she'd done and revel in it. "My father used to beat her. Every day. Any time he got drunk, or she did something he didn't like. He always made me go to my room, but I knew what he was doing. I could hear the screams. Saw the bruises my mother tried to cover up afterward."

"Why kill your grandfather?" Leon asked, stalling for time, too.

Maggie scanned the area, looking for an exit route. Something, anything, she could use to their advantage. So far, she was coming up short. Their boat was at the other side of the cemetery, leaving them stranded with no way out other than a body bag.

"I went to him for help." Angela's voice rose with anger. "Told him all about my worthless father and how he hurt my mother. Do you know what he said? That those things were between husband and wife and I should do as my father told me. He could have put an end to it. Stopped it before it was too late."

"But he didn't," said Isabella, Maggie only now noticing the welt across her face.

Angela narrowed her eyes. "No. Which was why he had to die, too. There was no other option once I learned he helped Stefano cover up Mother's murder, making it seem like she was mugged in the street instead of being beaten to death in her own home."

The woman closest to Maggie was just out of reach, and she inched towards her, eying the gun and calculating the risk of making it her own. "Carmella died years ago," she said to Angela, remembering what Guido had told her.

"When I was ten years old. Ever since that day, I vowed to make Stefano pay for what he did. I bided my time until I could make it happen. Waited all those years for the moment when he would peer into my eyes and know how much I hated him. Know why he was about to die, and that his precious daughter was the one to do it."

Maggie gave Angela a sad, knowing smile, doing anything she could to keep Angela talking instead of ordering her henchmen to tie up her loose ends. "I lost my mother when I was young, too."

Angela scrunched her nose. "I don't care about your fucking mother."

A raging calm settled over Maggie, as dangerous as it was silent. Up until then, Maggie understood why Angela went to great lengths to see the men in her life dead. She didn't blame the woman for wanting revenge. But those last words had been a mistake. They'd hit a sore spot in Maggie that unleashed the killer within.

Angela Rossi would live to regret pissing her off, but not for long.

"You're just like your father." Isabella stepped forward, her fists shaking. "A spoiled, damaged brat who I've had to suffer for six whole years. Your mother would be ashamed of you."

Angela slapped Isabella with the back of her hand.

Isabella's face twisted to the side, but she didn't flinch or show any sign that the blow hurt. "Silly girl," she said, somehow managing to be condescending despite the situation.

Even while surrounded with armed men and women, Isabella showed no signs of the fear Maggie knew she felt inside. Looking around the small island, she felt it too.

"You think I didn't know who you were?" said Angela. "Where you come from? You may have fooled my grandfather, but I saw right through you." Angela spat on the ground. "That's what I think of you and your government."

Isabella laughed. "You're going to die sooner than your father did."

"Is that so?" Angela's cheeks flushed in anger. Isabella knew just what to say to get under the younger woman's skin.

Back straightened, Isabella looked down her nose at Angela. "Yes."

Angela circled around Isabella, her heels crunching under the gravel. "Perhaps you're right. But you won't be there to see it." Angela pulled the trigger and shot Isabella pointblank in the head.

Blood and globs of brain matter splattered the gravel. Isabella collapsed to the ground in a crumpled mess. Maggie winced and closed her eyes. Isabella deserved better. She'd sacrificed so much to try and take the Rossi family down.

Angela kicked the dead body. "Bitch."

Maggie's nails dug into her palms. She wouldn't let Isabella's sacrifice be in vain.

"She was trying to take down Carlo and Stefano, just as you were," said Maggie, voice steady, refusing to show Angela even the tiniest hint of fear.

"No. She was trying to tear apart the Rossi empire. My empire," corrected Angela, smoothing her jacket and checking for blots of Isabella's blood, like it was merely spilled marinara sauce. "Now that those bastards are gone, I can lead the family in the right direction."

Maggie cocked her head. "If that direction is down the toilet, then I'd say you're doing a bang-up job."

Angela stopped in front of her, yet kept enough distance so Maggie couldn't strangle her throat. "You have a sharp tongue. I think I'll cut it out before I kill you."

Maggie tensed, knuckles cracking. "Don't make promises you can't keep, little girl. You're in way over your head."

"I don't know if you're Rebecca Sterling or another undercover bitch like her," said Angela, pointing a thumb at Isabella's dead body as it grew cold on the ground. "Either way, it ends the same for you." She raised the gun.

"What if Peter finds out about all this?" Leon asked in a clear attempt to stall the inevitable. "You think he'll want to make a deal with a backstabbing traitor like you?"

"I don't much care, to be quite honest." Peter West's voice announced his presence a moment before he stepped into view, flanked by two of his own guards.

Leon growled. "You."

"Yes, me," said Peter, pleased with himself. He wrapped an arm over Angela's shoulders. "Angela called last night after I left you two in Cannaregio with an offer I couldn't refuse. She's a better businessperson than her father could have ever hoped to be."

Angela's smug grin widened at his praise.

Maggie shook her head. Peter West was playing her, inflating her ego to get the best deal he could. He'd probably short changed her. Not that the new Mafia boss would care. It wasn't about money for Angela. It was personal.

For years, she had worked towards the day where she could bury those responsible for her mother's death, a vendetta that, as much as Maggie hated to admit, Angela had carried out to great effect.

"Should we get going?" Peter asked. "I'd like to arrange

the first shipment. I have an opening coming up for a delivery in Southampton."

"Let's take my boat. I've wasted enough time on these two." Angela turned on her heels and walked off with Peter and his two men. She called over her shoulder and left one final order.

"Kill them."

Chapter 15

The armed men and women closed in around them, ready to carry out their boss's orders.

"We're not dying in a cemetery," Maggie said, standing back-to-back with Leon. "Not today."

"Get on your knees," said the roof shooter, enjoying every second of his moment in charge.

Maggie stood her ground and waited for her advisories to narrow the gap between them. The closer, the better.

"I said, get on your knees," he repeated, lowering his gun. He strode towards her like he thought he could force her into submission.

Maggie shot the man a wicked grin. She may not have her Beretta, but she still had her knives. Slipping one out from under her jacket sleeve, Maggie threw it at the approaching man.

The blade spun in the air and buried in her target's chest.

The shooter made to step towards her but instead fell to his knees. His eyes rolled to the back of his head, and he slumped to the ground in a dead weight.

Maggie didn't waste any time celebrating her bullseye. She turned her attention to the rest of Angela's henchmen. Leon was already on them, disarming the man next to him.

Procuring his gun, Leon used the man as a shield as he fired at the other guards, hitting one of the women between the eyes. She collapsed into the pile of dead bodies on the gravel.

Leon broke his shield's neck, the bone snapping in the otherwise quiet air, and moved on to the others.

Maggie rushed toward one of the two remaining women before she had a chance to retaliate and drew her knife across her throat, the sharp blade slicing through skin to the sinewy muscles and tendons below.

Four down, two to go.

Only they were gone.

The remaining Rossi guards had disappeared in all the confusion, trying to avoid the same fate as their brothers and sisters in arms.

Leon made to run after them, but Maggie stopped him. "They're pawns."

He nodded, panting and eyes alight from the rush of fighting for their life, and they took off at a run, Maggie collecting one of the dead guards' guns on the way. Passing through the gravesites, weaving between rows of tombs and headstones, they made their way back to the entrance where they'd left their boat.

"They don't have much time on us," said Maggie as they rounded the final plot of graves.

An engine roared into life, and Maggie darted her head to the docking station to see Peter West and Angela Rossi take off into the lagoon in Angela's speedboat.

Angela waved to them as they set off, picking up speed.

"We need to hurry." Maggie leaped into their boat and took position at the bow, gun at the ready.

Leon followed and ignited the engine, reversing out of the docking station as fast as the boat would carry them.

A bullet ricocheted off the front of the boat.

"Fuckers," spat Maggie as the two runaway guards returned, expelling their magazines on them.

Leon ducked, still maneuvering the boat as he took cover.

Maggie leaned down and aimed her procured weapon at the remaining guards and fired.

She missed, a blast of stone puffing up between her two targets.

"Shit," she hissed, pulling back. Wasting bullets wasn't a good idea.

Leon spun the boat, put the gear in drive, and

slammed the accelerator. The engine rumbled underneath them, chasing after Angela and Peter.

The two guards sent more rounds at them, but the boat was too far out now.

Maggie turned her attention to the main threat, coming to stand beside Leon as he navigated through the lagoon.

Shielding her eyes from the spray, Maggie spotted her enemy's boat careening back towards the city. Her pulse quickened. "We can't let them reach the city."

"Too late," called Leon through the wind, surging the boat forward with everything it had.

Angela steered into a canal, turning against the waves and sending a crashing blast of water into the air.

Leon tailed them, the gap closing with each second.

The approaching turn forced him to slow down to avoid capsizing the boat.

A horn rang, followed by frantic yelling as Angela overtook a water taxi, forcing the craft to crash into a line of docked boats that ran along the left side of the canal.

The taxi driver cursed them as smoke rose from his engine, the whole front side dented from the collision.

Leon picked up the pace and passed the taxi, the patrons inside pale faced with hands over their hearts.

More honking came from up ahead as Angela tried to dodge between the buildings and a vaporetto blocking the way. But the waterbus didn't budge.

Angela gave up and turned into a connecting canal.

Leon followed, and Maggie spotted the back end of Angela's boat as she swerved again, taking a left into a smaller canal, narrowly missing a passing gondola.

The gondolier tried to keep his balance, but the resulting force of the water caused him to trip, and he stumbled into the water headfirst.

Maggie leaned over the side of the speedboat and pushed the gondola out of the way to let them pass through after Angela. The gondolier popped his head up through the surface, spluttering and swearing, more angered than hurt.

Before Leon could slip the boat through into the next turn, a bullet whipped past Maggie's ear and buried into the stone wall of the building nearest her.

A boat came up from behind them and continued forward, showing no signs of stopping.

"Watch out," Maggie yelled as the boat ran straight into the back of them.

The boat jolted forward, sending Maggie to her hands and knees.

Leon's biceps bulged as he fought for control, steering the boat into the turn and hitting the accelerator to carry on down the canal Angela had taken.

Peter and Angela were out of sight, but they had more pressing matters to deal with.

The attacking boat charged towards them again, the two leftover guards from the cemetery hell-bent on stopping Leon and Maggie from reaching their new boss.

Back on her feet, Maggie took in their surroundings, narrowing in on the street signs pinned to the corners of the buildings.

"I've got an idea."

Leon raised an eyebrow. "Uh, oh."

"Just keep following Angela and Peter. Don't stop." She nudged her head to the boat behind them. "I'll handle those two."

"Got it." Leon didn't need any further explanation, his trust in her never-ending.

With no time to waste, Maggie wriggled onto the front of the boat and waited for the right moment. Leon continued down the canal, fast enough to spot Angela's boat further ahead as it sped around yet another turn to try and throw them off.

Maggie waited for an opening and leapt in the air.

She jumped over the water and landed on the pathway running along the canal, breaking her fall as she collided into a group of screaming tourists.

Untangling herself from the frantic civilians, Maggie got to her feet and ran down the street, seeing the map of the city in her mind's eye, her time studying it during her flight coming in handy.

Maggie thundered down the street, heading away from the canal, and weaved between tourists. Taking a right, and another right after that, she rounded the square and arrived at a bridge connecting one tiny island to the next.

Catching a glimpse of Leon, Maggie ducked, her chest

heaving, and waited until the sounds of the boat's engine whipped past under the bridge.

Maggie climbed onto the side of the bridge and dropped over the edge to the water below, timing it just right.

She landed hard on her feet, acute jolts of pain shooting up her legs. Maggie ignored it, and before the man had time to react to her crashing the party, she swept his legs from under him and sent him careening into the canal.

The boat slowed as the woman left her station and grabbed for her gun.

Maggie ducked through the interior and charged into her before the guard could aim her weapon. They toppled back, and Maggie sent a tirade of blows to the guard's face, breaking her nose in a sickening crunch.

One final punch to the damaged bone, and the guard blacked out on the floor.

Maggie wobbled to her feet as sweat trickled down her back. She took the unconscious guard's place and moved the boat forward, catching up with Leon.

Leon never slowed, but shifted to the side to allow Maggie to pull up next to him. She hopped back onto their own boat and left the other to carry on forward until it collided into a row of parked vessels with a splintering crash.

"Where are they?" Maggie asked, catching her breath, thankful for the cool wind whipping her face.

"Just turned down the next left."

Maggie reorganized her thoughts, figuring out where exactly they were in the city and where Angela and Peter were headed. "That's good," she said. The canal had no other exits beside the one straight ahead of them. "It leads out into the lagoon at St Mark's Square."

They needed to lead Angela and Peter away from the tourist-filled streets, out into the safety of the vast lagoon.

Leon took the turn and stepped on it. They sped through the canal, Leon dodging passing boats and inching ever closer to their targets.

Two figures stepped out into the back of Angela's boat and set their sights on them.

"Peter's guards," Maggie said, as water sprayed in front of the boat as an assault of bullets splattered into the canal.

Leon steered the boat in a sharp left, dodging out of the line of fire, but there was nowhere to turn in the straight canal. No side streets or corner turns to hide behind.

The guards sent their next round of shots.

Maggie yanked Leon out of the way as a line of bullets tore into the front of the boat, travelling up to the helm where Leon had been standing. The windshield shattered into a thousand crystal pieces and scattered across the bow.

"All right." Maggie pulled out her procured gun. "That's it."

Getting down on one knee to steady herself, Maggie

used the boat as cover and aimed at Peter's men.

It was a long shot, especially for a handgun.

Angela and Peter were upfront, but Maggie's view of them was obstructed by the interior. Instead, she moved along to the guards and trained her weapon on them. Just like she did with Jason Stroud back in Poland, Maggie aimed the shot, held her breath, and emptied her magazine. She normally wasn't so wasteful with bullets, but under the conditions, the more shots the better her chances of striking true.

"Yes," whooped Leon, "you got one."

Maggie tossed the empty gun, useless to her now.

They passed under the Bridge of Sighs and sped out into the ending of the Grand Canal. Angela made to turn right and head into the main artery of the city, but Leon cut her off, forcing the drug dealers to head out into the open water.

Ignoring the remaining guard, Maggie dug in her jacket pocket and brought out the device.

"Closer," she told Leon as they moved further and further away from land.

Leon propelled them on, ripping the engine to shreds in the process, its aches and whines drumming against their ears. "They're heading for Lido."

Maggie wasn't worried. Angela and Peter may be heading for the long, thin island across the way, but they would never reach its shores.

She peered at the device, waiting until the little red

light stopped blinking.

"Closer," she urged again, her hair coming free from her ponytail and whipping behind her.

Leon careened forward, balancing the dual need to be close enough for their plan to work, but not so close as to cross into the line of fire.

The red light stopped blinking.

Maggie gripped the device in her hand, remembering her orders from Bishop, passed down from the Director herself.

Under no circumstance had the deal between the Rossi family and Peter West to go through.

Maggie pressed down on the detonator.

Two long seconds passed before all hell broke loose.

She caught one last look at Angela and Peter, too far off to read their expressions.

Then the boat exploded.

A wave of heat rushed over Maggie and Leon as the boat went up in a blast of burning orange and blood red.

Water rushed into the air, carried up with the boat as the earth-shattering explosion boomed across with lagoon.

A cloud of black smoke floated into the air as splinters of wood, human remains, and other debris plopped into the water around the black husk that was once Angela Rossi's speedboat.

Maggie and Leon watched as the remains slowly drowned under the waves and sank to their aquatic grave in the salty depths below.

Chapter 16

A few hours later, Maggie lay out on the front of the boat in her bikini, soaking in the glorious summer sun. There was no guarantee London would enjoy similar weather once she got back, so Maggie basked in the warmth while she could.

Leon steered the hotel's boat with a frosted beer in one hand, his skin shiny from the sun lotion she'd just rubbed over his naked torso, taking her time massaging it in. Not that Leon complained.

She held her phone to her ear and briefed Bishop on their successful mission.

"How did you know it was Angela Rossi?" her boss asked.

"When we learned the Marinos weren't involved, we had to reevaluate what we knew. At the meeting on the rooftop terrace, Angela injected herself into the conversation and stormed off when Carlo reprimanded her. Next thing we knew, her grandfather was dead. With her conveniently out of the way, no one would think to point the finger."

Maggie recalled the look Angela gave her grandfather before making her exit, a venomous glare that she had mistaken for tarnished pride. If only she knew then how deep the bad blood between them ran.

"You pinned her for the murders based on that?" Bishop asked.

Maggie moved onto her stomach and peered out into the lagoon, the water glittering under the rays like diamonds. "There were other factors," she said. "Angela was the only one with Stefano in the royal box at the orchestra, giving her the perfect opportunity to carry out her revenge. After Carlo's death, Stefano's security was on high alert, but no one thought about keeping the man safe from his own unassuming daughter."

Bishop slurped on his tea at the other end of the line. "The presence of the Marino brothers gave her the perfect distraction, too."

"I wouldn't be surprised if Angela had invited them for that very reason." Maggie recalled what Guido said about the brothers wanting to establish a business relationship. They would have gladly accepted Angela's invitation, viewing it as an olive branch between the two families.

Angela had them all fooled.

Maggie sighed. "In the end, it came down to who had the most to gain. The Marinos were after a deal with the Rossis, and Peter West had already made steps to secure one of his own. It didn't add up for either of them to take out Carlo and Stefano."

"Whereas Angela stood to gain control of the family empire, while simultaneously carrying out her vendetta to avenge her mother," added Bishop with just a hint of admiration in his voice. "Smart girl."

"Not smart enough." Angela's plans had exploded. Literally.

Bishop cleared his throat. "And your contact, Isabella?"

"Dead." Maggie closed her eyes behind her sunglasses. Watching allies die in the field was never easy. It wasn't the first-time Maggie had experienced it, but each time it broke a little piece of her inside. They all knew the risks, yet it never stopped a good agent from doing what was right, and Isabella was no exception. Death reared its ugly head all too often in their line of work.

"I'm sorry to hear that." Bishop knew better than most what it was like, being an agent himself since before Maggie was even born.

"She was a good agent." Maggie fought to control the wave of emotion in her chest. "We couldn't have done it without her."

Teaming up with Isabella before the meeting in the cemetery had been vital to Maggie's plan. She'd been wrong to suspect her involvement in the deaths, mistaking the woman's complicated relationship with Carlo as an indicator of guilt.

It couldn't have been further from the truth. Isabella was loyal to her government and her cause to the very end, planting the bomb in Angela's boat before attending the meeting in one last heroic act before her life ended too soon.

Maggie acted like she thought Isabella was the one behind the murders when she first turned up at the cemetery, needing to fool Angela into thinking they weren't onto her. Isabella had slipped the detonator to Maggie while Angela revealed her motives, allowing Maggie to end things with the press of a button.

It was a small consolation, but at least Isabella had completed her mission before she died, even if she didn't get to see it herself.

"I'll let her people know how key she was to the success of the mission," said Bishop after she outlined the details. "You did good, Maggie. You both did."

"Thanks," she said, not quite able to celebrate.

"Take a few days before reporting back. You deserve it."

They said their goodbyes, and Maggie hung up.

She padded over to Leon on bare feet. "Mission accomplished," she said.

Leon pulled her close and leaned his chin on her

shoulder, her rear rubbing against his groin. "Part of me doesn't want to go home."

Maggie tilted her head back and ran her hands over Leon's strong arms which clung around her waist. Neither of them said anything about their relapse. They didn't have to. It hung over them like a little dark cloud amid the sunshine. Their time together couldn't last forever.

The weekend in Venice didn't change their complicated relationship. At the end of the day, they were still agents, each more than aware of the instability and erratic nature of their lives.

It was a pipedream to think their lives would ever slow down enough—become stable enough—for them to be together. It was a dream, but it was one they didn't have to wake up from just yet.

"We don't have to go home," Maggie said, turning to face him. "Not for a few days, at least."

A smile tugged at Leon's lips. "I can get onboard with that."

He leaned down and kissed her, and Maggie lost herself in his embrace. The future wasn't certain, but she focused on the present. On the man she loved, and the beautiful city surrounding them.

Reality could wait.

For now, they were simply two lovers in one of the most romantic getaways in the world, and Maggie intended to make the most of it.

THE WITNESS

MAGGIE BLACK CASE FILES BOOK 2

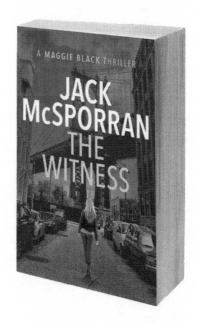

Chapter 1

Maggie Black leapt from the edge of the rooftop and flew through the air.

Below, boats passed through the canal, carting tourists around the crowded city as they snapped pictures with excited fingers.

Pain shot up Maggie's feet and travelled through her tired legs as she landed hard on top of the next building, muscles twitching in complaint. Maggie grit her teeth and continued her chase. The killer couldn't get away.

Quickening her pace, Maggie jumped the gap. But instead of reaching the next rooftop, the buildings faded into shadows and she found herself plunged into the ice-cold water of the lagoon. Rope bound her to a wooden post in the darkness. The tide was rising, inching closer and closer to her face, ready to devour her.

And Leon.

"I love you, Maggie."

From the murky, bone-chilling water, to the hot jets of a double shower, Maggie leaned into Leon as he kissed her neck. The rush of their near-death experience set fire to the simmering passion that had rekindled at the start of their mission in Venice.

Steam rose around them and washed away the image, reforming in the bed where they spent hours beneath the sheets, lost in the complete ecstasy of their insatiable need for each other.

Faces flashed in Maggie's mind. Two dead crime bosses. One with a bullet through his throat, the other stabbed in the back. A dead undercover agent, shot point blank after being discovered. A British drug dealer. And Angela Rossi, the woman behind it all.

The roar of an engine filled her ears. Wind whipped across Maggie's hair.

"Closer," she urged Leon, holding a detonator in her hand.

The speedboat rushed through the lagoon, the waves tossing the boat up and down as they crashed through the water, leaving a track of white foam in their wake.

Maggie pressed the button on the device, and the boat they were chasing—Angela's boat—exploded.

A blast of heat rushed over her face, and Maggie startled in her bed.

She blinked and cataloged the scene around her. The sun crawled over familiar walls, and she turned to find a bedside table—*her* bedside table—with an alarm clock announcing it was just after six in the morning. She was home. In her flat in London.

A wave of nausea coursed through her from the boat chase, making her head spin.

No, not the boat chase. That was two months ago now.

The nausea was something else.

Maggie stumbled to the bathroom, disorientated from her dream, and dropped to her knees by the toilet. Her body convulsed, and she heaved, reaching the bowl with not a moment to spare. Maggie lost track of time as she hugged the cool porcelain and her stomach emptied itself for the third morning in a row.

Sweat beaded her forehead, and she leaned against the corner of the bathtub, wiping her mouth with the back of her hand. She closed her eyes until her head stopped spinning, letting the feeling pass before she tried to get up.

On shaking legs, Maggie leaned over the sink and ran the cold water. She splashed it over her face and neck, avoiding the mirror. Her blond hair hung in a curtain over her face, tousled from another restless night of troubled dreams.

Maggie dabbed her face dry with a towel and flushed the toilet, plopping down on the closed lid. Her eyes drifted over to the plastic bag sitting by her toiletries. She'd purchased the item a few days ago, but she hadn't quite mustered the courage to use it.

A tremor shook her hands, and Maggie tucked them into her folded arms. She wouldn't show fear. Not even to herself. Still, she worried at her lip as she debated her next move.

Eight weeks had passed since her mission in Venice. It felt longer than that in some ways, each day without Leon stretching longer than the last. Yet the nightmares kept the horror of the trip fresh in her mind, like it had happened only yesterday.

With their mission complete, she and Leon had spent the rest of the week in the sinking city like a pair of newly-weds. They saw little of the city beside their shared hotel room, barely coming up for air as they enjoyed their temporary reprieve from their lives as secret agents.

Maggie's heart panged at the thought of him. Of his infectious smile and comforting presence. The way he looked at her with his dark, honest eyes. She missed his touch, missed the way he'd found all the places that made her moan.

She gave herself a shake.

Leon was off on a new assignment, disappeared to some undisclosed location doing something classified for the good of Queen and country.

Maggie had only just gotten back from a quick job in Dublin herself. She'd been tasked with taking out an IRA radical before he could meet up with a militia group in the Middle East. The job went smoothly, even with the queasiness that had followed her around like a stalker on the prowl, ready and waiting for her every morning without fail.

She stole another glance at the bag, a pit of dread forming in her stomach. She couldn't put it off forever. Maggie sighed and reached for the bag, pulling out the box within, and reading the instructions on the back. It was a straightforward process.

Maggie opened the box and looked inside, her fingers trembling. She closed the box.

It could wait another day.

Another day of wondering, of biting her fingernails and thinking about nothing else. Another day of not knowing.

Before she could change her mind, Maggie removed the little plastic stick and considered the terrifying apparatus. How could something so small have the power to turn a trained secret agent into such a nervous wreck? The weight of what it might reveal turned her already queasy stomach.

Maggie removed the cap and proceeded with the unglamorous process. Soon, she'd know the answer to the question she couldn't even vocalize. The question she couldn't even bring herself to admit to Ashton, her best friend and trusted confidant. She'd visited him the day before and hadn't said a word.

Now all she had to do was wait. Maggie replaced the cap and placed the test down by the sink. She studied the offending piece of plastic and paced the small bathroom.

Her palms grew clammy.

She hadn't paid much attention to the lull in her usual cycle, chalking it up to the stress of the job. Her body never ran a normal monthly routine anyway, not even back when she was a teenager.

In the months before Venice, Maggie had neglected her prescribed little white pill. Her social life was non-existent thanks to her work. Hopping from one place to the next without a word to anyone didn't exactly do wonders for a girl's love life. Not that she'd had any recent interest in one.

At least, not until she saw Leon again.

Maggie padded on bare feet into her bedroom and checked the time.

Three minutes felt like three hours.

A buzzing vibrated by her bed. Maggie flinched, reaching on reflex for the gun she kept under her pillow, but it was only her phone.

She sighed and placed a hand on her chest as she collected her phone, heart drumming with anticipation and dread.

"Bishop." Her boss was the only one who'd call that early.

"Morning, Maggie. I hope I haven't woke you."

Maggie ran a hand through her hair. "No, I was up." She glanced over her shoulder to the bathroom. "What's going on?"

Bishop sipped on something at his end, a morning cup of tea no doubt. "We have a situation. I need you to come in as soon as possible."

A jolt of panic coursed through her. "What's wrong? Is it Leon?"

"What?" Bishop asked, surprise coloring his tone. "No, no, he's fine. I need you on a new assignment. I'll tell you more when you come in."

Maggie's shoulders dropped, and she pinched the bridge of her nose, trying to calm herself down. "Okay, give me an hour."

"See you then." Bishop hung up without waiting for a goodbye.

The room grew silent again, and Maggie noted the time.

Her three minutes were up.

She returned to the bathroom on hesitant feet and readied herself for the result. Maggie peered down at the little plastic stick. Two blue lines stared up at her.

She was pregnant.

Chapter 2

Maggie reached the Unit headquarters in a blur, too lost in her troubled thoughts to take notice of how she got there.

She swiped her security pass at the doors of the five-story office building—which masked as a stationery supplier named Inked International—and continued past the foyer in a daze, not saying hello to anyone. The elevators dinged at her boss's floor before Maggie even registered she'd left the lobby.

Like always, Brice Bishop waited for her in the hallway when the doors pinged opened.

"Maggie," he said, placing a paternal hand on her back and leading her into his office. "Thank you for coming in."

"No problem." Maggie kept her leather jacket on, unable to scare away the chill that enveloped her. It was cold outside, and any residual heat from the two weeks of sunshine Londoners called summer had left weeks ago.

Bishop held up a teapot adorned with the British flag, steam trailing from the spout. "Tea?"

"Yes, please," Maggie said, taking a seat at the conference table.

Bishop wore a navy suit, the tailoring impeccable on his frame. For a man in his late fifties, he was in great shape. Despite trading in field work for his desk job years ago, the Unit Chief hadn't lost his edge. Even his chestnut hair was kept army regulation short from his days in the military.

After fixing her tea with milk and no sugar, Bishop sat across from her and slid the mug over the table.

Maggie cupped the warm ceramic and let the heat seep into her hands.

"Is everything all right?" Bishop paused with his mug hovering by his lips as he took her in, a little crease forming above his brow.

"Just tired, that's all," she lied, fixing her face into a smile. She should have known Bishop would sense the change in her mood; he knew her too well by now. After working together for eleven years—four in training and seven with Maggie as an official agent—they'd cemented an intimate knowledge of each other's emotions. They were abundantly familiar with the other's subtle ticks and tells. Maggie took a soothing sip of tea and hid her racing mind behind a cool façade.

Bishop studied her for a moment with his piercing brown eyes before getting back to business. "You can get some sleep on the plane."

"Where am I going?"

"New York City."

It had been a long time since she was in the United States. Americans took great pride in their covert intelligence work and rarely sought British assistance unless the situation impacted both nations.

Maggie sipped her tea, an English breakfast blend that soothed her stomach enough that she craved a solid meal. She placed her hand over her belly and fought the swell of emotion that grew inside her.

"What's the situation?" she asked, shaking her emotions aside. She couldn't give Bishop more room to draw suspicions.

Bishop gave a little laugh, though Maggie didn't miss the thinning of his lips. "I'm not quite sure, actually."

Maggie frowned. "What?"

"It's all very hush, hush." Bishop shrugged and laced his fingers together. "The Director left orders to send you across the pond for the official briefing."

For a moment, Maggie just sat there, blinking. She couldn't recall a time when Bishop wasn't briefed on an assignment. He oversaw every agent in the Unit, which meant he knew about all the missions Director General Helmsley and the other higher ups delegated to their intelligence agency. Given the covert nature of their work, sometimes agents weren't cleared to discuss their jobs with their colleagues. But Bishop always knew. At least, he was supposed to.

Maggie sat up in her chair, tea abandoned. "Why haven't you been briefed?"

"It's above my pay grade, it seems."

Part of her rigorous training involved reading people, a vital skill in the field, one that made sure you returned alive. But Maggie didn't need a degree in behavioral psychology to see how much Bishop bristled at not being privy to the job at hand.

"What *do* you know?" Bishop must know something. If only enough to choose the best agent for such a highly-classified mission.

Bishop leaned back in his chair and shook his head. "Only that it concerns a key witness to something important, and that the mission is of the highest priority. Apparently, our national security is in jeopardy and the Director wants my best agent on it as soon as possible."

Even after eleven years, Bishop's praise still invoked a sense of pride in Maggie. She'd worked hard during her time as an agent, never turning down an assignment or giving up and coming home when things got rough.

But could she accept the mission now?

Taking a prolonged drink of her tea, she considered her options. She had no idea what she was going to do about being pregnant. Having a child was never part of her plan. Never something she allowed herself to think about for too long, given her occupation.

There was so much to consider, and Maggie wasn't ready for any of it. There'd be time for that later.

"When do I leave?" she asked. Whatever was happening in America was clearly urgent. If her skillset was needed, then she would give all the help she could, just as she had always done. The rest could wait until she returned home.

"A car is waiting outside to take you to the airport."

Maggie pushed her chair back and stood. "I'll need to stop at my apartment for a few things first."

"Already taken care of," said Bishop with an apologetic smile. "Someone will be waiting at the airport with your things."

"Well," Maggie said, prickling at the idea of someone breaking into her apartment and rummaging through her belongings. "I guess I'm all set to go then."

Bishop walked her to the door. "Once you land, you'll report to the British Consulate."

Maggie shot him a raised eyebrow. "This is all very cloak and dagger. Even by our standards."

"Agreed," said Bishop, a little weary now. It wasn't even eight o'clock yet, and Maggie would bet the man had been at the office for hours already. If he even went home the night before.

"Thanks for the tea." Maggie placed a hand on his

shoulder before turning to leave. "I'll see you when I get back."

"Ring me if you need anything," Bishop called as she stepped into the elevator to take her down to the awaiting car. "Oh, and Maggie?"

"Yes?" she asked, as the cart doors began to close.

Bishop's face hardened, his eyes troubled. "Watch your back on this one."

Maggie nodded. "I always do."

Chapter 3

M aggie left London from Heathrow at eleven in the morning and touched down at JFK International Airport a little after two in the afternoon, thanks to the five-hour difference between time zones.

Despite the routine of hopping on a plane at a moment's notice and flying across the world being as normal for Maggie as taking the tube to work, even she couldn't avoid jetlag altogether. Over the years, she'd grown accustomed to the lethargic sluggishness that accompanied her travels.

As tired as she was, catching some sleep on the way to

the consulate was out of the question. Her mind hadn't stopped spinning since the test came out positive. Talk about a wakeup call.

Wheeling the carry-on suitcase one of her fellow agents had packed for her, Maggie made her way through security, putting on an air of excited tourist for customs. A driver stood outside the arrivals terminal carrying a little whiteboard with her name scrawled on it.

"Ms. Black?" he asked, no doubt having been provided a picture of her beforehand.

"The very one." Maggie handed him her luggage and followed him to his car. She swung open the Escalade's passenger door and slipped inside. The Cadillac stood out like fox in a hen house among the rows of yellow cabs, with its V8 engine and tinted windows. Apparently, subtlety wasn't a concern.

After stowing her case in the trunk, the driver settled behind the wheel and pulled into traffic. "I'm to take you straight to the consulate."

Maggie suppressed rolling her eyes. It wasn't the driver's fault, but the babysitting was a little ridiculous. She'd been sent in response to a request for the Unit's best operative; her US-based colleagues should trust her to make it from the airport to the consulate without getting herself killed.

Situated in Manhattan, the British Consulate General resided in the Turtle Bay neighborhood of Midtown East. The trip from the airport should have taken thirty minutes, but thanks to traffic, an hour passed and they were still on the road.

The driver slowed to a stop to pay the toll, and they crossed the East River through the Queens-Midtown Tunnel. The Empire State Building poked out from the skyline beyond, waving at them before the view vanished and was replaced with the mouth of the tunnel.

Phosphorescent lights glowed above them and guided the way through the underwater highway before it finally opened out into Manhattan. Taking the Downtown exit, they merged onto East 37th Street and turned right onto 3rd Avenue.

Maggie craned her neck to get a view of the towering buildings looming over them from every direction, their postures dominant and proud. There was something about the city that always made Maggie pause. She'd travelled the world twice over working for the Unit, spent time on every continent and experienced the cities each had to offer.

New York didn't have the gilded statues and ornate facades of Paris, or the ethereal decaying beauty of Venice. It didn't have the tranquility of Kyoto, or the deep-rooted history of Edinburgh with its castle perched on top of an ancient volcano.

Yet it had *something*.

A presence that could be felt more than seen. A confident energy that lived and breathed through the gridded streets and skyscrapers. A resilience in the people who stomped the sidewalks, from hard-nosed construction workers to high-end businesswomen in expensive heels. In both the old-timers who watched the city grow and polish itself over decades, and the new arrivals fresh off the bus with big dreams and a determined grit to succeed.

It was heard in the voices of performers in Harlem's Apollo Theater. Tasted in the dirty water hotdogs from the cart vendors around Times Square. Witnessed in the cut-throat world of the stock market on Wall Street. Experienced through the actors on the legendary stages of Broadway.

The city held no pretenses, and living there wasn't for the faint-hearted. The old adage held true: you could make it anywhere if you could handle the Big Apple. It was the very thing that made the place special.

It attracted tourists from every corner of the globe, each of them eager to experience that special, intangible *something*, if only for a day.

New York City was unlike any other place in the world.

The car pulled up at 845 3rd Avenue, and Maggie stepped out into the street. The front entrance of the large, modern office building greeted her with a British flag swaying from a pole on one side and the American stars and stripes hanging at the other.

The driver led Maggie inside, greeting the guards who manned the doors. The pair of guards ushered Maggie through a metal detector and passed her luggage across the conveyor belt of an x-ray machine before allowing her entry. Once satisfied she wasn't carrying a bomb or packing a gun, they formally welcomed Maggie to the consulate.

To the untrained eye, the foyer appeared pedestrian. Clusters of people sat around as they waited for their appointments and filled in forms. A loud and exasperated man at the front desk explained how he'd lost his passport.

Maggie spotted the cameras positioned throughout, some prominently displayed to deter misbehavior, others hidden and focused on strategic points. While consulates acted as safe havens for nationals, they were also potential targets, and the New York location wasn't taking any chances.

Security may appear lax on the surface, but a trained—and heavily armed—detail of marines or private contractors was undoubtedly standing by, ready to act if the need arose.

A woman spotted Maggie and approached.

"Maggie Black," she said, holding out her hand. "I'm Danielle Hawkins."

Like her demeanor, Danielle's shake was firm and professional. She nodded to the driver, who took that as a sign to leave, having passed his charge onto someone else.

"I appreciate the escort, but I could have made it here myself." Maggie's gaze trailed after the driver as he left, noting the way he paused to speak with the security guards at the x-ray machine.

"Just giving you a warm welcome," Danielle replied, herding her over to the elevators.

More like keeping an eye on her.

No older than thirty, Danielle kept her mouse-brown hair pulled back from her face, the spray of freckles across her nose giving her a juvenile appearance. Even the thick mascara and tight-fitting suit couldn't hide her youth.

Six stories up, Maggie trailed her case behind her as she walked through a busy cubicle-filled floor decorated with an art installation of the British flag running along one of the walls.

"I apologize for the lack of a proper welcome, but I'm afraid time is of the essence." Danielle led her into a small room in the back where two other suits waited for them.

Danielle shut the door behind her and closed the blinds of the glass office.

"Ms. Black." The eldest of the two men flashed a tight smile from his position at the top of a mahogany conference table.

"Maggie, this is the Consul-General, Jonathan Cole."

No one bothered to introduce the man at Cole's left, leading Maggie to conclude he was the Consul-General's secretary or personal assistant. Hierarchy was king in places like the consulate, and Cole wouldn't even think to introduce someone with such a low position.

Danielle sat to Jonathan's right, leaving Maggie to sit at the opposite end of the table like she was a schoolgirl sent to the headmaster's office. A deliberate move on their part, she was sure. Not that it intimidated her in the slightest.

"I understand the situation is time sensitive," Maggie said, uninterested in introductions. The Unit sent her there for a reason, and it was about time she learned why.

"Indeed." Jonathan's assistant slid over a document, which the Consul-General scanned through rimless glasses. "Which department did you say you came from?"

"I didn't."

At that, Jonathan Cole leaned back in his chair and folded his arms across his ample gut, the buttons of his shirt struggling against the pressure.

"Look." Maggie breathed deep and grasped at the final straws of her patience. "I'm here because the higher ups feel you need my help. Clearly, you aren't happy with an outsider joining whatever operation you have going on. I can't say I'm particularly thrilled, either, but given how tight-lipped everyone is about the situation, I assume something major has happened. So why don't we stop this little power play before it starts, and you tell me what I need to know."

Silence fell over the room, full of barely contained tension. Finally, Danielle cleared her throat and looked to Jonathan, who nodded his permission.

"The sole witness to the murder of a UN official has been abducted." Danielle let out a resigned sigh. "We need someone to get her back."

"Which is where I come in, I presume." Maggie knew

a thing or two about recovering hostages. "Where is she being held?"

"The Russian Consulate."

Maggie's eyebrows shot up. "Excuse me?"

Danielle fidgeted in her chair. "The Russians got to the witness before we could and are holding her inside. Our sources say they plan to move her tomorrow afternoon."

"So you expect me to infiltrate the consulate and do what exactly? Stage a break out?"

"We were told the higher ups were sending their best agent." Jonathan glanced up from his file, like it was nothing. Like accomplishing what they asked was as simple as a walk in Central Park. As if Maggie could just waltz up to the Russians and ask if they would be so kind as to go fetch the witness and hand her over.

"Who's the witness?" Maggie asked.

"Her name is Emily Wallace." Danielle passed over a photo, and the face of a young black girl smiled up at her. She was dressed in a school uniform, had braces covering her white teeth, and wore her hair in long braids that fell past her shoulders.

"She's just a kid." Maggie held out an expectant hand for the rest on the intel, and the three of them blinked back at her. "There's no file?"

Jonathan seemed to roll his words over in his mind before responding. "Due to the nature of the situation, we're not at liberty to disclose more about the witness."

"Fine. Who was the UN official?"

Again, neither of them seemed inclined to answer.

"You're not going to tell me that either?" Maggie shook her head and laughed. "I get it. The less I know, the less the Russians can torture out of me if I get caught trying to save Emily Wallace."

"If you are caught, the British government will not claim you as their own," Jonathan warned.

Maggie knew the drill. The chances of her succeeding in the monumental task laid before her were slim. Slim enough for them not to tell her anything other than the bare minimum.

"When did the Russian's kill the official?" Whomever the victim was, they must have been British, otherwise this impossible task would have fallen to someone else. Additional details about their identity would be useful but, ultimately, unnecessary.

"The incident happened last night," said the Consul-General. "The American's are doing what they can to stop the news reaching the press."

"Emily Wallace is the only person who saw the assassination," Danielle added. "Given the method used, there is nothing else to prove the death wasn't due to natural causes."

Maggie nodded. Without Emily, the Russians would get away with it. Emily was the only link to prove their guilt, and Maggie's government would need her testimony.

Jonathan sat up straight, his defensive guard replaced

with grave authority. "It is vital the witness make it back here alive. Failure to do so could result in the highest threat to national security in years."

No pressure then.

Maggie frowned. "Why haven't they killed her already?"

"The Americans are pursuing official channels to enter the Russian Consulate." Jonathan removed his glasses, exposing dark circles under his eyes. "We think the Russians don't want to risk killing Ms. Wallace inside the building as it could incriminate them. Especially with the US watching from outside. Better to slip her out unnoticed, take her somewhere unrelated, and kill her there."

Most civilians assumed consulates and embassies were built on foreign soil. Maggie blamed the movies. While the diplomats and ambassadors benefited from diplomatic immunity, the Russian Consulate was on sovereign territory belonging to the US.

The trouble came from entering the building itself. Strictly speaking, American authorities required the Consulate's permission to come inside. Barging in without the Russian Consul-General's consent would create a political nightmare and cause serious repercussions to foreign relations.

The Russians wouldn't be quick to open their doors with Emily Wallace inside. By the time the Americans got in, the witness would be long gone. Which meant Maggie was the only person who could save Emily and help prove that the Russians were responsible for the UN official's murder.

Maggie hesitated in her chair, hand hovering over the picture of Emily Wallace.

The Russian Consulate was a fortress. This was more than a simple case of breaking and entering to reach the witness. Assuming she even got that far. The Russians would be on high alert and were already planning on killing one person. They wouldn't think twice about adding Maggie to the list if they caught her.

Could she risk it?

Normally, Maggie wouldn't think twice. She'd sworn long ago to give her life for the good of her country. But if she failed now, it wouldn't just be her life forfeited. She had more than herself to consider.

Maggie picked up the photo and stared at the girl's innocent face. Emily was someone's child. Someone's baby. Maggie couldn't even begin to imagine what her parents must be going through. Their daughter stolen with no way to get her back. Standing helpless by the phone and unable to do anything.

Maggie wasn't helpless. *She* could do something.

She could get up and leave. Return home and forget all about it. It would be the smart thing to do. She ran an absent hand over her stomach and averted her eyes from the photo.

If she walked away now, Emily would be just as dead

as the UN official, and no one would be brought to justice for either of them.

Maggie caught Emily's kind eyes from the photo and sighed. Sometimes the right thing to do wasn't always the smart thing.

"Well, you've all been a wonderful help," she said, her words dripping with sarcasm. "Do I at least get a weapon, or is that too much to ask?"

Jonathan's assistant handed Maggie a rucksack.

She dug inside and brought out a 9mm Glock 19, extra magazines and rounds, and a foreign passport with her picture inside. Just another day at the office.

"You'll find a full biography in there as well," said Danielle. "I hear aliases are your specialty."

Maggie closed the Russian passport. "You heard right."

Chapter 4

The thirty-five-story condominium was just as Maggie expected: a lavish residence in the Upper West Side complete with a host of amenities, including its own swimming pool, basketball court, yoga studio, and sauna.

The glass tower on West 59th Street, resided in the heart of Lincoln Square, and Maggie unlocked the door to the apartment on the twenty-eighth floor.

Maggie let out a whistle as she took in her temporary digs, dumping her suitcase in the corner along with her new backpack and the supplies she collected on the way there. Ashton had called ahead with orders for the doorman to hand over the spare key when she arrived, her best friend refusing to let her stay in a hotel while she was in New York.

"It's not like I'm using the place," he'd said on the phone that morning before she left.

Ashton had several homes scattered around the world, all of them owned but none through legitimate means. Maggie may carry out illegal acts for the government, but Ashton preferred to do his nefarious business on his own terms, having left the Unit years ago without ever looking back.

He'd done well for himself since then. Most of Ashton's fortune came from ripping off criminals who had no idea he'd duped them. Maggie wandered around the two-bedroom apartment, everything furnished like a showroom —from the four-poster bed in the master suite, to the plush suede couches in the living-room which led out into a wide corner terrace—and took in the view of the Hudson River.

Maggie stepped outside and let the cool breeze sweep over her face. It had been a long day, and tomorrow was fast approaching.

When the sun dipped low and the air drew goose-bumps along her arms, Maggie returned inside and ran a hot bath, filling it high with bubbles. Steam rose from the water as she sank beneath the sudsy surface and let the heat seep in and loosen her tense muscles.

She closed her eyes and basked in the quiet.

The peaceful silence broke when her phone buzzed against the tiled floor. Maggie groaned and reached over the edge of the bath to put the caller on loudspeaker.

"Hello?"

"Mags, how you doing?" Ashton's Scottish brogue reverberated around the bathroom.

Her fingers brushed over her flat stomach and she stared down, the image of it swollen with her growing baby sweeping through her mind.

"Good," Maggie lied, giving herself a shake and pushing the image to the back of her mind. She sat up and folded her arms on the tub's ledge, leaning towards the phone and wishing Ashton was with her.

"You settled in okay?"

"The apartment's a little shabby, but I guess it'll do," she teased, making a better effort to hide her troubled mind with Ashton than she had with Bishop.

"Brilliant," Ashton said. A woman's voice spoke in the background, announcing several delays to upcoming flights.

Maggie frowned. "Where are you?"

"At a layover in Miami. I'm heading to Ecuador."

Maggie narrowed her eyes. "What are you doing down there?"

"You know me," Ashton said, all innocent. "A wee bit of this, a wee bit of that."

"Well, be careful. I'm tied up here, so I can't come and save your arse like I did in New Orleans." Ashton was no stranger to sticky situations, but that particular trip had been a close one. Too close.

Ashton laughed, like the trip had consisted of

gumbo, good jazz music, and one too many cocktails, instead of murder and mayhem. "I'll be on my best behavior."

"That's not promising much," Maggie chided, but she couldn't stop the grin tugging at the corners of her lips, despite her growing worry.

"Is something wrong?"

Maggie sighed. "It's just work. Nothing to worry about."

"You sure?"

"Yes, I'm fine," she assured, changing the subject. "Thanks for letting me stay here."

"Of course." Another airport announcement sounded in the distance. "I better go, my flight is boarding."

"Stay safe."

"You, too," Ashton replied, before hanging up.

Maggie shook her head. If there was trouble to be found in Ecuador, Ashton would find it.

Strictly speaking, Maggie shouldn't have told Ashton she was in the city on assignment. Especially given the sensitive nature of the job. Old habits die hard though, and they had always kept in touch, checking in with each other even after Ashton left the Unit. Besides, the Unit wasn't aware they'd remained friends; the entire agency had been ordered to cut all ties with the 'traitor.' Not that Maggie listened. As long as they kept their friendship covert, everyone was happy.

Laying back into the water, she indulged in a further

ten minutes of attempted relaxation before drying off. It was time to get to work.

Maggie wrapped a towel around her and sat in front of the dressing table in the master bedroom. She propped the background document of her new alias by the mirror.

Yana Kostina.

As far as the look went, it wasn't that difficult. Maggie could keep her natural hair if she wanted since the fake passport was several years old. Yana's hair was a lighter shade than hers, but people changed their hairstyle all the time. In the end, she decided to match the picture exactly. With a mission this sensitive, she couldn't risk any slip ups. Nothing to make the people inside the Russian Consulate pause or question her.

Tucking her real hair under a cap, Maggie put on the newly purchased wig she got from a little place in the East Village and pinned it in place. Teasing it out to give the hair more volume, she styled the platinum blond bob into a deliberate messy look to fit Yana's free-spirited personality.

Yana Kostina was born and raised in Cherepovets, the largest city in Vologda Oblast. The daughter of an architect and a notable oil painter, Yana grew to hold a deep appreciation and love for the arts. So much so, that it led her to study the subject at Saint Petersburg University where she earned a master's degree in art criticism.

"I work at a gallery in Cherepovets," Maggie said into the mirror. Yana returned home after she graduated and quickly became the associate art director for a thriving gallery known in the art world for its industrial inspired installations.

Yana's eyes were darker than Maggie's, a deeper, warmer shade than her ice blue irises. Nothing a set of contacts couldn't fix. Unscrewing the cap, Maggie slid the contacts over her eyes and blinked them into place.

"I've always wanted to visit New York," she said in Yana's native tongue.

Maggie repeated the phrase a few times, getting the accent just right. She had learned Russian from a Muscovite, and while the language was uniform across the country, there were subtle differences in tone and inflection. Yana's Northwestern roots should be apparent when she spoke, at least to fellow Russians at the consulate.

Playing a tourist was the ideal set up for Maggie's plan. She wasn't too concerned about infiltrating the Russian Consulate. Getting inside was one thing. It was getting back out that worried her.

Once they learned Emily Wallace had escaped their clutches, the Russians would stop at nothing to contain the situation, even if it meant killing Maggie and Emily on the streets.

Satisfied with Yana's appearance, Maggie rummaged in her shopping bags and brought out her outfit for tomorrow. She made sure to buy flats for the mission. The only thing worse than breakout missions, were breakout missions in heels.

The boots she chose were black leather with steel

toecaps. While not conventional footwear for a tourist, they fit with Yana's quirky style and could also come in handy if she found herself in a fight. Maggie matched the boots with some tightfitting black jeans, red cardigan, and a tank top with a picture of a little cartoon cat on the front.

Maggie slipped into the clothes and took in her new persona through the full-length mirror by the bed. While not to Maggie's taste, Yana was exactly what she needed to be: young, unassuming, and innocent.

She was ready for tomorrow.

Chapter 5

M aggie walked up Madison Avenue and turned left onto East 91st Street.

A light wind picked up, the trees along the sidewalks ruffling in a choreographed dance to the whistling breeze. The Russian consulate stood in the middle of the street, a grand four-story building which seemed welcoming from the outside with its potted plants by the windows. Inside would be an entirely different story.

Like the British Consulate, its Russian counterpart would have a specialized team on guard, waiting to end any potential conflicts, with lethal force if necessary. Surveillance cameras were deliberately visible at each corner of the building, two trained on the front door with the Russian flag hanging proudly above it. Another camera watched from the gate adjacent to the building where cars had to wait until they were permitted entry.

Maggie stored the layout and camera positions in her mind for later. Exit routes were a priority, and if the Russians were as prepared as the British, they could lock the building down in mere minutes.

Stopping at the consulate's neighbors next door, Maggie ducked under the scaffolding erected over the outer building and put the finishing touches to her disguise. Construction workers called to each other, men on the roof tossing bricks and other debris into a chute which travelled down the scaffolding and straight into a large dumpster. Cosmetic work from the looks of it. The city had cleaned itself up over the years, and residents so close to the park had to keep up appearances. It wouldn't do to be the shabbiest building on the block.

Maggie kept a fresh face to give herself a younger appearance, the only make-up on her face there to give the illusion of an injury, a new and reddening mark that promised to grow into a nasty bruise.

She bit down on the capsule in her mouth. The contents burst open, filling her mouth with the tang of cinnamon. Maggie let the liquid spill over her bottom lip and drip down her chin, the fake blood stark red against her pale skin.

Speeding up her breathing, she took short, shallow breaths. Her heartbeat quickened and pulsed in her chest, her body reacting to the deliberate signs of physical distress. She paced a little, back and forth, running a hand through her hair. It wasn't enough to simply act. You had to *be*.

Maggie forced herself back to when she was a child, bringing up memories that brought out the worst of her panic response. The day her mother died. The night she killed her first man in self-defense. Of when she was arrested for said murder and held in a police station. Of when she and Leon almost drowned in Venice, just weeks ago.

It didn't take long for the emotions to overtake her logical mind. Maggie welcomed the rising panic and had to force back the urge to shut those memories away. They were painful, but they also had their uses. Her past could very well help ensure her future.

Tearing her cardigan and letting one of the sleeves hang over her shoulder, Maggie limped the rest of the way down the street and stumbled through the front doors of the consulate.

"Help!" she cried in Russian as soon as she entered. "Somebody, please, help me."

A startled guard stood beside the metal detectors.

Maggie ran past him and through the detectors before he could stop her, the siren wailing as she passed.

Another guard approached her from her left. Maggie spotted him in her periphery, but Yana wouldn't have, given the state she was in. Instead, she rushed forward, unaware of his approach and headed past the front foyer and down an empty hallway.

"Wait, you can't go back there." The man grabbed her arm and yanked her back, his vice grip wrapping the whole way around her upper arm.

Maggie restrained herself. Normally, she'd punch the guard in the throat for touching her. But Yana didn't have the training or instinct for violence. "Please, you must help me," Maggie said in Yana's native tongue, her voice pitched high and shaking.

The man's burrowed brow vanished as he lay eyes on her face, spotting the scarlet trail of blood down her chin. His grip loosened, and he ushered Maggie back to the entrance, near the metal detectors.

"Are you okay?" He shifted on his feet and didn't seem to know where to put his hands, clearly unaccustomed to dealing with an upset and bloody woman.

"No," Maggie wept, her voice cracking as she covered her face with her hands.

The guard cleared his throat and spoke with his colleague who held a radio in his hand, ready to alert backup if needed. The second guard shook his head, and picked up a handheld device next to the door-shaped frame of the metal detector.

"I have to scan you," he said in a firm voice.

He motioned for Maggie to stand by the small x-ray machine for bags and other personal items and hovered the scanner over her body. It beeped around Maggie's hand, and the guard noted the bracelet around her wrist. She'd left her newly acquired gun back in Ashton's apartment. There was no way to get through security armed. All she had by way of weapons were her guile and her fists.

And that was all she needed.

"Personal belongings must go through the machine before we can let you in," the first guard advised.

"I don't have anything with me," Maggie snapped, turning to face him with her tear-streaked face.

The second guard returned the scanner and shared a look with his colleague, the meaning clear. He would deal with her. "Please, come with me," he said, offering a small and sympathetic smile.

At least her appearance worked on one of them. Maggie allowed the guard to lead her through an open door to the right, whimpering as they entered the front-of-house section of the consulate with a line of glass-covered kiosks along one wall.

A few people stood at the various kiosks, filling out forms and speaking in Russian to members of staff, much the same as it had been at the British Consulate. They all stopped when they spotted Maggie. One woman let out an audible gasp.

The guard took Maggie to a row of seats and sat her down with a gentle push. "What happened?" he asked.

"I," Maggie said, pausing to add a well-timed sniffle, "have been robbed."

"You poor thing," said an elderly woman, listening in from a few seats down.

Maggie let out a burst of tears at the woman's kind words, and tilted her head back in despair. A camera was stationed in the middle of the high ceiling, allowing those watching to get a full view of the entire room.

"Someone robbed me, and I don't know what do to," she continued, louder this time for the audio on the camera feed. All eyes were on her, and Yana was making quite the scene.

A voice called through the man's radio asking for him to check in.

He turned away from Maggie and lowered his voice. "We have a hysterical woman claiming she was mugged."

Maggie's eye twitched at the word 'hysterical,' a term men liked to throw around whenever a woman showed any display of unhappiness, anger, or distress. The guard was lucky she was undercover, or she would have shown him *exactly* what hysterical meant.

At the end of the row of kiosks, a door opened and distracted Maggie from her temporary rage. Maggie took a deep, shaking breath as another man walked over to them.

His gait said military, his gray eyes trained on her as he took in the situation.

Maggie did some assessing of her own. Six foot one. A lean, yet powerful build. Agile footing. A gun concealed under his suit jacket. His posture was confident and full of authority. Maggie was willing to bet he was head of security.

"Hello, Madam. My name is Aleksandar Petrov. Would you come with me?"

Yana flinched as he reached for her. "Where?"

Aleksandar pulled his hand back and bent down on one knee, lowering himself to her level like he was talking to a small child.

"I understand that you have been in an altercation. Please come with me to my office so we can get you cleaned up and take your statement."

Maggie sniffed and wiped at her tear-filled eyes. Aleksandar offered a small smile that softened his otherwise harsh face, his nose, jaw, and cheekbones a collection of sharp angles. He kept his dark brown hair long and tied back smartly from his face in a tight ponytail.

"Go with him, dear," said the elderly woman with an encouraging nod. "He'll make sure you're okay and looked after." She tutted and shook her head. "Americans. Stealing from a young, helpless girl."

Maggie was many things, but helpless wasn't one of them.

She looked from the woman to Aleksandar, showing

Yana's trepidation before finally agreeing. "Okay," she said, hugging herself.

"Right this way," said Aleksandar. They left the guard to return to his post by the door while Aleksandar led Maggie deeper into the large building. Maggie kept an eye on the cameras, instinct keeping her face turned to avoid a direct image. Not that it mattered. Her face on their CCTV was the least of her worries as she followed Aleksandar up a set of marble stairs and further into enemy territory.

Committing each step to memory, Maggie kept an eye out for anything out of the ordinary. For anything that might indicate a higher level of security.

Nothing.

The hallway on the first floor was like a fancy five-star hotel, lavishly decorated to impress visitors, no doubt. Their footsteps were muffled thanks to a pristine cream carpet, the walls covered in matching wallpaper veined with gold designs and large paintings surrounded by gilded frames.

They turned a corner and Aleksandar stopped by the next door. He swiped a card across the reader and the locks clicked open. "Ladies first," he said.

Maggie stepped inside, Yana careful not to touch Aleksandar as she entered past him. He followed, closing the door behind him, and she flinched at the noise.

"It's okay." Aleksandar held his palms out as if in surrender. "You're safe here."

He gestured for Yana to take the seat across from a maple desk and she complied, shuddering as the tears subsided. The room was much like any other office, computer, shelves filled with folders and files, a well-watered plant by the window. For all the office said, Aleksandar could have been an insurance salesman.

Before sitting down, Aleksandar walked into a connecting bathroom and came back out with a damp towel. "Are you hurt?" he asked, handing the towel over and examining her from a distance.

Maggie dabbed at her mouth and winced for good measure. "More shaken than anything else," she replied, voice meek.

"Nothing appears to be broken," he concluded, sitting down across from her once satisfied that her wounds were superficial. "Your face and neck will bruise, though. I'll call and get a doctor to examine you, just in case."

"Okay." Maggie made sure to leave a smear of blood at the corner of her mouth to distract him. The more Aleksandar saw her as a victim, as a scared and defenseless young woman in a big, strange city, the better.

"What's your name?" he asked, moving the mouse of his computer and typing in his password.

"Yana. Yana Kostina."

Aleksandar typed her false name into what Maggie assumed was an incident report. "Where are you from, Yana?"

Maggie cleared her throat, making a show of discomfort as she spoke. "Cherepovets."

"I have family there."

Maggie stayed quiet. Small talk was a dangerous route for her to take. Digging too much into the past of an alias led to slip ups, and she played on Yana's shock and fear to avoid any chitchat about a hometown she'd never visited.

"Yana, can you tell me what happened to you?" Aleksandar asked, repeating her name to ground her in the moment and calm her, a tactic she'd used before when dealing with people riddled with fear or shock.

"I was robbed." Maggie waved her hand in front of her face like she was about to cry again.

"It's okay," Aleksandar soothed. "Let's take it slow and start from the beginning. What brought you to New York?"

"I'm an art director at a gallery back home. Nothing big, but our latest exhibition got a glowing write up in the Media Center," she said in Yana's nervous prattling, having checked the name of the local newspaper in Cherepovets the night before. "I came here to visit the Guggenheim."

Aleksandar stopped typing and clasped his hands, giving Yana his full attention. "Can you believe I've been here nearly nine years and have yet to visit?"

Yana sat up straighter and met his eyes. She couldn't resist a discussion about art, even after what happened to her. Her true passion was a safe place, and much easier to discuss than her supposed mugging.

"Oh, but you must. They have the most comprehensive exhibition of Russian art outside of the homeland. Icons like the Virgin of Vladimir. Collections amassed by Peter and Catherine the Great. Shchukin and Morozov. Avant-Garde. Even Post-Soviet pieces." Maggie lowered her head and picked at her thumbnail, one of Yana's nervous ticks. "Not that I got to see any of it."

Aleksandar gave her some time to compose herself before asking the inevitable. "Is that where it happened?"

She nodded. "It all happened so fast."

"Why didn't you go to the police?"

"Would you? I watch the news. They don't like us, and I don't trust them," she said, not having to clarify who *they* were.

"You did the right thing." Aleksandar went back to his computer. More typing. "We'll do everything we can to find the ones who did this to you."

"And my things?"

"I wouldn't get my hopes up, Ms. Kostina. New York is a very big place, and even if we do arrest the ones responsible, your belongings will most likely be long gone."

Maggie sniffed, eyes filling with tears again. "They took everything. My phone, my money, the key to my hotel room."

"We can help you with all of that. Now, do you have anything to confirm your identity and citizenship, Ms.

Kostina? It's just a security precaution," he added when she frowned at his request.

"I have my passport." Maggie pulled out the counterfeit ID and passed it over.

Aleksandar checked inside, his eyes flitting between Maggie and the photo of Yana. "If someone stole your bag, how do you still have your passport?"

"My father told me to keep it in my pocket. He was always going on about American muggers and New York's dangerous streets. I didn't really believe what he said, but I did as he asked." Maggie rubbed at her throat again, her voice scratchy as she spoke and getting worse. "I can't believe he was right."

"Do you want a drink?" Aleksandar asked.

"Please," she rasped, coughing.

Aleksandar opened the door to a little fridge by his desk and brought out a cool bottle of water, condensation dripping down the plastic.

"Could I have something hot?" Maggie leaned her head to one side to show off the bruising on her neck. "My throat hurts from where they grabbed me."

Muscles twitched on Aleksandar's jaw as he peered at the handy work of the supposed muggers, a dark look sweeping past his eyes. "Of course. Stay here, and I'll be back in one moment with some coffee."

"Thank you," said Maggie with a weak smile. "You've been very kind."

Maggie waited until the door clicked shut behind him

and dashed from her seat to Aleksandar's. Grabbing the mouse, she caught the computer before the screensaver locked her out.

"Kind, but stupid."

M en always underestimated women. While irritating to the highest degree, the predictability of the phenomenon was useful and had helped Maggie during missions more than any other weapon. Being overlooked came with advantages, and she exploited them to the fullest.

A tab was already open on Aleksandar's computer, and she double clicked it into full-screen. Live video footage blinked back at her, a grid of squares for each camera in the building and the outside perimeter. Aleksandar himself came into view at the top left, heading down the hall and into what looked like a staffroom where a few people waited in line for coffee from a vending machine.

Scanning each square, Maggie searched for her target. Emily Wallace was somewhere inside, for now, and she needed to move before the head of security came back. Aleksandar would raise the alarm the moment he found Yana missing. Maggie needed to find Emily and get the hell out of there before that happened, which didn't leave her much time.

A feed at the bottom caught her attention. While not overtly different from the other rows of doors, two guards stood sentry outside. Something important must lay inside.

Or someone.

Using the feeds to plot the route to the guarded door, Maggie slipped out of the office and hurried down the corridor in the opposite direction from Aleksandar's coffee run.

The hallways were deserted. The upper floors of consulates weren't generally used by the public. The door in question lay on the ground floor at the back of the building. Maggie took a different set of stairs down to avoid the guards by the front entrance. They would intercept her on sight if seen without a chaperone.

With pricked ears, Maggie crept down the steps.

Pressing against the wall, Maggie inched to the corner and risked a glance around the edge towards what she hoped was Emily's prison. The guards were still there, postures rigid and alert despite their bored expressions. Professionals.

Maggie was no amateur, either, and without wasting another second, she rounded the corner into plain sight.

"Help," she called, running towards them and looking back over her shoulder like she was being chased. "Please, you have to help me."

"What's wrong?" The man stepped forward, abandoning his post.

"You can't be down here." The woman reached inside

her suit jacket, seeming unimpressed with Maggie's performance.

"He's going to kill me!" Maggie voice was wild with fear.

The male guard reached out to her, but the female guard held him back as she scrutinized Maggie with narrowed eyes.

"He's got Aleksandar," Maggie cried as she grew closer, not stopping.

Both guards paused at that and shared an alarmed look. It didn't matter if either of them believed her. All Maggie needed was a precious few seconds of distraction to bridge the gap between them.

Maggie sprung into the air and shot out her leg, catching the man in the temple with a roundhouse kick. The steel toecap on her boots worked like a charm, and he crumpled to the floor. His eyes rolled to the back of his head before he even registered her attack.

The woman wasn't so slow.

What Maggie thought was a gun, turned out to be a baton. The guard flicked it out to its full length and swung it at Maggie like her head was a piñata.

Maggie ducked just in time and slammed her fist into the woman's gut. The guard doubled over, the baton traveling with her momentum and catching Maggie in the arm with a sickening *thwack*.

The pain elicited a sharp hiss, and Maggie grabbed the bottom of the baton, yanking it forward. The guard stumbled, unable to catch her footing, and Maggie clipped her on the chin with an uppercut. Her head snapped back, and she staggered back, giving Maggie enough room to kick the woman square in the chest, sending her crashing back into the door.

The impact left a dent in the wood, and as the guard struggled to get back to her feet, Maggie caught her with a right hook and sent the woman to the floor beside her partner.

Listening for signs of new arrivals, Maggie turned the handle to the door. It didn't budge.

"Shit."

An electronic reader was positioned on the wall next to the door, the light red. Remembering Aleksandar's card, Maggie bent and rummaged through the unconscious guards' pockets. She found a keycard in the man's jacket and swiped it through the reader. The light switched from red to green and Maggie entered.

"Who are you?"

Emily Wallace stood up, abandoning the couch that took up most of the little box room. There were no windows, and empty bottles of water lay scattered on the carpet. They'd kept Emily there for a while.

"A friend." Maggie checked the hall for signs of back-up. The coast was clear, for now.

Emily's braids fell over one shoulder, dark eyes innocent yet untrusting. "You're British," she said, clearly expecting another Russian.

"Well spotted."

Emily crossed her arms. "I don't know you." Her blue dress sparkled underneath an oversized hoodie, which Maggie suspected belonged to one of her captors. Black leggings covered her legs, ending in a pair of well-loved Converse on her feet.

"I'm here to rescue you," Maggie said, her patience thinning.

Emily exhaled in relief. "Did my mom send you?"

"We don't have time to talk." Maggie reached out her hand. "Come with me. Now."

Maggie's sharp tone must have frightened the girl. She could see the cogs working in Emily's head, wondering if she could trust this stranger. One of many she must have come into contact since her abduction.

"If you prefer, you can stay here." Maggie shrugged. "Either way, I've got to go."

That did it. Emily reached out and took Maggie's hand, letting her pull her out of the room and into the hallway.

"Don't mind them," Maggie said, as she stepped over the guards and scooped up the woman's baton along the way.

Emily looked back at them, her short legs working double time to keep up with Maggie's pace. "Did you do that?"

Maggie shushed her. "Stay quiet."

Then the alarm began. A high-pitched wail screeched

throughout the hallway, screaming like a banshee in Maggie's ears.

"Bollocks," she swore, dragging Emily to the staircase.

Emily dug her heels. "Shouldn't we be running out the front door?"

"Quiet," Maggie hissed. "If they catch us, the only way we're leaving this building is in a body bag. Got it?"

Emily nodded, eyes wide.

"Good, now do as I say and we might make it out of this mess alive." Maggie forced a smile as her mind raced through her plans. She unclasped Yana's bracelet and fastened it around Emily's slender wrist.

"What's that for?"

"It's a tracker. If we get split up, I can find you." Not that Maggie intended to lose sight of Emily. The bracelet was strictly a safeguard for the worst-case scenario.

They travelled back upstairs and headed towards the front of the building. A flurry of confused and alarmed voices echoed down the hallway, originating around the corner. Lockdown protocols would already be in place. The guards would secure civilians in offices and safe rooms while the advanced security team searched the building to eliminate the imminent threat.

At the end of the hallway, Maggie led Emily into a room on their left and closed the door.

The lounge was brightly lit from the sun shining through the large windows and was likely used for meeting and entertaining foreign dignitaries. Plush sofas sat around well-polished tables with decanters of amber liquid and crystal glasses arranged like center pieces. Ornate paintings hung from the walls, and portraits of stern looking nobles stared down at them with disapproving eyes.

Marching footsteps approached outside the door, and Maggie's heart leapt in her chest.

Darting her eyes over the room, she narrowed in on the grand piano in the corner. "Help me move this," she ordered Emily, kicking the brakes up from the wheels of each leg.

Emily complied as the racket through the door grew louder. The handle on the door began to turn and Maggie shoved the piano the last few feet just in time to stop it from opening.

The handle moved to no avail. Muffled Russian curses penetrated the door. The wood shuddered as someone rammed their shoulder into the door, trying to break it down. Maggie kicked down the brakes on the piano and stepped back. It should hold them off long enough.

Shoulders were replaced with feet and the door rattled in its frame.

Emily's hands shook, and Maggie patted her shoulder. "They won't get in," she assured the frightened girl.

"Get the axe," called a rough voice in Russian.

Well shit.

It was time to get a move on.

The slamming grew louder and more violent as more guards joined the fray.

"It's a dead end," Emily squealed, circling the room. "We're trapped."

"Not quite." Maggie moved to the windows and peered outside. It was risky, but it was their best shot at getting out unnoticed. Grabbing the curtains draping to the floor, she wrapped her hand in the thick fabric. Maggie sucked in a breath and punched her covered fist through the window. The glass shattered to the floor around them like sharp-edged diamonds.

Clearing the rest of the glass away with her boot, Maggie swung her leg out over the window pane. No guards were outside the building yet, too concerned about who was inside rather than out.

Wind whistled past her and brushed her hair from her face. It wasn't a huge drop to the sidewalk, but it was enough to break or sprain an ankle if you landed wrong. Worse if you failed to land on your feet at all.

"Where are you going?" Emily flinched as the first blow from the axe collided with the door.

"I think we've overstayed our welcome." Maggie propped both feet on the window ledge. "Now watch what I do. I need you to copy me, okay?"

A tear slipped down the girl's cheek, panic threatening to take over.

Maggie clicked her fingers. "Emily, do you hear me? I need you to follow exactly what I do."

Emily nodded, wiping her face with the over long sleeve of her hoodie.

The scaffolding framing the building next door jutted out four feet away. It was a simple jump, but Maggie couldn't risk Emily falling. Especially given how shaken she was.

Another crash sounded against the door, a crack forming down the center as the axe chipped away at the wood piece by piece.

Careful of the glass, Maggie gripped the window frame to steady herself before moving. With her feet planted securely on the ledge, she inched over and reached out for the stone pillar framing the window. The ledge was barely wide enough for her foot, and she shuffled across to the edge of the consulate building. Maggie reached for the corner pole of the scaffolding next door and swung herself around until her feet found purchase on the wooden slate walkway.

Emily's head bobbed out from the window. "I can't do that."

"Yes, you can," said Maggie. "You have to."

Yelling echoed out of the window along with the collision of sharpened metal on wood. "They're breaking through!"

"Come on," Maggie urged. They were losing precious time. "Your mother's waiting on you."

Though Maggie didn't even know her mother's name, the white lie was enough for Emily. A steely look passed over her eyes, and she clenched a determined jaw.

"Take your time," said Maggie as the girl stepped out

onto the ledge. "Keep your eyes on your feet, but don't look down any further."

Emily was painfully slow, but Maggie refrained from rushing her. "That's it," she encouraged, checking behind her for any signs of the workmen. Drills and hammering rang from above amid light-hearted chatter. Most of them were on the upper levels but she'd be ready if they encountered any stragglers who tried to stop them or called attention to their presence.

A loud crash announced the shattering of the door from inside, and the guards' voices floated clear as crystal out the window.

"It's blocked. There's a fucking piano."

"Climb over it."

Emily heard it too, and she moved faster towards the scaffolding.

Maggie reached out her arms. "Almost there."

Emily fumbled forward. Her foot snagged and missed the ledge, falling out from under her. She screamed as she fell back into nothing but thin air.

Maggie dove out, using the corner rail of the scaffolding to steady her, and grabbed the scruff of Emily's hoodie. A jolt of pain ran up her arm as she bore the weight of Emily, her muscles burning under the strain of the hanging girl.

Emily kicked and flailed in panic, but Maggie dug her fingers into the fabric and hoisted her up with everything she had. When Emily cleared the edge, Maggie pulled herself onto the scaffolding, and they fell back into the safety of the walkway. "I've got you," panted Maggie. "You're safe."

It was the second lie she told Emily Wallace that day.

The danger was far from over.

Chapter 6

Maggie led Emily down the street from the consulate and turned onto 5th Avenue when the first group of Russians sped out the front door. The gates drew open and a detail of three SUVs with tinted windows pulled onto the road.

The traffic lights turned red, and Maggie and Emily weaved between vehicles as they crossed the road, ducking behind a delivery van to stay out of view. Scurrying across to the sidewalk, Maggie risked a glance as the lights flicked to green and the traffic crawled forward through the crowded city streets.

The SUVs growled with impatience at their red light, waiting with blinkers flashing and ready to give chase.

"We need to get off the street." Maggie scanned the buildings, connected the sights to the map of New York she'd memorized. The lavish Cooper-Hewitt museum sat directly across from them, once the mansion of industrialist Andrew Carnegie.

Across from the mansion stood the Church of Heavenly Rest, its neo-gothic arches and foreboding presence less than welcoming. Maggie wouldn't seek sanctuary there. The church's very name seemed like a bad omen.

Maggie forced her pace to slow to a brisk walk and kept Emily close as they continued down the street. A row of parked cars lined their left, the brick wall that encased Central Park by their right.

The park.

"This way," Maggie steered Emily past a hotdog cart and into the eastern entrance of Central Park.

The path through the park led them in the opposite direction of the British Consulate, but the direct route was too open. Too dangerous.

Two point three miles separated the consulates. Forty-seven minutes on foot. Less than that if running. It didn't sound long, but travelling the forty or so blocks would be tricky under normal situations, but with a scared kid, mounting morning sickness, and the Russians close behind, it felt as impossible right then as running the New York City marathon.

Taking 3rd Avenue would be the fastest, but not necessarily the wisest, route. Yet the longer Maggie kept Emily Wallace out on the streets, the longer the enemy had to track them down and kill them both.

That meant taking an alternative route.

The park was busier than Maggie expected on a weekday afternoon. A cluster of school kids huddled around a teacher who bellowed for them to gather around and get into pairs. The wind rustled through the trees and swept along the early fallen leaves that blanketed the pathways, rushing past Maggie's feet like a river of red and gold.

A vendor selling cheesy t-shirts and hats shouted his wares from the corner by the entrance. A cluster of straggling school kids harassed him, asking how much each t-shirt cost when the sign said everything was ten dollars.

"This isn't worth ten bucks," said a young haggler. "I'll give you five for it."

"Look kid, quit bustin' my balls. If the sign says ten, its ten."

Maggie brushed past the little stand and swiped an *I heart NYC* shirt and hat. The kids kept the vendor occupied and a smile tugged at her lips, wondering if her own child would be full of mischief.

"Put these on." She handed the clothes to Emily and tossed the girl's oversized hoodie into a nearby trash can. Maggie shrugged out of her cardigan and added it to the pile, along with her short haired wig.

"Who are you?" Emily asked. "Some kind of Jane Bond?"

"No," Maggie replied, running a hand through her real hair. "I like my martinis stirred."

Emily simply frowned.

Tires screeched and sent Maggie's heart to her throat. Grabbing Emily, they crossed East Drive, a road that allowed cars to drive through the park, and slunk into Bridle Path which lay parallel to it. They crouched behind a set of bushes that Autumn had visited early, leaving little gaps where the leaves had already fallen.

Two of the SUVs pulled into the park, barely slowing for pedestrians who rushed to avoid being hit.

The drivers slammed on the brakes, which squealed like the school children Maggie had seen before. The vehicles stopped a mere ten yards from Maggie and Emily's hiding spot, and Aleksandar emerged from the first one, followed closely by his men. He barked out orders, sending a group north on foot and directing the second SUV southbound down the drive. The third car was nowhere to be seen.

The head of security scanned the area by the first SUV, his body taught with barely controlled rage. Maggie had penetrated his fortress and stolen his witness, which not only undermined him and his job, but the country he served, too. Aleksandar was out for blood.

Unfortunately for him, Maggie was *not* easy prey.

"Come on," she whispered, helping Emily up. "We need to go."

Keeping hidden, they travelled up a set of stone steps and reached the Shuman Running Track which ran the circumference of the large man-made stretch of water. Beyond, the reservoir stretched out, taking center stage in New York's oasis, acting as a reprieve to the grimy urban streets and imposing gray skyscrapers. The sun glittered off the surface and winked back at them.

It was a beautiful sight, but Maggie and Emily couldn't stop and stare. Maggie nodded to her charge as a group of middle aged runners approached, and together they joined in the pack, heading south towards the bottom of the reservoir.

"What will happen if they catch us?" Emily asked, puffing.

"It won't come to that." Maggie kept her eyes trained for any signs they'd been found. The park was a big place, but Aleksandar had a whole crew of trained professionals after them.

Beads of sweat formed across Maggie's forehead as she ran. September in New York City wasn't like London, where the cold swooped in like an unwelcome house guest who stayed until Spring. The last of the Summer's sun bore down on them with each step, with only the breeze of the wind offering a light reprieve.

Five minutes later, the track opened out and they arrived at the south gate house. The stone building looked out into the park, a picturesque bridge rested at the foot of the main steps. But that wasn't what caught Maggie's attention.

Two men in suits spotted her and Emily from the footpath below. The men broke into a run the second they saw their targets, mouthing into earpieces, jackets flapping in the wind.

"Run!" Maggie urged Emily forward, back onto the running track. A cluster of tourists had stopped by the water to feed a family of ducks with torn pieces of pretzels, taking snaps of the little birds on their cellphones.

Maggie barged into them and cleared a gap for Emily, not stopping to explain. A few of the tourists fell into each other amid their rabble of complaints and cries, but Maggie didn't care. They'd create a diversion, blocking their pursuers, even if only for a couple of moments. Those precious seconds could be the difference between life and death.

Emily winced and gripped the side of her waist. "I can't keep running."

"You must," Maggie said, scooping her arm through Emily's and forcing her to move. She risked a glance behind them to see the men in suits. Two had become four, a second pair of Russians closing in quick.

They were fast. Faster than Emily.

Maggie grit her teeth and checked that the baton she'd stolen was still tucked in her waistband. It wouldn't do much against a set of guns, but it was better than nothing. As they ran, Maggie used innocent passersby as human shields and hoped the Russians wouldn't risk taking out a civilian. If only to avoid a very public international incident.

But no matter what Maggie tried, the pounding foot-steps and angry shouts drew closer. Maggie tugged on Emily's arm and merged them back onto Bridle Path.

"They're too fast. There's too many of them," cried Emily between pants. She was getting slower, the adren-aline from her fear losing the battle against her fatigue.

Maggie closed her eyes and focused on the map she studied on the flight over. The grid system made New York easier to navigate than most cities. They were at the bottom of the reservoir now, which put them five or six blocks south of the Russian Consulate.

"Left," said Maggie, warning Emily before they made the turn. There was no direct pathway from their position, causing them to barge through a thicket of trees and bushes. Bare branches snagged at Maggie's clothes, but she surged on, holding tight to Emily's hand.

"They're right behind us," Emily warned.

Maggie could hear their panting breathes, much more controlled than Emily's labored gasps. Like Maggie, the Russians could keep this pace for miles. They wouldn't slow down. They wouldn't stop. Not until they caught their targets. Not until she and Emily were dead.

"Jump!" Maggie yelled when the thicket stopped. She didn't wait for Emily to comply. Instead, she gripped the girl's hand tighter and pulled Emily over the edge of the bushes and dropped down into the middle of a street.

Emily screamed, but the drop wasn't far. She landed hard, tearing the thin material of her leggings and skinning her knees. Maggie pulled her up and crossed the street. Emily's injuries could wait. First, she had to keep the girl alive.

The 85th Street Transverse veined through the middle of Central Park, snaking from East 85th Street on one side, to West 86th on the other. Right smack in the middle of said street was the 22nd Precinct Police Station, which was exactly where Maggie was headed.

Two officers stood by the front gates of the precinct. While Maggie doubted the NYPD's finest boys in blue would be a match for Aleksandar's men, she was desperate and out of options.

Above them, ruffling came from the bushes and the first of the gang of Russians followed them into the street.

Maggie and Emily hurried towards the police, and Maggie slipped on a mask of terrified innocence. "Officers! There are men following us, and they have guns. They tried to force us into the back of a van."

One of the officers called for backup on his radio and stepped in front of Maggie and Emily, heading towards the approaching Russian security operatives.

The officer's partner turned to Maggie and opened the gate. "Ma'am, you and the girl go inside and stay there until it's safe."

"Thank you," Maggie said, stepping through the gates with an arm over Emily's shoulders. She backtracked as soon as the officer ran to meet his partner, and left the precinct as five more policemen and women came to help their colleagues.

The police couldn't protect them, but they did make for a good distraction while Maggie and Emily hurried down the street and headed towards the Upper West Side.

Chapter 7

By the time they emerged from Central Park, Maggie had come to a dangerous conclusion: Emily wouldn't last. Her feet dragged more with each step, her breathing grew labored, and her face winced with each step from the stitch in her side.

Maggie checked over her shoulder. Aleksandar and his men were nowhere to be seen, but that didn't mean they weren't close. Maggie needed to get Emily off the streets and out of sight as soon as possible.

Which meant the subway.

They walked all the way to the end of the block to use the crosswalk to avoid unwanted attention. Cops were everywhere, and no matter Maggie's views on the ridiculousness of ticketing for jaywalking, the last thing they needed was to get stopped and charged for being in a hurry.

The 86th Street station was closest, and Maggie and Emily merged with the crowd as they travelled to the terminal. Paying for two tickets with fresh bills, she and Emily waited for the C train and hopped on. Maggie double checked the lines depicted on the car's interior once they'd found a seat. Five stops and they'd be at 42nd Street. From there, the E train would take them to Lexington Avenue, leaving them a short two-minute walk from the British Consulate.

The car filled up fast, and Maggie kept an eye on each passenger who stepped inside, evaluating their threat level before moving on to the next. None of them were Aleksandar's men.

Passengers squeezed into Maggie's car like sardines even though the adjacent car lay empty. Having visited the city several times, Maggie knew that meant the smell was unbearable, thanks to what was usually vomit, excrement, or some unforgiveable combination of the two.

City life had its glamorous side, but public transport wasn't one of them.

Maggie turned to Emily, checking her red knees. The blood had stopped, but the open skin needed to be cleaned. "How are you holding up?"

Emily shrugged and wrapped her arms around her waist. Fear lined her young face, the remnants of childhood still in her round cheeks. She was holding up okay, all things considered. Homework and petty arguments with friends should be the extent of worries for a girl so young. Not running for her life.

If the Russians had their way, Emily wouldn't live to see another sunrise. A dark thought shadowed Maggie's thoughts and her nails dug into her palms.

"Emily, did anyone..." Maggie stopped, trying to find the right words.

"Touch me?" Emily finished for her. She shook her head. "No."

Maggie's tense muscles relaxed a little, grateful for that one small miracle at least. Emily seemed to calm a little while talking, so Maggie kept her chatting.

"How old are you?"

"Twelve, but I'll be thirteen in a few weeks."

"A teenager. Your mom must have her hands full." The idea of having an infant—never mind a teen—hit Maggie like a ton of bricks. Emily was her responsibility right now, but taking care of the life growing inside her would be a full-time job. Was she ready for that? Was Leon? A pang of guilt tugged at her heart.

She should tell him. As soon as the mission was over.

Emily sighed. "Yeah, I'm getting old."

"I know the feeling." Maggie grinned. "I like your dress."

"I don't." Emily groaned. "My mom made me wear it for the party. I still wore my Chucks, though." The hint of a mischievous grin tugged at the corner of her lips.

Maggie nudged her. "Rebel. What was the party for?"

"Some boring thing for some boring colleague of my mom's. She's a human rights lawyer."

Which explained why Emily found herself at a party with a UN official. It wasn't lost on Maggie that Emily could tell her more than Jonathan Cole and Danielle Hawkins had bothered to share.

"And you saw something?" Maggie asked. "Something bad."

Tears filled Emily's eyes. "Yes."

Maggie wiped Emily's eyes dry with the sleeve of her shirt. While Maggie's curiosity about the assassination was strong, she didn't want to upset her charge. Especially not in public with prying eyes.

"Do you work for the UN, too?" Emily asked.

Maggie shook her head, and filed the tidbits of information she'd learned with what else she knew.

"But you were hired to come get me?"

"Something like that," Maggie admitted. Even with the panic and deadly situation she found herself in, Emily didn't miss much. Her mother had raised her well, and although Maggie had been trained to keep charges at an emotional distance, she couldn't help but warm to the girl.

"I don't even know your name," Emily said.

"I'm Yan—" Maggie stopped. "My name is Maggie."

"Maggie, do you think I can go home now? I wanna see my parents."

"Soon." Maggie took Emily's hand and gave it a squeeze.

The car slowed down for the first stop at 81st Street, right by the Museum of Natural History. People got on and off, a mixture of bored looking locals and excited tourists trying out the famed underground system for the first time.

Four more stops, a line switch, then another four stops. They'd both be safe soon, and Maggie could return home to deal with her own predicament. So many things were about to change.

Just as the doors pinged in warning that they were about to close, three men in suits squeezed through in time before the train set off again.

Maggie tensed and swore under her breath. Aleksandar headed towards them, flanked by two men, with a sneer on his face.

There was nowhere to run. Nowhere to hide.

They were locked in until the next stop.

"Thanks for getting me out of there," Emily said, who hadn't noticed the approaching Russians.

"You're very welcome." Maggie stood and reached for her waistband. "It's all part of the job."

Emily stared up at her. "What *is* your job?"

Maggie grabbed the baton and flicked it open.

"To keep you safe."

Chapter 8

Maggie held out her hand. Emily took it without question and gasped when she spotted the Suits heading toward them.

Aleksandar and his men moved with a singular focus, their eyes trained on Emily.

"Come on," Maggie said, leading Emily down the packed aisle. She opened the doors separating one car from the next and slipped through the gap, the Russians closing in behind them.

Her heartbeat pounded loud in Maggie's ears with each step. Small, wall-mounted lights flew past the windows in a blur. They couldn't get out. Not until the next stop, and by then it could be too late.

They carried on from the empty, foul-smelling car and through to a third which was packed with people. Emily stumbled forward, tripping over their fellow passengers' feet and shopping bags.

Maggie closed her eyes when she spotted the problem, hitting a dead end sooner than expected. It was the last car on the train. "Shit."

"Maggie," Emily whimpered, as the car door opened and Aleksandar stepped inside with his goons. She pointed to the man in charge. "He's the one who took me."

There was no escape, and Maggie prepared herself for the inevitable.

"Go to the far corner and crouch behind the seats. Cover yourself as best you can and don't move." It was the best Maggie could do for now.

Emily complied and ran to the very back of the car. Maggie straightened her spine and stared down her opponents.

The air changed, and the passengers seemed to sense something was wrong. They looked up from their phones and stopped talking to their partners, each searching for the cause of their instinctual unease.

Aleksandar cleared his throat. "Ladies and gentlemen, this car is now closed to the public. Move to another car. Now."

New Yorkers didn't need to be told twice. Trouble was coming, and no one wanted to be around to get caught in the crossfire. There was a flurry of rustled fabric, zipping bags, and a crescendo of footsteps as the passengers hurried past Aleksandar and into the next car.

A young man in Timberland boots and a hoodie

stopped by Maggie as the others left. "Yo, ma'am, these guys don't look so happy to see you. Do you need help?"

Maggie kept her attention on the Russians. "They're the ones who're going to need help."

One of the goons lunged for her then, and the would-be-Samaritan sprung forward before Maggie could stop him. The goon dodged his uppercut with ease and took him down with a roundhouse kick that caught the young man's temple.

Aleksandar's laughter echoed through the empty car as the civilian crumpled to the floor. "All you're doing is slowing us down. You cannot stop the inevitable end."

Maggie straightened and twirled the handle of the baton, keeping it loose in her dexterous hands. "If you want the girl, you're going to have to go through me."

Aleksandar arched an eyebrow. "As you wish."

The three men charged forward, and Maggie waited until they were almost upon her. Without a second to spare, she leaped up and grabbed the metal bar above her. Using the momentum to her advantage, she swung forward and kicked the first man square in the chest.

The blow landed with an encouraging *whoosh* as the air knocked from his lungs. The man reeled back, colliding into Aleksandar. The pair stumbled and fell to the dirty floor in a pile of tangled limbs.

Maggie released the grab bar and dropped to her feet. But the third guard was there in an instant. He clipped

Maggie across the face with his fist, quicker than she could raise her hands in defense.

Something wet trickled from her nose, and Maggie tasted a familiar coppery tang on her lips. A wave of anger rushed through her. No one drew blood and got away with it.

Maggie ducked under the man's next jab and swung her baton. The weapon caught the man at the side of his face with a satisfying *crunch*. Spittle, blood, and teeth flew from his mouth and spattered across the glass window. He collapsed, clutching his face, and Maggie turned in time to find Aleksandar and his comrade clambering back to their feet.

The guard reached for the gun at his side. Maggie couldn't have him shooting off rounds in the small subway car. She lashed out with her baton, swinging it past his arm, hitting him hard enough to snap bone in two. A kick in the solar plexus sent him careening to the floor with his colleague, evening the playing field to one on one.

Hands grabbed Maggie's hair and pulled her back with enough force to send her stumbling back. Strands ripped from her roots, and she hissed in pain as Aleksandar dragged her towards him.

She pivoted to try and free herself, but the man's grip was unrelenting. Maggie kicked for his groin, but Aleksandar had more experience than his staff and easily dodged the strike.

The back of his hand smacked against her jaw and

sent her head spinning from the impact. He was strong. Much stronger than Maggie.

A fist caught her in the same spot, sending a second surge of pain through her jaw that rattled her teeth. Maggie blinked away the black dots in her vision and focused on her opponent.

One of the fallen guards—the one with the broken arm—was speaking in rapid-fire Russian into his radio, calling for help. But Maggie had no time to stop him, forced to counter a third attack from Aleksandar.

He aimed a brutal kick towards Maggie's stomach, and a surge of maternal fear pulsed through her. She flung out her arm, the clumsy block hurting just as much as taking the hit. Acute stabs of pain rang up her arm, causing her to drop her weapon, but at least the blow missed its intended target.

She fell back a step and eyed her enemy. Aleksandar never spoke. No jibes. No pompous shit talk. No gloating. He was all business, and he was winning.

Maggie couldn't allow that.

Her head ached and, from the throbbing in her gums, she was certain she was going to need some dental work. Spitting out a mouthful of blood, Maggie reset her stance and focused on her opponent's movements, looking for something, *anything*, she could use to turn the tide on their battle.

Aleksandar faked left and landed another sickening blow, sending Maggie reeling to the floor before she even realized she misjudged his target. Adrenaline coursed through her, clogging her mind and leaving her gasping for air as the shock of the punch subsided and the pain registered.

Her eyes watered. Aleksandar's blurry form loomed over her like a towering skyscraper, ready to finish her off with one final hit.

A high-pitched cry pierced the subway car, and Maggie gasped as little Emily charged the Russian. She swung the dropped baton like a baseball bat and smashed it with all her might against the back of Aleksandar's head.

Aleksandar swayed and placed a hand over the strike point, his fingers coming away slick with blood. His faced hardened and knuckles cracked in his tight fists.

Maggie gaped at the head of security, amazed he was still standing.

"Maggie," Emily cried, tossing the baton her way.

"Bitch," Aleksandar swore, reaching for Emily.

Getting to her feet, Maggie raced along the subway seats and jumped back to the floor, separating Emily and the Russian. Aleksandar threw another punch, the blow to his head making his movements sluggish.

Which only accentuated Maggie's sole advantage: her speed.

Air whooshed past her face as she dodged Aleksandar's punch. Quick as an alley cat, Maggie swung the baton, snapping several of the man's exposed ribs. He stumbled forward, a shout escaping his lips, and Maggie aimed a second blow for the same spot Emily had softened.

A sickening crunch proceeded a dull thud as Aleksandar collapsed to the ground..

"Are you okay?" Emily asked, running to Maggie.

"You shouldn't have stepped in," she chided.

"I got him good though," replied Emily with a sheepish smile.

That she had.

Maggie laughed as she slumped down onto a seat and wiped the sweat from her brow. It was a close one, and her head spun from the dizzying blows she'd sustained. "I don't know much about baseball, but I'd say that was a home run."

The train began to slow again, reaching its next stop. Maggie winced as she got up, using the handrail to keep her steady. One of the goons was still muttering into his radio on the floor, clutching his broken arm. A simple kick to the face put an end to his communications.

Maggie checked the good Samaritan on the way out, thankful to discover he was still breathing. He'd have one heck of a headache when he finally came to.

Staying on the train was out of the question now. It was time for plan B.

Chapter 9

Maggie battled the impulse to barge through the crowd. To push and shove anyone and everyone blocking their path. Each step felt like it took twice as long as it should, the brisk pace of New Yorkers too slow for her as she and Emily travelled through the station and out into West 72nd Street. Blending in was the best option. Running would get them noticed, and there was no telling where the rest of Aleksandar's team was.

It didn't take long for them to find out.

Brakes shrieked. Doors slammed.

Maggie snapped her head towards the sounds as one of the SUVs in Aleksandar's fleet pulled up from Central Park West. His team spilled from each side, and Maggie cursed herself for taking so long to shut up the man with the radio.

"Shit," Maggie hissed. "Run!"

Grabbing Emily, she high tailed it down the street in the opposite direction, heading towards Columbus Avenue.

"They must have called in our location," Maggie said, scanning the area for an escape route.

The Russians followed them on foot, the driver of the SUV blaring the horn at the traffic blocking his way.

Maggie cursed the lack of alleys, each of the buildings joined to the next, as she and Emily sprinted on. They approached the intersection with Columbus Ave, but something was wrong.

Her hearing perked up, and Maggie dug her heels into the ground, yanking Emily back just in time. A second SUV hurtled towards them from around the corner of the street. It bumped up over the sidewalk and crashed right where they'd been standing a split second before, blocking their path.

Maggie spun on her heels and dragged Emily back the way they came as more Russians rushed from the second vehicle to join the pursuit.

They were cornered from both ends.

"What are we going to do?" Emily cried, digging her nails into Maggie's hand. They were trapped.

The hum of an engine purred, growing louder as it approached. A motorbike. It wasn't anything special, an old Honda decked out with decals for a local pizza joint, but it might be enough.

Maggie made a silent apology to the delivery driver and hoped this wouldn't jeopardize their job. As the vehicle approached, Maggie stepped into its path and threw out her arm.

It caught the delivery guy's neck in a clothesline and he flew from the seat. The motorcycle skidded along the road with bright sparks as metal met asphalt.

Emily ran after their escape vehicle. Maggie spared a quick second to make sure the delivery guy wasn't injured before following her charge. Hoisting the bike up, Maggie swung her leg over the seat and revved the engine. Emily wrapped her arms around Maggie's waist, hopping on behind her without having to be told.

A bang ricocheted off the stone walls of the surrounding buildings as one of the Russians fired a warning shot into the air. Pedestrians dispersed like a flock of scared sheep, and Maggie didn't stay around for the next bullet either.

She hit the road full throttle and sped down the street towards the second SUV. The driver spotted her and reversed off the sidewalk, backing into the street—much to the annoyance of a speeding taxi. Maggie dodged the approaching car, leaning into the turn and missing the back bumper with mere inches to spare.

Cars honked in anger as Maggie weaved between them. The smash of metal and glass suggested the SUVs weren't being overly careful in their pursuit, but Maggie didn't look back. She leaned down into the bike and picked up the pace.

Columbus Ave was a wide street with four lanes and ample room for the SUVs to bully their way through the traffic. Car brakes skidded behind them with a symphony of horns, the deep rumbling engines of the SUVs unrelenting and getting closer.

"Maggie," Emily warned, as one of the two vehicles came up from behind.

It bumped the back of the bike.

Emily squealed, tightening her grip on Maggie as she tried to steady the bike. The SUV bumped them again and jolted them forward. The rear fender cracked and a piece fell off, crunching beneath the wheels of the SUV.

Checking her mirrors, Maggie swerved into the next lane and hit the brakes, slowing down to leave a gap between them and their hunters.

While the first SUV flew on past the bike, the second SUV caught on quick. They came into view from the rear, overtaking a cab on the lane to Maggie's right and forcing the car in front of them to speed up or be hit.

Three seconds later, the Russians were in line with the bike. Maggie risked a sideward glance and caught the driver spinning the wheel to the left.

The SUV crossed into Maggie's lane with a vicious screech. Maggie moved, inching as close to the opposite lane as she dared, and dodged a collision that would have sent her and Emily off the bike.

Two could play at that game.

Maggie kept pace with the SUV and reached for her baton. Keeping the motorbike steady with one hand and flipping the baton out with the other, Maggie shattered the driver's window. Most of the glass sprayed the driver, but a few errant pieces ricocheted back, cutting Maggie's cheek, but she didn't care.

The baton had done its job. A second jab of the weapon hit the driver with enough force to distract him from the road. By the time he noticed the parked garbage truck, it was too late. The SUV ran straight into the back of it in an explosion of shattered windows and burst trash bags.

A wicked grin spread across Maggie's face. One down. One to go.

They approached an intersection as the lights switched from green to red, and the surrounding cars slowed to stop. Maggie hit the gas.

"Hold on tight," she warned Emily, "and lean with the turn."

Clenching her jaw, Maggie picked up speed and weaved through the slowing vehicles. Traffic from West 68th Street drove through the intersection in one-way traffic.

There was no right turn, but that didn't stop Maggie.

She turned into the oncoming traffic, maneuvering the bike past a truck that almost collided right into them, and headed down the street amid the approaching cars.

The surviving pursuit vehicle tried to follow, but as it turned to tail them, the van Maggie had dodged hit the SUV side on and sent the car flipping onto its side and over onto its back.

Emily whooped and cheered, her braids whipping behind her in the wind. "You really are Jane Bond."

Maggie laughed and allowed a small cheer of her own, her heart warming to the brave little girl holding on to her.

The elation didn't last long though. They may have lost the Russians for now, but one of the SUVs was still out there, and it was a long way to the British Consulate.

Chapter 10

Too long.

Travelling across town was out of the question. By now, the city would be teaming with undercover Russian operatives along with the more obvious ones they'd just escaped.

While Maggie preferred to work alone, she knew when things were tight. Getting Emily to the consulate alone was too big a risk and, as much as her ego hated to admit it, she needed help.

Snaking through the streets, taking alleyways when she could, Maggie headed for Ashton's apartment on West 59th Street. She stopped around the corner on 10th Avenue and ditched the bike behind a dumpster.

"What are you doing?" Maggie asked.

Emily fiddled with the notch of a container on the

back of the bike and opened the lid. "There's pizza in here. You don't let perfectly good pizza go to waste."

With two pizza boxes in hand, Maggie led Emily down the street and into the apartment building. As far as she could tell, no one spotted them. Right now, Aleksandar's crew would be scattered around the city, watching and waiting for them to turn up. Perhaps even staking out the British Consulate. Right now, they needed to lay low.

"Nice place," Emily said, surveying in the apartment. She slumped onto the couch and sniffed the pizza boxes. "Mind if I watch some TV?"

"Sure." Maggie checked through the peephole in the front door. Her muscles were stiff, the impact from her fight with Aleksandar settling in now they weren't racing through the city for dear life.

After some searching, Maggie found pain killers in the bathroom and washed off the blood from her face. Her reflection was paler than usual, and her hand tremored. It took a moment for her to register the odd feeling. Fear.

Maggie would be lying if she said she didn't get a thrill from her work. An adrenaline-fueled high coursed through her in the heat of the moment, when all she could focus on was staying alive and taking down whatever adversary stood in her way. Yes, fear was a familiar companion, but it was also exhilarating.

This fear felt different.

Then again, she'd never been on a mission like this. Or rather, *she'd* never been like *this* on a mission.

Raising her t-shirt, she stood to the side and appraised her tummy. She wasn't showing yet, but it was only a matter of weeks before the beginnings of a baby bump blossomed there. Nothing in her life would be the same, and whether she was ready for it or not, change was coming.

Ashton kept a first aid kit in his bedroom, and Maggie dug it out from the fitted wardrobes. Her phone lay on the bedside table. It was time to call in.

"Maggie." Danielle Hawkins answered on the first ring. "What's your status."

So much for hello.

"I have the witness. We're safe for now, but the situation is too volatile to reach you."

"Then we'll come to you. What's your location?"

Maggie gave Ashton's address.

"It might take a while to get a detail together. Stay inside until we get there."

Maggie bristled. Regardless of what Danielle seemed to think, this wasn't Maggie's first time in the field. The whole reason she was even involved was because Danielle and the rest of Jonathan Cole's team couldn't access the Russian Consulate. Maggie would like to see Danielle survive what Maggie had accomplished so far.

Hanging up without a goodbye, Maggie pocketed her phone and returned to Emily with the first aid kit.

"Who were you talking to?" Emily asked, chewing with her mouth open.

"Help." Maggie sat down beside her. "We'll wait here until they come for us."

Emily's shoulders relaxed. "Then I can see my parents?"

"I expect they'll be desperate to see you." Maggie opened the first aid kit. "Let me take a look at those knees."

Emily complied, taking another bite of her pepperoni and cheese slice while she flicked the TV channels to some cartoons. The abrasions were nothing to worry about, but they still needed cleaning. Dirt and small bits of rubble were stuck to the skin from her fall.

"This might sting a little," Maggie said, uncapping an antibacterial spray. She covered the wound with it and wiped the dirt off with a clean cloth.

Emily hissed, but she didn't complain or jerk away. Maggie smiled, liking the girl more and more. Not many kids Emily's age could go through what she had and still put on a brave face.

"That was quite the swing back there," noted Maggie, moving on to the next knee.

Emily gave a sheepish grin. "I'm on the little league team."

"I'm not surprised with a shot like that." Had it not been for Emily's attack, the whole mission could have ended down there in the subway. "You're very brave, Emily."

Emily ducked her head. "I don't feel brave."

Maggie tilted Emily's chin with her hand and met her eyes. "But you are."

"I ran away," she whispered.

"When?" Maggie asked, getting up and sitting next to Emily on the couch.

"When the man was attacked."

"What man?" Maggie probed. She still didn't know the name of the dead UN official, and Maggie hated missing information.

Emily shrugged. "I don't know. He was at the party. I needed the bathroom, and the one downstairs was being used, so I went upstairs. Only it's a big house and I got lost. I went into the wrong room and that's when I saw it."

Maggie leaned forward. "What did you see?"

Emily's bottom lip shook. "They stuck a needle into the man's neck and he started shaking. Then he just stopped."

A needle. Danielle had said the means of the assassination were undetectable, which was why Emily was key to it all. Without her, the official's death could be passed off as a heart attack, or something similar. A shot of an untraceable substance into the bloodstream could induce cardiac arrest. It wouldn't be the first-time Maggie had come across the likes of it.

The Russians had covered their tracks. But they didn't count on Emily.

"I'm sorry you had to see that." Maggie wrapped her

arm over Emily's small shoulders. "Did you get a look at the attacker's face?"

Emily nodded. "I ran before they could get me, but the guy from the subway grabbed me when I got to the bottom of the stairs, and the next thing I knew, I woke up in the building with the Russians."

Aleksandar. He had been the one to take Emily away. Maggie was especially glad the little girl got the swing on him.

"Like I said, brave. And you're going to have to keep being brave." Emily was tough, and it would do her well for what lay ahead. Having to testify against a foreign government was the last thing a child should have to go through. Considering the magnitude of the crimes committed, Emily wouldn't be safe for a long time. At least not until she testified. Relations between Russia and the West were strained, and the Russians had already tried to remove Emily from the picture once.

"I'm scared," Emily whispered, her deep brown eyes glossy with tears.

Maggie gave her a squeeze and rubbed her arm. "That's okay. Being scared is part of being brave. What matters is that you keep going anyway, even if things seem bad. You're a fighter, and what do fighters do?"

Emily looked up at her. "Fight?"

"That's right." Maggie bumped her fist with Emily's. "We fight, and we keep on fighting."

Emily nodded, setting a determined jaw like she had done back inside the Russian Consulate. "I can do that."

"Good," said Maggie, closing the first aid kit and sinking into the sofa with Emily. "Now scoot over and quit hogging the pizza."

E mily regarded Maggie with an arched eyebrow. "You're out of your mind."

They'd been in the apartment for half an hour, and were tucking in for a second helping of lukewarm pizza. Maggie's stomach rumbled in pleasure, having been neglected since the night before. She'd never been able to eat much prior to an assignment, especially one as important as hostage rescue.

"I'm telling you," Maggie replied, goading Emily, "I think Chicago's got the upper hand with the deep dish."

Not that it stopped her from delving into her third slice. It was greasy, laden with cheese and pepperoni, and the perfect comfort food after an afternoon of running for your life.

"Nope." Emily swiped the air with conviction. "It's New York slice, or nothing at all."

Maggie shrugged and went in for another bite. The base was so thin that it dangled in front of her in a flopping mess and she had to maneuver her mouth down and around to catch it.

Emily giggled as she witnessed the spectacle. "Tourists. You're eating it all wrong."

Maggie put the slice down and sipped on some soda, kicking her boots off. "All right, smarty pants, show me the mystical ways of eating pizza."

"You fold it like this," Emily instructed, taking a new slice for herself and folding it so both sides of the crust touched, creating a sturdier hold. "That way, the topping doesn't splat on the sidewalk." Emily laughed and pointed to Maggie's lap where a big glob of cheese had landed on her trousers. "Or on your jeans."

Maggie collected the cheese and ate it, sticking her tongue out at Emily. "Okay, I'll give you that, but deep dish is still better."

Emily sniggered and tuned back into her cartoons playing on Ashton's flat screen.

"What is this rubbish," Maggie asked, forgoing a napkin and licking her fingers.

"It's not rubbish," Emily said, eyes glued to a chubby little boy and his superhero sausage dog. "It's Tommy and Sir Barksalot."

"Cartoons have gone downhill since I was young," Maggie said, enjoying their little back and forth. Maggie wasn't much of a people person, but she liked Emily more than most adults she'd come across.

"Maybe," Emily countered, not missing a beat, "but at least we have color TVs now."

"I'm not that old," Maggie scoffed, taking another bite of folded pizza.

As she watched Emily laugh along to the cartoons, Maggie's mind turned to her pregnancy. Would she have a daughter? Would she be brave and resilient like Emily? She might even look a little like Emily, with her dark skin like Leon's and those big, beautiful eyes that didn't miss much.

The idea that a new life was forming inside her was surreal. A life that would grow into a child with their own personality, thoughts, and feelings. Would they be kind like Leon? Always considering how others are doing? Would they be resourceful and able to look after themselves like Maggie? Or would they be completely different, and grow up to be an artist or a scientist? She certainly hoped so. The further away their child was from her and Leon's type of work, the better.

There was an entire realm of possibilities inside of her. Possibilities that could change Maggie's life forever.

"So, Emily," Maggie said, interrupting her show as the superhero sausage dog saved the day, "what are you going to be when you grow up?"

"Hmm," Emily said, brow creased in thought.

"A baseball player?" Maggie suggested, topping Emily's glass up with soda. "I'm sure a team would be glad to have you with a swing like that."

Emily took a gulp of her soft drink and swirled the

glass like she was sipping on an aged Bordeaux. "I like sports, but I don't think I'd want to play professionally."

"What about a lawyer, like your mom?" Maggie asked, certain Emily's mother held her wine glass the same way.

"I don't think so." Emily scrunched her nose. "She's super stressed all the time and she thinks her boss is an assho— I mean, he's a jerk. I think I'd like to be an entrepreneur. That way, I'd get to be the boss, and no one can tell me what to do."

Maggie leaned over and held her glass to Emily. "I like your style."

"I like yours, too, Jane Bond," Emily said, clinking her glass with Maggie's. "You're kinda a badass."

The doorbell rang a while later. Maggie wiped the pizza grease off on her already dirty clothes and whipped out the baton to full length.

She crept to the front door, ready to attack, and checked the peephole. She sighed in relief when she saw Danielle standing impatiently with a detail of armed men. The cavalry had arrived.

Maggie swung open the door and her allies ducked inside. They wore white jumpsuits, scattered in blobs of paint to masquerade as decorators, and carried cans of paint and a set of ladders.

"Thanks for coming," Maggie said, closing the door behind them before any of the neighbors got too nosey and noticed the host of people in the hallway.

"We have a van waiting in the underground garage to transport the witness," Danielle said.

"Maggie?" Emily called, coming to see who had arrived.

Emily stopped dead and eyed Danielle. The pizza box dropped from her hands and the entire apartment filled with her screams.

Chapter 11

Maggie ran to Emily and held her by the arms.

"Emily, what is it? What's wrong?"

Emily stabbed a finger at Danielle. "It was her. She was the one who killed that guy."

Maggie straightened and stepped between Danielle and Emily. Her mind raced to catch up, to figure out what was happening.

"It was her," Emily cried again. "She's with the British government, I heard her tell my mom at the party. She said she worked here in New York."

Danielle's crew lunged forward, shoving Maggie out of the way. Before she could retaliate, one of them snuck behind Emily and jabbed a needle into her neck.

Emily blinked a few times, her face a map of confusion, before she slumped forward. Maggie lunged and caught her before she fell, holding the unconscious little girl in her arms.

"What was in that?" Maggie demanded.

"Relax," Danielle said. "It's a sedative."

Maggie lay Emily on the floor and sprung to her feet. In two strides, she grabbed Danielle by the shoulders and pinned her to the nearest wall so hard the framed picture hanging there fell to the wooden floor. "Why the fuck are you drugging her?"

Danielle's men reached for their concealed weapons.

"It's okay, boys," Danielle assured, before turning back to Maggie. "She was hysterical. We can't exactly take her down to the van kicking and screaming."

Hysterical. There was that word again.

Maggie released her hold of Danielle and backed away. "Is what she said true? Were you the one she saw kill the UN official?"

"Yes," Danielle admitted, straightening her suit, the only one of the detail not wearing overalls.

Maggie glared at the woman, curling her hands into fists. "Which UN official?"

"Dimitri Udinov."

"The Russian ambassador?" The final puzzle piece clicked into place. Fury burned in Maggie's veins. "You tricked me. You let me believe the Russian's had killed a British official, but it was the other way around."

The woman frowned. "I don't remember telling you anything of the sort. We refrained from telling you the full story in case you were compromised, as you yourself pointed out in our first meeting."

Danielle and Jonathan Cole hadn't told any lies, which explained why Maggie hadn't suspected the deception. Emily was indeed a witness. What they failed to mention was that she was a witness to a British operation.

Maggie inched closer to Emily, her chest rising and falling in a chemically induced slumber. "Why did our government want Udinov dead?"

"He was spotted in multiple meetings with former KGB affiliates," Danielle said. "Our undercover intelligence reported plans to assassinate select world leaders at the next UN summit, including the Prime Minister."

"And the Americans were in on this, too?" Maggie guessed. They had to be to allow the operation to take place on their turf.

"The President was one of their proposed targets, too," Danielle confirmed.

Maggie counted six men in Danielle's detail. "And the Russians were holding Emily as proof against us?"

Us. The affiliation tasted like ash in her mouth.

Danielle's lips thinned. "They got to the girl before I could. We have reason to believe that was their intention. Thanks to you, now they won't be able to."

Aleksandar had grabbed Emily, but he never meant to kill her. He wanted to protect her. Protect her from the very people Maggie worked for.

Thinking back on it, the Russians had plenty of

opportunities to shoot Emily dead. In Central Park. On the Subway. Even during the chase through the streets, one of them could have leaned out the SUV and pulled the trigger. Maggie hadn't considered it at the time, too busy trying to escape and stay alive, but there it was. They didn't take the shot because they wanted Emily alive.

Seven sets of eyes stayed on her, and Maggie considered her odds at taking them all out. "Why kill Udinov if you had proof of his plans?" she asked Danielle, trying to understand. "You could have outed him publicly."

"It was a matter of national security." A coy smile played at the woman's lips. "I'm sure you understand."

Maggie laughed, but it was bitter and burning with rage. "You didn't have sufficient evidence to prove his plans, did you?" Or at least, no proof the British government could use. Not if they attained it through illegal means.

"His plot was a legitimate threat," Danielle said, voice sharpening. "Now it isn't."

Maggie couldn't bring herself to care about any of it. All she cared about was Emily's fate. "Where are you taking her?"

Danielle raised her chin. "The situation must be contained."

"Contained?" Maggie closed her eyes. She knew what it meant.

"We can't afford any loose ends."

"Her name is Emily Wallace," Maggie said through gritted teeth. "She's twelve years old."

"A pity," Danielle said, loftily, "but collateral damage is unavoidable sometimes."

Maggie balled her fists so hard her knuckles cracked. "It's entirely avoidable if you're even remotely competent at your job. What kind of assassin gets caught by a child?"

Danielle crossed her arms. "I regret what happened, believe me I do. But our hands are tied."

Maggie's mind raced for a solution. For anything that could save Emily. "There must be another way. A way that doesn't involve killing a little girl."

Danielle waved a hand at Emily sprawled on the floor. "You heard her. I was a guest at the party representing the consulate, and she witnessed me killing Udinov. She knows too much." Danielle stated, her words hard and unyielding. "The decision has already been made."

With Emily able to connect Danielle to Britain, it linked the government directly to the murder of Udinov. Emily was a risk they couldn't afford, no matter how deplorable it was to eliminate her.

"You're just going to kill an innocent child?" Maggie searched each of her colleagues faces, making sure to stare each of them in the eye.

She was met with blank stares.

"Why not have me do it back at the consulate?" Maggie asked, her blood boiling. The tremor from before was back, but it wasn't fear for herself or the life growing inside her this time. "Why have me break Emily out and keep her alive if you're just going to kill her anyway?"

"We need to question her," Danielle said. "Find out what the Russians already know and what they gleaned from her before you arrived."

Bile rose in Maggie's throat. "Interrogation first, then death."

"It will be quick and humane," Danielle assured, like a vet telling a bereaved owner their pet was going to be put down. "A doctor will administer a lethal injection tonight. It will feel like she's falling asleep."

"You can't do this," Maggie yelled, stepping forwards.

"Stand down," Danielle ordered, like she could ever be Maggie's superior.

In a wave of fury, Maggie swung at Danielle, but her men held Maggie back.

Danielle clicked her fingers and one of the men hoisted Emily's small frame over one shoulder. She stopped at the door and turned back to Maggie. "You did well, Agent. The Consul-General expects an in-person report tomorrow morning before you leave. We'll take things from here."

And just like that, Danielle and the man carrying Emily left the apartment, followed by the rest of her team.

Maggie fell to her knees as the door slammed closed.

Chapter 12

Maggie brought up the final bites of pizza and spat out a mouthful of bile that burned her throat on the way up.

Emily.

Maggie stood and rinsed out her mouth, splashing her clammy face with water. Her mind swam, trying to come to terms with what had happened. Right now, unconscious and alone, Emily was in the back of Danielle's van, being transported to a secure location.

Maggie's nails dug into her palms as she bit back tears.

Unknowingly or not, she had delivered Emily to her death.

She told Emily she would get her back to her parents. She promised to keep her safe.

Her fingers itched to wreck the place. To smash, and tear, and break everything in sight. Maggie paced the apartment, her thoughts racing. She completed the mission given to her, just as she always did. Did what was asked of her, even with the seemingly impossible odds.

Maggie had done plenty of things for Queen and country she wasn't proud of. Things that kept her awake at night. Things that haunted her dreams. Things she could never take back. The weight of it took a toll on her. A toll she gladly paid to do what must be done. To do what others could not.

The one thing that kept her going, that allowed her to do those things, was the knowledge that it was all for the greater good. Until now, she'd never felt like the enemy.

But what could she have done? Fought Danielle? Stopped them from taking Emily?

It wasn't Danielle she would be defying. It wasn't her boss Jonathan Cole, or even the entire consulate.

Maggie would be defying her country.

She was guilty of a whole list of crimes, but treason wasn't one of them.

Maggie collapsed onto the couch and ran a hand through her hair. The cushions were still warm from where Emily sat eating pizza, the noise of cartoons still played in the background. The weight of it bore down on her, threatening to suffocate her with tears. Maggie had taken many lives over the years, but never a child's. Most of the people she took out had done despicable things. Deplorable things. They deserved what came to them.

Not Emily.

Not a twelve-year-old girl who stumbled into the wrong place and the wrong time.

A set of tears slipped from her eyes and tracked down her face. Maggie wiped them away with an angry fist. She didn't get to sit around and cry or feel sorry for herself. Not after what she let happen. Not now, knowing what was going to happen to Emily before the night was over. Maggie may not be the one administering the lethal injection, but she might as well be. Danielle never would have retrieved Emily without Maggie's help.

Maggie worried at her nail, a habit she had gotten rid of back in training as a teenager. The whole situation was unraveling her.

Jonathan Cole and Danielle hadn't been exaggerating when they told Maggie her operation was of the highest priority for the sake of national security.

If the Russians had managed to use Emily as they planned, if she'd testified about what she saw and helped prove Britain was responsible, there was no telling the extent of the damage caused.

Relations between Russia and the UK and US were already tense. It was a delicate balance, and even the slightest thing could tip the scale, never mind something as damning as murder. If anyone caught wind of the assassination—especially during a UN party—all hell would break loose.

It would rip open Pandora's box, and the threat of war would be very, very real.

The testimony of a twelve-year-old girl could result in World War III. It was far too big a risk.

Not that it made things easier. Not that it made Maggie feel any better.

Intellectually and strategically, Emily Wallace couldn't be allowed to live.

But morally? Emotionally?

Maggie got up and paced the apartment again.

Nothing she could say would change the minds of her superiors. Bishop wasn't even privy to the mission. The Director General would know, of course, but she was the one who had Bishop send Maggie to New York in the first place.

Even Danielle was following orders given to her by Jonathan Cole, which would have been passed down from higher up, too. Something as classified as this would run all the way up the food chain. This was top level stuff, and there was no way any of them would discuss a change of plan with her.

Maggie stopped in the middle of the room and bit her lip as the idea crossed her mind.

No, she couldn't.

Her heart thumped in her chest. It was insane. Not to mention dangerous. She looked over her shoulder to where Emily had sat, a hand over her stomach. Maggie couldn't say anything that would help Emily.

But she could *do* something.

She had two phone calls to make. Maggie dialed the number before she changed her mind.

"Mags."

"Ashton, I need your help."

Chapter 13

What am I doing?

The question circled for the hundredth time since she'd made up her mind. It was the bracelet that sparked this insane idea of hers. Maggie had secured it around Emily's wrist back inside the consulate, but she never thought she'd use it for this.

The tracking device concealed inside the bracelet showed Emily's current location in Downtown Brooklyn.

Maggie, along with a team of Ashton's New York City contacts, crossed the Manhattan Bridge. Night had fallen, and the city lit up like a constellation of stars, the Empire State Building rising into the sky, a beacon of brilliant light. The cloak of darkness gave Maggie and her cohorts some much needed cover, but it also meant Emily was running out of time.

Danielle said a doctor would arrive that night to kill Emily by lethal injection. A fate that only the worst of America's criminals received. At least in some states. Emily was about as far from being a criminal as a person could get, and Maggie refused to sit back and let her life be cut short because of Danielle's incompetence.

"Thank you for helping me," Maggie said to the driver, who seemed like the leader of the small crew.

The gruff man, who refused to tell Maggie his name, chewed on his cigar and blew out a puff of smoke. "I'm only doing this because I owe Ashton a favor."

Maggie hadn't asked Ashton many questions about the ragtag group he assembled for her. If he trusted them, that was enough for her. Even if most of them operated on the other side of the law.

Ashton hadn't revealed any confidential information to his contacts, but from the looks of their faces in the back of the van, they knew enough to know things were about to get dangerous.

None of them were happy about Maggie's no gun policy. She may be willing to defy her country and colleagues, but that didn't mean she wanted any of them dead. Murder was strictly off the table, at least on their end.

The heavens opened, and rain battered against the windshield of the van. Above, the gray clouds blotted out the full moon. A superstitious person might consider a night like this to be a bad omen.

Good thing Maggie wasn't superstitious.

The baton she'd stolen earlier lay across her lap, and she gripped it with her gloved hands, focusing on her breathing. On what she was about to do.

Maggie didn't make a habit of committing treason. Her work required a variety of illegal acts, but treason was a line she never wanted to cross. One she'd never even considered.

Until now.

A quirk of a smile settled on Maggie's lips. Her actions could only be considered treason if she got caught, and she had no intentions of letting that happen.

There were six mercenaries in the back of the van: three women, three men. Including Maggie and the driver, that made them a team of eight. Danielle would have more guards at her disposal, but Ashton assured Maggie each of his contacts was worth two normal agents. She only hoped he was right.

They exited the bridge and headed to the New York Naval Shipyard. The NYNS was decommissioned in the sixties and had since reinvented itself as commercial property. It catered to a wide scope of industries, from farming and manufacturing to entertainment, and was home to the largest set of production studios outside of Los Angeles.

Emily's tracker placed her inside an abandoned warehouse at the edge of the yard that looked out into the East River from Wallabout Bay.

Maggie's phone buzzed in her pocket.

"Do you have everything you need?" Maggie asked, forgoing hellos.

"Yes."

"Good. Meet me at pier K in one hour. Don't be late." Maggie hung up and turned off the phone. She'd done all she could.

Her driver approached one of the yard's entrance gates and spoke briefly with the guy manning it. From the tone, Maggie assumed they knew each other. The driver passed the man a thick fold of bills before continuing inside.

"Let's abandon the van here," Maggie said, scanning the docks. "I want the advantage of surprise."

Danielle's crew would still be on high alert. Until the witness was silenced, the Russians looking for her would continue to be a concern.

If Maggie's plan worked, none of them would see Emily Wallace ever again.

Ashton's band of mercenaries got out the van in silence, each dressed head to toe in black. Maggie pulled the balaclava over her head, making sure to conceal her hair, and secured a pair of night vision goggles over her eyes. Concealing her identity was vital, especially tonight.

Motioning for her team to follow, Maggie led her temporary troops into the rain-soaked night and approached the abandoned warehouse.

Wind whistled across the bay and sent shivers down Maggie's spine, stinging like iced fingers clawing at her skin. The night air was warm, but still Maggie's teeth chattered. Clamping her jaw, she pressed forward until they reached the entrance of the warehouse.

The crew split into prearranged groups, leaving Maggie on her own—just the way she liked it—and they slunk into position like phantoms in the night.

Waiting for the driver's signal, Maggie leaned down on her knees and hid between a rough outcrop of bushes and tall grass. Through her goggles, the world was shades of green. Two of Danielle's agents made rounds of the perimeter, guns in hands and eyes watchful.

Not watchful enough.

The driver and his partner aimed their dart guns at the agents from their spots behind a SUV. Their accuracy was impressive, even to Maggie. Thin darts struck both guards in the thigh, the dark tips protruding from their flesh long enough for them to realize their mistake.

A second pair of Ashton's mercenaries appeared from the darkness and caught the agents before they could fall with unceremonious thumps. The pair dragged the unconscious guards to the side of the building to sleep it off, while the rest of the mercenaries narrowed in from all angles and surrounded the building.

Maggie waited until the first pair breeched the entrance and set off their smoke bomb before moving. Most of the windows were boarded and hid what lay within. Emily could be anywhere.

Yelling and gunshots echoed inside the cavernous

building, the whipping wind drawing the sounds outside to Maggie.

Circumventing the entrance, Maggie sprinted to the back of the warehouse. Like the front of the building, the windows at the back were boarded, too. Using her baton, Maggie wedged the weapon between the wood and the window frame and yanked it with all her strength.

The nails slid out without much fuss, the damp wood rotten with age and exposure.

Maggie risked a look inside to make sure the coast was clear. The familiar grunts of fighting reverberated through the bare brick walls, but the coast was clear. Sliding in, Maggie closed the wood back over the window as best she could and scanned her surroundings.

A two-story warehouse, Maggie found herself in a hallway at the foot of a set of stairs. The floor above was silent. She fiddled with her goggles and listened, the whole place pitch black thanks to one of her team dismantling the breaker and cutting the lights.

The floorboards creaked behind her. Maggie lashed out with her baton. The assailant dodged the attack and came in with one of his own. Maggie took the blow, a meaty fist striking her in the shoulder. Her arm rang with pain, but she held on to her baton and parried a right hook with it. As much as she would like to stand toe to toe with the big brute and let off some steam, Maggie had a job to do and didn't have time for distractions.

She and the brute circled in the little hallway, squaring

each other up. The agent didn't seem impressed with what he saw, but Maggie was used to that.

The man quirked a grin and lunged forward like a rugby player, going in for a takedown. Maggie twirled on the balls of her feet and spun, bringing the baton down like a whip, and bludgeoned the agent in the back of the head.

It had worked for her and Emily in the subway, and it worked for Maggie now. The agent fell to the floor and never got back up.

Maggie kicked him to make sure he was out, going over the options in her head. The fighting still raged on beyond the set of doors to her left, where Ashton's contacts were hopefully gaining the advantage.

Strategically, Danielle wouldn't place Emily anywhere near the entrance. She'd want her witness-turned-hostage as far away as possible. Somewhere they could keep her while they contained the breach.

That didn't leave many options, and Maggie ascended the steps on light feet, holding her baton close.

The top floor wasn't as big as the lower level. From what Maggie could tell, it took up a fraction of the space, and she passed two small offices as she crept down the hallway. Mold-covered carpet lined the floor, squishy under her feet and spotted with frayed holes and dark stains. A rat scurried away from Maggie, but she didn't squirm. She had bigger vermin to take care of tonight.

Only one more door remained. Unlike the others, it was closed, and a moving light shone under it.

Counting down from three, Maggie took a deep breath and rushed the door. Leaping into the air, Maggie kicked the wood and it flew open, breaking from its rusted hinges. It was a foreman's room, larger than the other two offices with a wide, one-hundred-and-eighty-degree window that overlooked the shop floor and the fighting going on below.

Maggie's heart leapt as she spotted Emily on the office table.

But she wasn't alone.

A man fumbled with a flashlight and aimed it at Maggie. In his free hand, he held a needle filled with a clear substance. A vicious rage bubbled inside of Maggie. If the agent downstairs had slowed her even a moment more, she would have been too late. She would have committed treason with nothing to show for it.

Liquid spurted from the end of the needle as the doctor dropped the flashlight and made for Emily on the table.

Maggie raced over the fallen door and yanked the man back by the scruff of his shirt. Taking her baton in both hands, she scooped it over the doctor's head and caught him by the neck, pressing the weapon against his windpipe.

The doctor wriggled in her grasp, but his attempts to break free only made the process quicker, expelling his oxygen until it became too much for his body. Maggie held on tight as he slipped into unconsciousness and his eyes rolled to the back of his head. She let the doctor slip under her arms and splay out on the ground.

"Sorry, Doctor, but your services will not be needed tonight."

Maggie didn't check on him. The doctor would live. Instead, she went to the table where Emily lay.

Maggie's heart stopped as she got close.

Emily's eyes were closed. She wasn't moving.

Chapter 14

Maggie tapped Emily's face as panic welled inside her. Was she too late? Had the doctor already administered a dose of something else? Something lethal?

"Emily. Emily wake up."

Emily didn't move.

"Emily," Maggie said again, louder this time.

Nothing.

Slipping off one of her gloves, Maggie placed the back of her hand above Emily's lips and held her breath. Waited until—

There. Shallow but there all the same. Emily was breathing. She was still alive.

Digging into her pockets, Maggie brought out a small vial and unscrewed the cap. She placed the smelling salts under Emily's nose and waited.

Emily's eyes shot open and her body jerked away from the smell. Maggie secured her by the shoulders as she came to, her clouded brain trying to catch up with where she was. They must have drugged her again after questioning.

Bastards. "It's me," Maggie whispered, wiping Emily's clammy face free from her braids. "Can you sit up?"

Emily groaned as Maggie hoisted her into a sitting position, holding a hand to her head. Maggie knew the feeling. Emily was in for a killer headache.

"Do you think you can walk?" They couldn't hang around any longer than necessary.

Emily's eyes widened, peering over Maggie's shoulder. "Watch out!"

Maggie spun in time to see Danielle striding towards her from the hallway. Maggie shoved Emily back and stood her ground, ready to face the woman whose botched mission caused all of this.

"Come on!" Maggie yelled in fluent Russian, springing forward to meet Danielle.

The women clashed in a collision of fists and anger.

Maggie evaded a kick aimed at her stomach and thrashed out with her baton. Danielle leaned back to dodge the swing, but it clipped her on the nose and she reeled back, swearing as blood oozed from her nostrils.

"You not take her," Danielle rasped, her Russian flawed and rudimentary. She charged Maggie again, slapping her in the face with an open palm.

The blow caught Maggie off guard, and Danielle used the distraction to swipe her leg under Maggie's ankles and send her to the ground.

Maggie careened back and slammed into the floor. The baton slipped from her hands and rolled out of sight.

The fall was awkward and knocked the air from Maggie's lungs. Before she had time to suck in a breath, Danielle was on her. The agent kneeled, using her momentum to put power into the fist heading right for Maggie's face.

Maggie rolled to the side just in time, Danielle's fist smacking against the moldy carpet. Both women rushed to their feet, and Maggie felt a twinge of unease. Their speed was evenly matched.

"Bitch," Maggie swore, her voice pitched low and gruff to conceal her identity. Danielle was expecting Russians, and that's what Maggie gave her.

With a cry, Danielle shot forward again and lashed out with a foray of jabs. Maggie took the brunt of them, each one sorer than the last as Danielle built momentum.

Despite her mishap with the assassination, Danielle was good. More than good.

But Maggie was better.

Not that she was going to give away that secret, not just yet. She let Danielle believe she was gaining the upper hand, stumbling backwards, inching closer and closer to the foot of the stairs at the end of the hallway. Danielle twisted her hips and raised her leg into a kick.

Spotting the perfect opportunity, Maggie moved in sync with the other agent, her perfect mirror, and scooped Danielle's leg into her arm. Maggie pinned Danielle in a death grip and reached for the collar of her jacket, pulling her forwards.

With her leg pinned, Danielle had to focus all her attention on staying upright. Maggie pivoted and shoved Danielle. Hard.

Danielle yelped as her first step yielded nothing but air, and she tumbled down the stairs, hitting every step and collapsing in a crumbled mess of limbs at the bottom landing. Maggie assessed her from her position at the top. A few broken ribs, maybe a fractured bone here or there in her arms and legs. Nothing that wouldn't heal in time.

Certain Danielle wasn't getting back up, Maggie ignored the guilty rumblings in her stomach and returned to the office.

"Maggie?" Emily asked, uncertain.

Maggie took off her balaclava and knelt by the table Emily was using to keep herself standing. "It's me. Are you okay?"

"I think so," Emily said, her voice sluggish from the drugs. "Are you?"

The fighting had ceased on the workshop floor. Maggie peered out the window and found Ashton's contacts binding the wrists of the fallen agents with plastic zip ties. That would keep them busy once they came to.

"I've had worse," Maggie said, holding Emily by the

255

waist and wrapping the girl's arm over her shoulder. "Now come on, let's get you out of here."

The agents may be down, but Maggie and Emily weren't out of hot water just yet.

Chapter 15

Maggie said her farewells to the nameless driver and the rest of Ashton's contacts. They fought well, and refrained from killing anyone like she'd asked, but Maggie would see the final part of her mission through alone. The less people who knew, the better.

The van drove off, wheels crunching on gravel as it exited the old shipyard, leaving Maggie and Emily in the pouring rain. The sky rumbled, the waves beyond the bay crashing amid a coming storm.

"Why aren't we going with them?" Emily asked, teeth chattering.

Maggie took off her jacket and wrapped it around Emily's shoulders. "We have somewhere else to be."

It wasn't too far from the warehouse, but it took longer

than Maggie liked, thanks to sedatives still coursing through Emily's veins.

They arrived at pier K with minutes to spare, and Maggie's racing pulse relaxed once she spotted the vessel tethered and waiting for them. The captain of the RBS-11 was an ex-marine and a current member of the US Coast Guard. His face matched the photo Ashton sent along earlier that night for confirmation, a stern looking man with a weatherworn face and a thicket of salt and pepper hair. If anyone could get the Wallaces out of the city, it was him.

A woman in a dark trench coat spotted Maggie and Emily walking up the pier and ran to them.

Emily was a young clone of her mother, a beautiful woman in her forties with high cheekbones and a regal air to her movements. She collected Emily in her arms and cried a wail into the wind

"My baby."

"Mom," said Emily, closing her eyes and snuggling into her mother's embrace.

Ms. Wallace looked up to Maggie with glistening eyes. "You did it."

Maggie cleared her throat and gathered herself together. "I promised your daughter I would keep her safe."

Mr. Wallace arrived close behind his wife and lifted Emily into his arms for a fierce hug.

"Thank you," he said, unable to say anything more.

"If there is anything we can do," said Ms. Wallace, shaking Maggie's hand, "Anything you need, just say the word."

Maggie looked both of Emily's parents in the eye. It was important they listened to her.

"I need you to follow through with the plans we discussed. Don't try to contact anyone you know. No relatives, no friends, and especially not anyone from work. Your old life is over, and if you want to make sure your daughter sees her next birthday, you must accept that."

The British, the Americans, and the Russians would all be searching for Emily. A key witness like her could not be allowed to disappear. They all needed her for their own reasons, and none of them would stop looking for her. Not for a long time.

Ms. Wallace nodded, her face serious. "It's a small price to pay to have our daughter back." Without warning, she wrapped her arms tight around Maggie, her rose scented perfume tickling her nose.

"Keep her safe," Maggie whispered. She had done all she could. It was up to them now.

"We will."

"And remember," Maggie said, staring Ms. Wallace in the eyes, "if you go public about the assassination, not only will you endanger Emily's life, but the lives of millions of people. You know the kind of people involved in all of this. It won't end well."

"I know what's at risk," Ms. Wallace assured, her stern

expression a mirror image of her daughter's. "And not only for my family. I understand why this truth must be buried."

Maggie believed her. She had to if she was going to follow through with her plan.

Mr. Wallace was by their side now, and Emily was back on her feet, still a little unsteady. The effects would wear off soon. All she needed was something to eat and a good night's rest.

Maggie released herself gently from Ms. Wallace's hold, all of them sodden in the rain. "All right, you better get going."

Emily stepped forward. "Thank you, Maggie."

A warmth spread over Maggie, and the urge to burst into tears sprung behind her eyes. She willed them back and leaned into the brave little girl who would soon be a young woman.

Emily peered over at the boat. "Where are we going?"

"Away," said Maggie, tugging her jacket closer around Emily. She needed to stay warm. "It's not safe for you here anymore."

"Are you coming with us?" Emily asked with innocent, hopeful eyes.

"No, but you'll be safe. I promise." Ashton wouldn't let Maggie down.

"Will I see you again?"

Maggie smiled. "Perhaps one day."

Emily stared down at her feet. "Can I call you once we get there?"

"It's best if I don't know where you are." If her colleagues or the Russians learned of Maggie's escapades, they'd torture everything they could out of her, but Maggie couldn't reveal a location she didn't know. She spoke to them all, trying but failing to keep the emotion from spilling into her voice. "Once you're safe, you'll be taken to a private airport. A plane is already waiting for you."

"What about passports?" Ms. Wallace asked, clutching her husband's hand. "Money?"

"It's all covered," Maggie assured. "A friend has arranged everything you'll need."

The Wallaces would soon have new names, taking on aliases like Maggie had done countless times before. It would be difficult for them at first, but they'd get used to it. They had to.

"And you trust this friend?" Mr. Wallace asked.

"With my life," said Maggie. And with theirs. Ashton had really come through for her on this one.

Emily hugged Maggie. "Goodbye, Jane Bond."

"Goodbye, brave girl," Maggie said, allowing a tear to fall and get lost amid the rain. She straightened up and held out a fist. "Remember, what do fighters do?"

Emily grinned and bumped her knuckles against Maggie's. "We keep on fighting."

Maggie stayed by the pier as the Wallaces boarded their boat. The engine rumbled to life and they zoomed across the East River until it disappeared in a blanket of darkness. Life was full of gray areas, and while she may have defied her government, she did not fail Emily Wallace.

Some things in life were more important than following orders. Even though she'd gone against her country's wishes, she had still eliminated any threat of war between the nations. While things didn't go as planned, the sole witness to Udinov's murder was gone. By the time the night was over, Emily Wallace would have vanished, never to be seen or heard from again. Her parents and the strings Ashton pulled would see to that.

Maggie didn't make a habit of placing her trust in others, but she put her faith in a mother and father's love. Without Emily, the Russians couldn't prove anything, and Danielle and her team were in the clear. Any threat caused by the chain of events had been removed, and Maggie pulled it off without ending the life of an innocent.

Resolute in her decision, Maggie left the shipyard and slipped into the shadows of the night.

Chapter 16

M aggie sat with folded arms across from Jonathan Cole the next morning.

"If this is a joke," she said, "I don't find it funny."

"I can assure you, this is far from a joke." Jonathan bristled and fidgeted in his chair. From the wrinkles in his untucked shirt and the bags under his eyes, the Consul-General didn't get much sleep last night.

As for Maggie, she slept like a baby once she fell into Ashton's king-sized bed. Her friend had called an hour ago to let Maggie know the Wallaces were safe and had made their way out of the US undetected.

Jonathan's assistant sat to his left, scribbling notes and keeping his head down, doing what he could to blend into the background and avoid his boss's wrath. Mr. Cole was like a bear with a sore arse, and that was before he spilled his coffee down himself.

Maggie turned her attention to Danielle, sitting to Jonathan's right. The day before hadn't left Maggie unscathed. Her muscles ached, and her skin was covered with several cuts and bruises, but it was nothing she couldn't hide under a long-sleeve shirt and some makeup.

Danielle didn't fare as well. Arm in a sling, she sat scowling in another bland suit, the one from the night before well and truly ruined. The best drycleaner in New York City couldn't have removed the blood and dirt from that ensemble.

One of her eyes was bloodshot and surrounded by a ghastly purple bruise that ran all the way across to her broken nose. Danielle winced as she coughed, her ribs likely wrapped up tight under her blouse, and left to heal on their own. If Maggie felt any remorse at causing Danielle pain, it was tampered by the satisfaction that she'd rescued Emily without outing herself as a traitor.

"You lost the witness again," Maggie spat, putting on a show for her colleagues. She slammed her fist down on the desk and tea sloshed from her cup. "After everything I went through to get Emily Wallace to you, you managed to lose her in less than ten hours."

"We were ambushed by the Russians," Danielle said. "They outnumbered us three to one."

Maggie raised an eyebrow. She wasn't the only one adding some flair to the real story. Then again, Danielle's pride wouldn't allow her to admit she had been bested by a detail half her size.

Jonathan mopped his head with a handkerchief and wrung his hands. "The situation is unfortunate."

"Unfortunate?" Maggie interrupted, waving her hands in exasperation. "What kind of half-baked operation are you running here?"

"I will remind you, Ms. Black, that you are not the authority here. You do not get to question me or my operatives."

Maggie balked at that and leaned forward. "Fine, but you can rest assured that Director General Helmsley will hear all I have to say about the shocking levels of incompetence from this office."

Letting her words settle, Maggie kicked her chair back and shrugged on her jacket.

"Where do you think you're going?" Jonathan demanded.

Maggie stopped by the door with a hand on the handle. "You're on your own with this one. I did what I was sent here to do, and I don't intend to board your sinking ship."

"You can't leave," Jonathan spluttered. "You haven't given your full report yet."

Opening the door, Maggie glanced over her shoulder. "I'll give it straight to the Director General herself. Besides, you don't have time to sit around asking me questions. I suggest you use what time you have left to prepare for your own debriefing."

Without another word, she walked out of Jonathan Cole's office and slammed the door. Her work there was done, and it was time to go home.

Chapter 17

Maggie arrived at the health center five minutes early. It was a crisp October Saturday, and she had wrapped up warm for the short walk across the Thames from her apartment.

"Hi, my name's Maggie Black. I have a follow-up appointment with Dr. Kahn."

The receptionist told her to take a seat, and Maggie joined the little cluster of women. The woman in the seat next to her looked like her water could break at any moment.

"You have this to look forward to," she huffed at Maggie, pointing to her swollen ankles and feet. Maggie tried to imagine her stomach that big. Stretch pants were definitely in her future. She couldn't wait.

A lot of things in her life were about to change.

Leaving the Unit was the biggest. Maggie had spent the last eleven years building her career and working non-stop, hopping from one country to the next. It was a dangerous and thrilling lifestyle. A lifestyle she could no longer live.

Though she'd miss parts of her old life, motherhood was her assignment now and, like every mission she completed before, she'd give it her all. Failing this job wasn't an option.

Ms. Wallace walked away from her career as an international human rights lawyer in a heartbeat for Emily. Maggie now understood why.

Working for the Unit wasn't like most careers. Plenty of women returned to work after having a baby, more than capable of juggling a career and motherhood, both full-time jobs in their own right.

But Maggie couldn't do both. She couldn't be there for a morning routine or spend afternoons in the park with her child if she was in a foreign country taking out bad guys. She couldn't return home from the office in time to collect her child from school. To make dinner, or kiss her little one goodnight.

Half the time, Maggie couldn't even tell anyone where

she was. It wasn't fair to do that to a child. To only be there between missions, not knowing if she'd ever make it back to see their sweet little face again.

Agents weren't known for long life expectancies.

Even her own mother died before her time, the car crash stealing her away from Maggie when she was just six years old. She knew what it was liking losing her mum, and she refused to let her child suffer the same fate.

If that meant walking away from the Unit, then so be it.

"What are you having," Maggie asked the heavily pregnant woman beside her.

"I don't know," she replied, pleasant and warm despite her clear discomfort. "We want it to be a surprise."

We.

Rummaging in her purse, Maggie found her phone and called Leon again. Bishop said he should be getting back from an assignment today, and she couldn't wait any longer to tell him. She wasn't sure how he'd take the news, but he needed to know. She wanted him to be the first person she told.

The voicemail picked up. He must not be back yet.

"Hi, it's me. I heard you'd be back today. I know we haven't spoken much since Venice, but I'd like to see you. I have something to tell you, and it's not the kind of thing you say over the phone. Anyway, ring me back once you get this."

Maggie hung up as the doctor called her name. She

tucked her phone away and followed Dr. Kahn into his office.

"Nice to see you again, Maggie. How have you been?"

"Great, thanks," she said, taking off her scarf and coat.

Keeping the baby turned out to be an easier decision that she expected. After New York, only one route felt right. While she didn't think badly of those who chose to terminate their pregnancy, it wasn't an option she could personally come to terms with.

Putting her child up for adoption was out of the question, too. Maggie knew firsthand how the system affected a child, and she wouldn't put someone through that if she could help it. In many ways, Maggie wouldn't have ended up in the Unit if she had a loving family and decent upbringing.

Dark thoughts surfaced from the recesses of her mind, taking her back to the night she first killed someone at the tender age of fifteen. Memories tried to push forward to remind her what led to that moment, to show her the domino effect it had on her life ever since.

Maggie forced the thoughts down and focused on the present. Focused on Dr. Kahn and her new future.

"We got the results back from your hCG blood test." Dr. Kahn straightened the tissue box on his desk, like he thought she might have need of them soon. *Why would she need tissues?* And then, seeming to realize what he was doing, he folded his hands on top of the file with her medical records.

Maggie sat up in her chair. A knot tightened in her stomach, her heart fluttering like a scared bird. "And?"

Dr. Kahn stared at the file instead of looking her in the eye. "I'm afraid I have some bad news."

"What?" Maggie's fists clenched, but this wasn't a battle she could win with violence. She forced herself to stay seated. "Is everything okay with the baby?"

Dr. Kahn sighed and finally looked up. The pull of his brow, and the supposedly comforting smile on his lips, reminded Maggie of the doctors on TV when they delivered terrible news. "Ms. Black, I'm sorry to say, but you are no longer pregnant. You've had a miscarriage."

"What?" Maggie blinked, her mind struggling to catch up to his words, to understand the full weight of his implications. *Miscarriage.* Fear, piercing and acidic, sent her heart racing. "Was it because of me?" she asked, her voice rising. Breaking. "Was it something I did?"

The fighting. Risking her life to save Emily Wallace. Had all that killed her unborn baby? Things had been fine when Dr. Kahn saw her last week, aside from some light bleeding. He said it was normal. That he needed to run some simple tests.

"No, no," Dr. Kahn said quickly, shaking his head. "Nothing like that. There were some chromosomal abnormalities that caused problems with the fetus's development."

The fetus.

Maggie covered her mouth with a shaking hand,

holding back the urge to be sick. "You promise me," she wailed, hating the pleading, broken one in her voice. "Promise this wasn't my fault."

"I promise you," Dr. Kahn assured, offering her a sad smile. "There's nothing you could have done. These things are unfortunately common in the first trimester."

A flush of relief spread through Maggie, but it fled just as quickly, shame filling the empty space in her heart. It didn't change anything. She had still lost her baby.

The life growing inside her wasn't there anymore.

Like it had never been there at all. Except that is was. Her whole life was going to change. *Everything* was going to be different. And now, that hope—that joy—was gone.

"I know the news can come as a shock. Is there anyone I can call?"

"No," Maggie heard herself say, but it was like she was somewhere else. Gone.

Her legs moved as if on their own accord, and she got up from the chair. A surge of nausea engulfed her and she stumbled into the wall.

Dr. Kahn rushed from his chair. "Ms. Black, are you okay?"

Maggie steadied herself against the wall. Her careful composure crumbling away. She would never be okay again. Never get back what she lost. Her ears rang, and the contents of her stomach churned dangerously.

"Please, sit down."

Maggie let the doctor lead her back to the chair. She didn't resist. Couldn't resist. Her mind was everywhere and nowhere at once. Her chest tightened and her vision blurred. "I need to be alone," she whispered.

"Are you sure?"

"Go!" Maggie yelled, barely holding on to any semblance of control.

Dr. Kahn nodded and headed for the door. "You can stay in here for as long as you need. I'll be outside."

A guttural cry escaped Maggie's lips as soon as the door closed. Reality stabbed through her chest like a physical pain, cracking, splintering, *shattering* her heart into a thousand unrepairable pieces.

Maggie fell from the chair and doubled over.

She cradled her belly and shuddered at the emptiness. At the hollow feeling growing inside her where her child should be. Tears flooded her eyes, hot and angry and unrelenting, until she feared she'd drown right there on the office floor. She didn't care if the world stopped spinning. She didn't care if she never got up again.

Maggie didn't know how long she sat there on the doctor's office floor. At some point, he came in to check on her and left a cup of tea in her hand. It was cold now.

She'd run out of tears, left with shaking hiccups that left her feeling sick and wrung dry.

A buzzing broke the silence in the room. Maggie searched for the sound and traced it to her handbag.

Reaching over, Maggie tipped the contents out until her phone landed on her lap. Her eyes were sore, and she couldn't make out the name of the person calling on the screen.

Was it Leon?

Oh god. What would she tell Leon? She couldn't tell him, couldn't break his heart the way hers was breaking. But she couldn't *not* tell him either. She had to say something.

"Hello?"

"Maggie, I have a new assignment for you. How soon can you get here?"

She closed her eyes. It wasn't Leon. Bishop's voice echoed in her ear, so matter-of-fact, so to-the-point, breaking what little was left of her. The pain was too much. Too real.

"Maggie?"

The concern in Bishop's voice was like a shot of adrenaline. Her training kicked in, her frantic mind building a wall around her heart to protect itself. It shoved down every feeling, every hope, every dream. Her training chipped away at everything that made Maggie a person, carved out every emotion until all that was left was a hollow shell with a singular purpose.

Brick by brick she restored the obliterated pieces of her protective walls and replaced them with impenetrable titanium. Nothing could get through. Nothing could be allowed in.

No one would ever get in again.

"Maggie, are you there?"

Maggie held her phone back to her ear, her voice crystal clear. "I'll be right in."

RVICE CARD

work+shop

PO BOX 413050

NAPLES FL 34101-3050

THE DEFECTOR

MAGGIE BLACK CASE FILES BOOK 3

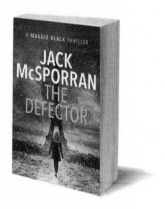

Chapter 1

Snow had visited the city of London.

It blanketed the streets and rooftops during the night, decorating the city like white icing on an intricate display of gingerbread. Maggie Black cupped her hands around her steaming mug of tea as snowflakes fluttered down from the heavens and swirled among passersby, each wrapped in warm scarfs and woolen hats to battle against the winter.

"Maggie?"

"Huh?" she asked, her breath clouding against the window pane.

Ashton slurped a gulp of his triple shot latte. "You were in a world of your own there."

The hum of chatter enveloped the little bookstore and coffee shop on Regent Street. People made the most of their time off to catch up with old friends. A few lone patrons sipped on cappuccinos in the corners as they clacked the keyboards of their computers, while others perused the shelves of hand-selected books curated by the owners.

Maggie pinched the bridge of her nose. "Sorry, what were you saying?"

"I missed you at the party," Ashton repeated, not quick enough to hide the glimmer of hurt behind his deep blue eyes.

"I meant to come," Maggie explained, "but I got back late from an assignment the night before and lost the entire day to jetlag."

Ashton eyed her over his mug, not buying any of it.

It wasn't a complete lie. Every spy knew the best tales were told in half-truths. Maggie *had* just returned home from a job on Christmas Eve, but it was only a two-and-a-half-hour flight away in Lisbon. Instead of heading over to Mayfair for Ashton's party, Maggie spent Christmas day curled up on her couch with a bottle of whiskey. Though she'd sat in complete darkness, she wasn't alone. Willow had stopped by to get out the rain and scrounge some turkey dinner, but the stray cat had to settle for a tin of tuna.

It was far from merry.

Maggie couldn't stomach anything else. Sitting around and pretending everything was okay required too much work, especially over the holidays. Better to slink away until the festivities were over.

Not that her best friend had any intentions of allowing her to skip seeing him.

"I got you a present," she said, changing the subject and sliding a hastily wrapped box in front of him. "It's not much. I was stuck in Portugal all of last week."

"Obrigado," Ashton said, tearing the wrapping paper off to reveal a bottle of his favorite aftershave. He took the cap off and spritzed himself with a half-dozen sprays, mortally offending a group of mothers behind him. "My favorite," he said, oblivious to them.

"I got it in duty free," Maggie admitted, the sweet scent tickling the inside of her nose. She had pushed the holidays to the back of her mind so much she'd almost forgotten to get him anything.

Ashton hadn't forgotten her. With his spare key, he'd snuck into her apartment while she was away and delivered a bundle of presents. He'd even dug her tree out from a closet and put it up in the living room, baubles and all, and left her gifts underneath. Never one to do anything by halves, Ashton had splurged on her with designer boots and matching handbag, a twenty-year-old bottle of whiskey which she'd emptied on Christmas day, and even the latest hardback from one of her favorite writers.

"Are you going to tell me what's wrong?" Ashton asked, his playful façade gone and replaced with real concern.

Maggie balked. "What do you mean?"

"When things are bad you hide, and you hop off on as many assignments as you can." Ashton sighed. "You haven't been yourself since you came back from New York."

"I'm fine," Maggie lied, forcing a smile before taking a prolonged sip of tea. "Work's just been busy, that's all." She didn't want to talk about New York, or what happened afterward.

Maggie's phone rumbled on the table and alerted her to an incoming call.

"Speaking of work," she said, answering before the third buzz. "Bishop."

Ashton scrunched his nose at the mention of his former boss.

"We have a situation," Bishop said, forgoing pleasantries.

Maggie sat up straight in her chair, unused to the panic that laced his words. "What is it?"

"Bomb threat. We have reason to believe it's legitimate."

"Where?" she asked, a pit of dread forming in her stomach.

"Trafalgar Square."

Maggie closed her eyes. The square would be filled

with civilians, out to enjoy the snow and gaze upon the twenty-foot tree, gifted by the Norwegians every year in thanks to the British for their help during the Second World War. "I can be there in less than ten minutes."

"Hurry," Bishop urged. "The bomb squad is on their way, but they were called out to another incident in Wembley."

"I'll call you when I get there." Maggie hung up and grabbed her coat.

"What's wrong?" Ashton asked, standing up as she fumbled with the jacket sleeves.

"We've got a situation," Maggie said, already calculating the quickest route to the square. "I have to go."

Leaving Ashton, Maggie barged out the door and took off at a run.

"Wait," Ashton yelled, following behind her. His long legs caught up to her in seconds.

"What are you doing?" Maggie quickened her pace, glad she'd chosen to wear boots for their coffee date.

Ashton steadied his pace to match hers. "I'm coming with you."

Maggie pressed her lips into a thin line. She didn't have time to argue. Together, they charged south-east down Regent Street, feet sloshing in the wet snow, grimy from a day's worth of travelers. The slush was a horrible mix of gray and brown along the edge of the pavement, shoved to the sides of the road in mounds to clear the way for traffic.

Ashton zipped his jacket up as he ran, snow dusting his jet-black hair. "Brief me."

Grit crunched under their boots as they crossed the road and continued onto Coventry Street, weaving through the crowded afternoon traffic.

"Bomb," Maggie said between puffs, her hot breaths like bursts of smoke. "Trafalgar Square."

"Fuck," Ashton hissed, picking up his pace. Maggie matched him, taking a right to remain on Coventry Street.

Bargain shoppers laden with overstuffed bags hobbled along the pavement, careful to avoid any underlying sheets of ice below the layer of snow. The soles of Maggie's sensible boots kept her steady as they sprinted through the shoppers, careful not to collide into them in an explosion of half-priced clothes and frivolous electronic goods.

Sweat trickled down Maggie's back as her body settled into the rhythmic surge of running. Counting the time in her head, she estimated a total of six minutes had passed before they reached the corner of Coventry Street and turned left into Pall Mall.

Traffic was congested, the never-ending lines of London vehicles especially thick from the added holiday tourists. The cars inched close to the backs of their neighbors, honking and waving frustrated fists at drivers who wouldn't allow them to merge in from Cockspur Street.

Maggie's heart sank as she and Ashton turned the bend and caught sight of Trafalgar Square.

Nelson's Column rose high above the crowded square,

the granite statue of the admiral looking down upon the mass of people. Majestic bronze lions languished on their stone pedestals at the column's base, and Maggie fought the urge to roar to the crowd, to warn them to run and get as far away from danger as possible.

Biting down on her lip, Maggie refrained. Alerting everyone would only worsen the situation, causing panic and mayhem as everyone tried to run to safety, pushing and shoving as the animalistic instinct to survive kicked in and ruled over all else.

"Where is it planted?" Ashton asked, hands on his knees.

Maggie ran a hand through her hair and looked around. "I don't know. Bishop never said."

Which meant he didn't know. The bomb could be anywhere.

"Let's split up." She pointed to the National Gallery with its steps and stone pillars, crowned with a dome on the roof. In the corner, St. Martin-in-the-Fields church sent a foreboding shiver down Maggie's spine. She wasn't the praying type, but they could use all the help they could get. "You take the north side. I'll take the south."

Ashton nodded, jaw set and eyes hard as he headed into the crowd and disappeared. Maggie wasted no time and rushed towards the nearest of the two fountains. Pigeons, rotund from the offerings of tourists, cawed and flapped away as Maggie stormed through their pecking grounds.

Scanning the area, Maggie searched for anything out of the ordinary. An abandoned bag. A suspicious looking man wearing a stuffed jacket to hide his suicide vest.

Nothing.

There was nothing at the other fountain, either. A well of panic rose within Maggie. Her palms grew clammy, and her head thumped as she rushed to think of where the would-be-bombers might place the device.

Somewhere that provided maximum exposure.

Somewhere that could do the most damage.

Big Ben chimed in the background, visible in the distance through Whitehall, the road that connected Trafalgar to Parliament Square. The bell rang and reverberated through the city, bellowing like the horn of war.

A sign caught Maggie's attention. A red circle with a white center. A blue stripe across the middle. The sign for Charing Cross station.

The underground.

The bell rang for the second time. Maggie turned from the fountain and made for the entrance of the station. Bishop said the bomb was in Trafalgar Square, but it could very well be *under* them.

The ground vibrated, sending trills through Maggie's feet and up her legs. She turned back to stare at the square as her mind caught up to the sensation a split second before it happened.

Big Ben rang for the third and final time.

And chaos erupted.

A surge of energy pulsed through the square like a tidal wave and sent Maggie reeling. An earth-shattering boom thundered all around her.

Maggie landed hard on her back, the fall sucking the air from her lungs.

Debris rained over her like hailstones. A cloud of dust and crushed ruble enveloped the surroundings in a dense, opaque fog. It clung to the back of Maggie's throat as she struggled to breathe.

Ringing swarmed her muddled thoughts as pain rattled through her ruptured eardrums.

An acute stabbing sensation punctured her side, and she knew from experience that at least one of her ribs was broken.

After the echoes of the explosion faded, an eerie silence fell over the square. It couldn't have been more than a few moments, but it felt like forever as Maggie lay there on the cold, wet ground.

Then the screams came.

Guttural, primal screams laced with pure anguish.

Pushing herself into a seated position, Maggie forced her eyes open, forced herself to bear witness to the destruction she should have stopped. The horror she could have prevented. If she were quicker. Smarter. Better at her job.

The dust settled and revealed a world splattered in red, white, and gray.

Blood trickled over the upturned ground and seeped

into the snow. Bodies scattered the square, crumpled and broken. Squirming in agony, or not moving at all.

The explosion had spilled out into the road, causing a collision of vehicles down the whole right side of the square. Windows were shattered, and damaged horns blared from upturned cars.

"Mummy?" came a whimper.

Maggie followed the sound, and her eyes latched onto a small hand poking through a pile of rubble further into the heart of the square. Getting to her feet, she limped over to the mound on shaking legs and began to dig.

Chunks of uprooted ground were all over the place. Their rough surfaces scratched at Maggie's palms. She ignored the discomfort and continued removing pieces from the pile.

A woman's eye peeked through the mound, bloodshot and vacant. Maggie ignored the dead woman, led by the soft groans coming beside her body.

Shoving a heavy clump of debris to the side, Maggie gasped as the tiny frame of a boy, no older than four, came into view. He was buried from the waist down.

"Mummy?" the boy called again, barely a whisper this time.

Maggie clamped a hand over her mouth and held back the cry building behind her lips. Her eyes travelled to the dead woman and back to the woman's small son.

Moving more wreckage away from him, Maggie inched closer and wrapped her arms lightly around the little boy's upper half, the rest of him pinned under a large, unmovable cluster of rock. She couldn't move him. Couldn't risk dragging him out in case his spine was broken.

"Maggie?" An unmistakable Scottish brogue broke through the choir of confused hysteria.

"Ashton!" Maggie yelled, her bottom lip quivering at the sound of his voice.

"Mags." Ashton broke through the smog like a specter, a layer of dust coating his skin and clothes. He stumbled to her side, a red gash poking through his ripped trousers. "Are you hurt?"

"I'm fine," Maggie croaked, hoarse from coarse dust in the air. "You?"

Ashton stared down at the boy in her arms and didn't answer. He fell to his knees beside her.

"I want my mummy," mumbled the little boy, disoriented and eyelids heavy.

"Hey, hey. It's okay." Maggie blinked back tears and brushed the boy's angelic curls from his dirt-covered face. "You're going to be okay."

She shared a knowing look with Ashton, his image blurred as a track of tears ran down her grubby cheeks.

It didn't take long. Ashton sat by Maggie's side while she held the boy. He took his last, shallow breath and then was gone, his life ended before it even started.

Sirens wailed all around Trafalgar Square as Maggie bowed her head and wept.

Chapter 2

His name was Oliver Clark.

The little boy's face was one of dozens to appear on the news, including his mother, Anna. Most of the victims hadn't been identified and released to the public yet, but the death toll continued to rise as emergency services worked the scene.

Maggie leaned back against the wall of the elevator as it ascended to the fourth floor of the Unit headquarters. Bishop had called all available agents to an emergency meeting, an event so rare there hadn't been one since Maggie's recruitment.

The early call didn't bother Maggie. Since the explosion, she was lucky if she managed more than two hours of fitful sleep, little Oliver's face watching her every time she closed her eyes, his whimpers echoing through her head.

Her reflection stared back at her in the elevator's mirrored interior. Blond hair pulled back in a tight ponytail. Face make-up free and paler than usual, accompanied by dark rings under her light blue eyes. Cuts and scrapes grazed her vulpine features, reminding her how lucky she was to be alive.

The elevator cart jerked as it stopped, and Maggie hissed at the stabs of pain in her side. Some injuries were less obvious in the mirror. The doors pinged open. Maggie stepped into the hall and nearly crashed into a fellow agent.

Leon.

Maggie sucked in a breath and froze, her legs rooted to the ground. Her throat tightened, and before she could walk away and retreat into the elevator, he turned around.

"Maggie." Leon wrapped his strong arms around her in a fierce embrace. "Are you okay?"

It took every ounce of her training to keep from falling to pieces in his arms. To bury the hurt and fears instead of dumping them all over his shoulders. A part of her almost laughed at his question. She wasn't okay. Hadn't been for a while now.

The familiar, masculine scent of him mixed with his woody aftershave and the mint-infused soap he always used. Maggie inhaled it like air and tried to keep a lid on the emotions bubbling inside her.

"I've been trying to call you," he said, still holding her, longer than a colleague should. A few of the agents waiting in the lobby eyed them, but Maggie didn't care. She held on, too, resting her forehead into his chest as her body tingled with the warmth of his touch. She'd been so cold lately. Cut off from everything. Frozen in her grief.

"I know." Maggie couldn't say more without everything, all her secrets, spilling out. She'd been avoiding him since her miscarriage. She couldn't even imagine where that conversation would start. Or how.

"That message you left. You said you had something to tell me?" Leon broke his hold but stayed close, their bodies inches apart. "Something you didn't want to say over the phone?"

Warm, deep brown eyes studied her. His brow furrowed at what he saw, concern mapping his beautiful, rugged face.

Leon deserved to know. Yet if she told him about her loss, about *their* loss... No. She couldn't hurt him like that. A piece of her had shattered when the doctor delivered the bad news. Maggie wasn't sure it would ever heal. She couldn't do that to Leon.

"I–" she began, scrambling for something else to say.

"All right, people," Brice Bishop called, saving Maggie from having to say more.

Everyone waiting in the floor lobby turned to their boss and chief of the Unit. "Now that we're all here, let's get started."

"We'll talk later," Leon said, holding the door of Bishop's office open for her as they entered.

Maggie nodded and slipped inside, crossing to the back of the office and sitting next to her fellow agent, and one of the few other women on the team, Nina Crawford.

The aroma of bad instant coffee filled the crowded room, some of her colleagues bleary eyed with rumpled clothes, showing signs of jet lag.

"Bishop called some of us in from the field," Nina whispered when Maggie took in her less than pristine appearance. "I'd just landed in Frankfurt and had to jump on a flight straight back. The director made it clear this took precedence over everything else."

Maggie nudged her head to the door. "Speak of the devil."

Director General Helmsley entered the crowded room, impeccable in her black skirt suit and wearing a grim expression. A sharp bob of gray hair framed her face, and she regarded her agents with sharp eyes that missed nothing. "All right, enough chit chat."

Agents took the seats at the large conference table and the rest lined the back wall as the room fell quiet.

Bishop stood to the director's right hand side and clicked on the projector. Images of the disaster in Trafalgar Square appeared on the wide screen. Maggie averted her eyes and focused on the Unit leaders. She'd seen enough in person yesterday.

The director addressed her agents. "As most of you

know by now, at exactly three p.m. yesterday, we experienced one of the worst terrorist attacks since the bombings in 2005. A self-proclaimed branch of ISIS, known as the Acolytes of the Holy War, has already claimed it as their own."

"Where are they from?" asked Zayan Asad. Of all the agents present, he had the most experience in dealing with terrorist cells. Infiltration mostly. Deep, and dangerous, undercover work.

Helmsley's lips thinned. "Unfortunately, this group is home grown. Radicalized right here in London."

Bishop pressed the remote again and the ruined square was replaced with blueprints. "The terrorists planted explosives in the disused Jubilee Line. It runs under the square, passing directly beneath the destroyed fountain."

"Why Trafalgar Square, specifically?" another agent asked, studying the screen.

Bishop flicked to an image of the Charing Cross entrance south of the square. "We believe they were targeting the tube station."

"Charing Cross is regarded as the notional center of London," Nina said, thumbing through copies of the images and blueprints left on the conference table. "It's the point from which distances from London are measured."

"They hit us at our core," Leon said from across the table, his voice almost a growl. "Right in the heart of our city."

Maggie leaned back in her chair and crossed her arms. "These aren't some explosion-happy, unorganized terrorists. They put thought into their target, picking a place that sends a message, not just to Britain, but the whole world. The Acolytes used the square as a symbol. These people are coming at us, but from within."

"This video certainly backs your theory, Maggie." Bishop pressed another button on his remote, and the screen switched to a loading video. "The Acolytes posted this online an hour ago."

The video played and revealed a bearded man dressed in miscellaneous military gear. The Black Flag was pinned behind him as he spoke in Arabic, a language Maggie recognized but didn't speak. A dark glint shone in his eyes, matching the smug grin slashed across his face.

Bishop paused the clip. "This is Dabir Omar. He's been on Counter Terrorism's radar for a while, but they were unable to formally tie him to anything. This is the first time he's shown his hand. He's not saying anything we haven't heard before. Disbelievers. Infidels. We're going to destroy the West. The usual rhetoric of these groups. What we're more interested in, is this man."

Fast-forwarding Dabir's vehement speech, Bishop stopped when the camera shifted to include another figure in the frame. The boy was no older than eighteen. Baby faced, with a mop of dark hair and a dusting of fluff across his jaw, evidence of a failed attempt at growing a beard.

"Hakim Hasan," Bishop continued. "You might recognize the surname from his brother, Khalid, who was responsible for a previous attack in Belgium two years ago, killing ten civilians and himself. It appears Hakim is following in his brother's footsteps."

Director General Helmsley caught each of their gazes and paced as she spoke. "Like many vulnerable Muslim youths, Hakim and his brother were targeted by The Acolytes online. They manipulated them, twisting their world view with their jihadist ideologies and recruited them into their ranks. Now he's being used to recruit others."

Bishop hit play again, and they all watched the remainder of the clip.

"My name is Hakim Hasan," the boy said in a thick Birmingham accent. "This is my plea to those of you like me. To those who are sick and tired of being treated like dirt. Too long has the West viewed us as second-class citizens. They've led us down an unrighteous path, and we're suffering because of it."

Hakim was dressed in a trendy t-shirt and jeans, likely a deliberate move on Dabir's part to make him appear more relatable.

"It's not too late," Hakim continued in the recording. "You know what's right. You know we can't let them keep their foot on our necks. I was blind, like you are, too busy worrying about getting with girls and my plans for the weekend. But I see now. It's time for us to rise against our enemies. We will not stop. We will not falter. The Day of Judgement is coming, and you owe Allah your allegiance."

Hakim reached for the camera and peered down the lens. "Au revoir."

The video ended there, and Bishop turned off the projector.

"Au revoir," Zayan mirrored. "That's rather bold."

Leon huffed. "Reckless, more like."

"Do we think this is another decoy," Maggie asked. "Like the false bomb scare in Wembley?" She was sure Dabir and his group were behind that, too, sending the bomb squad on a detour to allow them to attack unimpeded.

Director Helmsley shook her head, still pacing the room with pent up rage. "I don't think so. If they can so boldly hint that France is their next target and still pull it off, it makes them appear more powerful. Untouchable."

"Not to mention the terror it's already instilled in the French people," Bishop added, sitting down at the head of the table. He sipped from a cup of what must be lukewarm tea by now and winced.

"Paris is the most likely location," Nina said. She and Maggie were both familiar with the city after being taught French by a zealous Parisian back in their training days.

"The French government seem to agree," Bishop said.

Leon tossed the copied documents he was reading over

on the table and sighed. "What are the French doing about it?"

"They're on high alert and preparing as best they can," Bishop reported, refilling his cup with warm tea from the large teapot in the middle of the table. "Police are making their rounds through their watch lists as we speak."

"I don't care what the French are doing," Helmsley snapped, yanking her chair out and sitting down. "This group is our problem. They originated here, and *we* will be the ones to end them."

"Most of you will be placed here," Bishop said, filling the director's empty cup and sliding it in front of her. "We can't rule out the possibility of a repeat attack. Even if The Acolytes have left for France, their actions could spark a string of copycats."

Maggie agreed. It wouldn't be the first time a slew of smaller attacks happened in the aftermath of a hit. It awoke courage in their sympathizers, emboldening some of them enough to act.

Agent Sana Jafri let out a frustrated groan from across the table. "We'll also need to watch out for a rise in hate crimes. Muslims face enough Islamophobia in this country without people like Dabir adding fuel to the fire. An attack this size puts a giant bullseye on anyone who even *looks* Muslim or Middle Eastern." Sana glared at the screen, where Hakim's face stood frozen where Bishop paused the video. "If we're not careful, a lot of innocent people will be hurt, and any progress we've made toward building community will be ruined."

"You're right, Agent Jafri." Tea sloshed from the director's cup as she slammed in on the table. "As such, I want half of you working the streets and the rest with the online analysts. If they've left any virtual tracks, I want to know about them. These bastards need to be weeded out, once and for all."

Bishop mopped the spilled tea with a napkin. "The French made it clear they don't need, or even *want,* our assistance and are confident in their ability to find the terrorists before they strike. Quite frankly, we're not. Which is why one of you will go and find them first."

"Once found, you will alert the French to their location, but *we* want Hakim," Director Helmsley said. "And we want him brought in alive."

Some of the other agents stirred in their seats.

"After what he and the rest of them did?" spat Nina.

The director regarded Nina from the corner of her eye, unused to being questioned. "It's vital that we understand exactly *how* The Acolytes recruited Hakim. We can't afford for this problem to continue. Once the target has been apprehended, we'll send a team to transport him to a secure location."

They all knew what that meant. Helmsley and the higher ups wanted their hands on Hakim, but that didn't mean the rest of the country would know about it. Like the Unit itself, their apprehension of Hakim would remain a secret. As would their methods to extract the information they required.

Sana Jafri stood from her chair. "I'll go."

Bishop shook his head. "Under any other circumstance, I would gladly send you, Agent Jafri. But not in this case."

Sana's hands curled into fists, her voice shaking in controlled rage. "Why not?"

"Whoever goes needs to be able to stay under the radar," said Zayan Asad, sharing a knowing look with Sana. "Given the high alert and resulting profiling from the French, you and I would stick out like sore thumbs."

Director General Helmsley nodded. "Precisely. Besides, I need you both to lead the teams on the ground here."

"Very well." Sana let out a weary sigh and sat back down.

"In that case, this one's mine," Maggie said.

Everyone turned their attention to her.

"You're sure?" Helmsley asked, her boss's stare boring into her as she regarded Maggie's request.

Maggie gripped the edge of the table so hard it hurt. If anyone was going on the assignment, it would be her. "Positive."

"Stay behind then, Agent Black." Helmsley pointed to the door. "The rest of you get moving. I expect results, and fast."

Leon nodded in grim understanding to Maggie before

he got up and left with the others. Some things were personal, no matter how detached you tried to be.

Maggie had a score to settle, and she would not fail. She was going to track down the Acolytes and bring in Hakim Hasan.

Chapter 3

29 December
Paris, France

Maggie arrived at Charles de Gaulle airport a little after midday. The flight from London was a quick hour and fifteen minutes over the English Channel, which didn't give Maggie much time to dive into the chunky paperback she bought before boarding.

A rental car waited for her in one of the large parking lots, a sleek yet nondescript Peugeot 208 GTi Sport in all black. It was an ideal model for some of the city's narrower streets, fast with incredible handling. Maggie tossed her suitcase in the trunk, turned the interior heating on high, and put the keys in the ignition.

With a quick check of her phone, Maggie was relieved to discover there hadn't been any new word from the Acolytes. No attacks in Paris or anywhere else in France.

Yet.

The Acolytes were in the city; Maggie could feel it in her bones. Terrorist groups of their sophistication had large networks of allies, and it was only a matter of time before they struck again. Right now, they'd be working behind the scenes, high off their success and preparing for their next hit. A hit she intended to stop.

Maggie gripped the steering wheel and focused on the road, trying to keep little Oliver at the back of her mind. The seatbelt dug into her side and she shifted in her seat, her broken ribs complaining with every move. Digging around in her bag with her free hand, she grabbed the painkillers she'd been taking ever since the attack and gulped down two tablets.

Going out on an assignment injured, especially one as important at this, was never the best idea, but Maggie wasn't concerned. She'd been in worse states before and managed to complete the job. She didn't make a habit of failing, and she wasn't about to start now. She'd find the Acolytes and stop them even if it killed her.

The twenty-mile drive into Paris took longer than normal, the winter weather invoking an air of caution in her fellow drivers, at least by European standards. Most of the vehicles sported at least a few dents and scratches. People who complained about London traffic clearly had never driven in Paris. Maggie had found herself in many a car chase, yet even she took extra care on the Parisian streets.

Following the A3 most of the way, Maggie finally made it to Paris-Centre. Merging from the autoroute and into Quai de Bercy, she headed north-west and turned left over the Pont de Bercy. The river Seine coursed beneath her as she crossed the bridge, and Maggie stole a look at the water, releasing a deep sigh.

Despite her reasons for being there, Paris never failed to impress her with its regal beauty. As she ventured through the city, passing familiar avenues and boulevards lined with snow-dusted trees, she drank in the winter wonderland around her. Wind swirled the falling snowflakes through the air like Paris was incased in a snow globe, the light and fluffy flakes kissing Maggie's windshield before the wipers brushed them away.

The weather couldn't dampen French spirits. Cafés lined their terraces with outdoor heaters, allowing customers to enjoy the view as they cupped their warm drinks in gloved hands and snuggled into thick coats and scarves. Maggie let down the window as she passed and inhaled the aroma of rich coffee and buttery pastry that made her mouth water.

It took thirty minutes to cross the city's icy streets, but it was all worth it as she turned right from Avenue de

Suffren onto Quai Branly. The most famous sight in France had peeked out at her on the way, through gaps in apartment buildings and city parks, but seeing it up close was another thing entirely.

Standing proud and elegant, the Eiffel Tower sprouted from the ground on four legs and reached into the sky in a spear of wrought iron lattice. Snow rested over the metal, covering the outer parts of the tower in a frosted layer of white that glittered like diamonds when the sun touched it. Maggie craned her neck to take it all in, the tip just visible from inside her car.

Reluctant to tear her gaze away, Maggie focused on the road and slowed down to allow groups of excited tourists to scamper across the street. Maggie had visited the city more times than she could count, but the almost magical spark Paris stirred within her never changed.

The Pont d'Iena was guarded at each end by two valiant stone warriors and their noble steeds. Maggie crossed the Seine once more over the bridge and entered Trocadero, the sixteenth of twenty neighborhoods, or *arrondissements*, that Paris was split into.

Checking the address again on her phone, Maggie travelled down Avenue de President Kennedy, a lavish residential street that lined the Seine, and parked outside the building. Getting out the car, Maggie spun around and noted the Eiffel tower a mere hop, skip, and a jump away across the river. She dialed her friend's number and collected her suitcase from the trunk while it rang.

"Mags," Ashton answered, his hearty Glaswegian accent seeming out of place as she wheeled her luggage down the French street.

"You know," she said, using her shoulder to hold the phone while she punched in the passcode to enter the apartment building's lobby, "when you told me I could stay at your place, you failed to mention that it was on one of the most expensive streets in the city."

The Parisian apartment was one of Ashton's newer acquisitions, and she had yet to see it.

"Not expensive for me," Ashton chirped. "I won it in a poker game."

Maggie laughed and shook her head. "But you're terrible at poker."

Ashton was too much of a risk taker to play such a strategic game. He couldn't count cards the way he did at the blackjack tables on their first official mission as agents, and he had a habit of recklessly calling his rival players' bluffs every hand.

"Not when I cheat," Ashton said, and Maggie envisioned that mischievous smirk of his.

She waved at the concierge behind the front desk and entered the elevator to the sixth floor. "I can't win ten quid on the lottery, and you manage to finagle an entire apartment from someone."

"They were very drunk," Ashton explained.

"Clearly."

The elevator pinged, and the doors opened out into a

little hallway with a fire exit and one door. The apartment took up the entire floor, leading Maggie to estimate that Ashton's sleight of hand had won him at least a couple million euros in property.

"Right, I've got to go," Ashton said. "Talk to you soon."

Maggie said her goodbyes and slid the key into the lock. Before she could turn it however, the knob twisted of its own accord and the door opened from the inside.

"Bonjour madame," Ashton said, wiggling his eyebrows at her.

"Ashton?" Maggie stepped inside and closed the door behind her, lowering her voice on instinct. "What are you doing here?"

Ashton pulled her into a hug, wrapping his tattoo-covered arms tightly around her frame and planting a kiss on her forehead. "I've got some business to attend to."

Maggie eyed his sweatpants and bare feet. "Liar."

"Awright," Ashton admitted, taking Maggie's case and leading her into the main living area. "I thought I'd tag along. We've no had a wee trip away in ages."

Maggie being in Paris was hardly a 'wee trip.' Far from it. "You can't be here. If the Unit find out you're with me–"

Ashton cut her off with a wave his arm. "Relax, Mags. Those bunch of stiffs in London have enough to deal with as it is without checking to make sure their favorite agent isn't running around with a known traitor."

He shot her a wink at that last remark, but Maggie

caught the bitter tinge in the last word. Back when Ashton left the Unit, all agents were ordered not to associate with him. Maggie had made sure to keep their continued friendship a secret, especially from Bishop and Leon, who took Ashton's departure as a personal insult.

"Ashton–"

"Please," he replied, all hint of playfulness leaving his face. "I want to help. Those fuckers need to be taken down."

Maggie had never been able to blame Ashton for leaving like the others in the Unit had. Life as an agent required a certain type of personality, and though Ashton was more than qualified in intellect and skill level, his free-spirited nature didn't suit the job. It never had, even back in training.

He met her gaze with troubled, deep blue eyes. "I canny stop thinking about that wee boy."

It was easy to view Ashton as some wild playboy running around and stealing from the world's richest criminals, but Maggie knew him better than most. Back in training, he was like a little brother to her, younger than the rest and misunderstood. Deep down, he had a big heart and was always there for her when she needed him.

Maggie sighed and took off her jacket. "Okay, but we do this by the book."

Ashton saluted her. "Yes, boss."

Maggie ignored him and looked around. "Who did you

win this from, the queen?" The living room alone was the size of her entire apartment back in London.

Ashton followed her with his hands in his pockets. "Some tycoon from Dubai. From what I hear, he hadn't even stayed here once."

Like all his homes, Ashton had furnished the place with impeccable taste, no doubt with the help of some overpriced interior designer. It was minimal, making the most of the immense space, yet luxurious, with suede couches, marble flooring, and a large renaissance art piece hanging above a roaring fireplace. Overall, he'd kept it very French, which was just as well considering he had one of the best views in the city.

Maggie shook her head. If she had a place like this, she would never leave. "Idiot. He deserved to have it taken from him if he wasn't using all this."

"Agreed," Ashton said, putting an arm over her shoulders. "Want the grand tour?"

"Maybe later. Right now, I need to get out there and track down those bastards."

Maggie couldn't afford to waste any time. Not when the Acolytes were out there somewhere getting ready to deal out more devastation.

She walked over to the glass door which lead out to the full-length balcony. Boats coasted down the Seine, filled with unsuspecting tourists out exploring for the day. Beyond the Eiffel Tower, the rest of the city stretched out before her with rooftops crowned in snow. In a few hours, the sun would set and lights would twinkle to life, illuminating the horizon like a constellation of stars.

Amid all the beauty, a gray cloud still loomed over Maggie's head. The city she loved wasn't safe, and neither were the people who called it home.

"What's the plan?" Ashton asked, standing next to her.

Maggie nudged him with her elbow, trying to lighten the situation. "Careful, Ash. You're starting to sound like you miss your old agent days."

Ashton snorted. "Aye right. I'll crack the jokes, Mags."

"We're going to need supplies." Maggie wasn't taking any chances on this one. If the Acolytes learned she and Ashton were after them, the mission could turn deadly in a heartbeat.

Ashton took her hand and led her into the master bedroom. A row of fitted wardrobes were installed against one wall, but there weren't just clothes inside them. Ashton opened the center doors and revealed an arsenal fit for a small revolution.

"Will these do?" he asked.

Maggie ran her eyes along the rows of knives, guns, communication devices, night vision binoculars, grenades, and if she was right, blocks of packed explosives stacked like bricks in the corner. Ashton had better hope he never had a fire.

"You had all this lying around?" Maggie asked.

Ashton shrugged. "You keep a fridge full of food, the

bar filled with drinks, and your secret stash of weaponry loaded and ready to go. It's called being a good host."

The packed blocks caught Maggie's eye again and the cogs turned in her mind. There was no way the Acolytes could have transported explosives with them. Not in the volume needed to carry out another attack like Charing Cross. They'd need to restock, and the number of vendors who supplied that level of power in Paris would be a short list indeed.

Maggie turned to Ashton, who had a habit of blowing things up. "If you needed to get your hands on the kind of explosives the Acolytes use, who would you go to?"

It didn't take Ashton long to answer.

"Gabrielle Legrand."

Chapter 4

Maggie tossed the keys for her rental to the valet and took in their meeting place. Situated in Avenue Montaigne, Gabrielle Legrand's restaurant shared an exclusive address with Paris's most high-end and, in Maggie's opinion, absurdly overpriced designers. The Palais de Legrand sat nestled between Dior a few doors down at one end, and Ashton's favorite, Louis Vuitton, at the other.

"Nice, isn't it?" Ashton asked, right at home amid the extravagance. He wore a sleek dinner jacket under his tan cashmere coat, and his polished leather loafers winked up at her.

Maggie regarded the fine establishment with a raised eyebrow. "Restaurants and explosives. Bit of an odd mix in business ventures."

"Yes," Ashton said, holding the front door open for her,

"but places like these are ideal for laundering black-market money."

Stepping inside, Maggie was met with the soft melodies of a grand piano and a delicious waft from the kitchen that made her mouth water.

The maître d' was upon them immediately with a dulcet tone and warm smile. "Monsieur Price, so nice to see you. And Mademoiselle, how beautiful you look. May I take your coats?"

Maggie obliged and shrugged out of her winter coat. Ashton hadn't lied when he said Gabrielle's place was up-market. She was glad she took his advice and wore the royal blue cigarette trousers and matching tailored jacket.

Storing their coats away, the maître d' returned. "Please come with me, Madame Legrand is waiting."

He led them through the restaurant, avoiding the center floor where most of the diners sat. The décor was pristine and white, embellished with mirrored glass and crystals that sparkled in the light. The chairs were plush and high-backed, the glassware and crockery as fine and elegant as the food on the plates.

A small set of stairs brought them to a raised section with private booths that overlooked the rest of the restaurant. A woman sat alone in one of the finer booths and watched them approach. In front of her, a wide-necked man stood sentry, dressed in a well-fitted suit that did little to hide the bulging muscles of his arms and legs.

Maggie noted the surrounding tables were left empty, most likely to avoid any prying ears.

"Gabrielle, my dear," Ashton called, walking straight past the brute without so much as a nod and heading straight for their host.

"Ashton," Gabrielle replied, standing from her seat to air-kiss both of his cheeks. Her eyes never left Maggie as she did so, sizing her up with an unreadable expression. Maggie merely stared back, thanking the maître d' as he left them to their discussion.

"This is my friend, Eva," Ashton said, using one of Maggie's aliases. While not going full undercover for the meeting, they both thought it prudent to avoid using her real name.

Maggie made the first move and held out her hand to the older woman. "Bonjour."

"Hello," Gabrielle replied, accepting her hand with a smile that didn't reach her sharp gray eyes. They all sat around the booth, Ashton taking a seat right next to Gabrielle as Maggie took her place across from them.

Gabrielle Legrand was striking. In her early forties, her long raven hair fell in waves down the back of her slender frame, her high cheekbones and scarlet lips predominant features on her sculpted face. Like Maggie's alias Eva, Gabrielle could have been a model in her younger years, had she not decided to enter a far more nefarious profession.

"What happened to Henry?" Ashton enquired, nodding back to the grim looking guard.

Gabrielle let out an exaggerated sigh and placed a hand on Ashton's leg. "He disappointed me."

Maggie had the distinct impression that Henry was more than off the payroll.

"You can't find good staff these days," Ashton agreed, allowing the woman's hand to remain on his leg, even though his tastes didn't lean that way. Flirting was one of his specialties.

"You have a lovely restaurant," Maggie said in perfect French.

"You must try the house wine," Gabrielle replied. "From my own vineyard." She clicked her fingers and a sommelier bustled up the stairs. He served each of them a glass of red and bowed before leaving.

"Superbe," Maggie said, meaning it. The wine was dry and had subtle fruity notes that tickled her taste buds on the way down. She took another sip before placing it on the table, keen to keep a clear head. They hadn't come for drinks, and Maggie was determined to learn who supplied the Acolytes.

Gabrielle leaned back and swirled her glass, the red wine like blood in her hands. "So, what brings you both to me? It's not often I have the pleasure of your company," she said to Ashton, almost accusingly.

Ashton shot her a grin and waited until her lips tugged

up before responding. "You know me, all work and no play."

Both Maggie and Gabrielle scoffed at that.

"Well, it's not a social visit this time, I'm afraid."

"A pity," Gabrielle responded, though she seemed far from surprised.

Maggie bit her tongue and allowed Ashton to start things off. It was his contact after all. "I'm in need of some information regarding a particular group of people."

Gabrielle cocked her head to the side, allowing her hair to drape over her shoulder. "And what makes you think I can help you?"

Ashton kept it casual. He leaned back in his chair and rested an arm over the back of the seat while he enjoyed the crimson wine. "These people would have been looking to shop in your particular niche of the market."

Gabrielle tutted at him, her eyes alight with interest. Whether it was over the topic of discussion or Ashton himself, Maggie couldn't quite decipher. "You know I can't discuss my clients. You wouldn't want me telling every handsome man who walked in here about the items you've acquired from me, would you?"

Ashton smirked. "Depends on how handsome."

Gabrielle let out a high-pitched laugh and leaned into him. She was very hands on, even for a Frenchwoman, and Maggie suppressed the urge to yank her away from her friend.

"They call themselves the Acolytes of the Holy War,"

Ashton continued. "You might have seen them on the news recently?"

Gabrielle sipped her wine and quickly sobered. "Terrible business in London. Just terrible."

"I hear they're in Paris now," Maggie added, watching Gabrielle's face for any hint of recognition.

Gabrielle remained calm and relaxed as she turned her attention to Maggie, at home on her own turf. "So everyone seems to think."

"But not you?" Ashton asked, observing her too.

Gabrielle shrugged her small shoulders, bare from the strapless red dress that clung to her lithe figure. "I wouldn't know one way or the other."

"They didn't approach you?"

Their host bristled. "Come now, Ashton. People like them know there's no point in asking me for anything. Even those such as you and I must have some morals. There is a firm line I won't cross." Gabrielle flourished her point with a swipe across the air.

"Aye, you're right there." Ashton tossed back the rest of his wine, face etched in annoyance as he refilled his glass from the bottle the sommelier left. "But someone must be in bed with them."

It seemed Maggie wasn't the only one accustomed to Ashton's care-free demeanor. "I am curious," Gabrielle said, lowering her voice. "Why you of all people is interested in this group?"

"It's not good for business, having people on edge.

Everyone watching their backs. How is a man like me supposed to make a dishonest living with bloody terrorists running amok?"

Gabrielle nodded and patted his arm, keeping her jeweled hand there. "I'm sorry I couldn't be of more help to you. You'll both stay for lunch though, yes? I'll have my head chef prepare us something exquisite."

"As long as you're in the sharing mood when it comes to information on your competitors," Ashton said, the mischief back in his tone.

A sly smile twitched across Gabrielle's face, illuminating the cunning behind the woman's beauty. "If you intend to make business difficult for them, then you have my full disclosure on that front."

Ashton clinked his glass with hers. "Deal."

"Excellent." Gabrielle brightened and got up from the booth. "I'll go and have a word with the chef on the way to the little girls' room. Please excuse me."

"Well, if she didn't give the Acolytes what they need, that leaves only two more leads," Ashton said after Gabrielle left with her bodyguard in tow. "Fingers crossed she can tell us more about them."

Maggie ran a finger around the rim of her glass, staring at Gabrielle's empty seat.

"What?" Ashton asked, knowing her well enough to spot when her mind was running.

"I'll be right back." Maggie got up and took her clutch bag with her. "Nature calls."

Following Gabrielle's path, Maggie walked past the rest of the diners and through a set of doors. Signs for the bathrooms navigated Maggie past the entrance for the kitchens and down a wide set of stairs. The old building retained its original moldings which encompassed the high ceilings. The thick stone walls, covered with a golden filigree wallpaper, blocked out the noise from the floor above.

Gabrielle's guard stood outside one of three doors, indicating which one was the ladies' room. Maggie made to enter, but the big man's wide frame blocked the door. "Excuse me. I need to use the bathroom."

The brute shook his head.

"This is ridiculous," Maggie went off, speaking in rapid French as she opened her clutch. "Is this how your boss expects you to treat her guests? I expected more from a place that charges thirty euros for a bowl of soup. Just you wait until I get home. I'm leaving a scathing review of this restaurant on every website I can think of."

Maggie checked over her shoulder to make sure no one was wandering down the stairs, then snatched the Taser out her bag. She aimed it at the man's thick neck and clamped her thumb on the button.

Electricity crackled out the device and hit the body-guard with enough volts to render him useless.

Using the momentum of his fall, Maggie shoved the convulsing man, pushing him past the men's toilet and into the third door. It swung open to reveal a closet filed with cleaning supplies and piles of spare napkins and tablecloths.

The volts continued to course through the bodyguard, and Maggie waited until a wet patch expanded across the center of his gray trousers before relenting. He slid down the wall, unconscious and, thanks to Maggie, soon to be unemployed.

Maggie popped the Taser back in her bag and returned to the hallway. With no one guarding the bathroom anymore, she slipped inside and locked the door behind her. Only one stall was occupied, and Maggie busied herself by the sink as she waited, reapplying her lipstick.

The toilet flushed and Gabrielle came out, seeming more than a little annoyed to find Maggie there. She frowned at the door, no doubt internally cursing her bodyguard, before plastering on that fake smile of hers.

Her heels clicked on the tiled floor, and she stopped to wash her hands. "It's not like Ashton to bring along friends. Have you been seeing him long?"

Maggie smacked her lips and dropped the lipstick into her bag before snapping it closed. "I don't have time for this."

Gabrielle blinked. "Excuse me?"

"Drop the bullshit, Gabrielle," Maggie said, crossing her arms. "When did the Acolytes come to you?"

"I already told Ashton–" Legrand began.

"Yes, yes, you're a convincing liar," Maggie interrupted, stepping towards her with each word. "Unfortunately for you, I'm better, and I know you're not telling the truth."

Gabrielle stepped back until she was pressed against the wall. She made to bite back, but Maggie held up a finger.

"We can do this the easy way or the hard way. Your guard didn't seem to like the hard way, but I must admit it was nice to let off some steam."

"You're crazy," Gabrielle said, unable to mask the alarm behind her eyes. She made to leave, but Maggie blocked her path.

"I'll give you one last chance to tell me everything you know about the Acolytes before I force it out of you."

"I'm leaving, and I want you out of my restaurant. Claude!" Gabrielle barged forward, calling for her bodyguard as she tried to shove past Maggie.

Maggie caught Gabrielle's hand and gave it a vicious twist. "Claude's sleeping right now, but I promise I'll keep you awake for every painful minute."

Gabrielle groaned, but to her credit she refrained from screaming. Her jaw clenched in anger, but Maggie saw the fear there, too, and she held her with ease.

"This could have gone a lot easier," Maggie said. She wasn't the tallest, but she had a few inches on the petite woman, and she made the most of it.

Gabrielle's lips curled with venom, and she spat in Maggie's face.

Maggie had tried to keep her cool, pushing down the rage that lingered just under the surface. Oliver Clark's face flashed in her mind. The cries of pain and horror echoed in her ears. The acrid smell of used explosives, blood, and destruction that surrounded the square in the aftermath of the explosion filled her nostrils.

She wiped the spittle off her cheek and took a deep, shaking breath.

Then she snapped.

Maggie dragged Gabrielle by the wrist, holding her in a painful lock that would send sharp stabs up her arm. Cold water poured from the faucet while Maggie jammed in the plug with her free hand and waited for the levels to rise.

"I've met some sick people in my life," Maggie said as Gabrielle squirmed in her hold, "but for the life of me, I don't understand how you can deal with monsters like them. They plan to blow up your own city for god's sake."

"Let me go," Gabrielle cried, the pain intensifying in her wrist each time she tried to pull back.

Maggie relished the panic in Gabrielle's eyes. The shuddering of her body as she stared at the filling sink.

"I was there, in the London bombing," Maggie said in Gabrielle's ear. "A toddler died in my arms. An innocent little boy who didn't deserve to suffer like that. None of them did."

Maggie grabbed the back of Gabrielle's head and dunked her under the water.

Gabrielle fought against her hold, trying to launch her head back and out of the water, but Maggie held steadfast. Water sloshed over the sink as Legrand thrashed around, glistening over the gleaming white tiles.

"Please," Gabrielle rasped when Maggie yanked her hair and pulled her head out of the water.

"You want more? Okay." Maggie forced her back under, Gabrielle's pleading nothing but gurgles and air bubbles.

People like Gabrielle were the scum of the earth, profiting from people's terror. They supplied groups like the Acolytes the tools they needed without the slightest thought or concern for the victims. As long as the price was right. As long as they were able to fill their pockets.

Maggie let Gabrielle up again, holding on longer this time. Gabrielle gasped for air, her makeup running down her face. "I don't know anything," she yelled between coughs of water that dripped down her chin. Her dressed was soaked, the red deepening to the color of all the blood that would be spilled if the Acolytes attacked again.

"Lies!" Maggie yelled, shoving her back down as the tap kept on running to replenish the sink. Water soaked into the sleeves of her jacket and ran up the arms, Gabrielle's scratching fingers sliding off the slick fabric.

The noises were horrible, but nothing compared to the whimpers of little Oliver. His unanswered calls to his mother. He was dead, and Gabrielle was in business with the people responsible. She didn't deserve mercy.

"Maggie? Are you in there?" Ashton banged his fist against the door.

Maggie snapped her head towards his voice and the locked door. Gabrielle wriggled in her arms and managed to raise her head out the sink amid the distraction.

"Help!" Gabrielle cried.

A bang clattered against the door, and it thrashed open on the second hit as Ashton kicked it in, busting the lock.

"What are you doing?" he called, running through the puddles of water to Maggie.

"She gave them the explosives," Maggie said, not letting Gabrielle go. "I know it."

"I don't know what she's talking about," Gabrielle pleaded. "Ashton, get her off me."

Maggie cut Gabrielle off and submerged her head again.

"Maggie!"

"She's in on this," she said above the splashing.

Ashton came behind Maggie and pried her fingers from Gabrielle's hair. "If she is, she's not going to be any use to us dead."

Gabrielle came back up, coughing water from her lungs. Maggie shoved her to the floor, and Legrand slid across the wet tiles, landing with a hard slap.

"I'll deal with her," Ashton warned, as Maggie stood panting.

"Keep her away from me," Gabrielle cried, whimpering from behind the mop of sodden hair that curtained her face.

Ashton walked over to Gabrielle and squatted down next to her. He tucked some of her hair behind her ear and pointed over to Maggie. "I'd start talking if I were you. My friend here seems to believe you supplied these Acolytes, and I don't know what will happen if I let her at you again."

"All right." Gabrielle's shoulders slumped in defeat, her fingers tremoring as she clutched her neck. "I did it. I gave them what they wanted."

Maggie stepped forward, balling her fists. "You piece of shit!"

Gabrielle backed away and quivered against the wall as Ashton interjected and held Maggie back.

"How much?" Maggie demanded. How much did the lives of innocent people go for these days?

"Enough." Gabrielle's voice cracked as fear-ridden tears ran mascara tracks down each side of her face.

"For what?" Maggie asked, refraining from hoisting Ashton off her and lunging for Gabrielle. "An attack like London?"

Gabrielle's bottom lip quivered. "Bigger."

Ashton, making sure Maggie stayed where she was, returned to Gabrielle and muttered about his new shoes getting wet. "When did you meet with the Acolytes?"

"Everything was done over the phone," Gabrielle

cried, the words tumbling out her mouth. "I spoke with their leader, Dabir, yesterday."

"And where are the explosives now?"

"They wanted them delivered. I sent them this morning."

Ashton brought out his phone from inside his dinner jacket. "I'm going to need an address."

Maggie filed away the address as Gabrielle filled them in, her sights already turning to Dabir and his soldiers. There was a special place in hell for the Gabrielle's of the world, but she was just a supplier. The real threat was still out there, and now they were armed.

Ashton straightened his jacket and motioned for Maggie to leave with him. They had the address. They needed to get going. Maggie collected her clutch and opened it again, stalking towards Gabrielle.

"Wait," she stammered, trying to crawl away from Maggie. "What are you doing? I told you what you wanted to know."

"Don't worry. You won't have to sit here long." Maggie took out the handcuffs and dragged Gabrielle to the nearby radiator. She swung the cuffs around the metal pipe and secured both of Gabrielle's wrists, locking her in place and making sure to fit the bracelets extra tight. "The police will come and pick you up soon."

Maggie would keep the location of the Acolytes a secret from the French until she had Hakim in custody, but that didn't mean she needed to keep them in the dark about Gabrielle. "I hope you can take better care of your-self in prison. Even the worst of criminals in there won't take too kindly to terrorist enablers."

Spinning on her heels, Maggie made for the door.

"But –"

Maggie shushed Gabrielle and glanced at her over her shoulder. "Oh, and don't give the police that address. I'd hate to have to repay you a visit."

Chapter 5

Beyond the City of Lights lay suburban areas the French refer to as *banlieues*. Many of these communities reminded Maggie of the council estates back home. Run down, underfunded, and tossed from the minds of the more fortunate like yesterday's trash.

"It's like night and day," Maggie said to Ashton as they drove through Saint-Denis, one of the more notorious banlieues on the outskirts of Paris. A mere thirty minutes away by train, it lay north of the city and was a far cry from Ashton's fancy French neighborhood.

"It's worse than Easterhouse," Ashton replied, sitting in the passenger seat of their rental car. While wealthy now, Ashton hadn't come from money, and from the stories he'd told Maggie, he grew up in a place not unlike this one outside of Glasgow.

Their car had earned more than a few envious and suspicious glances from those they passed. Ideally, Maggie would have acquired a more fitting vehicle to blend in, but they were short on time now that the Acolytes had what they needed from Gabrielle Legrand.

Concrete towers loomed over them as they snaked through uneven roads, bleak and industrial looking. The gray apartment towers housed some of the most impoverished people in the area, a lot of them immigrants from war-torn places like Syria. Weeds grew between the cracked tarmac of the carparks below, the surrounding playparks desolate and filled with loitering drug dealers instead of happy children on swings.

Maggie had spent time in similar places during her youth. Seeking shelter in abandoned squats and in the stairwells of high-rise flats to stay off the cold, rainy streets. Occasionally, someone would take pity on her and allow her sleep on their couch, but she never overstayed her welcome. Certain people expected things in return, things she would not give them.

Maggie brushed the thoughts of her past away and focused on the present. According to the Sat-Nav installed in the car, the address Gabrielle gave them was around the corner.

"Saint-Denis," Ashton said as Maggie parked the car and killed the engine. "The name rings a bell."

"It made the news during the 2015 attacks," Maggie said. Paris was no stranger to terrorist activity, and the slew of attacks that occurred on the thirteenth of November that year were some of the worst to ever hit the city. "Abdelhamid Abaaoud was killed here in a raid after orchestrating the deaths of one-hundred-and-thirty people." Not to mention the hundreds of people injured.

"Let's hope we can find this Dabir before he pulls off something similar," Ashton said, getting out the car and collecting their supplies from the trunk.

A cold shiver ran through Maggie that had nothing to do with the winter weather. She locked the car as they left, knowing it would do little to prevent would-be thieves from taking off with it, but a stolen car was the least of their worries at the moment.

The Acolytes were shacked up in an abandoned electronics store along a row of unused shops. Battered shutters covered most of the shopfronts, French and Arabic graffiti scrawled across them and the crumbling brick walls.

Maggie and Ashton circled the building to avoid being seen, stopping at intervals to plant surveillance cameras, and slipped into the building across the street from the back entrance. No one was there. The building was once a two-story house and had suffered a fire some years back from the state of it. Black, charred burn marks covered the walls, the furniture and appliances reduced to pieces of burned wreckage and melted plastic.

They set up their watch, positioning themselves near

the window of the upstairs bedroom to give them the best view of the electronics store.

Ashton tinkered with the settings of the cameras on his computer while Maggie placed a final one on the windowsill. They were too close to risk blowing their cover by using binoculars. If spotted, the Acolytes would either evacuate or come to take them out, and Maggie couldn't be sure how many of Dabir's men lay inside. Maggie was sure of one thing though: the terrorists would be armed and unafraid to pull the trigger.

"Are we going to talk about what happened back at the restaurant?" Ashton asked, keeping his eyes on the camera feeds playing on his laptop. The other cameras they planted showed the store at different angles, front and back. If anyone entered or left, they'd know about it.

"What's to talk about?" Maggie asked, hunkering down for what could be a long wait.

"It's not like you to lose your cool like that."

Maggie pulled her gun from her waistband and checked it over, giving her something to focus on other than Ashton, the friend who always saw too much. "Gabrielle deserved it."

"I'm not going to argue with you there, but you nearly drowned her. Not the best move when you knew she had intel we desperately needed."

Maggie sat the gun on her lap and closed her eyes. "This whole thing has me on edge."

"You've faced this kind of thing before," Ashton noted, stretching out his long legs.

"Yes, but this isn't like those other times. I've seen plenty of people die, and a lot of them by my hand at that. But Oliver–" Maggie cut herself off, hating the tremor in her voice. She gave herself a shake and allowed the uncomfortable sadness to turn into rage. Rage, she could handle. "I can't get my head around wanting to blow up innocent people. Especially from those like Hakim. He's British for god's sake."

Ashton sighed. "I don't think we'll ever understand what it's like for some of these kids. To be born British yet feeling like they don't belong. Like they're not welcome in their own country. A lot of white people don't exactly treat them like equals. Do you think kids like Hakim would turn to extremists if they weren't so ostracized?"

Maggie balked at the note of sympathy in Ashton's voice and sat up. "That doesn't mean they should join a fucking terrorist group and destroy the lives of others."

Ashton held up his hands. "Look, I'm not saying it excuses their actions, but they're not signing up to these groups because their life is fine and dandy."

"Nobody's life is perfect," Maggie countered, scrunching her face. "That's not an excuse."

"I'm not saying it is," Ashton replied, his temper rising to match her own. "But imagine growing up and seeing people like you demonized on the news every day. You're never the hero in any of the movies or TV shows you watch. You're always a villain. Just like you're the real-life villain in the eyes of half your neighbors, who equate being Muslim to being a terrorist. And it's not just the media. Politician's sprout that shite, too, knowing it'll get them votes."

"Ashton—"

"Look at Brexit! Look at all those hate-fueled debates over immigration. And don't even get me started on the rise in hate crimes. Britain is rife with Islamophobia, and until we address that, it'll only add to this problem."

Maggie made to retaliate but found she couldn't. It wasn't often Ashton got heated over something, but his cheeks had flushed red and his brows furrowed. She leaned back against the wall and considered his points. "I've never really thought of it like that." In truth, she'd never really thought much about it at all.

"Imagine how alienated these kids must feel, how hopeless to change their fate when everyone already thinks they're a terrorist anyway. Society pushes them down so hard they believe their best option is to join people like Dabir," Ashton continued. "These groups know how alone these kids feel. They know how lost, and vulnerable, and angry they are, and they take advantage of that to radicalize them."

Maggie's initial reaction was to disregard what her friend was saying. To fight against any attempt at humanizing the same people who murdered Oliver and the other innocents at Trafalgar Square. Yet his words mirrored

Director General Helmsley's. When the director said the Acolytes were home grown, maybe this is what she meant. That Britain had broken them down and left them vulnerable to Dabir's manipulations.

Helmsley's reasons for wanting Hakim brought in alive shifted in Maggie's mind. Became something more than simple revenge or interrogation. "The director wants to learn to understand defectors like Hakim."

"It's not that difficult," Ashton said, calmer now. "The same thing happened to you and me. Bishop recruited us just like Dabir did to Hakim and his brother. He made us feel wanted. He made us feel like we *belonged* to something greater than ourselves."

Thinking back on it, Maggie wasn't given much of a choice when it came to her recruitment. Facing a murder charge at the time, it was either go to prison or join the Unit. The decision was simple. Bishop would have known that, too.

"Yes," Maggie admitted, a wave of unease coming over her, "but we were recruited for something good, not evil. We're on the right side."

"And they believe they're on the right side," Ashton said. "From their point of view, we're the bad guys in all this. We're the reason there's so much violence against Muslims in the U.K. We're the reason they don't fit in anywhere else."

Maggie pinched her nose. "The whole thing is a mess."

"Aye," Ashton said with a sigh, pulling a flask out from his jacket. "No wonder I like a drink."

They sat in silence for a while after that, watching the screens. Maggie's head ached, and the bitter cold seeped through her jacket down to her bones. An hour passed with no activity from the electronics store, and she worried that the Acolytes had already left for their next attack. It was too early for that, though. They'd only gotten the explosives that morning.

"It's not just Oliver and the attack," Ashton said after a while. He shifted on the floor to meet her eyes. "You were like this before then."

"Like what?" Maggie scoffed.

"On edge and irritable," Ashton said, clouds puffing in the air as he spoke. "Something else is bothering you. What is it?"

"It's nothing." A muscle twitched in Maggie's jaw as she clamped her mouth shut and shook her head, afraid it might all spill out.

"Maggie..."

Maggie's heart leapt in her chest. "It's Hakim." She scrambled to her feet and grabbed her gun, pins and needles shooting up her legs from sitting so long.

Ashton frowned, watching her fumble. "What?"

Maggie pointed to the man on the camera feed. "There. He's going out the back."

Chapter 6

Maggie hurried after Hakim on foot while Ashton raced for the car. She circled around the long way to avoid being seen by anyone else in the Acolyte's temporary camp. Hakim was the target in this chase, and Maggie wasn't about to have the tables turned on her if Hakim's comrades caught her tracking him.

Her pulse quickened. Her legs itched to stride faster, to run, but that would only draw unwanted attention. At least she and Ashton had come prepared. Maggie dug into her jacket pocket for her earpiece and slipped it into her ear.

"I've got eyes on the target," she murmured, crossing the road as Hakim turned right and headed down a side street. At least he wasn't jumping into a car. Tailing someone in a vehicle could easily result in losing them to traffic, especially in Paris. "He's heading south-west."

"Roger that," Ashton replied, the sound of a car door closing in the background. "I'll be right behind you."

From a distance, Hakim looked much the same as he did in the video. He wore jeans and a puffer jacket, his long strides indicating he was in a hurry to get to wherever he was going.

Maggie held back as much as she dared. His superiors must have warned Hakim to watch his back. He checked over his shoulder more than once in the few minutes she tailed him.

Police presence was scarce in Saint-Denis compared to the city, but they had a reputation for being heavy handed and unfair when they did turn up. The last time Maggie was in Paris on a mission, a story made the headlines of a young man in the area being raped by the police during a violent arrest.

Then there were the residents themselves. Crime was no stranger here, and it wasn't uncommon to be mugged or threatened, even at this time of day.

Hakim walked for a mile or so before reaching a small supermarket. Maggie headed for a shopping cart to blend in as Hakim gave a final check before ducking inside.

Maggie spotted Ashton down the street in her rental, parked behind a delivery truck to stay out the way. "I'm going in."

"Be careful."

Fluorescent lights hummed above her as Maggie wheeled the cart through the store, stopping to look at the labels of random items she picked up before tossing them in. Hakim made his way towards a refrigerated unit and filled a basket with a dozen premade sandwiches and bottles of water, no doubt for his fellow Acolytes hauled up inside the abandoned store. Not that they'd ever eat them. Hakim wasn't making it back to the electronics store. Not on her watch.

"What's happening?" Ashton asked in her ear.

"He's shopping," Maggie replied, barely moving her lips as she bagged some apples. "I'm going to make an approach."

Waiting for the right moment was key to initiating contact. While usually best to allow the target to approach you, it wasn't always possible. Given the beads of sweat across Hakim's forehead and the edge in his demeanor, he was hardly in any mood to spark up conversation with a stranger.

He was a lanky guy, looking younger than his years. He was still very much a child in the face and in the awkward way he carried himself, like he hadn't gotten used to a sudden growth spurt.

Maggie bided her time and gripped the handle of her shopping cart. She may not get a second chance if she botched her first approach. Hakim already appeared spooked.

When his basket was full, Hakim headed for the

check-out counter up front. As he spun, Maggie came up behind him and crashed straight into his chest in a mock collision. The bag slipped through her fingers and apples rolled out of it and across the sticky floor.

"Sorry," he stammered, bending down to catch some of the runaway fruit. "I mean, um, pardon."

"It's okay," Maggie replied in heavy accented English, her smile genuine.

Hakim hadn't even felt the prick of her needle in all the confusion. It was quick, and the needle was barely the length of a tack, but it struck true as she noted the tiny bead of blood on the back of his hand.

Apologizing again, Hakim handed over the last apple and left for the check-out counter with his back to Maggie.

"I got him," she said to Ashton, leaving her trolley in the middle of the isle. "Meet me out front."

It wasn't over yet, and the next part wasn't as easy as a pin prick. Hakim wobbled on his feet as the clerk rang up his items. He wiped his brows and blinked a few times, the sedative kicking in full speed ahead.

Maggie was thankful there wasn't a line at the counter, otherwise Hakim may not have lasted. If he fainted in the store, she'd fail. She still might.

Wiping her clammy palms on her trousers, Maggie headed for the exit as Hakim pocketed his change and grabbed his stuffed shopping bag. The snow ensured the streets weren't busy, which was a small gift in what was an overall shitty week. No one was near the supermarket, and she loitered by the sliding doors as Ashton pulled the car around front.

An unsteady Hakim stumbled out the store, his feet dragging as he struggled to put one foot in front of the other. Maggie came up behind him and wrapped his arm around her shoulders in aid. Hakim was too far gone to protest, and only his confused face showed any signs that he registered something was up. He tried to speak, but his words came out slurred.

Ashton opened the trunk while still in the driver's seat, keeping the engine running. "Taxi for two," he said in her ear.

Maggie lead Hakim to the back of the car and helped him pack his bag away, double checking over her own shoulder to make sure no witnesses were around.

Certain the coast was clear, she forced Hakim into the trunk in a tangle of limbs and slammed it shut as his eyes rolled to the back of his head.

Maggie smirked, ignoring the aches from her broken ribs, and got into the passenger seat.

Hakim was hers now, and whatever plans Dabir had for his little protégé were about to go up in smoke.

*

They took Hakim to a lock up a couple of miles from the electronics store. Maggie closed the door and kicked away the busted lock. From the rust covering it and the screech the door made upon opening, no one had used the small garage in a long time.

It was pitch black inside the small confines. Ashton turned on the light, and the single lightbulb blinked on with a buzz, swinging above the chair where they'd secured Hakim.

Though protocol dictated that Maggie needed to call in the successful apprehension of her target, she needed to make sure there was no imminent threat of an attack first. And if there was, she needed to gather all she could from her captive.

Maggie opened one of the bottles of water Hakim had purchased and took a long drink. Then she tipped what was left over Hakim's head.

Hakim's eyes blinked open, sluggish and delayed, and the water trapped in his thick eyelashes dripped down his cheeks like tears.

"Wake up," Maggie ordered, the sharpness in her tone winning her a cautious glance from Ashton, who was likely worried about a repeat performance of the restaurant's bathroom.

Hakim groaned and winced at the harshness of the bare bulb. He tried stretching his long legs only to find them trapped within tight binds of rope. His eyes opened fully then, the effects of the injected drugs unable to contain the wild panic that coursed through him like electricity. Maggie saw it in the tightening of his muscles, and in the hollowed expression etched across his features.

His breathing grew frantic, chest heaving as he took in the little room. The bare bricks were covered in cobwebs. Cardboard boxes with long forgotten belongings were stacked to one side, Ashton watching from the sidelines at the other.

"Nice of you to finally join us," Maggie said, securing his full attention. She crossed her arms and stepped closer, forcing him to crane his neck to meet her eyes.

"You're British," Hakim said, though not seeming particularly surprised at the fact.

Maggie sighed in exasperation, the disturbed layers of dust irritating her nostrils. "Well spotted."

"Are you Counter Terrorism?" he asked. There wasn't the scorn Maggie expected to find in his voice, though Hakim seemed far from happy to be there. His jaw clenched, and his knuckles were bone white against his brown skin.

Maggie leaned down and came level with his face. "I'm your worst fucking nightmare if you don't cooperate and answer all of my questions."

Hakim kept his mouth shut, wide eyes darting from side to side like his brain was on overdrive. Weighing his options. It wouldn't take long to choose one, since there were so few available. He was trapped, and either he would talk or he wouldn't. And if he decided to keep his mouth shut? Well, Maggie had more than a few ways to loosen his tongue if it meant saving lives.

"Where is Dabir Omar?" she demanded.

Hakim raised his chin. "I don't know."

Maggie swung and smacked a back hand across Hakim's face. "This will go a lot faster, and a lot less painful for you, if you don't lie to me. So I'll ask again, where is Dabir Omar? Is he inside the electronics store?"

Hakim spat out a mouthful of blood on the floor. "He left this morning, but he doesn't tell me where he's going."

"Is he planning another attack?" Ashton asked, leaning against the wall, his face free from that mischievous grin of his. He could look more than a little intimidating when he wanted.

"Yes," Hakim said, keeping his attention on Maggie. They'd removed his puffy jacket while tying him up, and his teeth chattered as he spoke, whether from the cold and his soaking shirt or fear, Maggie didn't know. Or care.

"Where and when?" she asked, keeping her alarm under the surface. She couldn't show any signs of weakness in front of her captive. "Is he setting it off right now?"

"No," Hakim replied. "We'd all be with him if he were, but most of us aren't told much until closer to an attack."

"Why wouldn't he tell you if you're part of his group?" Ashton asked, he and Maggie settling into a flow. They'd done this more than once in their many years of friendship.

"He tells those closest to him. Those he trusts. The ones who have been with him longer than I have." Hakim nodded to the bag of bottled water and sandwiches. "I'm a new recruit. He sends me on errands most of the time."

Maggie unzipped her jacket and swept a hand into her trouser pocket, making sure her gun peaked out at Hakim. "What do you know?"

"The next attack will be soon, and it's going to be bigger than London. Much bigger."

Ashton frowned. He kicked off the wall and came to stand by Maggie's side. "You're a bit too chatty for a terrorist. In my experience, people like you need a little persuasion before you betray your Brothers."

"I am not a *terrorist*." Hakim's voice was guttural, almost a growl.

"Of course not," Maggie said, her words dripping with sarcasm. "You joined the Acolytes of the Holy War to make new friends and fill up some free time."

"I joined to get closer to him," Hakim retorted, his breathing deep and angry now as opposed to the panicked panting before.

"Your brother, you mean?" Ashton asked.

Maggie startled. Had he really joined the Acolytes for something as sentimental as that? To somehow feel closer to his dead brother by following in his footsteps?

"No," Hakim spat. "Dabir."

"Why?" Maggie narrowed her eyes, her suspicion still on high alert. "Did he tell you he liked you? Did he listen to your problems and welcome you into his gang with open arms?"

Hakim's temper rose with each question, and Maggie continued, pushing him closer and closer to the edge. She raised her voice, almost shouting now, and shook him by the shoulders.

"He filled your head with bullshit, and you ate it up because he made you feel like you were a part of something. Didn't you?"

"You don't get it!" Hakim screamed, finally reaching his breaking point. "I joined to destroy Dabir Omar," he yelled, the vein on his neck throbbing. "From the inside."

A track of tears slipped down his face. Maggie had imagined a lot of motives for Hakim, but that was never one of them. At least now she could use his anger to get the answers she desperately needed. "Oh, I get it. You're on a one-man crusade to take out a highly connected, fanatical extremist organization by fetching them sandwiches."

"Shut up," Hakim spat, freely crying now.

"You're not even doing that right," Maggie said, stomping on one of the sandwich boxes. The plastic wrapping popped and the filling oozed out between the bread like spilled guts.

"I know more about Dabir and how he works than *you* do." Hakim pulled at his bindings, but they held fast. "If you and the rest of Counter Terrorism had done your jobs, I wouldn't have needed to do any of this."

"Why would you want to take Dabir down?" Ashton asked, his voice not harsh like Maggie's, yet not showing any hint of remorse either.

"Khalid died because of him," Hakim said, his voice breaking at the mention of his older brother. A drip of saliva hung from his lip, and despite everything, a hint of empathy rose within Maggie. Not that she could allow it to show. They had him talking now.

"Your brother died because he chose to blow himself up in order to kill ten innocent civilians in Belgium," Maggie pointed out, crossing her arms.

"On the orders of Dabir. He brainwashed my brother, just like he tried to brainwash me." Hakim sniffed and tried to steady himself, his eyes red and wet with tears.

Maggie noted how tired Hakim looked. His face was drawn, like he hadn't eaten much in a while. Dark circles hung under his eyes, and he had an air of mental instability about him. No wonder he broke so easily. The eighteen-year-old, more a teenager than a man, was exhausted and living among people he considered his enemy.

If what he said was true.

"Khalid was a good guy before he met Dabir," Hakim continued, shaking his head like he still couldn't believe what had happened to his brother. "He was studying to become a doctor. He was going to make something of himself before he let Dabir poison his mind. It's just me and my mum now, and she's never gotten over his death. I'm going to make Dabir pay."

Maggie couldn't decide if Hakim was more brave or stupid. He was a good dose of both, either way. "Not from here you're not," she said, playing her role. "You'll be back in Britain by tonight."

"You have to let me go. I've worked too hard to get close to Dabir. I can help you get to him before anyone else gets hurt." Hakim fought against his restraints, so hard the chair almost reeled back.

Maggie caught the seat of the chair with her foot before Hakim toppled back to the floor. The legs clicked on the concrete floor, the sound echoing off the bare walls. "Prove it," she said. "Prove you're not lying about all of it."

Hakim looked up at her, his face defeated and pleading. "I can't."

"Then you can't possibly expect me to believe a word you say," Maggie said. As convincing as he was, the risk was too high to go on his word alone. She had orders to hand him over to the director, and she would need a very good reason to defy that command.

"The video," Hakim said with a desperate look of hope. "Did you see the video?"

"I did," Maggie said, recalling his vitriol towards the West. "You gave quite the speech."

Hakim blanched at that, knowing how he must have sounded and how it hardly helped him plead his case now. "Then you heard my clue at the end. Au revoir. Is that how you found me here?"

Maggie didn't respond, sharing a masked look with

Ashton. Had what she and the rest of the Unit considered a pompous, arrogant move on the Acolytes' part actually been Hakim's plot to give away their next target?

"I tried to warn you about Trafalgar Square, too," he continued, eager now. "I called in and reported the bomb, but I don't think they took me seriously. Dabir had already called one in at Wembley to lure the bomb squad away from the area. You have to believe me. I didn't want any of it to happen."

Bishop had said they received word of a bomb scare when he called her that day. Maggie had never asked where, too consumed with reaching the square before anything happened. After the fact, she'd forgotten about that small detail, more concerned with bigger picture.

"It'll happen again if you don't do something. I can stop this if you let me go."

Maggie stared at Hakim for a long time. Her gut said he was telling the truth, but she couldn't rely on that alone. Not with stakes as big as they were.

"I trust him," Ashton said, finally breaking the silence.

Maggie shot Ashton a glare. So much for a unified front.

"I can't let him go on mere trust," she shot back, worrying at her thumbnail. Dabir was still out there. Even if Hakim was lying about infiltrating the Acolytes to avenge his brother, he still didn't know where Dabir was. That at least, she believed. There was no way someone like Dabir would allow Hakim into their inner circle in such a short period of time. Hakim would need to prove himself before he'd be privy to such intimate details.

But could he truly help? While he may not be in-the-know about everything, Hakim had gotten close to Dabir. The men had sat side-by-side in the video the Acolytes put online. Dabir was using Hakim to lure other impressionable kids to his cause.

"What's the worst that can happen if he is lying?" Ashton said with a shrug. "He tells Dabir that Counter Terrorism is after him? He already knows that."

Ashton wasn't wrong there. Hakim still believed they were with Counter Terrorism, and Maggie wasn't inclined to correct him. Dabir had been a threat long enough to know the British Government would chase him down after the attack in London. She had Hakim in her custody as ordered, but right now, Dabir was the one capable of dealing the most damage.

Maggie turned to Ashton. "We can keep Hakim here and go back to the electronics store. If Dabir isn't planning to attack today, we wait there until he returns and ambush him."

"He doesn't stay with us there," Hakim interrupted. "He stays away from our location as much as possible in case we're found out and raided. Dabir doesn't like to get his hands dirty. He uses people like my brother for the messy work."

Bishop had said as much during their briefing. Dabir was on Counter Terrorism's radar before Trafalgar Square, but he was smart, never incriminating himself in anything and pulling the puppet strings from afar.

"But you said he was there earlier," Maggie accused Hakim. "That he left this morning."

Hakim nodded. "Yes, he arrived to inspect a delivery of explosives. There's a lot of it."

Maggie dug her nails into her palm. She should have drowned Gabrielle Legrand after all.

"Where are the explosives now?" Ashton asked. "Are they still back at the electronics store?"

"Dabir took it all with him," Hakim said. "He didn't trust the supplier and wanted to move it as soon as possible. I helped pack the van he left in with his lieutenants."

"Shit," Maggie hissed, pacing the room now.

"If you're going to let me go, then you better do it quick," Hakim said with growing impatience. "They'll notice if I don't get back soon."

He had a point. The supermarket wasn't far from the electronics store, and by all accounts he should have been back by now. While he may not be the most important member in the group, someone would eventually note his absence, especially if Hakim was in charge of bringing the rest of them food and water.

"We can have him wear a wire." Maggie hated being backed into a corner like this. She was out of options, and she didn't like any of the ones that remained open to her.

"Dabir's not an idiot." Hakim sighed. "Everyone entering the building is frisked and searched."

Maggie swore again and refrained from hitting something. That ruled out a tracker, too, which was a pity. A tracker had come in handy on her recent assignment in New York. Without a tracker or wire, they wouldn't be able to keep track of Hakim's whereabouts or watch his discussions for signs of betrayal or hints on where the attack would go down.

Leaps of faith didn't come easy to Maggie. Yet her current predicament didn't leave her much choice.

"Fine," Maggie said, moving to untie Hakim before she changed her mind. She whispered in his ear, steady and crystal clear. "But I promise, if you fuck me over, I won't stop until I find you. I will hunt you down and kill you, and it won't be a quick death."

"I'm not lying," Hakim assured, rubbing his wrists once they were free.

"That's good," Maggie replied, "for your sake." She looked between Hakim and Ashton, the three of them the only thing standing in the way of Dabir and his next attack. "Now, let's come up with a plan."

Chapter 7

Maggie was at her wits end. After a sleepless night of no news, her nerves were rattled and she had picked her fingernails down to the quick.

"Why hasn't he gotten in touch with us?" she asked for the hundredth time, pacing along the length of Ashton's living room. The city stretched out before them through the balcony's glass-paned doors, quiet and untouched in its blanket of snow. For now.

Dabir could be out there, preparing for his attack, and they would be none the wiser. Hakim should have discovered *something* by now. Maggie's stomach lurched at the thought of being wrong about him. Had he played them for fools?

"He'll contact us when he has news," Ashton assured her, lounging on the couch with his feet up, sipping an espresso. "Until then, sit down and have some breakfast."

Maggie sat at the dinner table and reached for the set of knives she'd been sharpening instead of the breakfast spread of pastries and good coffee Ashton had laid out. "What if something's happened to him?" she worried, tapping a finger on the tip of one of the blades. "What if they know he's working with us?"

"How could they come to that conclusion?" Ashton licked a drop of espresso from his lower lip. "They don't even know we're here, or who we are for that matter. Hakim will reach out once he's gotten something we can use."

Ashton had left Hakim with his phone to contact them. While Hakim couldn't risk trying to smuggle it into the electronics store, he hid it nearby so he could slip outside for a few moments and text them.

But a text hadn't come through.

Perhaps no news was good news. Dabir could have cancelled his plans, whatever they were. Or something could have delayed his schedule. Not that the thought did much to calm Maggie's nerves.

Her phone buzzed and rattled against the wooden table, and she and Ashton jumped. Maggie grabbed the phone and read the message on the screen.

Notre-Dame. 40 mins. It's happening today.

The phone trembled in Maggie's hands, flashes of the destruction in Trafalgar Square flooding her mind. It couldn't happen again. She couldn't allow it.

Maggie did the math, going over the quickest route to the cathedral. They could make it in time if they left immediately. Maggie gathered the knives spread out on the table, securing them to the inside of her jacket and strapping them around her ankles. She checked to make sure her gun was secured in its holster by her hip.

Ashton shoved his feet into his boots and flung on his jacket, both of them in all black with tactical clothes designed for ease of movement. They didn't talk as they rushed from the apartment and out into the cold streets. They knew what was at stake.

Travelling by car would take too long to reach their destination. On foot, even longer. Instead, Maggie and Ashton sprinted to the Gare D'Avenue du President Kennedy and descended into the Métro.

Maggie checked her phone for more messages as they caught the C train and whizzed underneath the city. No more came.

Four stops and thirteen agonizing minutes later, they arrived at the Saint-Michel – Notre-Dame station. Forgoing all niceties, Maggie and Ashton shoved their way through the crowds and emerged above ground, charging across the Petit Pont bridge to the Ile de la Cité, one of the two natural islands in the river Seine, where the cathedral lay.

Maggie's heart sank as they approached the west façade. Hundreds of tourists were outside the gothic building, braving the weather to get a glimpse of the magnificent medieval architecture of the Notre-Dame de Paris. *Our Lady of Paris*. Gargoyles and chimeras glared down at them from their perches by the bell towers, birds scattering off into the air on frantic wings as if they knew what was to come.

"Ashton..." Her voice caught in her throat. There were so many people. So many innocent lives. And there'd be just as many, if not more, inside.

"I know," said her friend, taking her hand in his. "Come on."

They entered through the far right of the three front doors, known as the Portal of Saint Anne, and broke through huddles of gaping visitors with tour guides in hand.

A table lay beyond the door, filled with candles available for purchase to burn in memory of lost loved ones. The flicker of flames twinkled star-like throughout the expansive ground floor. Maggie grimaced at them. If Hakim was right about the level of explosives Gabrielle Legrand had sold Dabir, then an inferno of naked flames was not a good idea.

The sun shone through stained glass, purple hues from the three rose windows blessing everything it touched with a warm glow. The beauty felt out of place to Maggie amid the impending danger, the depiction of Jesus hanging on the cross by the high altar more fitting to the situation.

"Where would they have planted the bomb?" Ashton asked.

Maggie moved to a framed map of their location and scanned it. There was the crypt, of course. Dabir could be mirroring Trafalgar Square by placing the explosives underground. The main floor itself had plenty of nooks and crannies, not to mention the highest density of people if maximum casualty was the goal.

"I don't know," Maggie said, the time ticking down in her head. They had less than ten minutes now, the commute taking longer than expected thanks to the weather and slippery pavements.

The bomb could be anywhere, and if they didn't find it soon, they'd all be dead.

Sweat trickled down Maggie's back. She shivered despite the stuffy warmth of her jacket. She gazed out over the crowd and watched for anything out of the ordinary. Anything that could help her narrow their search. A whole minute passed before she saw anything.

Two men, one white and the other middle eastern, slunk out of a door and hurried toward the exit. Everyone else around them peered toward the heavens, their necks arched toward the windows and ceiling, or examining the placards explaining the various artifacts that circled around the rows of pews. True tourists spoke in hushed tones or took in the history in respectful silence.

But these men were most definitely *not* tourists. The white man made eye contact with Maggie from across the pews and startled, pulling his friend into a run, shoving people out of their path.

"The north tower," Maggie said, pointing the way for Ashton. There was no time to chase after the terrorists. Grabbing her gun, Maggie sent three shots into the air as they crossed the floor.

The bangs reverberated through the cathedral, amplified by the acoustics, and sent everyone into a panic. Pandemonium erupted. People screamed and stampeded towards the nearest exit. It wasn't the best method of evacuation, but it was all Maggie could do given the circumstances, and she could only hope everyone made it out in time.

She and Ashton backtracked along the terrorists' path and barged through the door to the north tower. A man in caretaker overalls lay splayed near the foot of the stairs, his throat slashed like a garish, grinning mouth. They stepped over him and took the stone steps two at a time.

Unlike its neighbor, the north tower wasn't open to the public, making it the perfect place to go unnoticed. The muscles in Maggie's legs burned as she travelled up and up and up, passing the Virgin's Balcony and then the Colonnade. Almost four hundred steps later, they finally reached the tower.

Maggie wiped her brow as she caught her breath, searching for the explosives. "There!"

A large trunk-sized box sat in the corner by the balcony.

Maggie ran to the box and dropped to her knees. Wind whipped her hair back from her face and bit at her skin, the chill much colder this high up.

"Wait," Ashton warned, blocking her hand from opening the lid. "What if opening it triggers the fuse?"

Maggie squeezed Ashton's hand. "It's going to blow anyway."

Ashton gave her a stiff nod and kneeled beside her.

"There might still be time to get out," she said to Ashton. It wasn't exactly true if the countdown in her head was accurate, but there was no way of surviving the blow sitting this close. If he made it to the bottom of the tower, he might get out alive.

"Enough of the heroic shite, Mags. We're in this together."

Maggie didn't argue. There wasn't time. She tried to say something heartfelt but found the words trapped in her throat. She wiped her eyes and focused on the box.

Her heartbeat drummed in her ears, and she held her breath as she pried open the lid.

Both she and Ashton gasped.

It wasn't a bomb.

Maggie picked up the single piece of paper inside the otherwise empty box and read the scrawled note.

You're too late. -Dabir

"Too late?" Ashton said, reading over her shoulder. "What does he mean 'too late?'"

The answer came three seconds later when a cataclysmic boom resounded over Paris.

Chapter 8

Maggie snapped her head towards the eruption.

A surging wave of heat pulsed through the air, slamming her and Ashton back against the wall of the north tower.

Below them, water flew into the air from the Seine, blasting over the sides of the riverbanks onto the pavements and surrounding roads.

Chunks of metal and shredded bits of wood followed the flood waters, obliterated pieces of the boat that moments ago carried passengers along the Seine. The shrapnel rained from the sky in burning meteors and plummeted back into the river, hissing as flames met water.

Nausea coursed through Maggie as she struggled to her feet, using the balcony to steady her. "That was a tourist boat," she said, recognizing the shape of the bow as it slowly submerged with what was left of the vessel.

The boat was gone. All those people... No one could have survived that.

Odd colored debris emerged from the water and bobbed among the sloshing waves. Maggie let out a cry when she realized what it was. Bile burned the back of her throat, and she covered her mouth to hold back the building scream.

The bodies, or what was left of them, floated like life-jackets among the wreckage.

Ashton wrapped an arm over Maggie's shoulder, his eyes glistening as they relived what happened in Trafalgar Square all over again. They'd failed, and all they could do was watch.

Sirens wailed in a mournful choir, emergency services narrowing in from all areas of the city. But their speed was in vain.

The damage was done.

*

Fifty-eight people. All of them dead.

Ashton handed Maggie a double whiskey with ice and plopped down on the couch beside her. They had returned to the apartment, leaving the French police and ambulances at the scene. It was a clean-up job now. There wasn't anything for them to do.

Maggie ran a hand through her hair, fingers still shaking.

Hakim betrayed them. He wasn't trying to take down Dabir. All of his crying and rage over his brother Khalid was bollocks, and Maggie let him lead her right up the garden path. He'd tricked her, and she fell for it like an amateur.

Now people were dead, and it was all her fault.

Maggie tossed back the amber liquid, and the sweet burn travelled down to her chest. The whiskey didn't fill her with its usual warmth, though. Inside she was bitter cold, frozen numb with the shock of everything she'd seen in the two attacks. Those kind of memories dug deep, like carvings etched in marble. They never went away. Not even when she closed her eyes to sleep.

She pulled the woolen throw closer to her chin and leaned her head on Ashton's shoulder. "I was a bloody idiot," she admonished, the guilt heavy as an anchor, weighing her down.

"*We* were bloody idiots you mean. We both let Hakim go, and I was the one who said I trusted him first." Ashton threw his empty glass into the roaring fire, which crackled and snapped as it consumed a pile of wood. The crystal glass shattered, and the pieces turned black as the flames licked over them.

Notre-Dame was a decoy. A very deliberate decoy chosen so Maggie and Ashton could witness the devastation of the Acolytes' latest hit.

"They wanted us to see it." They'd made sure to lead them on a wild goose chase across the city, positioning them with a front row seat to their heinous attack.

Ashton refilled Maggie's glass and drank a swig straight from the bottle. "No doubt. The sick fucks."

One minute, the tourists were enjoying a river cruise down the Seine, a perfect way to take in the Parisian sights with the interior of the boat offering warmth and drinks to sweeten the deal. The next minute, they were gone. Wiped from the earth in mere seconds.

The news played on mute in the background, and in the hours since, the death toll continued to rise. Passersby had been injured, too. An unfortunate few who were strolling by the banks of the river, or walking along the pavements above. Cars had crashed into each other in all the confusion, including one driver who had been hit with a piece of shrapnel that pierced through the windshield and killed her on impact.

The more they watched, the more Maggie and Ashton drank. It was self-pitying, she knew, but it was about all Maggie was capable of at that moment. There was only so much a person could take. Only so much death and destruction she could handle.

"Dabir and Hakim planned it all." Ashton glared at Dabir's note, which lay in front of them on the coffee table.

Maggie sipped her drink. "They could be long gone by now." So far, no video had surfaced of the Acolytes claiming the attack, but it was only a matter of time. Right now, they'd be celebrating, reeling with the high of executing another attack. This time right under their noses.

Hakim had given the French plenty of warning, yet they still managed to carry out their plans. His lies about trying to help, about giving them a clue to their next target, was utter bullshit. It had been a taunt. A boastful display of their confidence. And they'd been right. They attacked Paris unchecked, even with the advanced warning.

The Acolytes had delivered the world a message: they could destroy you, wherever and whenever they wanted, and nothing, not even the police or the government, could do anything to protect you from their wrath.

Maggie's phone rang, and Bishop's name popped up on the screen. She stared at it for a moment, the buzzing impatient and angry.

"Bishop," she said, waiting for the tirade to come. She put the phone on loudspeaker, Ashton staying silent as he listened.

"What happened?" Bishop asked, voice tight.

"My efforts failed." Maggie kept things succinct and to-the-point. "Dabir and his soldiers arranged a decoy explosive in the Notre-Dame cathedral, and I fell for it."

Maggie left out Hakim and his betrayal. She wasn't quite ready to discuss her foolishness with Bishop, to admit the complete incompetence she displayed in allowing a known terrorist to walk away from her grasp and return to his leader.

For all Maggie knew, Hakim had contacted Dabir the second he stepped into the electronics store and told him about her and Ashton. They could be the reason Dabir chose to act so quickly. Pushed to carry out the attack before she got close enough to stop them. Hakim's acting skills was enough to escape them once, but Dabir wouldn't risk a second meeting.

Bishop sighed over the phone, and Maggie pictured him pacing his office. "We've been tracking Dabir on our end to no avail. French intelligence haven't gotten anything substantial either."

"Has there been a video yet?" Maggie asked. If there was, the Unit would know about it long before the news channels did.

"No," Bishop said. "If they're following the pattern they carried out over here, they'll be moving on to their next location before releasing anything. I expect one will show up tomorrow."

"I'm sorry, Bishop."

"Are you hurt?" he asked, still concerned despite how she failed him. Failed everyone.

Her ribs ached from all the running, but she didn't complain. It was nothing compared to what the victims suffered. "No, I was far enough from the attack to avoid the blast." But close enough to see every second of it.

"Very well. Come home tomorrow. The director expects a full report in the afternoon. I don't need to warn you that she's in one hell of a mood."

Bishop didn't reprimand her or yell or shout. There was no need. He knew Maggie well enough to know she'd beat herself up enough for the both of them. Knew that nothing he said would be worse than what Maggie was telling herself.

"Okay," she said, not trusting herself to say much more. "I'll see you tomorrow then."

As soon as she hung up, Maggie burst into tears.

"Hey," Ashton said, pulling her into a hug. "It's all right, Mags."

"No, it's not." Maggie covered her face with her hands. Nothing was all right. It hadn't been for a long time now. "People are dead because of me."

"Those lives are not on you. They're on the Acolytes. Dabir and Hakim did this. You tried to stop them. You did what you could."

"But it wasn't good enough." The Acolytes could be anywhere now. Preparing for yet another attack she couldn't prevent.

Ashton rubbed her back, his affection only leading her to cry more. "You can't blame yourself. You put yourself in harm's way to defuse what you thought was the bomb. You risked your life to do the right thing."

All the secrets Maggie had hidden from Ashton, all the private pain, bubbled up to the surface. She tried to push it back down, but the failure at the cathedral left her without any strength to fill the cracks in her mask. Her dam was about to burst, and she let it.

"Just before I left for that New York assignment, I found out I was pregnant."

The words spilled out, toppling from her lips. There was no taking them back. Ashton sat up and pulled off their blanket to look at her stomach.

"No," Maggie said, covering her flat tummy and unable to look at it. "I'm not anymore. I lost it. I lost my baby."

The last words came out in a wail, all pretense of strength gone. She couldn't keep it up any longer. Couldn't pretend that everything was fine and act like nothing had happened.

Ashton held her as she sobbed. She wasn't sure how long she wept. Too lost in the throes of her grief. Once she let the floodgates open, she didn't think the tears would ever stop.

They did, though. Eventually.

Ashton wiped her damp cheeks with the cuff of his sleeve, and Maggie saw her sadness reflected in his eyes. "Is, I mean, was Leon the father?"

"Yes." Maggie stared at her hands. "But I haven't told him. How can I tell him?"

She couldn't bring herself to do it. To say the words out loud to him. To pass on the pain that had rampaged through her entire being since the doctor delivered the fatal news like a virus. Leon wouldn't take it well. Maggie knew him enough to know how much it would crush him. How much he'd always wanted a family.

"I knew something was up, but I had no idea." Ashton brushed her hair away from her face. "You could have told me. You don't need to go through this alone."

Maggie accepted the handkerchief Ashton offered and blew her nose. "I didn't want to think about it. If I told anyone else, I'd have to admit it really happened, that it wasn't just a terrible nightmare."

Maggie was good at running away from her problems. Detaching herself from reality and focusing on her missions. Playing the roles of her many aliases as if she was another person entirely. But there were some things you couldn't run from.

"When little Oliver died in my arms, it ripped open the wound again," she continued. "He was gone, just like my baby, and I couldn't do anything to save them. Just like I couldn't stop Dabir and Hakim today."

Maggie had been harsher than usual with Gabrielle Legrand. As much as the explosives dealer deserved what she got and more, it was unlike Maggie to resort to that level of violence based on a gut feeling that the woman was lying.

"I have this anger inside me. It's burning everything to ash, and I can't stop it. The Unit trained us to cope with all sorts of situations, but nothing prepared me for this. I was willing to change my entire life, Ash. I wanted my life to change. For a moment, I was going to be a mother. No fighting. No death. I was going to leave the Unit."

Ashton took her hands in his. "I can't imagine what you're going through. I'm sorry that happened to you."

"I suppose it wasn't meant to be," Maggie said, shaking her head. "Maybe I'm not cut out to be a mum, or have a normal life like everyone else."

"You can still have that normal life, if you want it." Ashton eyes were intense, his dislike for the Unit burning even brighter than usual. "You can walk away whenever you want."

"I'm afraid that if I walked away, I'd have nothing left. I don't know if I could go through that again." Maggie laughed, but there was no humor in the sound. "And it's not like Leon and I are this perfect, happy couple. Our fling in Venice shouldn't have happened. We know things will never work out between us. I couldn't even look him in the eye at the Unit briefing."

Seeing him, feeling his touch, had only solidified her decision not to tell Leon about the miscarriage. He didn't need to know.

"For what it's worth," Ashton said, reaching for a new glass in his little bar trolley by the couch. "I think you're going to be a brilliant wee mammy someday."

"You think?" Maggie asked, finishing off her latest double measure.

"Of course. Plus, I want some little nieces and nephews running around causing havoc."

Maggie allowed herself a small smile. "Uncle Ashton, eh?"

"Aye. And I'll apologize in advance for spoiling them rotten."

"No kids of your own then?" The topic of children didn't come up often since neither of them had any plans to start a family. Until she fell pregnant, Maggie hadn't allowed herself to consider it.

Ashton scoffed. "Are you kidding? I can barely look after myself."

Maggie actually laughed at that. Though the pain was still there, it wasn't quite as sharp with Ashton by her side.

"You'll get through this, you know," Ashton said, more confident than she was about the matter. "Just like you do everything else. And I'm here to help you in any way I can."

Maggie held out her empty glass. "Well in that case, how about you pour me another drink."

Ashton complied, and the TV caught Maggie's attention. The news carried on in the background, and an update flashed over the screen. Another victim had died in the hospital, bringing the death toll to fifty-nine.

"What are we going to do?" Ashton asked. As they watched, faces of confirmed victims appeared on the screen.

There wasn't much they *could* do. Maggie raised her glass, and they drank to the dead. She and Ashton sat there on the couch long into the night, until the fire had dimmed to embers, drowning their sorrows and drinking themselves into oblivion.

Chapter 9

Maggie stood over her friend, a glass of water and two painkillers in hand.

"Ashton."

It was still dark outside, the winter sun sleeping in late. Unlike Maggie. After a fitful few hours of sleep, she dragged herself out of bed, her troubled mind unable to rest.

"Ashton," she said louder this time, flicking on the light by his king-sized bed.

"What?" Ashton sat up, eyes still closed and his usually pristine hair suffering from a severe case of bedhead. "What's wrong?"

"Your phone."

Ashton rubbed the sleep from his eyes and peered up at her with a scrunched face. "Eh?"

"Your *phone*," Maggie repeated. "Is it registered in your name?"

"Come on, Mags. Nothing's in my real name."

"Good, then we can trace it." If the phone couldn't be linked back to Ashton, it was safe to have the Unit techs track it. If they asked any questions about the strange name of the owner, Maggie could say she stole it. They'd be too busy hunting the terrorists to ask much more than that.

"You want to go after the Acolytes?" Ashton asked, stretching his arms into the air and stifling a yawn. The tattoos covered both his arms in sleeves of black and grey, Maggie's favorite, a beautiful siren dragging an entranced sailor down into the depths of the ocean, catching her eye.

"We're going to find them," Maggie vowed.

"They could be anywhere by now."

"Then we'll hunt them down." Maggie would follow them to the ends of the earth if that's what it took. They were not slipping away from her that easily. She handed the water and tablets to Ashton. "Take these. Coffee's brewing as we speak."

Ashton was useless without caffeine in his system, and she needed him at his best.

"What if Hakim tossed the phone?" Ashton asked. "He'll know we can trace it, too."

The thought had occurred to Maggie earlier, as the beginnings of her plan stewed in her mind. It was a long shot, but she had to try something. She wasn't prepared to give up. Not after everything the Acolytes had done. They didn't get to walk away from this.

"Right now, it's all we've got. Now get ready. Please," she said, checking her watch. "I want to be out of here within the hour."

Maggie was already dressed and ready to go. Her cold shower and painkillers were enough to sober her from last night's whiskey. The time for feeling sorry for herself was over. The victims of the attacks deserved vengeance, and Maggie intended to get it for them.

Ashton didn't protest. He rolled out of bed and padded across the room to open the drapes in nothing but his birthday suit. "Don't you have to report to crabbit old Helmsley this afternoon?"

Maggie may have made a mistake with Hakim, but she wouldn't be fooled a second time. She wasn't returning home until she righted her blunder and put an end to the Acolytes. She was out for blood, and this time it was personal.

"The director will have to wait." Maggie tossed Ashton his clothes. "We've got terrorists to catch."

*

Twenty minutes and three espressos later, Maggie and Ashton were in her rental. Ashton drove while Maggie called in the trace.

It didn't take long for the techs to hack into the phone's network provider and find an address. Like Maggie, they had been trained to be the best in their respective field and could cause as much damage with their keyboards as Maggie could with her fists.

"Thanks, Gregg. Say hello to Liz for me." Maggie hung up and typed the address into the Sat-Nav, anticipation building inside her like sparks of electricity. "They're still in Paris."

Ashton checked the directions and took a right turn. "Is that a good thing or a bad thing?"

Maggie stared out the window at the unrelenting snow. "I guess we'll find out."

Their destination in Belleville was only six miles from Ashton's place, but it took them a full forty minutes to get there. The snow made the traffic worse than usual, and Ashton drove an extra five minutes out of the way to avoid the Rue de Rivoli. Maggie didn't complain. She didn't want to pass the spot of yesterday's disaster.

A somber tone had befallen the city. Parisian's were resilient though, and this wasn't the first time they'd found themselves the targets of hate. Already people were gathering with signs of love and solidarity, heading to the Arc de Triomphe where the news showed a growing crowd coming out in the cold to be together during their time of sorrow.

Ashton parked a safe distance away from the phone's location and reversed into a graffiti-covered alleyway. They got out of the car, and Maggie had them recheck their weapons. She carried her knives, gun, and an extra magazine in case things got messy.

Other than pickpockets, Belleville was relatively safe during the day when hipsters opened their boutique coffee shops and secondhand clothing stores. It was at night, when the shutters closed, that a very different type of vendor took over. Drug dealing and prostitution generally made the neighborhood a place to avoid, especially the narrow side streets.

The butcher's shop rested at the end of a dead-end street and took up the entire building. Like the rest of the surrounding stores, it was closed for the day and darkness lay beyond the windows. Deals were written on the glass in French and Arabic, offering the usual items as well as halāl ready cold cuts and rotisserie chickens.

Maggie motioned for Ashton to follow her around the back, and they crept along the building's walls, keeping an eye out for scouts or spies. A butcher's shop wasn't what Maggie expected, but she trusted the techs were correct with the location.

Someone had threaded a heavy chain through the metal double doors, the lock new and well-oiled. Even if Maggie and Ashton could pick the lock, a parked van blocked their access to the entry. The windows at this end of the building were narrow and frosted, too, giving no hint of what lay inside. Ashton tapped Maggie's shoulder and pointed above them.

A raised skylight protruded from the slanted roof, a ground level section that connected to the main two-story building that housed the shop floor. With a silent nod, they hoisted themselves onto a large dumpster and shimmied up to the roof with the help of a drainpipe.

Maggie rolled on top and waited for Ashton before crawling to the corner of the skylight. Snow melted under the heat of her body and soaked into her clothes, layers of grime covering her jacket and trousers as she slid across to get a look inside.

The snow covered the skylight glass too, and Maggie risked wiping a small section away to peek inside. Shadows lingered across the floor, odd shapes that didn't make sense until she swiped away more snow. Animal carcasses hung on hooks, their bodies stripped and flayed, ready to be sliced and diced into cuts of meat. The animals lined in macabre rows of red muscle and sinew.

The animal bodies weren't alone, though. Maggie recognized the two men from Notre-Dame standing between the rows, speaking with someone. Muffled voices emanated from within, and Maggie pressed her ear against the glass pane, making room for Ashton to get a glimpse inside.

The slap of a fist meeting flesh echoed in the chilled chamber.

"Stop it, Assad. Dabir wants him alive." The white man grabbed his partner and shoved him back before returning his attention to the person sitting before them. Maggie sucked in a gasp when she saw who it was.

Hakim.

The white guy grabbed Hakim's face in his meaty hand. "Dabir wants to kill you himself. Streaming live online for everyone to see. The world will learn what happens when you betray your Brothers."

Blood oozed from Hakim's nostrils, his nose swollen like the rest of his face. Garish purple bruises replaced the bags under his eyes, the white surrounding one of his irises turned red and bloodshot.

Betrayed?

Maggie shared a look with Ashton as they listened on.

"I only have one brother," Hakim said, tied to a chair much the same as he had been when he was in Maggie's detainment.

Hakim's resistance earned him another blow, this one to his gut.

"You aren't half the man Khalid was. *We* were his Brothers. He wouldn't acknowledge someone as weak as you."

"Khalid fell for the same self-righteous crap you both did. You're nothing but a bunch of fanatics, man. Allah wouldn't want this. Dabir has you all fooled."

That earned him two blows, this time from Assad. Hakim took them without crying out, though he couldn't hide the pain from his face.

"You can shit talk all you want," said Assad, "but we're not going to stop until you tell us who you're in contact with. Who were you trying to warn about yesterday's attack?"

Hakim titled his head back and let out a sardonic laugh.

Maggie knew that laugh. Had bellowed it herself a few times when the chips were down. It was the laugh of someone who had resigned themselves to dying. The Acolytes wouldn't let him live now that he'd betrayed them, and Hakim knew it. Keeping the truth from them was his last rebellious act. The only piece of power he had left.

She closed her eyes. Hakim hadn't lied to them. He'd been found out.

A wash of relief came over her, selfish as it was. She hadn't been wrong to trust Hakim. His plan to infiltrate the Acolytes had been true enough. Only Dabir and the others had caught him in the act before he could contact Maggie.

"What's the plan?" Ashton asked in her ear, coming to the same conclusion.

Maggie thought it over, weighing the options to achieve the cleanest outcome. They couldn't let him stay there much longer. Assad and the other guy were quickly running out of patience with him. "I'll cause a distraction. When the room is clear, break in and get Hakim out."

Ashton nodded, and Maggie maneuvered to the edge of the roof and slipped back down.

Returning to the front of the shop, Maggie risked checking inside, cupping her hands to get a better look. She didn't see anyone else inside. A pit of unease burned in her stomach. Where were the other Acolytes?

Maggie gave herself a shake and focused on the task at hand. A bike sat chained up against a railing a few shops down. It likely belonged to the resident in the flat above. She used one of her many knives, picking the lock without much trouble, and wheeled the bike over to the butcher's shop.

She had been trained in the delicate art of breaking and entering. Taught how to pick locks and slip into even the most rigorously guarded fortresses. To sneak around unnoticed and leave without a single trace of her presence. Silent. Cautious.

Now wasn't one of those times.

Hoisting the bike up over her head, Maggie lurched back and threw it with everything she had. Her ribs protested the movement, but her aim was true.

The bike soared through the air and crashed into the front window in a cacophony of shattered glass. The windowpane clung to shards of glittering glass, giving her improvised entrance the look of a gaping mouth with jagged teeth.

Maggie stepped into the store with a knife in each hand, glass crunching under her boots. No alarm went off, but she'd made enough racket to draw the wanted attention. Quick footsteps drew near, coming from the back.

Assad bounded through the door a second later, wide shoulders barely fitting between the frame, and spotted her. Maggie sent one of her knives spinning through the air.

The blade closed the distance between them and imbedded itself into Assad's chest. He stared down at the hilt and blinked twice before crumpling to the ground with a massive *thump*.

A second set of footsteps grew louder, Assad's partner falling for her trap. Maggie crossed the room and pressed her back against the wall by the door as she waited for him, crouched down on the balls of her feet.

Maggie let him thunder into the room and see his fallen Brother. Then, lashing out with her second blade, she sliced, deep and precise across the backs of his ankles.

Blood spurted from the cut flesh. The big oaf dropped to his knees and screamed as the pain of his butchered tendons registered.

The screams were short lived. Maggie lunged onto his back and slit his throat with vicious efficiency.

She didn't wait to watch him die. It wouldn't take long for someone to call the police, and they'd already be on high alert after yesterday. Ashton met her in the back, more glass covering the floor from his own makeshift entrance from the skylight.

Hakim looked even worse up close.

"How did you find me?" he asked as Ashton freed him from the chair.

"Ashton's phone," Maggie said, keeping an eye out by the door for any unwanted arrivals.

Hakim groaned as he got to his feet. "They took it off me in the van on the way here yesterday morning." The van that was left parked out back, which was just as well for Hakim. Not so good for Assad and his friend, though. "Dabir text you the wrong location for the bomb right in front of me."

"Where's Dabir and the rest of the Acolytes now?" Ashton asked as he helped lead Hakim to the door. Maggie walked in front of them, primed and ready for any surprises.

"I heard Ben and Assad talking," said Hakim, his grave tone making Maggie stop and turn around to face him. "Dabir's going to attack the city again. Tonight."

Maggie's heart plummeted. "Where?"

"The Champs-Élysées."

Chapter 10

Maggie stomped around Ashton's living room with her phone pressed against her ear.

"Are you fucking kidding me?"

"They're not bending on it." Bishop sighed, and Maggie pictured him running a hand down his face. "If they move people away from the Champs-Élysées, or try to evacuate the city, it would only show the Acolytes that they'd won."

Maggie was all for showing no fear in the face of adversity, especially against those whose aim was to instill terror in the hearts of people, but things were getting serious now. Deadly.

"Bloody French," she muttered. They were almost as stubborn as the British.

Maggie watched the news coverage, reporters coming in live from the scene as what looked like half the city congregated on the famous street, clustering around at the Arc de Triumphe.

"They're on high alert and have as many people on the ground as they can," Bishop said.

Maggie had called in the news to Bishop, bringing him up to speed about Hakim's true motives and Dabir's plans for an impending attack. "They were on high alert yesterday, but Dabir still succeeded. What's going to stop him from doing it again this time?"

"They have the location this time," Bishop replied, though he didn't sound convinced.

Maggie sat down at the dinner table where Hakim devoured a bowl of soup and bread. She tapped her fingers on the wood. The past few hours of phone calls and waiting grated on her nerves. "I still don't like it. I'm going to make sure I'm there. I don't trust anyone else with this."

"Be careful," Bishop warned. She'd barely escaped two bombings now and, if what Hakim said was true, Dabir was planning quite the bang with his third.

"I'll try," she said with a deep sigh. "Call me with any updates." Maggie tossed the phone on the table and rubbed her aching head.

"They're not moving them, are they?" Hakim asked. After a hot shower and some new clothes, he looked a bit better than how they found him. Still, his so-called Brothers Ben and Assad had done a number on him. One of the cuts on his cheek needed stitches, and Ashton had to dig out the first aid kit. Hakim was stronger than he looked though, accepting the stitches without a fuss.

"No, they're not." Maggie said, topping up on her painkillers. Her ribs hadn't fared well with all the climbing and killing at the butcher's shop, but she couldn't sit back and rest now.

The Champs-Élysées was flooded with people. No police detail could be one hundred percent vigilant with a crowd like that. The tourists would provide more than enough cover for Dabir and the Acolytes to go unnoticed. Maggie needed to be on the ground.

"What are we going to do?" Hakim asked, chewing on a bread roll. The Acolytes hadn't given him so much as a sip of water since yesterday, and he was making up for it now, already on this third bowl of soup.

"*We* aren't doing anything," Maggie corrected. "You've done enough."

More than enough. Not many people Hakim's age had the guts or the cunning to infiltrate a terrorist organization. He'd spent almost a year with the ones who brainwashed his brother, never losing sight of his craving for vengeance. It couldn't have been easy.

"But –"

"But nothing," Ashton said calmly, coming in with two steaming cups of tea for them both. "You'll stay here until we get back."

Hakim's face grew sullen, and he swirled his spoon in his soup instead of meeting their eyes. "Let me help. I messed up yesterday. Because of me, more people are dead."

"That's not on you," Maggie said, echoing Ashton's words to her the night before. She refrained from reaching out and placing a hand on his shoulder, afraid that it would hurt after Ben and Assad's handiwork. "Dabir is to blame for this, and I'm going to make sure he pays for it."

Ashton sat down next to Hakim. "We wouldn't know anything if it wasn't for you. It took guts to do what you did."

Maggie agreed. If Bishop were there, he'd already be sizing up Hakim as a possible candidate for agent training. His intellect and evident skills in infiltration would make him very appealing to the Unit.

Maggie reached out and squeezed his hand. "Let us use your intel to end this."

Hakim gave a short nod. He appeared less than happy about being left out, but he ducked his head and went back to his meal without comment.

"Any word on our friend Gabrielle?" Ashton asked.

Maggie sipped her tea before she spilled the only good news Bishop had for her. "She's been charged with enough offenses to keep a judge very busy. The French plan to make an example of her."

Ashton grinned at that. "She's going to hate those prison jumpsuits." His face sobered when he looked over Maggie's shoulder and out to the city beyond. "There should be fireworks in the sky by now."

Given recent events, the police had cancelled the traditional New Year's Eve fireworks and banned the use of private displays as well. They'd already received an overwhelming number of frightened calls, scared Parisians reporting sounds of an explosion or shifty strangers roaming in their neighborhoods. The city had accepted the request, leaving the night sky dark and untouched.

The Eifel tower across the river should be twinkling like a Christmas tree, too. Instead, it stood tall and unlit in mournful remembrance to yesterday's victims.

"Come on," Maggie said, gulping down the rest of her tea. "It's time we head out."

Dabir was out there somewhere, and Maggie was going to find him.

Chapter 11

The Champs-Élysées was the place to be on New Year's Eve. An annual grand parade marched down the length of the famous street culminating in a magnificent lightshow at the Arc de Triomphe to usher in the new year.

It was a different story this year.

The parade had been cancelled, and in its place a small vigil had grown into a mass gathering of mourners coming to pay their respects to those who'd lost their lives. The Arc de Triomphe served as a central altar, its lightshow changed to display the names of each of the confirmed victims instead of wishing everyone a *Bonne Année*.

As Maggie searched for the Acolytes, a sea of candles bathed placards and handmade signs in soft light. Some were commemorative, others angry or political. All displayed the unrelenting strength of Paris. Times may be hard, but they would stand tall and carry on.

Maggie shook her head and gestured out to the crowd. "This is impossible, Ash. All Dabir and the Acolytes need to do is mask as mourners. We'll never be able to pick them out in this."

They'd been there for hours now and had completed several sweeps through the crowd to no avail.

Ashton dropped his binoculars and nudged his head over to a nearby woman standing guard with an assault rifle. "Maybe those lot scared them off."

The French government had brought in military reinforcements to help contain the situation. Most wore their uniforms as an outward show of their presence. There were groups dressed as civilians, too, dispersed throughout the crowd. Dabir wasn't an idiot, though. He would have planned for the increase in security.

"No, he's here somewhere." Maggie felt it in her gut. According to Hakim, destroying the boat hardly made a dent in the truckload of explosives Dabir had acquired from Legrand. The Acolytes retained more than enough power to obliterate the entire vicinity and everyone in it.

"We should go," Ashton said. "You'll drive yourself nuts waiting here."

Ashton was right, but weaving through the crowd wasn't going to help. Dabir was a strategist. Based on the previous attacks, his plans were airtight. Nearly impossible to stop.

"We need to think." Maggie massaged her aching forehead and tried to concentrate. "Hakim said they had a shitload of explosives, right? Dabir would need someplace to conceal them."

There were plenty of buildings lining the street, but the police had already checked most of them. While Dabir and his followers could hide in plain sight, that volume of explosives would be harder to hide.

"Wherever they are, we need to find them quick. It's forty minutes to midnight." Ashton shifted on his feet, the anticipation of disaster putting them both on edge. And they weren't the only ones. Tension made the police fidget and the soldiers stand with especially rigid postures. They'd all been briefed; they all knew what was coming.

Maggie had to stop it. "You think he's waiting until the bells ring?"

"Looks like it. He certainly has an air for dramatics."

"Yes," Maggie agreed, thinking of the first attack back home.

Nina and Leon had spoken about the symbolism of hitting London's heart. The Arc de Triomphe de l'Étoile lay in the center of the Place Charles de Gaulle, a large road junction with twelve radiating avenues, hence the name: Triumphal Arch of the Star. It was the pinnacle of French patriotism, there to commemorate fallen soldiers, with an eternal flame burning for the unidentified who had died in the wars.

"Wait, that's it." Maggie grabbed Ashton's arm and yanked him down the stairs.

"What?"

Maggie pushed and shoved her way through the thicket of people, ignoring their protests as she headed straight for the opposite end of the Arc de Triomphe. "Dabir used the underground to plant his bomb below Trafalgar Square. What if he's done the same here?"

Ashton's gaze slipped to the ground as he kept pace beside her. Acknowledgement lit his eyes. "The underpass."

Maggie nodded and charged forward. If Ashton was right about the bomb going off at midnight, they had no time to politely travel between the huddles of people.

An underpass tunnel lay at the Avenue de la Grande Armee side of the circle, directly opposite the Champs-Élysées. It gave pedestrians a safe way to cross the round-about and reach the Arc de Triomphe without risking their lives crossing the notorious road that circled it. With no road marks and traffic coming from the twelve encompassing boulevards, attempts to cross the road were as good as suicide.

Thanks to the crowd, Maggie and Ashton had no vehicle traffic to worry about. When they finally reached the entrance to the pass, they took the steps leading down to the opening two at a time.

"Maggie! Ashton!" came a voice behind them. "Hey, Maggie, wait."

Maggie spun on her heels. "Hakim? What are you doing here?"

"We told you to stay in the apartment," Ashton yelled.

Hakim descended the steps to reach them, limping and favoring his right leg. "I know, but I was watching the coverage on the TV and it came to me. Dabir's going to do what he did at—"

"Trafalgar Square. Yes, we know," Maggie said.

Hakim deflated. "Oh."

Ashton checked his watch, panic in his voice. "Thirty-five minutes left, Mags."

"Go back to Ashton's, and be quick about it," Maggie ordered. "If we're right, the bomb's about to go off at midnight."

Hakim raised his chin and continued down the stairs. "I'm coming with you. This is my fight as much as yours."

Maggie didn't have time to argue. Time was ticking, and each second she wasted could mean the death of thousands. "Fine, but stay behind us. If things get bad, I want you to get out of there, okay?"

"Yeah, no heroics," Ashton said, handing Hakim one of his guns. "If we tell you to run, you run."

Hakim cocked the gun and gave a firm nod. "Fine."

It seemed Hakim hadn't wasted his time with the Acolytes. Bishop really would be interested in recruiting the boy. They set off without another word, keeping close.

Their pounding footsteps echoed off the walls, the ceiling arched and low to the ground. Shadows splayed out showing their approach thanks to the brightness of the lights that shone off the cream tiles.

"There," Maggie said, pointing to a jut in the wall: a service door lined within the tiles, its discreet handle the only thing indicating its presence.

Ashton grabbed the handle, and Maggie stood with her gun at the ready. The door had only opened a crack when it swung open from the inside.

An Acolyte barged though, the door hitting Ashton and knocking him back. The man charged straight for Hakim, but Maggie was ready for him. She shot him point blank in the back of the head and sent his brains splattering against the wall.

The gun shot reverberated through the tunnel. So much for the element of surprise.

The man's presence at least confirmed they were right about Dabir going underground. Motioning with a wave, Maggie took the helm and led her small team into the darkness beyond the door.

There were no lights here, and Maggie waited for her eyes to adjust before venturing too far in. Where there was one Acolyte, more would follow. "How many Brothers are left?" she asked Hakim, keeping her voice to a whisper.

"Eight," Hakim said from behind Ashton. "Nine if Dabir's here."

"Oh, he's here all right," Maggie said. He wouldn't want to miss his grand finale.

The narrow pathway was only wide enough for two

people, the surrounding walls bare and bitter cold to the touch.

Ashton rummaged in his pocket and brought out a small flashlight. It flickered to life and illuminated the faces of two approaching Acolytes.

Afraid to fire in such close proximity, Maggie holstered her gun, reached for her knives, and dove forward.

Maggie collided with the first man, knocking him to the ground and pinning him down. Her ribs screamed with pain, but she couldn't let up without losing her advantage. Ashton and Hakim were busy with the second attacker, the flashlight clattering to the ground with a crack. The light blinked out, and Maggie battled blind, aiming to stab the man beneath her.

Her opponent caught Maggie's wrist before the blade could penetrate. The Acolyte tried to pivot under her, but Maggie squeezed her thighs against the brute's sides and held steady.

Both their hands shook as they struggled. The man was stronger than Maggie, but she had the better position. She pushed with all her might, and he gasped as the tip of Maggie's knife met his flesh.

He wriggled under her, adrenaline giving his superior strength the edge it needed to push the blade back out. Maggie's arms shook, but she couldn't let him turn the blade. If he did, the tides would turn. She tightened her grip and dropped forward, pushing her entire weight into the hilt.

For a second, nothing happened. The blade quivered in the open air between them. Then the man sucked in a breath as his strength failed him and the knife plunged into his chest, glancing off his ribcage.

Warmth coated her hands, and a single sigh marked his final breath.

Sliding out her blade, Maggie got to her feet and wiped the slick blood onto her trousers.

"You good?" Ashton asked as he and Hakim came into view.

"Yes," Maggie said, catching her breath. "You?"

"Two down," Hakim reported. "Seven to go."

A shuffle of feet caught in Maggie's ear, and she spun in time to grab an approaching Brother. Maggie twisted away from his grabbing arms and caught him in a headlock.

His fingernails dug into her jacket, but she didn't relent. Then, with a vicious snap, she twisted his head and let his convulsing body fall to the floor.

"Make that six."

Hakim blinked in astonishment. "Wow."

Conscious of the literal ticking clock, Maggie ventured further down the pathway. A screeching noise rumbled beyond the walls, and the floor vibrated under their feet. It whizzed passed them in a rush of sound and carried off into the distance.

"The Métro," Maggie explained to Ashton and Hakim. It must have been a train passing on the Charles de Gualle – Étoile line that passed underneath the Arc de Triomphe.

The pathway grew wider, and after thirty more feet or so, it opened out into a generator room. Voices echoed from further down, but the noises coming from the Métro lines stopped them from being clear.

But Maggie knew who the voices belonged to, no matter the muffled sounds. She inched closer to the end of the pathway's wall.

Glancing back at Ashton and Hakim, who nodded their assent, Maggie rearmed herself and darted into the room.

Chapter 12

Everything happened in a flurry of bright flashes.

As soon as Maggie came into view, five Brothers holding guns released a tirade of bullets in her direction.

She lunged to the ground, ducking behind a piece of machinery and skinning her palms on the landing.

Ashton and Hakim made the most of the distraction and charged after her, gunshots deafening as bullets ricocheted off the metal shells of the generators.

Springing back up, Maggie swung out from the other side of the machinery and fired. The first bullet clipped an Acolyte in the shoulder. He fell back, but not before she planted another bullet in his chest.

A second body fell at Maggie's feet, and she turned to see a grinning Hakim lowering his gun. He shot her a wink before another Acolyte aimed at him and he ducked out of the way.

Maggie followed suit and pressed against one of the machines. Risking a look, she spotted Dabir heading towards a door at the far end of the room.

"Oh no you don't."

Leaping over a dead Acolyte, Maggie aimed fire. Dabir moved at the last minute, and the bullets imbedded in the door with a clang.

The terrorist leader abandoned the exit and dodged out of sight. Maggie made to follow him, but an Acolyte grabbed her from the back. He yanked her hair, and Maggie hissed as her blond locks tore from her scalp.

Maggie lashed out and caught him with a fist to the face. In his shock and pain, Maggie wriggled free and disarmed the gun from his hands.

The Acolyte recovered quick. He dodged her next punch and spun, kicking Maggie in her already broken ribs.

Acute pains stabbed up her side, and she doubled over. The Acolyte caught her with an uppercut and sent her flying back, her gun slipping from her grip and skidding across the floor.

Ashton's screams echoed through the room, and Maggie's stomach lurched. She gazed over at the exit door from on her back, dizzy with the throbbing pain in her ribs. Ashton was grappling with one of the terrorists, blood running down his face.

A fist caught Maggie across the jaw, forcing her attention back to her own opponent. She reached into her jacket and lashed out with the knife concealed there, slicing the blade through the air as the Acolyte swung again.

He pulled his fist back and roared in anger. Maggie jumped to her feet, and they circled the floor. She feinted an attack, but he didn't fall for it, holding back to avoid the edge of her blade.

Every move Maggie made sent shooting pains across her ribs. She went for another attack, but the Acolyte dodged and came in with one of his own.

The kick was hard, and Maggie was too slow to block it. It caught her in the ribs again, and fear thundered in her chest as she let out another cry of pain. The Acolyte knew she was injured. Knew her weak points.

Nausea coursed through Maggie, and she barely refrained from retching, forcing down bile as she stumbled to get back up. Hands reached out for her, and at first she thought it was her opponent.

Only when her original opponent returned did Maggie realize one of his Brothers had arrived to help end her life.

Still clutching to her knife, Maggie squirmed out of the new attacker's grip and brought her knife down on his boot. The newly sharpened blade made light work of the leather, and Maggie gave the knife a savage twist once it was in his foot.

Her original opponent grabbed her hair again and pulled her away from his Brother. Maggie let him drag her up, still holding onto her blade. A spray of blood covered her face from the second man's sliced foot, and she swung the knife up, using the momentum the first man provided.

Maggie roared and lodged the knife under the first Acolyte's chin. The blade went right through the skin, and the glint of metal winked at her as the Acolyte opened his mouth in shock.

His hold on her loosened. Maggie pulled out the knife and shoved the Acolyte back. He toppled over, and she left him to bleed out while she dealt with his Brother.

The second Acolyte was still holding his foot. Maggie jammed her knife in his back, the blade slicing through his spine.

He wasn't too fussed about his foot after that.

A gunshot rang out behind her, and Maggie's heart hammered in her ears. Her mind went to Ashton, and she raced for the door, afraid she'd find him bleeding out. Instead, she found him standing over another dead Acolyte. He checked his gun and, finding the clip empty, tossed it to the ground.

From her count, all of the Acolytes were down, except for one. "Where's Dabir?" she asked Ashton, giving him a quick check for wounds requiring immediate attention. Like her, he hadn't come out unscathed, but the cut on his head appeared superficial.

"I see you brought your friends, Hakim."

Maggie and Ashton snapped their heads towards the voice and found Dabir stepping out from one of the generators. He held Hakim at gunpoint, using him as a shield as he inched towards the middle of the room.

"Dabir," Maggie growled. She and Ashton spread out, angling in on the last living member of the Acolytes of the Holy War.

"Don't come any closer," he warned, pressing the end of the gun into Hakim's temple.

"Shoot him," Hakim spat, his words strangled by Dabir's muscled arm locked around his throat.

Maggie reached for her weapon, but she'd lost it during the fighting. She eyed the pile of explosives behind Dabir and Hakim, packed like a crate of bricks and wired to a detonator. A timer sat on top, running down the minutes, second by second.

"I would've preferred to be long gone before the main event, but you leave me no choice." Dabir followed Maggie's alarmed gaze to the wired device and punched in a series of numbers, his gun still trained on Hakim.

The timer went from twenty-nine minutes remaining to five.

A train rushed by through the walls, likely the very one Dabir and his men had planned to catch to make a quick exit before time ran out on the bomb, giving them a full half hour to escape to safety.

Maggie inched cautiously forward, arms held out.

"Dabir, it isn't too late. You can stop the bomb. You don't need to die down here."

Four minutes and twenty seconds.

"Foolish bitch. You think you can talk your way out of this? I'm not afraid to die. I'll be treated as a king in the afterlife, rewarded for my services to Allah."

"You're going to Jahannam," Hakim rasped, condemning Dabir to hell. "Allah will see you punished for the lives you've taken. There's no place in paradise for people like you."

Maggie stared at the timer.

Three minutes and forty-nine seconds.

Dabir reached behind him with his gun hand and grabbed something from the pile of explosives. "I guess we'll find out."

It was a detonator.

Maggie and Ashton moved to stop him, but they were too far away. Until now, Maggie had been afraid to throw her knife in case it hit Hakim, but it was a risk she'd need to take.

Dabir's thumb reached out to press down on the detonator, ready to manually override the timer and set the bomb off three minutes early.

"No!" Hakim cried. He bit down on Dabir's arm as Maggie threw her blade.

Dabir jerked back, shaking off Hakim's attack, inadvertently saving himself from taking Maggie's knife to the face.

Free from Dabir's clutches, Hakim dropped down next to a fallen Acolyte and took the gun he held in his dead hands. Dabir saw what Hakim was doing and aimed his weapon at the boy, dropping the detonator in the process.

Two guns fired.

But only one bullet found its target.

Chapter 13

Hakim's gun slipped through his fingers.

"No!" Maggie screamed. Hakim's eyes widened as he held a hand against his chest. His fingers came back wet and dripping red.

Hakim missed the shot, but Dabir hadn't.

Ashton ran to Hakim's side, but Maggie only had eyes for Dabir, a blast of fury igniting within her.

Dabir's maniacal laughter boomed through the room, and he returned his attention to the detonator.

Maggie dove, hitting the ground in a roll. On the way back to her feet, she grabbed Hakim's fallen gun and released three rapid shots.

The bullets reached their intended target, and Maggie smirked in dark satisfaction to see each of the deliberately placed holes in the terrorist's body.

Dabir's right hand no longer held the detonator, the device falling to his feet. In fact, his right hand ceased to exist. All that was left was a bloody, torn mess. The oozing hole in his chest mirrored the one in his forehead, and Dabir was dead by the time his body collapsed to the ground.

Maggie lowered her gun but didn't stop to process what happened.

She returned to her team, the rising panic clear in her voice. "Ashton." She pulled her friend up from Hakim as the boy lay on the floor with blood pooling around him. "Ashton, the bomb!"

Ashton stumbled to his feet, the blood draining from his face as Maggie led him to the pack of explosives.

Two minutes and thirty-one seconds.

They were all going to die.

"Can you stop it?" Maggie asked, shaking Ashton by the shoulders when he wouldn't respond, shock leaving him still as marble.

Ashton blinked once. Twice. Then with a shake of his head, he was himself again. He examined the bomb, each passing second bringing them closer to death. Wires jutted out and wrapped around the explosives in all directions, each of them a different color.

Maggie knew enough about bombs to know not all of them were necessary, placed there to confuse anyone trying to defuse it. One wrong cut of a decoy wire and the thing would blow instantly.

"Give me a knife," Ashton said, picking through the wires with blood soaked hands.

Maggie complied, handing him the one strapped to her ankle. "Do you know which wire to cut?"

"I'm not sure."

"You have to be sure. Or we and the thousands of people above us are going to be obliterated."

Ashton mopped his brow and let out a hollow laugh. "No pressure then."

Maggie paced behind him, trying not to add to his nerves, but they were running out of time. "Fifty seconds, Ash."

"I know, I know." Ashton fumbled with the wires, tracing them along their winding course around the explosives.

Forty seconds.

"It's between the blue one and the green," Ashton announced, his brow burrowed in concentration.

Maggie stood beside him, her mind turning to thoughts of Leon, and if she would ever get to see him again. "Which is it?"

"I don't know."

Thirty seconds.

"Hurry, Ashton. It's going to blow!"

Ashton let out a shaky breath, the knife in his hand hovering next to the green wire.

Twenty seconds.

"Do it!" Maggie urged, her muscles tightening as she

prepared for the worst.

Ashton went to cut the green, but at the last moment, he switched and grabbed the blue, pulling the knife up and snapping the wire in two.

The timer read eleven seconds and stayed there.

Maggie and Ashton stared at the clock. The seconds ticked on, but the clock didn't move. Finally, then tension melted out of Maggie's shoulders as their victory settled in.

"How did you know it was the blue wire?" Maggie leaned against the wall, her body going limp as her muscles relaxed, overcome with relief.

Ashton shrugged. "I didn't."

Maggie started, eyes wide and mouth agape. "You guessed?"

"Life's a gamble, Mags," Ashton said, like he just bet money on black or red at a roulette table instead of gambling the lives of thousands of people on a whim.

Maggie couldn't help but laugh. She shoved Ashton back a step then pulled him into her in a bear hug, not caring about the pain it caused her aching ribs. Blue was definitely her new favorite color.

They released each other and let out a triumphant sigh. They'd done it. They saved everyone. Maggie turned back to Hakim.

Well, almost everyone.

Maggie knelt down beside her old target.

"You did it," he said, staring up at them.

"We did it," Maggie corrected and took his hand with a squeeze. Ashton helped her bring him up to a sitting position.

Hakim smiled, his teeth stained red from the blood filling his mouth. "I'm glad you found me when you did. I couldn't have taken out Dabir on my own."

Maggie bit back tears and waited until she trusted herself to reply. "Thousands of people are alive because of you." Without Hakim, they would have never have found Dabir. His reign of terror would have continued with disastrous results.

"I'm going to die, aren't I?" Hakim asked.

He had already lost too much blood. There wasn't enough time to get him help, and Maggie couldn't lie to him. Not after everything he'd been through. He deserved the truth. "Yes."

A tear slid down his face as he accepted his fate, brave as ever. "Can you guys do something for me?"

"Anything," Ashton said, wiping at his eyes.

Hakim gave them his last request, and Maggie took out her phone.

It didn't take long after that. They stayed with him, Ashton cracking jokes all the while to distract him from the pain. His breathing grew weak, and Maggie stroked his hair, holding him, just as she had held little Oliver only days before.

Hakim finally slipped away in her arms, the light going out from those fiery, determined eyes of his. Maggie closed them shut and bowed her head over his body.

He was gone.

Chapter 14

Maggie brushed the hair from her bruised face as the wind picked up across the grave-yard. She stood at the top of the hill, watching the mourners below say their final farewells to Oliver Clark and his mum, Anna.

The city had come out in support, touched and saddened by the story of the little boy and his young mother who had died at the hands of the now eliminated terrorists. Or at least, Dabir's branch of the organization. Groups like the Acolytes were like the mythical hydra. You chopped off one head and two more grew in its place.

Maggie hadn't attended the church service. People were lined all the way outside and around the church gardens for the Clarks. Part of her was glad so many people cared for Oliver and Anna, and another part was relieved there wasn't room for her in the church. She didn't think she could have made it through the whole ceremony.

Maggie hugged herself against the cold as the snow continued to fall, cradling an absent hand over her stomach. Her ribs were in the process of healing; the Acolyte she'd fought added an extra break to the existing two. Still, she bore the pain. Pain meant she was alive.

The Clark funeral was one of many to take place over the last few days as the victims of the Trafalgar Square attack were laid to rest. The French were currently in the process of making sure all the bodies of the tourists on the Seine riverboat made it home so their friends and family could say a proper goodbye. It wasn't possible for all, given the nature of the attack.

"Thought I'd find you here."

Ashton walked over to her, and they stood shoulder to shoulder as they watched Oliver's tiny coffin being laid into the ground. Maggie knew he'd come, even if he hadn't expected to find her there. Though he tried to mask it behind his usual care-free front, the last week had taken as much of a toll on him as it had her.

"You okay?" she asked.

"Aye," he lied. "You?"

Maggie leaned her head into his shoulder. "Yeah."

"Look at this." Ashton handed his new phone to her. "Our boy Hakim's gone viral."

Hakim's beaten face appeared on the screen, the image jarring. Her heart panged at the sight of him, and she made a mental note to ask Bishop for Hakim's mother's address. She deserved to know how brave her youngest son had been from someone who had been there with him. While it wouldn't bring her son back, Maggie hoped it would give her some comfort to know Hakim had died a hero.

Maggie hit play on the video.

"My name is Hakim Hasan. I'm eighteen years old and from Birmingham. I love my mum, like wasting hours playing video games, and support Birmingham F.C., even though we're shit and never win anything."

Maggie laughed at that and wrapped her free arm around Ashton's.

"A few years ago, a terrorist group targeted my brother, Khalid. They manipulated him. Warped his brain into believing their lies. Looking back on it, I think Khalid was feeling lost. He had a bright future ahead of him and was the first person in our family to go to uni. Me and my mum were so proud of him."

Hakim coughed, and Maggie's hand came into view on the screen as she wiped the blood from his lips.

"Khalid killed ten people, and himself, in a suicide bombing. They say he yelled 'Allahu Akbar' before he did

411

it. Some of you watching won't know what that means, but you've probably heard it on the news and stuff. It's a term we Muslims use to remind ourselves every day that god is greater than the ugliness of the world. Terrorists like Dabir Omar and the Acolytes are part of that ugliness. They're so filled with hate and use God's name in vain to carryout horrible acts."

Maggie sniffed, seeing the pain in Hakim's face as he struggled on, knowing he was about to die. Even in his last moments, Hakim had wanted to try and help. To make a change.

"I want to make it clear to you all, that they don't speak for us. Islam is a peaceful and beautiful faith, and every-thing they do goes against our beliefs. I know you're afraid. We are, too. But please don't lump us in with them in your mind. We're just like you."

Hakim was crying now, but he continued on, Maggie recalling how cold he was laying there on the hard floor.

"I'll never see it, but I hope that one day everyone will come together instead of breaking further apart. It's the only way to stop this mess from happening over and over again."

Hakim was visibly shaking now, his lips growing a cold shade as his body tremored.

"And to those out there who are doing what the Acoltyes did to my brother; You will not win. Fear will not prevail. One day the world will unite as one, and on that day, you will fall."

The video stopped, and Maggie handed the phone back to Ashton. So far, Hakim's final words had been viewed over three million times. Maggie didn't know if it would make a difference, if things really would change for the better, but like Hakim, she had hope.

And as long as she had hope, she could continue to fight against those who want to see the world burn.

"Come on," she said, turning from the graveyard below as the funeral ended. "I could use a drink."

"Now there's a plan," Ashton said, brightening up. "You buying?"

Maggie grinned and shook her head. "I was going to, but then I remembered you have that big expensive apartment in Paris."

Ashton laughed. "Touché."

Maggie didn't know what her future would hold. So much had changed over the last few months. Life altering things that made her a different person to the woman she was before. Things were far from perfect, but time would pass and help heal some of the wounds she'd collected.

And until then, she had her dear friend and some good whiskey to keep her company.

NEVER MISS A RELEASE!

Thank you so much for reading the Maggie Black Case Files. I hope you enjoyed it!

I have so much more coming your way. Never miss a release by joining my free VIP club. You'll receive all the latest updates on my upcoming books as well as gain access to exclusive content and giveaways!

To sign up, simply visit
https://jackmcsporran.com/vendettasignup

Thank you for reading the Maggie Back Case Files collection! If you enjoyed the books, I would greatly appreciate it if you could consider adding a review on your bookstore of choice.

Reviews make a huge difference to the success or failure of a book, especially for newer writers like myself. The more reviews a book has, the more people are likely to take a shot on picking it up. The review need only be a line or two, and it really would make the world of difference for me if you could spare the three minutes it takes to leave one.

With all my thanks,

Jack McSporran

KILL ORDER IS OUT NOW!

Check out the first full-length instalment of the gripping
Maggie Black series.

Deadly. Beautiful. On the run.

When secret agent Maggie Black agrees to protect the
Mayor of London, she thinks she's in for a boring night of
babysitting. The simple job gets a lot more complicated
when an assassin arrives and takes out the Mayor, framing
Maggie as the killer.

Unable to explain the evidence against her, Maggie is
branded a traitor and hunted by the very people she once

fought beside. With no one to turn to, Maggie relies on the one person who has always had her back—herself.

From the hidden nightclubs of Madrid, to the dark streets of Moscow, Maggie must delve into the depths of the criminal underworld to unearth the truth, and fast. Because time is running out and the enemy is closer than she thinks...

Get your copy of Kill Order today!

A SNEAK PEEK INSIDE KILL ORDER...

CHAPTER 1

CANNES, FRANCE

18 MAY

Maggie Black scanned the top deck of the luxury yacht and searched for her target.

A sea of people crowded the open space. Everyone from A-list actors and rock stars to wannabes and groupies were all there for the annual Cannes Film Festival. Even the patient onboard staff seemed impressed as they waited on Hollywood royalty.

The security guards were less impressed. Maggie made sure to keep an extra eye on them. They wandered among the guests in suits that strained against muscled arms, their postures rigid and wires barely hidden in their ears. Blending in wasn't on their list of priorities – unlike Maggie's.

"What did you say your name was again?" asked an irritating brunette to Maggie's left. The stench of cigarette smoke and vodka assaulted her with the woman's every breath.

"Eva," Maggie replied, swirling her glass of water on the rocks. She leaned against the rails of the balcony and looked over the woman's shoulder, feigning interest in whatever it was she was saying.

Music blared from a deejay booth in the center of the partial deck as people well past drunk danced under the glow of the moon, its light glittering off the water as the yacht bobbed a half mile out from the port.

"And what do you do?" the brunette asked, who'd introduced herself as Brooke. Or Becky. Or something like that.

"I'm a model." Maggie didn't bother looking at her conversation partner. She was far more interested in the guard nearest her, and the flash of his pistol as he adjusted his jacket. A black Smith and Wesson from the looks of it. Her hand itched for her own 9mm Glock 19, but it was back in her hotel room.

The crew had searched everyone before coming onboard, and her tight-fitting red dress could hardly conceal a weapon like that. Tonight, Maggie was armed with her wit and her fists.

"Funny, I don't recognize you," Brooke said, the hint of a sneer edging at the corner of her ruby lips.

"Most of my work is international. I did a shoot in Japan last week."

The shoot – two bullets in a Japanese businessman. One in his chest and one in the head to make sure. The British government didn't take too kindly to those caught selling malware to their enemies. In this case, a militia group planning a cyber-attack against the National Health Service.

Maggie flipped her waves of long blond hair to the side and turned to gaze over the deck below.

Plush sofas sat in clusters around glass tables, each of them covered with champagne bottles and bowls of suspicious-looking white powder piled high in the center.

She moved from face to face, evaluating then discarding them one by one. None of them matched the image of the reporter she'd memorized.

Then she saw him. Adam Richmond. Investigative reporter, trust fund playboy, and seller of classified information.

Brooke yapped in Maggie's ear about some movie producer she was seeing, but Maggie paid her no mind. She focused all her attention on the tall, dark, handsome man chatting up a beautiful woman near the bar.

The woman touched his arm and laughed at whatever Adam said. Her clear interest seemed to bore Adam, and his gaze moved from the woman to the rest of the party.

Condensation dripped down Maggie's glass as she took a sip. The day's heat lingered into the night, making Maggie's pale skin glow amid the humid air. The sky had bled out and bruised to a dark purple, promising another ideal day for the film festival. Though not everyone onboard would see the sun rise.

Adam's eyes traveled towards the top deck and landed on Maggie. He grinned at her, the woman beside him forgotten. Maggie watched him with open interest and tucked a strand of hair behind her ear.

He gestured to the bar, where a barman placed two glasses of bubbling champagne on the counter. *Smooth.*

Maggie abandoned her spot at the railing, leaving a flustered Brooke behind without a goodbye, and made her way to him. She took her time travelling down the stairs, allowing her leg to peek out from the slit of her dress, feeling his eyes take her in from head to toe.

As she reached the bottom step, Adam dug into his jacket pocket and brought a cellphone to his ear. His face grew serious as he spoke, his attention stolen from her. Maggie frowned. She made for the bar, but a group of partiers interrupted her path and blocked her view of the target.

When they dispersed, Adam was gone.

Maggie picked up her pace and reached the bar. "The man who was just standing here, where did he go?"

The barman shrugged, busy shaking cocktails and hounded with calls for service from the other guests.

Maggie scanned the bar, but Adam was nowhere to be found. *Shit.*

She scoured the whole deck in search for him, heat rising to her cheeks. A drunk man stumbled into her and stood on the bottom of her dress, pinning her to the spot. Maggie yanked the dress back and shoved the guy away from her. If only she could have worn trousers instead of an insufferable dress.

Holding the train away from her feet, she weaved through the party and headed inside, closing the heavy watertight door behind her.

The bass from the speakers outside hummed through the wooden floors, adding to the rocking of the water as Maggie hurried down the corridor. Her sea legs had suffered much worse than the tame waves of the Mediterranean, allowing her to move with ease, even in killer heels.

Passing a lounge area with a grand piano nestled in the corner, she smiled at those standing around it, singing songs and taking shots of amber liquid. *At least someone gets to enjoy the cruise,* she thought as she continued deeper into the heart of the yacht.

Maggie rounded a corner and took a flight of stairs leading down to the sleeping quarters on the deck below. Voices made her freeze.

"No," said a muffled voice. "I don't want to."

"Yes, you do." The second voice was deep. Slurred. "You've been hanging over me all night."

"Please."

"Shh," the male voice cooed. "You know you want it."

Maggie leaned down to get a look.

A man in his fifties had a young girl pinned against the wall, a meaty hand covering her mouth to stop her from calling out or screaming.

Maggie's nails dug into her palm. She continued down

the stairs and marched up behind the man. "Hey," she called, grabbing the man's shoulder.

"We're busy here." His scowl was soon replaced with a sloppy smile. He whistled, looking Maggie up and down. "Want to join in?"

Maggie grimaced at the man, whose shirt was soaked through with sweat. "Get your hands off her."

The man laughed and returned his focus to the frightened girl. "If you're not interested, piss off before I lose my patience."

Maggie took a deep breath. She couldn't afford to cause a scene or waste time. She needed to find Adam.

The man laughed at her and shook his head. "Stupid bitch."

Maggie grabbed him again and spun him around to face her. She smashed her fist into his bulbous nose, the bone cracking with a delicious snapping sound.

Blood flooded from his nostrils and ran down his chin.

"You broke my fucking nose!" The man lunged at her, but Maggie was ready for him. She caught him with a mean right hook, sending him crashing to the floor with a thump.

The girl leaned against the wall and blinked at Maggie. Her eyes were dilated, and black hair stuck to the sides of her face.

"You okay?" Maggie asked.

The girl stared at her knocked-out attacker and gave a little nod.

"Good. Get out of here and don't tell anyone what happened."

"What about him?" she asked.

"I'll deal with it. Now go, and make sure you drink plenty of water until the yacht gets back to the port." Cocaine and alcohol was one cocktail the girl could do without.

"I will. Thanks." The girl backed away then ran upstairs and out of sight.

Maggie rested her hands on her hips and sighed. She kicked the big lump with the tip of her shoe, then hoisted him up by the arms and dragged him into a nearby supply closet. Maggie shut the door and allowed herself a brief moment to catch her breath before moving on. The dead weight of the man, combined with the heat, sent trickles of sweat down her back.

The lower deck was deserted, the hum of the party echoing from above. Maggie walked towards the aft until the music died enough to hear waves sloshing against the sides of the yacht. She reached a wide hallway with numbered rooms running along either side. Someone had left a door ajar, which revealed a large suite with a king-sized bed and a private balcony.

Her reports said Adam Richmond was staying onboard the yacht during his stay in Cannes. One of his many high roller friends owned the vessel, an investment banker on Wall Street. Adam must have a private room. Somewhere.

Maggie strained her ears and listened for any signs of

life. She tried the first door, but it was locked. As was the next.

This is taking too long. Maggie felt around for the light switch. She flicked off the lights and allowed her eyes to settle. There. At the end of the row to the left.

Light emanated in a thin strip from under the bedroom door. She grinned. *Bingo.*

Maggie turned the lights back on and crept toward the door. She pressed her ear against the wood, careful to stay out of view from the peephole. Footsteps. She was sure of it.

Maggie gripped the door handle, hoping it wasn't locked, and turned it. The door swung open and she stumbled inside, pretending to lose her balance.

Adam jumped in his chair, closing his laptop before turning to face her.

"Oh," Maggie said, wobbling on her feet, "this isn't Brooke's room."

"No, it's not." Adam got up from his chair and ushered her towards the door. He stopped when he got up close to her, his face brightening. "You're the woman from the top deck."

"And you're the man from the bar." Maggie let out a laugh. "I'm sorry. I was looking for my friend, and I got the room numbers mixed up."

"A happy coincidence." Adam crossed the room and opened a minibar, taking out a bottle of cognac. "How about that drink?"

Maggie looked back out into the hall. "I should really be getting back."

"Oh, come on. Just one drink. I insist." Adam shot her a wide smile, his schoolboy charm laid on as thick as his upper-class drawl.

Maggie pretended to consider his offer and shrugged. "Well, if you *do* insist." She closed the door behind her with a soft *click*.

She eyed the closed laptop as Adam poured the drinks into curved crystal glasses. Maggie didn't know what secrets lay inside the hard drive or who the reporter planned on selling them to, but she knew one thing. The transaction would never take place. Not on her watch.

Adam returned and handed her a filled glass. He held his own to hers and they clinked their glasses.

"I'm Adam, by the way."

"Eva," Maggie said, biting her lip. She tossed back her glass in one gulp, and the cognac burned down her throat in a comforting warmth.

Adam's eyebrows rose and then he followed suit, smacking his lips.

"The party couldn't hold your attention?" Maggie asked, brushing her hand against his.

"Let's just say things have certainly picked up, thanks to you."

Maggie gave him a playful push. "Charmer."

He grinned at that, and Maggie suppressed the urge to roll her eyes. A light breeze swept in from the balcony, the curtain sweeping up like a phantom warning of things to come.

"I don't mean to be forward," he said, stepping closer so his chest pressed against hers, "but what would happen if I tried to kiss you right now?"

Maggie raised her head and whispered into his ear. "Why don't you try and find out?"

Adam closed his eyes and moved his head towards her with parted lips.

Maggie placed her hands at either side of his face and leaned towards him. Before Adam Richmond's lips could touch her own, she tightened her grip and jerked her hands with a savage twist.

His neck snapped. A clean, precise break.

They always were.

Maggie let go, and Adam collapsed to the floor, his head lolling to the side.

She stepped over him and sat down at the desk, the seat still warm from the reporter's body, which now grew cold on the floor.

She opened the laptop, took out a portable USB stick from her bra, and plugged it into the port at the side.

Taking a quick glance at the folders stored in the hard drive, Maggie transferred the files onto the USB.

Five percent complete. The green bar grew longer as each file downloaded. *Ten percent.*

A loud knock rapped on the door. "Mr. Richmond, are you okay? We heard a crash."

Maggie's heart leapt in her ribcage. The man's phrasing was not lost on her.

We.

Maggie tapped the side of the laptop. "Come on, come on."

Twenty percent complete.

Sliding out of her heels, Maggie slipped off her dress and stripped down to the thermal bathing suit concealed beneath. She leaned down and collected one of her heels.

Fifty percent complete.

Maggie stared at the body. The man behind the door called again. "Mr. Richmond? I'm coming in."

Bollocks.

The door swung open as Maggie charged across the room. She surprised the first guard, swinging her shoe to meet his head. The heel hit his temple, and blood spurted out like oil from a well.

The next guard was ready for her.

She sent a punch to Maggie's gut, forcing the air out her lungs. The woman reached for her gun, but Maggie charged into her side and rammed her against the door. Their impact slammed the door shut and they tripped over the fallen guard, who squirmed around like a fish out of water, holding his head to keep his brain inside.

Maggie scrambled to her feet, but the woman grabbed her hair and sent her reeling back.

She went with the momentum, hissing as hair ripped

out from her scalp. Maggie rolled into the fall and kicked up, her bare heel connecting with the woman's jaw.

The guard collapsed beside her now unconscious partner.

Maggie returned to the laptop, picking up the woman's gun as she went.

Eighty percent complete.

Footsteps sounded outside, coming closer. She counted four different gaits before she sent six rounds through the door.

Ninety-five percent complete.

There was a commotion outside the door, and it barged open, hitting the fallen guards.

Ninety-eight percent complete.

Someone grunted on the other side of the door as they shoved, sliding the fallen guards forward across the floor.

One-hundred percent complete.

Maggie pulled out the USB and scooped up the laptop. Behind her, the guards shoved the door open enough to fit through.

She reached the balcony and launched the laptop overboard. It landed in the water with a satisfying splash and sank to the murky depths below.

A call came from behind her as the first guard slipped through the gap. Maggie aimed and shot the guard through the thigh. He fell to the ground as three more entered the room and more guards shouted in the corridor.

Maggie dropped the gun and turned back to the

balcony. She ran forward and leapt in the air. Her body passed over the railings, and she positioned herself into a dive and met the water as gunshots carried out through the night.

CHAPTER 2

LONDON, GREAT BRITAIN

19 MAY

Maggie turned the keys in the lock and entered her apartment. A pile of letters lay on the floor waiting for her. She bent down with a groan, her muscles aching from the events of the night before, and nudged the door shut with her foot.

Bills, junk mail, bank statements, take out menus. Nothing important. She tossed them onto the kitchen counter with her keys, kicked off her boots, and wheeled her suitcase into her bedroom. She'd unpack later.

The air in the apartment was stale from disuse. Maggie lit a lemon scented candle, sitting it on the table beside the large living room windows. She peered out at the city skyline, the River Thames flowing past The O2 arena, illuminated like the towers behind it, which belonged to Canary Wharf's most influential banks.

Her reflection stared back at her. She looked tired, her

hair pulled back from her face and bags resting under her ice blue eyes.

Maggie turned away, taking off her coat and draping it over her leather corner couch. A red flickering light caught her attention, the answering machine blinking to alert her of a new message.

Just one. She hadn't been home for over two weeks.

Maggie played the message and plodded over to the fridge to appease her grumbling stomach. Empty, aside from a jar of pickles and a container of something that had long since passed its sell by date. Maggie dumped the container in the bin and ran a hand over her head.

The message played and a woman's voice filled the open plan living space.

"Hi, this is Laura from First Class Travel. I'm calling to fill you in on some of our latest deals as you bought a holiday from us eighteen months ago. I guess you're at work right now, so phone me back when you can. Remember, life isn't all work and no play. You deserve some down time, and we have the perfect hot spots for you to choose from. Bye for now."

Maggie deleted the message and stared at the now empty answering machine. It felt like all she did was travel, though never for pleasure. Even the trip Laura the travel agent mentioned went unused; Maggie was stuck undercover in Morocco at the time.

A familiar shadow crossed the floor of her balcony and pressed up to the sliding door.

Maggie let the black cat in, her only visitor to the riverside apartment since she bought the place last year.

"Hello, Willow." Maggie scratched the cat behind the ears.

Willow rubbed herself against Maggie and circled around her legs, purring up at her. For a stray, Willow was a rather affectionate feline.

Maggie rummaged through the cupboards in the kitchen in search of a can of tuna to feed her furry friend, but like the fridge, they were a barren wasteland.

Willow meowed.

"Chinese food it is then."

Maggie called the restaurant around the corner and placed her usual order. Thirty minutes later, her chicken chow mein and spring rolls arrived, along with steamed fish for Willow.

She switched on the TV, but nothing held her attention for long. There was a spy film showing on one of the movie channels, and Maggie laughed at the ridiculous gadgets featured. Give her an old-fashioned gun or knife any day.

Turning off the TV, Maggie finished her meal in peaceful silence. She fell back on her couch, still smelling as new as the day it arrived, and pulled her bare feet up, closing her eyes as Willow snuggled into her.

A few minutes later, Maggie was back on her feet, pacing around her unused home. It was always like that after a mission, especially one that involved wet work.

Unlike her television, Maggie couldn't simply press an off switch. She'd lost count of how many lives she'd taken over the years, her first at the ripe young age of fifteen. Perhaps she didn't want to know the number.

She could ring Ashton, but he would be busy. The man had never seen a Friday night he didn't like; not that he needed the weekend as an excuse to get up to no good. Besides, she hadn't spoken to him for almost a month. Hopping from one job to the next was a sure-fire way to annihilate any resemblance of a social life.

Her thoughts travelled to Leon, but Maggie was fast to shove them aside.

Fed and watered with a belly full of fish, Willow gave herself a shake, leapt off the couch, and left the way she came in, back out into the night and leaving Maggie alone.

It took all of five minutes before Maggie collected her computer from the coffee table and fired it up. She inserted the USB stick from her mission and downloaded the files she copied off Adam Richmond's computer.

Hours passed as Maggie combed over the contents, reading articles the reporter had penned himself, scrolling through emails from his work and personal accounts, and clicking from one image to the next in his photo folder.

It was almost midnight when she came across something that caught her eye, though it wasn't what she had expected to discover.

Maggie grabbed her mobile and rang one of the few

numbers stored in her contacts. The person at the other end answered after three rings.

"We need to meet."

Chapter 3
20 May

M aggie arrived at Westminster Station by way of Canning Town, maneuvering through the crowds of eager tourists and early risers, and up the stone steps out onto Bridge Street.

Big Ben watched her as she buttoned her jacket and crossed Parliament Street, continuing down Great George Street. A mass of enraged gray clouds hung over her, threatening rain in typical British fashion for the approaching summer.

She stopped into a café for a much-needed coffee and then cut through St. James's Park. Maggie stopped by the bridge and sipped her drink while she watched some children feed the ducks. Boisterous pigeons swooped down and stole the pieces of bread from their little hands with the skill of London's best thieves.

Maggie arrived at her destination soon after, staring up at the five-story office building on King Street that served as the Unit's headquarters. Disguised as Inked

International, a global stationery supplier, the boring nature of the business gave those not in-the-know no reason to walk through the doors.

The only time anyone ever tried to enter was when they stumbled home from The Golden Lion, an old-school pub next door where Maggie spent one too many nights drinking her way through their collection of whiskies in her early years as an agent.

Maggie swiped her security pass at the entrance. The locks clicked open, and Maggie walked to the elevators, her heels clacking on the marble floor. She entered the empty cab, pressed the button for the top floor, and waited.

"Hold on," came a voice before a foot wedged between the closing doors. The man pried them open and stood beside her in the confined space.

Maggie focused on keeping her face expressionless, her heart fluttering at the sight of him. She cleared her throat, the familiar woody scent of his favorite aftershave dancing in her nose.

"Hi, Leon."

"How you doing, Maggie?" he asked in his deep, gravelly voice.

"Just back from an assignment last night. You?"

"Can't complain." Leon hit the button for the fourth floor. "I thought you just came back from Japan the other week?"

"Are you keeping tabs on me?" Maggie craned her

neck to meet his dark brown eyes for the first time. At six foot three, Leon Frost had over half a foot on her.

"I worry, that's all," he said, his white shirt crisp and bright against his black skin. "Every agent needs some downtime after being out there."

"I'm a big girl, I can look after myself."

Leon sighed and rubbed a strong hand over his close-trimmed beard. "I didn't mean it like that."

It was always like that these days. Both with so much to say to each other, yet saying nothing at all.

They stood in awkward silence until the elevator pinged and opened at Leon's floor. He stepped out, and the cab felt empty without him.

Leon stopped and turned back to her. "You look good, Maggie."

"You too," she said, gripping onto her jacket sleeve.

The doors closed between them, and Maggie took a deep, shaking breath. Seeing Leon was never easy, especially when she wasn't prepared for it.

Straightening her back, she swept her feelings to the side as the elevator stopped on her floor. By the time she stepped out, she was back to normal, her training kicking in.

Never let anyone see you sweat.

Brice Bishop was waiting for her in his office with a cup of tea in his hand.

"Maggie," he said, the remnants of a Manchester accent still in his inflection. "Nice to have you back."

Maggie sat down across from his desk. "Thanks."

Bishop's office was clean and Spartan, the result of a long career in the military before he joined the Unit. His phone buzzed and he read the message, tossing it back on the desk with a heavy sigh.

"Everything okay?"

"June," said Bishop, needing no further clarification. The divorce with his wife had been a long and messy one, their relationship barely civil and only so because of their kids.

"What now?"

"I finally get the girls next weekend, and she's trying to cancel."

"Why?"

"She and *Brian*," he said, the distain for his ex-wife's new fiancé clear from the way he growled the man's name, "decided to take a family holiday that week. If I cancel, I don't get to see them for at least another three weeks."

"And if you don't, you're the bad one for cancelling their holiday," Maggie finished. It had taken a while for Bishop to get back on good terms with his teenage daughters, both girls siding with their mother during the divorce.

Bishop leaned back in his chair. "June's design, of course. She should have been an agent."

"I'm sorry, Bishop."

Bishop tried to shrug like it was nothing, but he didn't quite pull it off.

For a man in his late fifties, he still clung to his brown

hair which he kept cropped at the sides like he was still a soldier. Crow's feet perched at the corners of his eyes, his skin tough as leather, and nose bent out of shape from when Maggie had broken it during her first official mission.

To the untrained eye, Bishop appeared as just another businessman living in London who looked after himself and wore expensive suits. It was all deliberate, of course. Brice Bishop was so much more than that, and stories of his days as an agent still passed around the Unit like folktales. He was one of the best.

"Enough about that. I trust everything went well?"

Maggie nodded. "All according to plan."

"Excellent."

"There was one thing."

"Oh?"

"I couldn't find any of the stolen secrets on Richmond's laptop." Not one file. She searched for hidden folders and encrypted documents disguised as something else, but the laptop was empty.

"You read the computer files?"

"I figured I should check what the secrets were, in case any of them were an imminent threat to national security." And out of sheer curiosity to find out what was so classified that Richmond had to die, but Maggie kept that to herself.

Bishop nodded. "Good thinking."

Maggie leaned forward in her chair. "But that's just it. I didn't find any."

"Nothing?" Bishop frowned.

"Not nothing, but not what we were looking for."

Maggie got up and turned on the computer. It was linked to a projector Bishop used when hosting meetings. Like she did at her apartment, she plugged in the USB stick and selected some of the files of note.

"I trolled through every file on here. Junk for the most part, but one folder in particular stood out." Maggie clicked the first file and it appeared on the projector screen on the wall. "Richmond was working on a story, investigating a private and commercial property developer named Brightside Property and Construction Limited."

Bishop clasped his hands. "What was his angle?"

"Corruption. Apparently, the company applied for planning permission on a plot of land in the East End, but it was declined." Richmond had acquired a copy of the application to prove it.

"Why?"

Maggie brought up an article that had made it onto the BBC News website. "The land is home to a row of government assisted houses owned by the local council. The residents are refusing to move."

"Where does the corruption come in?" Bishop asked, his tea growing cold on the desk.

"Brightside recently purchased the houses from the government, which now makes the homes private rentals.

Brightside increased the rent payments to unaffordable levels to push the residents out."

Bishop shook his head. "Legally evicting them. Sly bastards."

"It's worked for the most part," Maggie continued, "but a few of the residents are causing a stink about it and going to the press. There have been reports of intimidation, too. Residents claim men knocked on their doors in the middle of the night and threatened them, warning them to move."

Richmond had gathered some written testimonies and a few names, but nothing concrete. It didn't take long for Maggie to find a way into the Metropolitan Police's records and hunt down police reports to corroborate the stories.

"I did some digging. Similar reports have been made against Brightside in other developments in London and surrounding areas over the years."

Maggie clicked on another file. A photo of a body appeared on the screen, an old man beaten to death, his face purple and swollen.

"Eric Solomon was found dead in his home, the victim of a supposed break-in."

Bishop examined the photos on the screen. "What makes you think he wasn't?"

"The week before his body was found, Mr. Solomon turned down a substantial financial offer from Brightside to move. He'd purchased the council house he was living in before Brightside took over and procured the surrounding land. His refusal to move would have stopped their plans to knock down the houses and build a shopping center on the land."

Maggie brought up the proposed plans for the construction. Richmond had really done his homework.

"With the old man dead, Brightside could carry on with their plans," Bishop said, tying up all the pieces with a neat bow.

"That's what I'm thinking." Maggie pulled the USB from the computer. "Though it seems strange for someone like Adam Richmond to investigate all this while preparing to sell classified documents to the highest bidder."

"Perhaps it was part of his cover," ventured Bishop. "He was an investigative reporter after all."

Bishop could be right. Maggie sat back down and slid the USB across the desk to him. "I don't know all the big players yet, but I will soon enough. I'm pretty sure Richmond was on to something here. Something big."

"Great work. Really." Bishop leaned back in his chair. "I'll speak with the Director General and see if she can dig anything up from the guys at MI5. They might already be looking into the dealings of this company." He shook his head. "Richmond must have kept the stolen files somewhere else."

"I can contact Ms. Helmsley if you want," Maggie offered. The Director General was known as a pit bull in a power suit around the Unit, but Maggie liked her. She had a knack for seeing through bullshit and kept the men running around for her like they were little boys and she their headmistress.

"No, that's all right, I'll do it." Bishop slid a manila folder in front of her. "I have a favor to ask of you in the meantime."

"What?" Maggie eyed the folder but didn't pick it up.

"The Mayor of London is the keynote speaker at an international business conference in the financial district and has requested a chaperone."

Maggie sighed. "When?"

"Tonight," said Bishop. "Nina will be there, too, following the same orders for the Foreign Secretary."

"Why can't another agent do it?" The last thing Maggie wanted to do was go back out on a mission. She'd only just gotten home. "I saw Leon coming in."

"Leon is already assigned to another case. All my other agents are tied up."

Maggie remained quiet. If she wanted a career in babysitting, she would've been a nursery teacher.

"It's only for a couple of hours," added Bishop, giving her that pleading look she hated.

Maggie drooped her shoulders. "I can look after them both on my own. No need to send two agents for this type of job." If she wasn't getting the night off, at least Nina could.

"Nina is going, too. You really need to learn to work

with others," Bishop said, not for the first time. "You can't do everything on your own."

Maggie folded her arms. It wasn't that she didn't like Nina. They had known each other since they joined the Unit at sixteen. She just worked better alone. "Fine, but I'm taking my annual leave after this."

"Of course." Bishop handed her the file containing what she would need to know for the evening's event. "Thanks, Maggie."

Maggie took the manila folder and left Bishop's office. Maybe she would call that travel agent back after all.

CHAPTER 4

The taxi took a left from Leadenhall Street and turned into St Mary Axe, where a swanky new hotel had opened on the corner of Bevis Marks, right next to The Gherkin.

Maggie paid the fare and stepped out into the cold. The sky's earlier promise of rain came through, and huge droplets plummeted down from the heavens.

She ducked under the covered entrance to the Baltic Hotel and shook her umbrella out.

"I'll take that for you, Madam," said a man by the door, ushering her inside.

"Thank you," she said. "I'm here for the conference."

The man pointed across the room to where a sign stood for the event. "Straight ahead."

Maggie walked through the foyer and arrived at a large and glamorous conference room, decked out with chandeliers hanging from the high ceilings that overlooked round tables. At the back of the conference room, Maggie noted the podium where the mayor would give his talk.

The tables were set with fine porcelain dishes, crystal glassware, and golden cutlery. The staff had even arranged the napkins into elegant swans. Ten seats a piece were tucked under the tables, upholstered in fine gold suede to match the intricate filigree design of the wallpaper.

Along the bar sat buckets of champagne resting on ice, ready for when the attendees arrived.

The organizers had spared no expense, appropriate given the high-profile guests could bring millions of pounds in foreign investments into London's private sector.

Nina stood waiting for her near the bar as staff milled around the room making final touches to the pristine layout.

"I've scoped out the place," announced Nina by way of hello. "Everything's in order."

She wore a sleek gown with a plunging neckline, the emerald fabric bringing out the green in her hazel eyes. It also did a good job of hiding the knives Maggie knew would be strapped to Nina's thighs. She had a fondness for getting up close and personal with her enemies.

"Good," replied Maggie, taking a quick look around. "Where are our charges?"

"Upstairs in one of the suites," Nina said as she headed out to the foyer and climbed the stairs.

Maggie followed, cursing the dress code. Why did she always find herself stuck in a dress? At least the black number she wore tonight wasn't hugging her hips. Her gun sat in its holster around her thigh, the familiar weight like a deadly comfort blanket.

"Here's your ear piece." Nina handed it over to Maggie along with a clipboard, both playing the role of event coordinators for their cover.

"It's already wired in to the right frequency." Nina spoke into the little microphone of her own device. "Testing."

"One, two, three," Maggie replied, securing hers around her ear, careful not to disturb her chignon hairdo. If she had to wear a dress, the least her hair could do was to stay out of her face.

"How was Cannes?" Nina asked, slowing down to walk by Maggie's side.

They were around the same height, but where Maggie was curved with vulpine features, Nina was lithe and all sharp angles, from her cutting cheekbones to her pointed nose.

"A pain in the neck," Maggie said. "The weather was nice though."

Nina shook her head. "Bishop really needs to stop sending me to places that require thermals."

"That's what you get for speaking Russian."

Nina huffed, a playful grin edging her lips. "You speak it, too, and you got to party on a yacht."

Maggie held up her hands. "Hey, I'm not complaining."

"Must be nice being the favorite," Nina teased, nudging her.

While preferring to work alone, if Maggie had to work with anyone, she was glad it was Nina. They were both teenagers when Bishop recruited them. Though they viewed each other as rivals at first, it didn't take long for them to become good friends. There weren't many women in the Unit, so they bonded quickly.

Like most old boys' clubs, the Unit had some work to do to bridge the gender imbalance. One too many meetings suffered from an overload of alpha-male testosterone. Not that Maggie or Nina had any trouble being heard. They just had to trample on a few toes first.

When they reached the third floor, Nina led Maggie to the corner suite, walking past two armed men who stood sentry before the entrance. Nina stopped in front of the door. "Fair warning, the Foreign Secretary is rather sloshed."

"Some boys just can't handle their drink," Maggie said with a sigh.

Nina ran a hand through her locks of straight chestnut hair and gave Maggie a wink.

The suite was as expected, given how the rest of the Baltic Hotel was decorated. The designers were fans of gold and rich creams, the primary colors of the sitting area that separated the bedrooms and bathroom. White lilies bloomed in several vases around the space and filled the air with their light floral scent.

A man got up from the couch on unstable legs. Nina was right, George Moulton was drunk, and from the triple measure in his hand, he had no intentions of stopping.

"Very nice indeed," he said, his voice loud and irritating. He studied them with glassy eyes, his fake tan a shade too orange to fool anyone into thinking it was real. "Why does Bishop only recruit sexy girls?"

Maggie responded with a raised eyebrow, biting her tongue to refrain from assassinating him with a response. At least she wasn't in charge of babysitting him for the night.

Nina stiffed at the mention of Bishop. "Is anyone else here?" she hissed.

"Relax, it's just us," said Moulton, shaking his head.

Nina glared at him.

Knowledge of the Unit was strictly classified due its propensity to cross the line of what was legal. Only those with a high enough clearance were made aware of its existence. Most of those working for the Secret Intelligence Service weren't even privy to their clandestine faction.

Ignoring the Foreign Secretary, Maggie walked over to the other man in the room. The Mayor of London was busy reading over notecards by the window. "Nice to meet you Mr. Worthington," she said and offered her hand. "I'm Maggie Black."

"A pleasure, and please, call me James," he said, his shake nice and firm. "Thank you for doing this on such short notice. I'm afraid our little event resulted in some anonymous threats, and Brice felt some extra security was in order."

"He doesn't like to take any chances," replied Maggie, cursing Bishop. She could be curled up on her couch in her pajamas, reading a good book with a nice glass of wine right about now.

George Moulton cackled behind them, Nina giggling a polite yet strained laugh along with him. James scowled at the man's back and offered Maggie an apologetic shrug.

"Ready for your speech?" Maggie asked.

"As I'll ever be." James released a heavy exhale. "I'm not good with these things."

James Worthington was new in his role as mayor. His predecessor Edgar Johnston died at the beginning of the year.

The new mayor was a handsome man, in a stiff upper lip sort of way. Not a hair was out of place on his head, his face clean shaven. He wore a smart suit, yet nothing too flashy like the Armani suit Moulton had squeezed into.

Moulton continued spluttering behind them, cracking jokes and lighting a cigar. Maggie had heard better one liners from Christmas crackers. The tendrils of smoke from his cigar circled around the room, drowning out the fresh lilies.

Maggie lowered her voice. "I'm sure you'll do better than him."

That won her a smile. "Yes, well, there's that at least."

"I'm going to take Mr. Moulton down to his table," called Nina. Moulton wasn't due to talk until after the dinner. Hopefully by then he would have the ability to stand, never mind give a speech on UK business.

"See you down there." Maggie turned back to the mayor when the door closed behind Nina. "We've made a sweep of the hotel and surrounding areas and cleared the conference room itself. You're good to go."

"Excellent." James held out his arm. "Shall we?"

Maggie indulged him and linked her arm in his. "It's a nice hotel," she said as they walked downstairs, the armed men following close behind. Voices travelled up from the foyer as the guests arrived in time for the mayor's speech. And the free booze and food.

"Yes, named after the Baltic Exchange. Terrible business."

Maggie was too young to remember the bombing of the building, right on the very street they were in now, but

Bishop had worked on the case. Three people had died that day, and another ninety-one injured.

"The drunken idiot is seated and behaving himself," came Nina's voice in Maggie's ear. "No signs of trouble."

The podium was to the back of the conference room and had its own entrance. The mayor stood behind the curtain, going over his notes one last time before going out.

The real event coordinator was behind the podium, too, ordering helpers around, her cheeks flush and movements flustered.

Maggie watched everyone who came and went, taking in faces and checking all access points.

"All clear here," Maggie said into her microphone just as a man caught her eye.

He strode backstage, but not in an organized rush like the others around him. He moved with a purpose, and that purpose became clear as he approached and reached into his jacket.

Maggie was about to shout when the man lunged at the mayor.

The man pulled out his gun and aimed at his target. Maggie dived in front of the mayor, blocking the man's path. His finger inched toward the trigger, but Maggie got to him first, thrusting his arm into the air. The gun went off and shot into the ceiling, flecks of plaster falling around them like snow.

Screams erupted from the other side of the curtain as guests heard the shot echoing off the walls of the large room. Chairs scraped on the floor and footsteps stampeded as people spilled out of the conference room and into the foyer.

The man was fast, and before the mayor's two personal guards could move three paces, he shot bullets into each of their heads. They crumbled to the floor like lifeless dolls, blood already seeping out of the bullet holes.

Maggie jabbed at the assailant, but he blocked her punch, sending a ringing pain through her arm. He pointed his gun at the mayor once again, but Maggie timed a perfect roundhouse that sent the weapon flying from his grasp.

The gun landed out of sight and Maggie squared up to the assassin, making sure to stay between him and James. If he wanted to reach the mayor, he would need to go through her.

The assassin swung a fist at her, and Maggie ducked back avoiding impact. She reached for her own gun, concealed around her thigh, but the man was on her again, this time catching her in the jaw with a right hook.

Maggie's head snapped to the side, the metallic tang of blood filling her mouth.

With a yell, she bounded forward and kneed him in the stomach, doubling him over. When he straightened back up, he had a knife in his hand, the silver glinting under the light.

The mayor stepped toward her, but Maggie shoved him back out of the way.

The assassin took advantage of her distraction and sliced at her. Maggie noticed the knife at the last second and flinched back, the blade catching on the fabric of her dress. She grabbed his wrist and thrust her palm into the man's elbow, aiming for a break. The bone didn't snap, but the assassin yelped and dropped his weapon.

But the loss of his weapon didn't slow him down. The man spun and rammed into her with his shoulder, forcing Maggie back. He swept his foot across the floor and swiped his leg into hers, sending her careening to the floor in a graceless fall.

He made for the mayor, but Maggie scrambled to her feet and grabbed him by the back of his collar, using his momentum as he stumbled back to trip him up. He fell on the arm she damaged and hissed.

Maggie seized the moment and threw all her weight into a brutal kick to his abdomen. The man groaned a curse and rolled away, holding his stomach as he bounced back up on agile feet. Maggie made for him again, but he turned and ran, heading back the way he came.

"Stay here. Don't come out until I come back for you," she ordered the mayor. "Got it?"

James nodded, wide eyed and panting, leaning against the wall to keep him steady.

Certain he was okay and had heard her, Maggie abandoned her heels, leaped over the dead bodies of the guards, and sped off after the assassin.

The foyer was pandemonium, people pushing and shoving each other out of the way to race from the hotel, all pretense of civility gone. An old man lay on the floor covering his head as others trampled over him to get to safety.

Nina spoke in Maggie's ear. "Maggie what the hell is going on? I heard gun shots."

"Someone tried to take out the mayor," she replied. "I'm in pursuit."

"Where are you? Do you need my help?"

"No. Get the Foreign Secretary out of here. He could be a target, too."

"Copy that," Nina said, her voice cutting in and out. "Go catch the prick."

The alarm interfered with the wire's signal, and it screeched in Maggie's ear. She took it out and tossed it, continuing her chase.

Maggie fought her way through the crowd, eyes set on finding the one responsible for the chaos. Black hair, light brown skin, an unassuming face that blended in well. Spanish from the way he cursed, though she could be mistaken on that. Spanish wasn't on her list of fluent languages.

The alarms wailed through the hotel. New and louder

screams followed, the sirens only panicking the people more.

Event Security tried to settle everyone down and restore order, but it wasn't working. The flight instinct in the guests was well and truly in effect. But not for Maggie. She was in full fight mode.

Maggie spotted Nina across the foyer in a splash of emerald among the crowd, heading out the front door with George Moulton. They met each other's eyes, and Maggie nodded for her to go on. George could be in danger.

Maneuvering her way through the panicked people, Maggie scanned every inch of the room.

There.

The assassin had made it through the crowd and was running up the stairs Maggie had taken with the mayor. The man looked over his shoulder and spotted her moving his way.

Maggie ran, feet cold on the marble floor, and fought her way through the guests. She reached the stairs and took them three at a time, releasing her gun from its holster and gripping it with a firm hold.

She turned the safety off and made it to the second floor.

A door to her left was closing, but no one had come racing out to head downstairs. Maggie caught it before it clicked shut and ducked inside, weapon at the ready.

The tail of a black jacket flashed down the hall as someone turned the corner at a run.

Maggie sprinted after them, her heart pounding and hair slipping out from behind her head. She rounded the corner and laid eyes on her target. Aiming with both hands, Maggie kept running and shot at the assassin.

The bullets missed his head by inches, embedding into the wall. He made a right down another hall of the hotel floor, and Maggie heard a crash.

Sprinting after him, she spotted the busted door to one of the rooms, the wood split off the frame. Gun at the ready, Maggie stepped inside. Something cold brushed against her bare foot, and she stole a glance down. A card. She bent to collect it, keeping her weapon pointed into the darkness of the room. It was a room key, but not for that one, or any other on the second floor. It was for the level above.

"I know you're in here," Maggie said, stepping inside.

Glass shattered further in, and she stormed through, ready to attack.

The assassin was at the window, the cold air blowing in through the broken pane. He took one last look at her before Maggie pulled the trigger.

The man jumped from the window and fell out of sight.

Maggie moved to the window and looked down. He wasn't there.

"Shit."

Things were still up in the air when she returned to the foyer, red faced and kicking herself at failing to apprehend the assassin.

She went to the back of the podium to return to the mayor and report what happened. So much for an easy couple of hours.

Maggie walked in to find the place deserted other than the two bodies lying in a heap on the ground.

She froze.

Not two bodies. Three.

James Worthington, Mayor of London and her charge, was dead.

Get your copy of Kill Order today!

Made in the USA
Middletown, DE
13 March 2018